CAT TALES FO

Also available from Headline

Dog Tales for Christmas
Murder for Christmas
Ghosts for Christmas
Chillers for Christmas
Mystery for Christmas

CAT TALES FOR CHRISTMAS

edited by
Mark Bryant

HEADLINE

Introduction and collection copyright © 1993 Mark Bryant

The right of Mark Bryant to be identified as the Editor of the Work has been asserted by him in accordance with the Copyright, Design and Patents Act 1988.

First published in 1993
by HEADLINE BOOK PUBLISHING

Reprinted in this edition in 1993
by HEADLINE BOOK PUBLISHING

10 9 8 7 6 5 4 3 2 1

All rights reserved. No part of this publication may be reproduced, stored in a retrieval system, or transmitted, in any form or by any means without the prior written permission of the publisher, nor be otherwise circulated in any form of binding or cover other than that in which it is published and without a similar condition being imposed on the subsequent purchaser.

All characters in this publication are fictitious and any resemblance to real persons, living or dead, is purely coincidental.

British Library Cataloguing in Publication Data

Bryant, Mark
 Cat Tales for Christmas. – New ed
 I. Title
 823 [FS]

ISBN 0-7472-0955-3

Printed and bound in Great Britain by
Mackays of Chatham PLC, Chatham, Kent

HEADLINE BOOK PUBLISHING
A division of Hodder Headline PLC
Headline House
79 Great Titchfield Street
London W1P 7FN

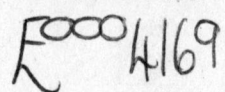

For my mother

Contents

The Trinity Cat *Ellis Peters*	1
Tobermory *Saki*	17
The Garden of Stubborn Cats *Italo Calvino*	25
The Tom-Cat *Colette*	35
Pains and Pleasures *L. P. Hartley*	39
The Cat that Walked by Himself *Rudyard Kipling*	51
Abner of the Porch *Geoffrey Household*	61
Ming's Biggest Prey *Patricia Highsmith*	69
The White Cat *Countess D'Aulnoy*	79
The Cyprian Cat *Dorothy L. Sayers*	111
The Yellow Terror *W. L. Alden*	125
Edward the Conqueror *Roald Dahl*	135
The Squaw *Bram Stoker*	155
The Cat in the Lifeboat *James Thurber*	167
The Paradise of Cats *Emile Zola*	169
Puss in Boots *Charles Perrault*	175
Lillian *Damon Runyon*	181
The Black Cat *Edgar Allan Poe*	195
Spiegel the Cat *Gottfried Keller*	205
The Cat *Mary E. Wilkins Freeman*	235
Acknowledgements	243

Introduction

Cat tales for Christmas – what a cosy image. A full moon outside, not a footprint in the snow, the doors well sealed and every window-pane rimmed with frost. Beneath the dark oak beams a quiet figure sits by a log fire, a grandfather clock chimes a late hour and all eyes look up as she begins to read. At her feet, blinking in the gloaming and purring contentedly as the aged voice unfolds the story, lies the household cat, smiling a quiet approval . . .

Cats have featured in stories from time immemorial. Though there were no cats in the Ark (and indeed there are none in the Bible at all), they do crop up in many works of antiquity, from the Greek tale of Galanthis and Juno to the Indian legend of Patripatan the celestial cat, and from Gunduple and the Golden Mouse of Borneo to the great Egyptian cat goddess Bast. In addition, there are countless anecdotes about the remarkable adventures of real cats, often considerably embroidered in the telling, but captivating reading none the less.

This book, however, concentrates exclusively on fictional short stories featuring cats and I have tried to make the collection as balanced as the limitations of length and copyright availability have allowed. Many of the stories are set in autumn or winter and the opening tale, 'The Trinity Cat', actually takes place at Christmas. The authors selected include both men and women from Italy, France, Switzerland and the USA as well as Great Britain, and from the seventeenth century to the present day. The stories themselves feature cats in churches, at sea, in the wild, on rooftops and are in a wide variety of genres from fable and fairytale to comedy and detective thriller. And for horror fans there are macabre

CAT TALES FOR CHRISTMAS

offerings from Edgar Allan Poe and Bram Stoker.

It would be tempting to give a flavour of some of the stories in this short introduction, but as any good storyteller knows, the real magic lies in letting the writers' words weave their own spell. So, unplug the telephone, turn off the TV and settle down with a mug of cocoa. And then, as night draws on – in bedsit, caravan, house or hotel – drift away to the sound of that old, comfortable voice in a cosy Christmas farmhouse telling tales and spinning stories, as the log-fire crackles and the cat purrs contentedly on the hearthrug...

Mark Bryant

THE TRINITY CAT
Ellis Peters

He was sitting on top of one of the rear gate-posts of the churchyard when I walked through on Christmas Eve, grooming in his lordly style, with one back leg wrapped round his neck, and his bitten ear at an angle of forty-five degrees, as usual. I reckon one of the toms he'd tangled with in his nomad days had ripped the starched bit out of that one, the other stood up sharply enough. There was snow on the ground, a thin veiling, just beginning to crackle in promise of frost before evening, but he had at least three warm refuges around the place whenever he felt like holing up, besides his two houses, which he used only for visiting and cadging. He'd been a known character around our village for three years then, ever since he walked in from nowhere and made himself agreeable to the vicar and the verger, and finding the billet comfortable and the pickings good, constituted himself resident cat to Holy Trinity church, and took over all the jobs around the place that humans were too slow to tackle, like rat-catching, and chasing off invading dogs.

Nobody knows how old he is, but I think he could only have been about two when he settled here, a scrawny, chewed-up black bandit as lean as wire. After three years of being fed by Joel Woodward at Trinity Cottage, which was the verger's house by tradition, and flanked the lych-gate on one side, and pampered and petted by Miss Patience Thomson at Church Cottage on the other side, he was double his old size and sleek as velvet, but still had one lop ear and a kink two inches from the end of his tail. He still looked like a brigand, but a highly prosperous brigand. Nobody ever gave him a name, he wasn't the sort to get called anything fluffy or familiar.

Only Miss Patience ever dared coo at him, and he was very gracious about that, she being elderly and innocent and very free with little perks like raw liver, on which he doted. One way and another, he had it made. He lived mostly outdoors, never staying in either house overnight. In winter he had his own little ground-level hatch into the furnace-room of the church, sharing his lodgings matily with a hedgehog that had qualified as assistant vermin-destructor around the churchyard, and preferred sitting out the winter among the coke to hibernating like common hedgehogs. These individualists keep turning up in our valley, for some reason.

All I'd gone to the church for that afternoon was to fix up with the vicar about the Christmas peal, having been roped into the bell-ringing team. Resident police in remote areas like ours get dragged into all sorts of activities, and when the area's changing, and new problems cropping up, if they have any sense they don't need too much dragging, but go willingly. I've put my finger on many an astonished yobbo who thought he'd got clean away with his little breaking-and-entering, just by keeping my ears open during a darts match, or choir practice.

When I came back through the churchyard, around half-past two, Miss Patience was just coming out of her gate, with a shopping-bag on her wrist, and heading towards the street, and we walked along together a bit of the way. She was getting on for seventy, and hardly bigger than a bird, but very independent. Never having married or left the valley, and having looked after a mother who lived to be nearly ninety, she'd never had time to catch up with new ideas in the style of dress suitable for elderly ladies. Everything had always been done mother's way, and fashion, music and morals had stuck at the period when mother was a carefully brought-up girl learning domestic skills, and preparing for a chaste marriage. There's a lot to be said for it! But it had turned Miss Patience into a frail little lady in long-skirted black or grey or navy blue, who still felt undressed without hat and gloves, at an age when Mrs Newcombe, for instance, up at the pub, favoured shocking pink trouser suits and red-gold hair-pieces. A pretty little old lady Miss Patience was, though, very straight and neat. It was a pleasure to watch her walk. Which is more than I could say for Mrs Newcombe in her trouser suit, especially from the back!

'A happy Christmas, Sergeant Moon!' she chirped at me on sight. And I wished her the same, and slowed up to her pace.

'It's going to be slippery by twilight,' I said. 'You be careful how you go.'

'Oh, I'm only going to be an hour or so,' she said serenely. 'I shall be home long before the frost sets in. I'm only doing the last bit of Christmas shopping. There's a cardigan I have to collect for Mrs Downs.' That was her cleaning-lady, who went in three mornings a week. 'I ordered it long ago, but deliveries are so slow nowadays. They've promised it for today. And a gramophone record for my little errand-boy.' Tommy Fowler that was, one of the church trebles, as pink and wholesome-looking as they usually contrive to be, and just as artful. 'And one mustn't forget our dumb friends, either, must one?' said Miss Patience cheerfully. 'They're all important, too.'

I took this to mean a couple of packets of some new product to lure wild birds to her garden. The Church Cottage thrushes were so fat they could hardly fly, and when it was frosty she put out fresh water three or four times a day.

We came to our brief street of shops, and off she went, with her big jet-and-gold brooch gleaming in her scarf. She had quite a few pieces of Victorian and Edwardian jewellery her mother'd left behind, and almost always wore one piece, being used to the belief that a lady dresses meticulously every day, not just on Sundays. And I went for a brisk walk round to see what was going on, and then went home to Molly and high tea, and took my boots off thankfully.

That was Christmas Eve. Christmas Day little Miss Thomson didn't turn up for eight o'clock Communion, which was unheard-of. The vicar said he'd call in after matins and see that she was all right, and hadn't taken cold trotting about in the snow. But somebody else beat us both to it. Tommy Fowler! He was anxious about that pop record of his. But even he had no chance until after service, for in our village it's the custom for the choir to go and sing the vicar an aubade in the shape of 'Christians, Awake!' before the main service, ignoring the fact that he's then been up four hours, and conducted two Communions. And Tommy Fowler had a solo in the anthem, too. It was a quarter-past twelve when he got away, and shot up the garden path to the door of Church Cottage.

He shot back even faster a minute later. I was heading for home when he came rocketing out of the gate and ran slam into me, with his eyes sticking out on stalks and his mouth wide open, making a sort of muted keening sound with shock. He clutched hold of me and pointed back towards Miss Thomson's front door, left half-open when he fled, and tried three times before he could croak out:

'Miss Patience... She's there on the floor – she's bad!'

I went in on the run, thinking she'd had a heart attack all alone there, and was lying helpless. The front door led through a diminutive hall, and through another glazed door into the living-room, and that door was open, too, and there was Miss Patience face-down on the carpet, still in her coat and gloves, and with her shopping-bag lying beside her. An occasional table had been knocked over in her fall, spilling a vase and a book. Her hat was askew over one ear, and caved in like a trodden mushroom, and her neat grey bun of hair had come undone and trailed on her shoulder, and it was no longer grey but soiled, brownish black. She was dead and stiff. The room was so cold, you could tell those doors had been ajar all night.

The kid had followed me in, hanging on to my sleeve, his teeth chattering. 'I didn't open the door – it was open! I didn't touch her, or anything. I only came to see if she was all right, and get my record.'

It was there, lying unbroken, half out of the shopping-bag by her arm. She'd meant it for him, and I told him he should have it, but not yet, because it might be evidence, and we mustn't move anything. And I got him out of there quick, and gave him to the vicar to cope with, and went back to Miss Patience as soon as I'd telephoned for the outfit. Because we had a murder on our hands.

So that was the end of one gentle, harmless old woman, one of very many these days, battered to death because she walked in on an intruder who panicked. Walked in on him, I judged, not much more than an hour after I left her in the street. Everything about her looked the same as then, the shopping-bag, the coat, the hat, the gloves. The only difference, that she was dead. No, one more thing! No handbag, unless it was under the body, and later, when we were able to move her, I wasn't surprised to see that it wasn't there. Handbags are where old ladies carry their money. The sneak-thief who panicked and lashed out at her had still had greed and presence of mind enough to grab the bag as he fled. Nobody'd have to describe that bag to me, I knew it well, soft black leather with an old-fashioned gilt clasp and a short handle, a small thing, not like the holdalls they carry nowadays.

She was lying facing the opposite door, also open, which led to the stairs. On the writing-desk by that door stood one of a pair of heavy brass candlesticks. Its fellow was on the floor beside Miss Thomson's body, and though the bun of hair and the felt hat had prevented any great spattering of blood, there was blood enough on the square base to label the weapon. Whoever had hit her had been just sneaking down the stairs, ready to leave. She'd come home barely five minutes too soon.

Upstairs, in her bedroom, her bits of jewellery hadn't taken much finding. She'd never thought of herself as having valuables, or of other people as coveting them. Her gold and turquoise and funereal jet and true-lover's-knots in gold and opals, and mother's engagement and wedding rings, and her little Edwardian pendant watch set with seed pearls, had simply lived in the small top drawer of her dressing-table. She belonged to an honest epoch, and it was gone, and now she was gone after it. She didn't even lock her door when she went shopping. There wouldn't have been so much as the warning of a key grating in the lock, just the door opening.

Ten years ago not a soul in this valley behaved differently from Miss Patience. Nobody locked doors, sometimes not even overnight. Some of us went on a fortnight's holiday and left the doors unlocked. Now we can't even put out the milk money until the milkman knocks at the door in person. If this generation likes to pride itself on its progress, let it! As for me, I thought suddenly that maybe the innocent was well out of it.

We did the usual things, photographed the body and the scene of the crime, the doctor examined her and authorized her removal, and confirmed what I'd supposed about the approximate time of her death. And the forensic boys lifted a lot of smudgy latents that weren't going to be of any use to anybody, because they weren't going to be on record, barring a million-to-one chance. The whole thing stank of the amateur. There wouldn't be any easy matching up of prints, even if they got beauties. One more thing we did for Miss Patience. We tolled the dead-bell for her on Christmas night, six heavy, muffled strokes. She was a virgin. Nobody had to vouch for it, we all knew. And let me point out, it is a title of honour, to be respected accordingly.

We'd hardly got the poor soul out of the house when the Trinity cat strolled in, taking advantage of the minute or two while the door was open. He got as far as the place on the carpet where she'd lain, and his fur and whiskers stood on end, and even his lop ear jerked up straight. He put his nose down to the pile of the Wilton, about where her shopping-bag and handbag must have lain, and started going round in interested circles, snuffing the floor and making little throaty noises that might have been distress, but sounded like pleasure. Excitement, anyhow. The chaps from the C.I.D. were still busy, and didn't want him under their feet, so I picked him up and took him with me when I went across to Trinity Cottage to talk to the verger. The cat never liked being picked up; after a minute he started clawing and cursing, and I put him down. He stalked away again at once, past the corner where people shot their dead flowers, out at the lych-gate, and straight back to sit on Miss Thomson's doorstep. Well, after all, he used to get fed there, he might well be uneasy at all these queer comings and goings. And they don't say 'as curious as a cat' for nothing, either.

I didn't need telling that Joel Woodward had had no hand in what had happened – he'd been nearest neighbour and good friend to Miss Patience for years – but he might have seen or heard something out of the ordinary. He was a little, wiry fellow, gnarled like a tree-root, the kind that goes on spry and active into his nineties, and then decides that's enough, and leaves overnight. His wife was dead long ago, and his daughter had come back to keep house for him after her husband deserted her, until she died, too, in a bus accident. There was just old Joel now, and the grandson she'd left with him, young Joel Barnett, nineteen, and a bit of a tearaway by his grandad's standards, but so far pretty innocuous by mine. He was a sulky, graceless sort, but he did work, and he stuck with the old man when many another would have lit out elsewhere.

'A bad business,' said old Joel, shaking his head. 'I only wish I could help you lay hands on whoever did it. But I only saw her yesterday morning about ten, when she took in the milk. I was round at the church hall all afternoon, getting things ready for the youth social they had last night, it was dark before I got back. I never saw or heard anything out of place. You can't see her living-room light from here, so there was no call to wonder. But the lad was here all afternoon. They only work till one, Christmas Eve. Then they all went boozing together for an hour or so, I expect, so I don't know exactly what time he got in, but he was here and had the tea on when I came home. Drop round in an hour or so and he should be here, he's gone round to collect this girl he's mashing. There's a party somewhere tonight.'

I dropped round accordingly, and young Joel was there, sure enough, shoulder-length hair, frilled shirt, outsize lapels and all, got up to kill, all for the benefit of the girl his grandad had mentioned. And it turned out to be Connie Dymond, from the comparatively respectable branch of the family, along the canal-side. There were three sets of Dymond cousins, boys, no great harm in 'em but worth watching, but only this one girl in Connie's family. A good-looker, or at least most of the lads seemed to think so, she had a dozen or so on her string before she took up with young Joel. Big girl, too, with a lot of mauve eye-shadow and a mother-of-pearl mouth, in huge platform shoes and the fashionable drab granny-coat. But she was acting very prim and proper with old Joel around.

'Half-past two when I got home,' said young Joel. 'Grandad was round at the hall, and I'd have gone round to help him, only I'd had a pint or two, and after I'd had me dinner I went to sleep, so it wasn't worth it by the time I woke up. Around four, that'd be. From then on I was here watching the telly, and I never saw nor heard a thing. But there was nobody else here, so I could be spinning you the yarn, if you want to look at it that way.'

He had a way of going looking for trouble before anybody else suggested it, there was nothing new about that. Still, there it was. One young fellow on the spot, and minus any alibi. There'd be plenty of others in the same case.

In the evening he'd been at the church social. Miss Patience wouldn't be expected there, it was mainly for the young, and anyhow, she very seldom went out in the evenings.

'*I* was there with Joel,' said Connie Dymond. 'He called for me at seven, I was with him all the evening. We went home to our place after the social finished, and he didn't leave till nearly midnight.'

Very firm about it she was, doing her best for him. She could hardly know that his movements in the evening didn't interest us, since Miss Patience had then been dead for some hours.

When I opened the door to leave, the Trinity cat walked in, stalking past me with a purposeful stride. He had a look round us all, and then made for the girl, reached up his front paws to her knees, and was on her lap before she could fend him off, though she didn't look as if she welcomed his attentions. Very civil he was, purring and rubbing himself against her coat sleeve, and poking his whiskery face into hers. Unusual for him to be effusive, but when he did decide on it, it was always with someone who couldn't stand cats. You'll have noticed it's a way they have.

'Shove him off,' said young Joel, seeing she didn't at all care for being singled out. 'He only does it to annoy people.'

And she did, but he only jumped on again, I noticed as I closed the door on them and left. It was a Dymond party they were going to, the senior lot, up at the filling-station. Not much point in trying to check up on all her cousins and swains when they were gathered for a booze-up. Coming out of a hangover, tomorrow, they might be easy meat. Not that I had any special reason to look their way, they were an extrovert lot, more given to grievous bodily harm in street punch-ups than anything secretive. But it was wide open.

Well, we summed up. None of the lifted prints was on record, all we could do in that line was exclude all those that were Miss Thomson's. This kind of sordid little opportunist break-in had come into local experience only fairly recently, and though it was no novelty now, it had never before led to a death. No motive but the impulse of greed, so no traces leading up to the act, and none leading away. Everyone connected with the church, and most of the village besides, knew about the bits of jewellery she had, but never before had anyone considered them as desirable loot. Victoriana

The Trinity Cat

now carry inflated values, and are in demand, but this still didn't look calculated, just wanton. A kid's crime, a teenager's crime. Or the crime of a permanent teenager. They start at twelve years old now, but there are also the shiftless louts who never get beyond twelve years old, even in their forties.

We checked all the obvious people, her part-time gardener – but he was demonstrably elsewhere at the time – and his drifter of a son, whose alibi was non-existent but voluble, the window-cleaner, a sidelong soul who played up his ailments and did rather well out of her, all the delivery men. Several there who were clear, one or two who could have been around, but had no particular reason to be. Then we went after all the youngsters who, on their records, were possibles. There were three with breaking-and-entering convictions, but if they'd been there they'd been gloved. Several others with petty theft against them were also without alibis. By the end of a pretty exhaustive survey the field was wide, and none of the runners seemed to be ahead of the rest, and we were still looking. None of the stolen property had so far showed up.

Not, that is, until the Saturday. I was coming from Church Cottage through the graveyard again, and as I came near the corner where the dead flowers were shot, I noticed a glaring black patch making an irregular hole in the veil of frozen snow that still covered the ground. You couldn't miss it, it showed up like a black eye. Part of it was the soil and rotting leaves showing through, and part, the blackest part, was the Trinity cat, head down and back arched, digging industriously like a terrier after a rat. The bent end of his tail lashed steadily, while the remaining eight inches stood erect. If he knew I was standing watching him, he didn't care. Nothing was going to deflect him from what he was doing. And in a minute or two he heaved his prize clear, and clawed out to the light a little black leather handbag with a gilt clasp. No mistaking it, all stuck over as it was with dirt and rotting leaves. And he loved it, he was patting it and playing with it and rubbing his head against it, and purring like a steam-engine. He cursed, though, when I took it off him, and walked round and round me, pawing and swearing, telling me and the world he'd found it, and it was his.

It hadn't been there long. I'd been along that path often enough to know that the snow hadn't been disturbed the day before. Also, the mess of humus fell off it pretty quick and clean, and left it hardly stained at all. I held it in my handkerchief and snapped the catch, and the inside was clean and empty, the lining slightly frayed from long use. The Trinity cat stood upright on his hind legs and protested loudly, and he had a voice that could outshout a Siamese.

Somebody behind me said curiously: 'Whatever've you got there?' And there was young Joel standing open-mouthed, staring, with Connie Dymond hanging on to his arm and gaping at the cat's find in horrified recognition.

'Oh, no! My gawd, that's Miss Thomson's bag, isn't it? I've seen her carrying it hundreds of times.'

'Did *he* dig it up?' said Joel, incredulous. 'You reckon the chap who – you know, *him*! – he buried it there? It could be anybody, everybody uses this way through.'

'My gawd!' said Connie, shrinking in fascinated horror against his side. 'Look at that cat! You'd think he *knows*... He gives me the shivers! What's got into him?'

What, indeed? After I'd got rid of them and taken the bag away with me I was still wondering. I walked away with his prize and he followed me as far as the road, howling and swearing, and once I put the bag down, open, to see what he'd do, and he pounced on it and started his fun and games again until I took it from him. For the life of me I couldn't see what there was about it to delight him, but he was in no doubt. I was beginning to feel right superstitious about this avenging detective cat, and to wonder what he was going to unearth next.

I know I ought to have delivered the bag to the forensic lab., but somehow I hung on to it overnight. There was something fermenting at the back of my mind that I couldn't yet grasp.

Next morning we had two more at morning service besides the regulars. Young Joel hardly ever went to church, and I doubt if anybody'd ever seen Connie Dymond there before, but there they both were, large as life and solemn as death, in a middle pew, the boy sulky and scowling as if he'd been press-ganged into it, as he certainly had, Connie very subdued and big-eyed, with almost no make-up and an unusually grave and thoughtful face. Sudden death brings people up against daunting possibilities, and creates penitents. Young Joel felt silly there, but he was daft about her, plainly enough, she could get him to do what she wanted, and she'd wanted to make this gesture. She went through all the movements of devotion, he just sat, stood and kneeled awkwardly as required, and went on scowling.

There was a bitter east wind when we came out. On the steps of the porch everybody dug out gloves and turned up collars against it, and so did young Joel, and as he hauled his gloves out of his coat pocket, out with them came a little bright thing that rolled down the steps in front of us all and came to rest in a crack between the flagstones of the path. A gleam of pale blue and gold. A dozen people must have recognized it. Mrs Downs gave tongue in a shriek that informed even those who hadn't.

'That's Miss Thomson's! It's one of her turquoise ear-rings! *How did you get hold of that, Joel Barnett?*'

How, indeed? Everybody stood staring at the tiny thing, and then at young Joel, and he was gazing at the flagstones, struck white and dumb. And all in a moment Connie Dymond had pulled her arm free of his and recoiled from him until her back was against the wall, and was edging away from him like somebody trying to get out of range of flood or fire, and her face a sight to be seen, blind and stiff with horror.

'You!' she said in a whisper. 'It was you! Oh, my gawd, *you* did it – *you* killed her! And me keeping company – how could I? How could *you*!'

She let out a screech and burst into sobs, and before anybody could stop her she turned and took to her heels, running for home like a mad thing.

I let her go. She'd keep. And I got young Joel and that single ear-ring away from the Sunday congregation and into Trinity Cottage before half the people there knew what was happening, and shut the world out, all but old Joel who came panting and shaking after us a few minutes later.

The boy was a long time getting his voice back, and when he did he had nothing to say but, hopelessly, over and over: 'I didn't! I never touched her, I wouldn't. I don't know how that thing got into my pocket. I didn't do it. I never . . .'

Human beings are not all that inventive. Given a similar set of circumstances they tend to come out with the same formula. And in any case, 'deny everything and say nothing else' is a very good rule when cornered.

They thought I'd gone round the bend when I said: 'Where's the cat? See if you can get him in.'

Old Joel was past wondering. He went out and rattled a saucer on the steps, and pretty soon the Trinity cat strolled in. Not at all excited, not wanting anything, fed and lazy, just curious enough to come and see why he was wanted. I turned him loose on young Joel's overcoat, and he couldn't have cared less. The pocket that had held the ear-ring held very little interest for him. He didn't care about any of the clothes in the wardrobe, or on the pegs in the little hall. As far as he was concerned, this new find was a non-event.

I sent for a constable and a car, and took young Joel in with me to the station, and all the village, you may be sure, either saw us pass or heard about it very shortly after. But I didn't stop to take any statement from him, just left him there, and took the car up to Mary Melton's place, where she breeds Siamese, and borrowed a cat-basket from her, the sort she uses to carry her queens to the vet. She asked what on earth I wanted it for, and I said to take the Trinity cat for a ride. She laughed her head off.

'Well, *he*'s no queen,' she said, 'and no king, either. Not even a jack! And you'll never get that wild thing into a basket.'

'Oh, yes, I will,' I said. 'And if he isn't any of the other picture cards, he's probably going to turn out to be the joker.'

A very neat basket it was, not too obviously meant for a cat. And it was no trick getting the Trinity cat into it, all I did was drop in Miss Thomson's handbag, and he was in after it in a moment. He growled when he found himself shut in, but it was too late to complain then.

At the house by the canal Connie Dymond's mother let me in, but was none too happy about letting me see Connie, until I explained that I needed a statement from her before I could fit together young Joel's movements all through those Christmas days. Naturally I understood that the girl was terribly upset, but she'd had a lucky escape, and the sooner everything was cleared up, the better for her. And it wouldn't take long.

It didn't take long. Connie came down the stairs readily enough when her mother called her. She was all stained and pale and tearful, but had perked up somewhat with a sort of shivering pride in her own prominence. I've seen them like that before, getting the juice out of being the centre of attention even while they wish they were elsewhere. You could even say she hurried down, and she left the door of her bedroom open behind her, by the light coming through at the head of the stairs.

'Oh, Sergeant Moon!' she quavered at me from three steps up. 'Isn't it *awful*? I still can't believe it! *Can* there be some mistake? Is there any chance it *wasn't*...?'

l said soothingly, yes, there was always a chance. And I slipped the latch of the cat-basket with one hand, so that the flap fell open, and the Trinity cat was out of there and up those stairs like a black flash, startling her so much she nearly fell down the last step, and steadied herself against the wall with a small shriek. And I blurted apologies for accidentally loosing him, and went up the stairs three at a time ahead of her, before she could recover her balance.

He was up on his hind legs in her dolly little room, full of pop posters and frills and garish colours, pawing at the second drawer of her dressing-table, and singing a loud, joyous, impatient song. When I came plunging in, he even looked over his shoulder at me and stood down, as though he knew I'd open the drawer for him. And I did, and he was up among her fancy undies like a shot, and digging with his front paws.

He found what he wanted just as she came in at the door. He yanked it out from among her bras and slips, and tossed it into the air, and in seconds he was on the floor with it, rolling and wrestling it, juggling it on his four paws like a circus turn, and purring fit to kill, a cat in ecstasy. A comic little thing it was, a muslin mouse with a plaited green-nylon string for a tail, yellow beads for eyes, and nylon threads for whiskers, that rustled and sent out wafts of strong scent as he batted it around and sang to it. A catmint mouse, old Miss Thomson's last-minute purchase from the pet shop for her dumb friend. If you could ever call the Trinity cat dumb! The only thing she bought that day small enough to be slipped into her handbag instead of the shopping-bag.

Connie let out a screech, and was across that room so fast I only just beat her to the open drawer. They were all there, the little pendant watch, the locket, the brooches, the true-lover's-knots, the purse, even the other ear-ring. A mistake, she should have ditched both while she was about it, but she was too greedy. They were for pierced ears, anyhow, no good to Connie.

I held them out in the palm of my hand – such a large haul they made – and let her see what she'd robbed and killed for.

If she'd kept her head she might have made a fight of it even then, claimed he'd made her hide them for him, and she'd been afraid to tell on him directly, and could only think of staging that public act at church, to get him safely in custody before she came clean. But she went wild. She did the one deadly thing, turned and kicked out in a screaming fury at the Trinity cat. He was spinning like a humming-top, and all she touched was the kink in his tail. He whipped round and clawed a red streak down her leg through the nylon. And then she screamed again, and began to babble through hysterical sobs that she never meant to hurt the poor old sod, that it wasn't her fault! Ever since she'd been going with young Joel she'd been seeing that little old bag going in and out, draped with her bits of gold. What in hell did an old witch like her want with jewellery? She had no *right*! At her age!

'But I never meant to hurt her! She came in too soon,' lamented Connie, still and for ever the aggrieved. 'What was I supposed to do? I had to get away, didn't I? *She was between me and the door!*'

She was half her size, too, and nearly four times her age! Ah well! What the courts would do with Connie, thank God, was none of my business. I just took her in and charged her, and got her statement. Once we had her dabs it was all over, because she'd left a bunch of them sweaty and clear on that brass candlestick. But if it hadn't been for the Trinity cat and his single-minded pursuit, scaring her into that ill-judged attempt to hand us young Joel as a scapegoat, she might, she just might, have got clean away with it. At least the boy could go home now, and count his blessings.

Not that she was very bright, of course. Who but a stupid harpy, soaked in cheap perfume and gimcrack dreams, would have hung on even to the catmint mouse, mistaking it for a herbal sachet to put among her smalls?

I saw the Trinity cat only this morning, sitting grooming in the church porch. He's getting very self-important, as if he knows he's a celebrity, though throughout he was only looking after the interests of Number One, like all cats. He's lost interest in his mouse already, now most of the scent's gone.

TOBERMORY
Saki

It was a chill, rain-washed afternoon of a late August day, that indefinite season when partridges are still in security or cold storage, and there is nothing to hunt – unless one is bounded on the north by the Bristol Channel, in which case one may lawfully gallop after fat red stags. Lady Blemley's house-party was not bounded on the north by the Bristol Channel, hence there was a full gathering of her guests round the tea-table on this particular afternoon. And, in spite of the blankness of the season and the triteness of the occasion, there was no trace in the company of that fatigued restlessness which means a dread of the pianola and a subdued hankering for auction bridge. The undisguised open-mouthed attention of the entire party was fixed on the homely negative personality of Mr Cornelius Appin. Of all her guests, he was the one who had come to Lady Blemley with the vaguest reputation. Someone had said he was 'clever', and he had got his invitation in the moderate expectation, on the part of his hostess, that some portion at least of his cleverness would be contributed to the general entertainment. Until tea-time that day she had been unable to discover in what direction, if any, his cleverness lay. He was neither a wit nor a croquet champion, a hypnotic force nor a begetter of amateur theatricals. Neither did his exterior suggest the sort of man in whom women are willing to pardon a generous measure of mental deficiency. He had subsided into mere Mr Appin, and the Cornelius seemed a piece of transparent baptismal bluff. And now he was claiming to have launched on the world a discovery beside which the invention of gunpowder, of the printing-press, and of steam locomotion were inconsiderable trifles. Science had made bewildering strides in many directions during recent decades, but this thing seemed to belong to the domain of miracle rather than to scientific achievement.

'And do you really ask us to believe,' Sir Wilfrid was saying, 'that you have discovered a means for instructing animals in the art of human speech, and that dear old Tobermory has proved your first successful pupil?'

'It is a problem at which I have worked for the last seventeen years,' said Mr Appin, 'but only during the last eight or nine months have I been rewarded with glimmerings of success. Of course I have experimented with thousands of animals, but latterly only with cats, those wonderful creatures which have assimilated themselves so marvellously with our civilization while retaining all their highly developed feral instincts. Here and there among cats one comes across an outstanding superior intellect, just as one does among the ruck of human beings, and when I made the acquaintance of Tobermory a week ago I saw at once that I was in contact with a 'Beyond-cat' of extraordinary intelligence. I had gone far along the road to success in recent experiments; with Tobermory, as you call him, I have reached the goal.'

Mr Appin concluded his remarkable statement in a voice which he strove to divest of a triumphant inflection. No one said 'Rats', though Clovis's lips moved in a monosyllabic contortion which probably invoked those rodents of disbelief.

'And do you mean to say,' asked Miss Resker, after a slight pause, 'that you have taught Tobermory to say and understand easy sentences of one syllable?'

'My dear Miss Resker,' said the wonder-worker patiently, 'one teaches little children and savages and backward adults in that piecemeal fashion; when one has once solved the problem of making a beginning with an animal of highly developed intelligence one has no need for those halting methods. Tobermory can speak our language with perfect correctness.'

This time Clovis very distinctly said, 'Beyond-rats!' Sir Wilfrid was more polite, but equally sceptical.

'Hadn't we better have the cat in and judge for ourselves?' suggested Lady Blemley.

Sir Wilfrid went in search of the animal, and the company settled themselves down to the languid expectation of witnessing some more or less adroit drawing-room ventriloquism.

In a minute Sir Wilfrid was back in the room, his face white beneath its tan and his eyes dilated with excitement.

'By Gad, it's true!'

His agitation was unmistakably genuine, and his hearers started forward in a thrill of awakened interest.

Collapsing into an armchair he continued breathlessly: 'I found him dozing in the smoking-room, and called out to him to come for his tea. He blinked at me in his usual way, and I said, "Come on, Toby; don't keep us waiting"; and, by Gad! he drawled out in a most horribly natural voice that he'd come when he dashed well pleased! I nearly jumped out of my skin!'

Appin had preached to absolutely incredulous hearers; Sir Wilfrid's statement carried instant conviction. A Babel-like chorus of startled exclamation arose, amid which the scientist sat mutely enjoying the first fruit of his stupendous discovery.

In the midst of the clamour Tobermory entered the room and made his way with velvet tread and studied unconcern across to the group seated round the tea-table.

A sudden hush of awkwardness and constraint fell on the company. Somehow there seemed an element of embarrassment in addressing on equal terms a domestic cat of acknowledged dental ability.

'Will you have some milk, Tobermory?' asked Lady Blemley in a rather strained voice.

'I don't mind if I do,' was the response, couched in a tone of even indifference. A shiver of suppressed excitement went through the listeners, and Lady Blemley might be excused for pouring out the saucerful of milk rather unsteadily.

'I'm afraid I've spilt a good deal of it,' she said apologetically.

'After all, it's not my Axminster,' was Tobermory's rejoinder.

Another silence fell on the group, and then Miss Resker, in her best district-visitor manner, asked if the human language had been difficult to learn. Tobermory looked squarely at her for a moment and then fixed his gaze serenely on the middle distance. It was obvious that boring questions lay outside his scheme of life.

'What do you think of human intelligence?' asked Mavis Pellington lamely.

'Of whose intelligence in particular?' asked Tobermory coldly.

'Oh, well, mine for instance,' said Mavis, with a feeble laugh.

'You put me in an embarrassing position,' said Tobermory, whose tone and attitude certainly did not suggest a shred of embarrassment. 'When your inclusion in this house-party was suggested Sir Wilfrid protested that you were the most brainless woman of his acquaintance, and that there was a wide distinction between hospitality and the care of the feeble-minded. Lady Blemley replied that your lack of brain-power was the precise quality which had earned you your invitation, as you were the only person she could think of who might be idiotic enough to buy their old car. You know, the one they call "The Envy of Sisyphus", because it goes quite nicely uphill if you push it.'

Lady Blemley's protestations would have had greater effect if she had not casually suggested to Mavis only that morning that the car in question would be just the thing for her down at her Devonshire home.

Major Barfield plunged in heavily to effect a diversion.

'How about your carryings-on with the tortoiseshell puss up at the stables, eh?'

The moment he had said it everyone realized the blunder.

'One does not usually discuss these matters in public,' said Tobermory frigidly. 'From a slight observation of your ways since you've been in this house I should imagine you'd find it inconvenient if I were to shift the conversation on to your own little affairs.'

The panic which ensued was not confined to the Major.

'Would you like to go and see if cook has got your dinner ready?' suggested Lady Blemley hurriedly, affecting to ignore the fact that it wanted at least two hours to Tobermory's dinner-time.

'Thanks,' said Tobermory, 'not quite so soon after my tea. I don't want to die of indigestion.'

'Cats have nine lives, you know,' said Sir Wilfrid heartily.

'Possibly,' answered Tobermory; 'but only one liver.'

'Adelaide!' said Mrs Cornett, 'do you mean to encourage that cat to go out and gossip about us in the servants' hall?'

The panic had indeed become general. A narrow ornamental balustrade ran in front of most of the bedroom windows at the Towers, and it was recalled with dismay that this had formed a favourite promenade for Tobermory at all hours, whence he could watch the pigeons – and heaven knew what else besides. If he intended to become reminiscent in his present outspoken strain the effect would be something more than disconcerting. Mrs Cornett, who spent much time at her toilet table, and whose complexion was reputed to be of a nomadic though punctual disposition, looked as ill at ease as the Major. Miss Scrawen, who wrote fiercely sensuous poetry and led a blameless life, merely displayed irritation; if you are methodical and virtuous in private you don't necessarily want everyone to know it. Bertie van Tahn, who was so depraved at seventeen that he had long ago given up trying to be any worse, turned a dull shade of gardenia white, but he did not commit the error of dashing out of the room like Odo Finsberry, a young gentleman who was understood to be reading for the Church and who was possibly disturbed at the thought of scandals he might hear concerning other people. Clovis had the presence of mind to maintain a composed exterior; privately he was calculating how long it would take to procure a box of fancy mice through the agency of the *Exchange & Mart* as a species of hush-money.

Even in a delicate situation like the present, Agnes Resker could not endure to remain too long in the background.

'Why did I ever come down here?' she asked dramatically.

Tobermory immediately accepted the opening.

'Judging by what you said to Mrs Cornett on the croquet-lawn yesterday, you were out for food. You described the Blemleys as the dullest people to stay with that you knew, but said they were clever enough to employ a first-rate cook; otherwise they'd find it difficult to get anyone to come down a second time.'

'There's not a word of truth in it! I appeal to Mrs Cornett—' exclaimed the discomfited Agnes.

'Mrs Cornett repeated your remark afterwards to Bertie van Tahn,' continued Tobermory, 'and said, "That woman is a regular Hunger Marcher; she'd go anywhere for four square meals a day", and Bertie van Tahn said—'

At this point the chronicle mercifully ceased. Tobermory had caught a glimpse of the big yellow tom from the Rectory working his way through the shrubbery towards the stable wing. In a flash he had vanished through the open french window.

With the disappearance of his too brilliant pupil Cornelius Appin found himself beset by a hurricane of bitter upbraiding, anxious enquiry, and frightened entreaty. The responsibility for the situation lay with him, and he must prevent matters from becoming worse. Could Tobermory impart his dangerous gift to other cats? was the first question he had to answer. It was possible, he replied, that he might have initiated his intimate friend the stable puss into his new accomplishment, but it was unlikely that his teaching could have taken a wider range as yet.

'Then,' said Mrs Cornett, 'Tobermory may be a valuable cat and a great pet; but I'm sure you'll agree, Adelaide, that both he and the stable cat must be done away with without delay.'

'You don't suppose I've enjoyed the last quarter of an hour, do you?' said Lady Blemley bitterly. 'My husband and I are very fond of Tobermory – at least, we were before this horrible accomplishment was infused into him; but now, of course, the only thing is to have him destroyed as soon as possible.'

'We can put some strychnine in the scraps he always gets at dinner-time,' said Sir Wilfrid, 'and I will go and drown the stable cat myself. The coachman will be very sore at losing his pet, but I'll say a very catching form of mange has broken out in both cats and we're afraid of it spreading to the kennels.'

'But my great discovery!' expostulated Mr Appin; 'after all my years of research and experiment—'

'You can go and experiment on the short-horns at the farm, who are under proper control,' said Mrs Cornett, 'or the elephants at the Zoological Gardens. They're said to be highly intelligent, and they have this recommendation, that they don't come creeping about our bedrooms and under chairs, and so forth.'

An archangel ecstatically proclaiming the Millennium, and then finding that it clashed unpardonably with Henley and would have to be indefinitely postponed, could hardly have felt more crestfallen than Cornelius Appin at the reception of his wonderful achievement. Public opinion, however, was against him – in fact, had the general voice been consulted on the subject it is probable that a strong minority vote would have been in favour of including him in the strychnine diet.

Defective train arrangements and a nervous desire to see matters brought to a finish prevented an immediate dispersal of the party, but dinner that evening was not a social success. Sir Wilfrid had had rather a trying time with the stable cat and subsequently with the coachman. Agnes Resker ostentatiously limited her repast to a morsel of dry toast, which she bit as though it were a personal enemy; while Mavis Pellington maintained a vindictive silence throughout the meal. Lady Blemley kept up a flow of what she hoped was conversation, but her attention was fixed on the doorway. A plateful of carefully dosed fish scraps was in readiness on the sideboard, but sweets and savoury and dessert went their way, and no Tobermory appeared either in the dining-room or kitchen.

The sepulchral dinner was cheerful compared with the subsequent vigil in the smoking-room. Eating and drinking had at least supplied a distraction and cloak to the prevailing embarrassment. Bridge was out of the question in the general tension of nerves and tempers, and after Odo Finsberry had given a lugubrious rendering of 'Melisande in the Wood' to a frigid audience, music was tacitly avoided. At eleven the servants went to bed, announcing that the small window in the pantry had been left open as usual for Tobermory's private use. The guests read steadily through the current batch of magazines, and fell back gradually on the 'Badminton Library' and bound volumes of *Punch*. Lady Blemley made periodic visits to the pantry, returning each time with an expression of listless depression which forestalled questioning.

At two o'clock Clovis broke the dominating silence.

'He won't turn up tonight. He's probably in the local newspaper office at the present moment, dictating the first instalment of his reminiscences. Lady What's-her-name's book won't be in it. It will be the event of the day.'

Having made this contribution to the general cheerfulness, Clovis went to bed. At long intervals the various members of the house-party followed his example.

The servants taking round the early tea made a uniform

announcement in reply to a uniform question. Tobermory had not returned.

Breakfast was, if anything, a more unpleasant function than dinner had been, but before its conclusion the situation was relieved. Tobermory's corpse was brought in from the shubbery, where a gardener had just discovered it. From the bites on his throat and the yellow fur which coated his claws it was evident that he had fallen in unequal combat with the big Tom from the Rectory.

By midday most of the guests had quitted the Towers, and after lunch Lady Blemley had sufficiently recovered her spirits to write an extremely nasty letter to the Rectory about the loss of her valuable pet.

Tobermory had been Appin's one successful pupil, and he was destined to have no successor. A few weeks later an elephant in the Dresden Zoological Garden, which had shown no previous signs of irritability, broke loose and killed an Englishman who had apparently been teasing it. The victim's name was variously reported in the papers as Oppin and Eppelin, but his front name was faithfully rendered Cornelius.

'If he was trying German irregular verbs on the poor beast,' said Clovis, 'he deserved all he got.'

THE GARDEN OF STUBBORN CATS
Italo Calvino

The city of cats and the city of men exist one inside the other, but they are not the same city. Few cats recall the time when there was no distinction: the streets and squares of men were also streets and squares of cats, and the lawns, courtyards, balconies and fountains: you lived in a broad and various space. But for several generations now domestic felines have been prisoners of an uninhabitable city: the streets are uninterruptedly overrun by the mortal traffic of cat-crushing automobiles; in every square foot of terrain where once a garden extended or a vacant lot or the ruins of an old demolition, now condominiums loom up, welfare housing, brand-new skyscrapers; every entrance is crammed by parked cars; the courtyards, one by one, have been roofed by reinforced concrete and transformed into garages or movie houses or storerooms or workshops. And where a rolling plateau of low roofs once extended, copings, terraces, water tanks, balconies, skylights, corrugated-iron sheds, now one general superstructure rises wherever structures can rise; the intermediate differences in height, between the low ground of the street and the supernal heaven of the penthouses disappear; the cat of a recent litter seeks in vain the itinerary of its fathers, the point from which to make the soft leap from balustrade to cornice to drainpipe, or for the quick climb on the rooftiles.

But in this vertical city, in this compressed city where all voids tend to fill up and every block of cement tends to mingle with other blocks of cement, a kind of counter-city opens, a negative city, that consists of empty slices between wall and wall, of the minimal distances ordained by the building regulations between two constructions, between the rear of one construction and the rear of the next; it is a city of cavities, wells, air conduits, driveways, inner yards, accesses to basements, like a network of dry canals on a planet of stucco and tar, and it is through this network, grazing the walls, that the ancient cat population still scurries.

On occasion, to pass the time, Marcovaldo would follow a cat. It was during the work-break, between noon and three, when all the personnel except Marcovaldo went home to eat, and he – who brought his lunch in his bag – laid his place among the packing-cases in the warehouse, chewed his snack, smoked a half-cigar, and wandered around, alone and idle, waiting for work to resume. In those hours, a cat that peeped in at a window was always welcome company, and a guide for new explorations. He had made friends with a tabby, well-fed, a blue ribbon around its neck, surely living with some well-to-do family. This tabby shared with Marcovaldo the habit of an afternoon stroll right after lunch; and naturally a friendship sprang up.

Following his tabby friend, Marcovaldo had started looking at places as if through the round eyes of a cat and even if these places were the usual environs of his firm he saw them in a different light, as settings for cattish stories, with connections practicable only by light, velvety paws. Though from the outside the neighbourhood seemed poor in cats, every day on his rounds Marcovaldo made the acquaintance of some new face, and a miaow, a hiss, a stiffening of fur on an arched back was enough for him to sense ties and intrigues and rivalries among them. At those moments he thought he had already penetrated the secrecy of the felines' society: and then he felt himself scrutinized by pupils that became slits, under the surveillance of the antennae of taut whiskers, and all the cats around him sat impassive as sphinxes, the pink triangle of their noses convergent on the black triangles of their lips, and the only things that moved were the tips of the ears, with a vibrant jerk like radar. They reached the end of a narrow passage, between squalid blank walls; and, looking around, Marcovaldo saw that the cats that had led him this far had vanished, all of them together, no telling in which direction, even his tabby friend, and they had left him alone. Their realm had territories, ceremonies, customs that it was not yet granted to him to discover.

On the other hand, from the cat city there opened unsuspected peep-holes onto the city of men: and one day the same tabby led him to discover the great Biarritz Restaurant.

Anyone wishing to see the Biarritz Restaurant had only to assume the posture of a cat, that is, proceed on all fours. Cat and man, in this fashion, walked around a kind of dome, at whose foot some low, rectangular little windows opened. Following the tabby's example, Marcovaldo looked down. They were transoms through which the luxurious hall received air and light. To the sound of gypsy violins, partridges and quails swirled by on silver dishes balanced by the white-gloved fingers of waiters in tailcoats. Or, more precisely, above the partridges and quails the dishes whirled, and above the dishes the white gloves, and poised on the waiters' patent-leather shoes, the gleaming parquet floor, from which hung dwarf potted palms and tablecloths and crystal and buckets like bells with the champagne bottle for their clapper: everything was turned upside-down because Marcovaldo, for fear of being seen, wouldn't stick his head inside the window and confined himself to looking at the reversed reflection of the room in the tilted pane.

But it was not so much the windows of the dining-room as those of the kitchens that interested the cat: looking through the former you saw, distant and somehow transfigured, what in the kitchens presented itself – quite concrete and within paw's reach – as a plucked bird or a fresh fish. And it was towards the kitchens, in fact, that the tabby wanted to lead Marcovaldo, either through a gesture of altruistic friendship or rather because it counted on the man's help for one of its raids. Marcovaldo, however, was reluctant to leave his belvedere over the main room: first, as he was fascinated by the luxury of the place, and then because something down there had riveted his attention. To such an extent that, overcoming his fear of being seen, he kept peeking in, with his head in the transom.

In the midst of the room, directly under that pane, there was a little glass fish-tank, a kind of aquarium, where some fat trout were swimming. A special customer approached, a man with a shiny bald pate, black suit, black beard. An old waiter in tailcoat followed him, carrying a little net as if he were going to catch butterflies. The gentleman in black looked at the trout with a grave, intent air; then he raised one hand and with a slow, solemn gesture singled out a fish. The waiter dipped the net into the tank, pursued the appointed trout, captured it, headed for the kitchens, holding out in front of him, like a lance, the net in which the fish wriggled. The gentleman in black, solemn as a magistrate who has handed down a capital sentence, went to take his seat and wait for the return of the trout, sautéed *à la meunière*.

If I found a way to drop a line from up here and make one of those trout bite, Marcovaldo thought, I couldn't be accused of theft; at worst, of fishing in an unauthorized place. And ignoring the miaows that called him towards the kitchen, he went to collect his fishing tackle.

Nobody in the crowded dining-room of the Biarritz saw the long, fine line, armed with hook and bait, as it slowly dropped into the tank. The fish saw the bait, and flung themselves on it. In the fray one trout managed to bite the worm: and immediately it began to rise, rise, emerge from the water, a silvery flash, it darted up high, over the laid tables and the trolleys of hors d'oeuvres, over the blue flames of the crêpes Suzette, until it vanished into the heavens of the transom.

Marcovaldo had yanked the rod with the brisk snap of the expert fisherman, so the fish landed behind his back. The trout had barely touched the ground when the cat sprang. What little life the trout still had was lost between the tabby's teeth. Marcovaldo, who had abandoned his line at that moment to run and grab the fish, saw it snatched from under his nose, hook and all. He was quick to put one foot on the rod, but the snatch had been so strong that the rod was all the man had left, while the tabby ran off with the fish, pulling the line after it. Treacherous kitty! It had vanished.

But this time it wouldn't escape him: there was that long line trailing after him and showing the way he had taken. Though he had lost sight of the cat, Marcovaldo followed the end of the line: there it was, running along a wall; it climbed a parapet, wound through a doorway, was swallowed up by a basement... Marcovaldo, venturing into more and more cattish places, climbed roots,

The Garden of Stubborn Cats

straddled railings, always managed to catch a glimpse – perhaps only a second before it disappeared – of that moving trace that indicated the thief's path.

Now the line played out down a walkway, in the midst of the traffic, and Marcovaldo, running after it, almost managed to grab it. He flung himself down on his belly: there, he grabbed it! He managed to seize one end of the line before it slipped between the bars of a gate.

Beyond a half-rusted gate and two bits of wall buried under climbing plants, there was a little rank garden, with a small, abandoned-looking building at the far end of it. A carpet of dry leaves covered the path, and dry leaves lay everywhere under the boughs of the two plane-trees, forming actually some little mounds in the yard. A layer of leaves was yellowing in the green water of a pool. Enormous buildings rose all around, skyscrapers with thousands of windows, like so many eyes trained disapprovingly on that little square patch with two trees, a few tiles, and all those yellow leaves, surviving right in the middle of an area of great traffic.

And in this garden, perched on the capitals and balustrades, lying on the dry leaves of the flower-beds, climbing on the trunks of the trees or on the drainpipes, motionless on their four paws, their tails making a question-mark, seated to wash their faces, there were tiger cats, black cats, white cats, calico cats, tabbies, angoras, Persians, house cats and stray cats, perfumed cats and mangy cats. Marcovaldo realized he had finally reached the heart of the cats' realm, their secret island. And, in his emotion, he almost forgot his fish.

It had remained, that fish, hanging by the line from the branch of a tree, out of reach of the cats' leaps; it must have dropped from its kidnapper's mouth at some clumsy movement, perhaps as it was defended from the others, or perhaps displayed as an extraordinary prize. The line had got tangled, and Marcovaldo, tug as he would, couldn't manage to yank it loose. A furious battle had meanwhile been joined among the cats, to reach that unreachable fish, or rather to win the right to try and reach it. Each wanted to prevent the others from leaping: they hurled themselves on one another, they tangled in mid-air, they rolled around clutching each other, and finally a general war broke out in a whirl of dry, crackling leaves.

After many futile yanks, Marcovaldo now felt the line was free, but he took care not to pull it: the trout would have fallen right in the midst of that infuriated scrimmage of felines.

It was at this moment that, from the top of the walls of the garden, a strange rain began to fall: fish bones, heads, tails, even bits of lung and lights. Immediately the cats' attention was distracted from the suspended trout and they flung themselves on the new delicacies. To Marcovaldo, this seemed the right moment to pull the line and regain his fish. But, before he had time to act, from a blind of the little villa, two yellow, skinny hands darted out: one was brandishing scissors; the other, a frying-pan. The hand with the scissors was raised above the trout, the hand with the frying-pan was thrust under it. The scissors cut the line, the trout fell into the pan; hands, scissors and pan withdrew, the blind closed: all in the space of a second. Marcovaldo was totally bewildered.

'Are you also a cat-lover?' A voice at his back made him turn round. He was surrounded by little old women, some of them ancient, wearing old-fashioned hats on their heads; others, younger, but with the look of spinsters; and all were carrying in their hands or their bags packages of left-over meat or fish, and some even had little pans of milk. 'Will you help me throw this package over the fence, for those poor creatures?'

All the ladies, cat-lovers, gathered at this hour around the garden of dry leaves to take food to their protégés.

'Can you tell me why they are all here, these cats?' Marcovaldo enquired.

'Where else could they go? This garden is all they have left! Cats come here from other neighbourhoods, too, from miles and miles around...'

'And birds, as well,' another lady added. 'They're forced to live by the hundreds and hundreds on these few trees...'

'And the frogs, they're all in that pool, and at night they never stop croaking... You can hear them even on the eighth floor of the buildings around here.'

'Who does this villa belong to anyway?' Marcovaldo asked. Now, outside the gate, there weren't just the cat-loving ladies but also other people: the man from the petrol pump opposite, the apprentices from a mechanic's shop, the postman, the grocer, some passers-by. And none of them, men and women, had to be asked twice: all wanted to have their say, as always when a mysterious and controversial subject comes up.

'It belongs to a Marchesa. She lives there, but you never see her...'

'She's been offered millions and millions by developers for this little patch of land, but she won't sell...'

'What would she do with millions, an old woman all alone in the world? She wants to hold on to her house, even if it's falling to pieces, rather than be forced to move...'

'It's the only undeveloped bit of land in the downtown area... Its value goes up every year... They've made her offers—'

'Offers! That's not all. Threats, intimidation, persecution... You don't know the half of it! Those contractors!'

'But she holds out. She's held out for years...'

'She's a saint. Without her, where would those poor animals go?'

'A lot she cares about the animals, the old miser! Have you ever seen her give them anything to eat?'

'How can she feed the cats when she doesn't have food for herself? She's the last descendant of a ruined family!'

'She hates cats. I've seen her chasing them and hitting them with an umbrella!'

'Because they were tearing up her flowerbeds!'

'What flowerbeds? I've never seen anything in this garden but a great crop of weeds!'

Marcovaldo realized that with regard to the old Marchesa opinions were sharply divided: some saw her as an angelic being, others as an egoist and a miser.

'It's the same with the birds; she never gives them a crumb!'

'She gives them hospitality. Isn't that plenty?'

'Like she gives the mosquitoes, you mean. They all come from here, from that pool. In the summertime the mosquitoes eat us alive, and it's all the fault of that Marchesa!'

'And the mice? This villa is a mine of mice. Under the dead leaves they have their burrows, and at night they come out...'

'As far as the mice go, the cats take care of them...'

'Oh, you and your cats! If we had to rely on them . . .'
'Why? Have you got something to say against cats?'
Here the discussion degenerated into a general quarrel.
'The authorities should do something: confiscate the villa!' one man cried.
'What gives them the right?' another protested.
'In a modern neighbourhood like ours, a mouse-nest like this . . . it should be forbidden . . .'
'Why, I picked my apartment precisely because it overlooked this little bit of green . . .'
'Green, hell! Think of the fine skyscraper they could build here!'
Marcovaldo would have liked to add something of his own, but he couldn't get a word in. Finally, all in one breath, he exclaimed: 'The Marchesa stole a trout from me!'
The unexpected news supplied fresh ammunition to the old woman's enemies, but her defenders exploited it as proof of the indigence to which the unfortunate noblewoman was reduced. Both sides agreed that Marcovaldo should go and knock at her door to demand an explanation.
It wasn't clear whether the gate was locked or unlocked; in any case, it opened, after a push, with a mournful creak. Marcovaldo picked his way among the leaves and cats, climbed the steps to the porch, knocked hard at the entrance.
At a window (the very one where the frying-pan had appeared), the blind was raised slightly and in one corner a round, pale blue eye was seen, and a clump of hair dyed an undefinable colour, and a dry skinny hand. A voice was heard, asking: 'Who is it? Who's at the door?', the words accompanied by a cloud smelling of fried oil.
'It's me, Marchesa. The trout man,' Marcovaldo explained. 'I don't mean to trouble you. I only wanted to tell you, in case you didn't know, that the trout was stolen from me, by that cat, and I'm the one who caught it, in fact the line . . .'
'Those cats! It's always those cats . . .' the Marchesa said, from behind the shutter, with a shrill, somewhat nasal voice. 'All my troubles come from the cats! Nobody knows what I go through! Prisoner night and day of those horrid beasts! And with all the refuse people throw over the walls, to spite me!'
'But my trout . . .'

'Your trout! What am I supposed to know about your trout!' The Marchesa's voice became almost a scream, as if she wanted to drown out the sizzle of the oil in the pan, which came through the window along with the aroma of fried fish. 'How can I make sense of anything, with all the stuff that rains into my house?'

'I understand, but did you take the trout or didn't you?'

'When I think of all the damage I suffer because of the cats! Ah, fine state of affairs! I'm not responsible for anything! I can't tell you what I've lost! Thanks to those cats, who've occupied house and garden for years! My life at the mercy of those animals! Go and find the owners! Make them pay damages! Damages? A whole life destroyed! A prisoner here, unable to move a step!'

'Excuse me for asking: but who's forcing you to stay?'

From the crack in the blind there appeared sometimes a round, pale blue eye, sometimes a mouth with two protruding teeth; for a moment the whole face was visible, and to Marcovaldo it seemed, bewilderingly, the face of a cat.

'They keep me prisoner, they do, those cats! Oh, I'd be glad to leave! What wouldn't I give for a little apartment all my own, in a nice clean modern building! But I can't go out . . . They follow me, they block my path, they trip me up!' The voice became a whisper, as if to confide a secret. 'They're afraid I'll sell the lot . . . They won't leave me . . . won't allow me . . . When the builders come to offer me a contract, you should see them, those cats! They get in the way, pull out their claws, they even chased a lawyer off! Once I had the contract right here, I was about to sign it, and they dived in through the window, knocked over the inkwell, tore up all the pages . . .'

All of a sudden Marcovaldo remembered the time, the shipping department, the boss. He tiptoed off over the dried leaves, as the voice continued to come through the slats of the blind, enfolded in that cloud apparently from the oil of a frying-pan. 'They even scratched me . . . I still have the scar . . . All alone here at the mercy of these demons . . .'

Winter came. A blossoming of white flakes decked the branches and capitals and the cats' tails. Under the snow, the dry leaves dissolved into mush. The cats were rarely seen, the cat-lovers even less; the packages of fish-bones were consigned only to cats who came to the door. Nobody, for quite a while, had seen anything of the Marchesa. No smoke came now from the chimney-pot of the villa.

One snowy day, the garden was again full of cats, who had returned as if it were spring, and they were miaowing as if on a moonlight night. The neighbours realized that something had happened: they went and knocked at the Marchesa's door. She didn't answer: she was dead.

In the spring, instead of the garden, there was a huge building site that a contractor had set up. The steam shovels dug down to great depths to make room for the foundations, cement poured into the iron armatures, a very high crane passed beams to the workmen who were making the scaffoldings. But how could they get on with their work? Cats walked along all the planks, they made bricks fall and upset buckets of mortar, they fought in the midst of the piles of sand. When you started to raise an armature, you found a cat perched on the top of it, hissing fiercely. More treacherous pussies climbed onto the masons' backs as if to purr, and there was no getting rid of them. And the birds continued making their nests in all the trestles, the cab of the crane looked like an aviary ... And you couldn't dip up a bucket of water that wasn't full of frogs, croaking and hopping ...

THE TOM-CAT
Colette

I had a name once, a short, furry name, a Persian Angora's name. But I left it on the roofs, in the gurgling hollow of the gutters, and on the rubbed moss of the old walls. I am the tom-cat.

What need have I of any other name? This one satisfies my pride. Those for whom I was once 'Sidi', the Lord Cat, no longer call me; they know that I obey no one. When they talk of me they say 'the tom-cat'. I come here when I please, and the masters of this dwelling are not my masters.

I am so beautiful that I hardly ever smile. My Persian fleece is shot with silver, the greyish mauve of wistaria faded by the sun, and the stormy violet of new slate. I have a broad, flat skull and lion-cheeks. And as for my beetling eyebrows and the superb, sad, red-brown eyes beneath them! In all this severe beauty there is just one frivolous detail, and that is my delicate nose, too short, like the noses of all Angoras, and as blue and moist as a little plum.

Even when I play I hardly ever smile. When I condescend to break some ornament with my royal paw, I give the impression that I'm chastising it. And if I raise the same heavy paw against that irreverent princeling, my son, you would think it was to cast him into outer darkness. You surely didn't expect that I would simper about on the carpet like the She-Shah, my little Sultana whom I neglect?

I am the tom-cat. I lead the restless life of those whom love has created for his hard service. I walk alone, blood-thirsty by necessity, and doomed always to be the victor. I fight as I eat, with a controlled appetite, like an athlete in perfect condition who wins without haste or rage.

I never return to your house until morning. Down I drop at dawn, and as blue as the dawn, from the top of those bare trees where a moment ago I looked like a nest in the haze. Or sometimes I glide over the sloping roof until I come to the wooden balcony; then I take up a position on the sill of your half-open window, looking like a winter nosegay from which you can drink in all the scents of a December night, with its tang of a cold graveyard. Later, when I fall asleep, my hot, feverish body will give off an odour of bitter boxwood, dried blood and musk.

For beneath the silky cloak of my fleece, I bleed. There is a burning wound in my throat; but I do not even lick the torn skin of my paw. All I want is to sleep and sleep and sleep, to shut my eyelids tight over my beautiful night-bird's eyes, and to sleep no matter where, like a tramp on his side, inert, clotted with mud, and bristling with twigs and dry leaves like a sated faun.

I sleep and sleep. Sometimes an electric shock makes me sit up, but after a rumbling growl, like distant thunder, I fall back again. Even when I wake up in earnest towards the end of the day, I seem absent and still haunted by dreams. I have an eye on the window and an ear on the door.

After a hasty wash, with stiff and aching bones, I cross the threshold every evening at the same hour, and off I go with my head down, looking more like an outcast than one of the elect. Off I go, threading my way like a sluggish caterpillar between the icy puddles, and flattening my ears against the wind. I make my way indifferent to the snow. If I stop for a moment it is not because I hesitate; I am listening to the secret rumours of my empire. I consult the dark air, hurling into it those solemn, rhythmic, despairing howlings of the wandering, defiant tom-cat. Then, as though the sound of my voice had lashed me into sudden frenzy, I spring. You catch sight of me for a second on the top of a wall, you have a vague impression that I'm up there, fur on end, blurred and floating like a shred of cloud, and then you see me no more.

Now is the wild season of love, which blinds us to all other joys, and by some black magic multiplies the lean females in the gardens. Impossible to choose between this one, white and thin, that one blazing like a brown and orange tulip, and the other, black and gleaming like a wet eel. Alas, I want all of them, this, that, and the other! If I don't subdue them, my rivals will take them. I want them all, not preferring any or even distinguishing them. Already I cease to hear the sob of this one who is enduring my cruel embrace. I am listening to a voice which reaches me over the roofs and across the winds, the voice of the she-cat who is calling me, and whom I don't know.

How beautiful she is, that far-away beloved, invisible and groaning with desire! Surround her with walls, keep her from me as long as you will, let her scent and her voice alone possess me! Alas, for me there is no such thing as an inaccessible lover, and this one too will leap over the walls to join me. It may be that my teeth will find again, in the bushy fur of her scruff, the marks that they left there last year.

The nights of love are long. I remain at my post, ready for action, punctual and morose. The little wife I have deserted sleeps in her house. She is blue and gentle and looks too much like me. Lying in the depths of her scented bed, is she listening to the cries that rise up to me? And when the struggle is at its height, does she hear my beast-name roared out by some wounded male, that name of mine which no man has heard?

Yes, this night of love is long drawn out. I feel sad and more solitary than a god. In the middle of a laborious vigil, I am suddenly aware of a simple longing for light and warmth and rest. Will dawn never come to pale the sky, reassuring the birds and putting an end to the midnight revels of the frenzied cats? For many years now I have reigned and loved and killed; and I have been beautiful for a very long time. Rolled in a ball on the wall icy with dew, I dream . . . I am afraid of looking old.

PAINS AND PLEASURES
L. P. Hartley

There is always room for improvement, but there is not always time for it. Henry Kitson had reached and over-reached the allotted span. In his youth he had been something of a teleologist. An immense and varied field of ambition lay open to him. He would become one with his desires; he would achieve an important and worthwhile aim in which his whole self, all the contents of his personality, such as they were, would be completely and for ever expressed.

These aims took different forms. He would climb the Matterhorn (in those days a considerable feat) and, if he had known about it, he would have wanted to climb the north face of the Eiger. He would also play the 'Moonlight Sonata' quite perfectly: the last movement would have no terrors for him. Adding to these achievements he would learn to read, and to speak, at least five languages; his Aunt Patsy, his father's eldest sister, had done so, so why not he? He would reduce his handicap at golf, which was 12, to scratch or even to plus something. He would write a book (he couldn't decide on what subject) that would be a classic, immortal: the name of Henry Kitson would resound down the ages.

And he had other ambitions.

Alas, none of them had materialized, and here he was, in his early seventies, with nothing to show for them. He was comfortably off, with a pension from the firm in the City who had employed him for nearly half a century, and with the money he had saved up – for he had not, mentally, grown old with the years; he was not, and could not be, 'his age'; he still regarded himself as the impecunious, ambitious young man he was at twenty-five.

Apart from the tendency which often overtakes elderly men to regard himself as penniless, his situation was most fortunate. He had, as general factotum, a retired policeman, who cleaned his cottage, cooked his meals and drove his car. Wilson ('Bill' to Henry Kitson) was perfect: he did everything he should, and nothing he shouldn't. In this he was very different from some of his predecessors, who had done everything they shouldn't, and nothing that they should.

Coming at the tail-end of this procession of mainly unsatisfactory characters ('character' was a word used in the old days, but in a different sense, when a prospective employer was asking for a reference) Bill had, of course, for Henry, an overwhelming advantage. After many years of domestic darkness, Bill was the light. Whenever Henry thought of him he gave (if he could remember to) thanksgiving to heaven for Bill.

At the same time it was a great temptation, as it always is if the opportunity arises, to flog the willing horse. Bill, like Barkis, was willing; and Henry sometimes asked Bill to do jobs that he would never have dared to ask of any of Bill's less amenable forerunners.

With the advent of Bill, 'a soundless calm', in Emily Brontë's words, descended on Henry. Domestic troubles were over; nothing to resent; nothing to fight against; no sense of Sisyphus bearing an unbearable weight uphill. No grievance at all. Had he lived by his grievances, was a question that Henry sometimes asked himself. Had his resistance to them, his instinct to fight back and assert himself and show what he was made of, somehow strengthened his hold on life, and prolonged it?

Now he had nothing to resist. What Bill did with his spare time – if he occupied it, as Henry suspected, at the pub and the betting-shop, was no business of his. As far as he was concerned, Bill could do no wrong.

But just as someone who has always carried a weight on his shoulders, or on his mind or on his heart and who is suddenly relieved of it, feels in himself a void, an incentive to living suddenly taken away, even so Henry, lacking this incentive, found his life empty, almost purposeless.

Gratitude to Bill was his major preoccupation, but how to express

Pains and Pleasures

it? Bill was by no means indifferent to money – he liked it and he knew more about it than Henry, with a lifetime's experience of business, did.

Little presents, Bill was not averse to them; but they didn't represent to Henry even a small part of his indebtedness to Bill. Perhaps a bonus of ten per cent for honesty?

Undoubtedly, Henry Kitson's retired and retiring life was the happier for Bill's presence, and for his presents to Bill, but it was also the emptier, now that his grievance had been taken away. Most people need something to live against, and if this objective, positive or negative, is removed, they suffer for it. Henry had friends in the neighbourhood whom he saw as often as he could; but they did not supply him with that extra-personal incentive.

'Live with one aim, but let that aim be high' – or low – which he had had when X, and Y, and Z were ill-treating him, and whose malfeasances, he felt, must be resisted to the ultimate extent of his emotional if not his personal prowess.

With Bill in charge of his domestic affairs, there was nothing at all to be resisted, nothing to aim at – for Bill was a placid, self-contained character, who had seen a lot of the ups and downs of life, and had little to learn from it which Henry, with the best will in the world, could supply.

So this life stratified itself into a routine, pleasant but nearly featureless. There were, however, two features in his day which had an emotional content and significance, and to which he clung, for they represented what he liked, and what he disliked: as long as he stuck to them and could look forward to or dread them, he knew he was keeping the advance of senility at bay.

One was concerned with Bill. Bill in common with many other men, rich and poor, criminal and honest, liked a drink: and Henry saw to it that Bill's 'elevenses' should be a tot of whisky. With all the variations of vocal expression at his command, he would ask Bill if he would like a drink; and Bill, with all the variations of expression at his command, would say 'Yes'. From the time when he was called, at eight o'clock, Henry looked forward to this little episode. At the word 'drink' Bill's dark eyes would glow, like coals that had suddenly been set alight. 'Good health!' he would say, before he took his glass into the kitchen. Henry never failed to get pleasure from his simple interchange of amenities, just as he never failed to get pain from the other cardinal event of his day, and unfortunately he had longer to anticipate it. This was to put out his cat, Ginger, at bed-time. He was fond of Ginger, but Ginger was old and set in his ways, and did not like being put out. Being a neuter, he did not have the same motive that many cats have for prowling about at night, growling and yowling and keeping everyone within earshot awake. He wanted to be warm and comfortable; and although there was a shed and an outhouse in the garden which he must have known about, he preferred Henry's fireside, and when Henry opened the garden door to put him out he would streak past through Henry's legs and sit down in front of the fire, purring loudly and triumphantly.

Henry found this daily or rather nightly ejection of Ginger very painful, but it was inevitable, for with age he had lost whatever house-training he ever had, and misbehaved accordingly. It fell to Bill's lot to deal with these misdemeanours, which always happened in a certain place, on some stone flags by the cellar-door. Perhaps Ginger thought that his oblations would be more acceptable there than anywhere else; and as someone said, 'it is impossible to make a cat understand that it should do what you want it to do'.

When bed-time approached, Henry picked Ginger up and carried him towards the garden-door, the fatal exit. Then Ginger would purr ingratiatingly, as though to say, 'You can't have the heart to do this.' Sometimes, in rebellious moods, he would struggle and claw and scratch: but the end was always the same; he made a desperate dash to get back into the house. Often the hateful process had to be repeated more than once and Henry peering through the glass door (which he couldn't resist doing) would see Ginger's amber eyes fixed on him with a look of heart-rending reproach.

Henry knew what the correct solution was: *he* should clean up the mess that Ginger made, and not leave it to Bill. But how tempting it is to flog the willing horse! And if ever he yielded to Ginger's protests, whether in the form of purr or scratch, and let him stay indoors, he refrained from asking Bill what had happened outside the cellar-door. Not that Bill ever complained. When Henry surreptitiously went down to the cellar-door and saw and smelt the unmistakeable traces (however carefully cleaned up) of Ginger's nightly defecations, not a word was said between them.

But as time passed, and the pension-supported Henry came to rely more and more on his daily routine of living, with nothing to jerk him out of it, the problem of pleasure and pain, as exemplified by Bill's whisky elevenses in the morning, and Ginger's compulsory expulsions at night, began to assume undue importance. Henry simply did not want his septuagenarian happiness to depend on these two absurd poles of emotional comfort and discomfort.

What *could* he do? Human beings were (so it was generally thought), more valuable and more important than dumb animals (a ridiculous expression, for many animals including Ginger were far from dumb). Certainly Bill was much more valuable to him than Ginger was: Bill was an asset of the highest order whereas Ginger (except for Henry's affection for him) was merely a debit. He was very greedy; he did nothing to earn his keep; he could not, and did not try, to catch the most unsophisticated mouse; he was just a liability and a parasite. Bill, though such a mild-mannered man, must in his time have been a tough character, and used to dealing with tough characters, criminals, murderers and such, as policeman have to be.

'I wish I knew what to do about Ginger,' Henry said. 'He makes such a fuss when I turn him out at night. But you know better than I do, I'm sorry to say,' (and Henry was genuinely sorry) 'what happens when he stays indoors. It's not his fault, he doesn't mean it, he can't help it, but well, there it is.'

'I know what you refer to, sir,' said the ex-policeman with an instinctive delicacy of utterance, 'and I think I know the solution. Indeed, I have been turning it over in my mind for some time. It's really quite simple.'

'You mean it would be simple to have Ginger put down?'

'Oh no, sir,' said Bill, horrified. 'Nothing as drastic as that. Ginger is a good old cat, he wouldn't hurt a mouse.' (This was only too true.) 'I am attached to him, just as you are, and when I said the solution is quite simple, it *is* quite simple, if you know what I mean.'

'I'm not sure that I do. What *is* the solution?'

'Just this, sir. Give him a box with sawdust in it, and put it where he usually – where he usually does his business, if you know what I mean – and I'll show it to him and then if he doesn't understand at *once* – but he *will*, all cats do, I'll put his paw in it, and he will soon know what it's for – and, and act accordingly.'

'What an excellent idea,' said Henry, a little patronizingly. 'I wonder that I never thought of it. There is an empty seed-box in the greenhouse, I think, that would be just right for the purpose. And sawdust, I suppose, is quite easy to get hold of.'

'Well, not all that easy, sir,' said Bill. 'But having in mind the ash-tree that fell down, which I am cutting up for firewood, it shouldn't be difficult, in fact I've got nearly enough already.'

'Thank you very much, Bill.'

Ginger was duly introduced to the box, and his paw gently embedded in the sawdust. This he took very well, purring all the time; but when the ceremony of initiation was over, he did not use the box for its intended cloacal purpose, but settled down in it, with his forepaws tucked under him, and his tail neatly curled round his flank, and went to sleep.

Next day he was discovered still asleep in the sawdust box, but alas, only a few inches away were the extremely malodorous vestiges of Ginger's digestion or indigestion, which the box had been intended to absorb.

'Never mind,' said Bill, 'he'll learn in time.'

But Ginger didn't learn. He spent many hours, sometimes all day, slumbering on his sawdust mattress, purring to himself, no doubt, instead of sitting in front of Henry's comfortable fireplace purring to *him*.

'I'm afraid Ginger isn't going to learn, Bill,' said Henry.

'It looks like not,' said Bill. 'You can't teach an old cat new tricks.' He laughed at this sally. 'But we can give him a few days' grace.'

The few days passed, but Ginger did not learn. He still regarded the sawdust box as his bed; and like a well-conducted person, he did not wish to pollute it. It was woundingly evident that he still preferred it to Henry's fireside and that his adjacent loo was very convenient to him. Henry knew that he himself ought to undo what Ginger had done; but somehow he couldn't bring himself to. 'I am over seventy,' he reasoned, 'and why should I sacrifice myself to the selfish whims of a cat, especially when it has been given every opportunity to satisfy the needs of Nature in other ways?' All the same, he didn't relish the nightly ordeal of turning Ginger out.

'I'm afraid our experiment with Ginger hasn't been successful,' he said to Bill. 'He goes on making a nuisance of himself. I wonder if *you* would mind putting him out at night? He doesn't like it, he claws and clutches at me, but I dare say that with you he would be more – more sensible. Would you mind?'

'Of course not, Mr Kitson,' replied Bill, who when he remembered, preferred to call Henry 'Mr Kitson' rather than 'sir'.

Days passed; Henry saw little of Ginger, so content was he on his sawdust bed that he didn't bother to visit Henry in the sitting-room. Henry caught fleeting glimpses of him in the garden, tail-twitching, intent on birds which he was far too old to catch. 'Blast him!' thought Henry. 'Ungrateful beast!'

One day there was a knock at his study door. 'Come in!' said Henry, who had always asked people not to knock. 'Come in! Who is it?'

'Oh, *Bill*!' he exclaimed, instantly welcoming. 'What can I do for you?'

He hadn't noticed how upset and how unlike himself Bill looked.

'It's like this, sir,' Bill began and stopped.

'Like what, Bill?' asked Henry, and his heart turned over with a presage of disaster.

'It's like this,' Bill paused, and repeated more slowly and with a note of authority in his voice that reminded Henry that he had once been a policeman, 'It's like this.'

'Like what?' Henry asked again.

'It's like this,' Bill said, and he looked taller under the toplight of Henry's study, and almost as if he was wearing uniform, 'I want to give in my notice. I want to ask for my cards.'

'But why, Bill?' Henry asked, aghast.

'Well, Mr Kitson, you may think it silly of me, but it's because of Ginger.'

'Because of Ginger?' Again Henry's heart smote him. 'You mean because of the messes he still makes?'

'Oh no, Mr Kitson. I don't mind them at all. They're all in the day's work, if you know what I mean.'

'Then what *do* you mind?'

'I mind putting him out at night, sir. He claws and clutches and scratches me – you wouldn't believe it. Not that I'd mind with a human being, I've had plenty of people to deal with much worse than he is – after all, he's only got his claws, and I think he's lost most of his teeth, but all the same, I don't like it, sir, and that's why I'm giving in my notice and asking for my cards.'

Henry was not too distraught to ignore the dignity of Bill's resignation.

'What will you do now, Bill?' he asked.

'Oh, well, sir, I shall find something. There are jobs waiting for a single man. I'm not a single man, really, I'm a widower, which is the nearest thing, and I have no ties. I haven't put an advert in the paper yet, but I shall find a job, you may be sure.'

Henry, too, was sure he would find another job; but where would he find another Bill? It was all too wretched, but he knew men of Bill's type and they didn't change their minds easily once they were made up.

'Listen!' he said loudly, as if Bill was deaf. 'I don't mind cleaning up the mess that Ginger leaves and I don't mind putting him out at night. I know the way he claws and scratches, but I thought that with you who feeds him, he would behave better than he does with me. It seems that he hasn't, and I am very sorry, Bill, but I shall be only too glad to take him on, eating, sleeping, and whatever else he wants to do – and relieve you of the responsibility.' (Just as Ginger relieves *himself*, he thought but did not say.)

'I couldn't ask you to do that, sir. You have been very good to me, but I shall find a job where there aren't any animals to work for.'

At this rather ungracious remark Henry Kitson groaned again.

'I know I ought not to have left the dirty work to you, Bill,' he said, with the belated contrition that most people feel at one time or another. 'I know I shouldn't have, and if you agree to stay I'll be responsible for everything to do with Ginger, by day or by night.'

'Oh no, sir, I couldn't let you do that, a gentleman in your position. And in any case, it isn't *that* that I mind.'

Henry groaned again. He was utterly at a loss.

'Then what do you mind, Bill?'

'I mind putting him out at night, Mr Kitson. He creates so, you wouldn't believe it, but yes, you would, you've had it so often yourself. It isn't his scratching and mauling I mind, it's when he purrs and tries to pretend I'm doing him a kindness. I'm not that tender-hearted, but I know what it's like to spend a night in the open,' the ex-policeman added.

Henry's eyes grew moist.

'Well, I'll put him out tonight.'

'Oh no, Mr Kitson, I'll see to him.'

But Henry displayed unexpected firmness.

'No, no, let's leave him indoors. And if anything happens, I'll take care of it.'

'Very good, sir,' said Bill, smartly. 'Good night, sir,' he added, on a note of finality that echoed through the room when he was gone.

Ginger was lying in front of the fire, on one of his rare visits to Henry's study since he had yielded to the superior attractions of the sawdust box. He purred, as he always did when Henry so much as looked at him. Every now and then he stretched out his paw, as though trying to make himself more comfortable than he already was. Every now and then he half opened his eyes and looked at Henry with what Henry called his 'beatific' expression, suggesting his mysterious but not unkindly insight into the past, the present, and the future.

I won't disturb him, Henry thought, turning out the light. Let him stay here if he wants to, and if he prefers the cellar-door he knows the way.'

At eight o'clock the next morning Bill appeared as usual, bringing Henry's early morning tea. He drew the curtains.

'There it is!' he said.

Henry had heard this aubade before, but he was always foxed by it.

'Where is what?' he asked.

'The day,' said Bill.

Henry, nursing again his discomfiture at not having foreseen this obvious answer, sat up and looked out of the window. It was a dreary November day, but Bill didn't seem uncheerful.

'I'm afraid I've some bad news for you,' he said.

Henry tried to collect his waking thoughts. A pall enveloped them. How could Bill be so unkind?

'I suppose you mean that you are leaving?' he said, stretching out his hand for the teapot.

'Oh no, Mr Kitson, it's much worse than that.'

What can be worse? thought Henry miserably, and uttered his thought out loud. 'What can be worse, Bill?'

'It's much worse,' said Bill.

Eight o'clock in the morning is not the best time to receive bad news, and especially if one doesn't know what it is. Henry relinquished the teapot and sank back on the pillow.

'Tell me,' he said.

'Well, Mr Kitson,' said Bill, with his back to the light, while he was arranging Henry's clothes on a chair, 'to tell you the truth—'

'Oh, do tell me, Bill.'

'To tell you the *truth*,' Bill repeated, as if one sort of truth was more valuable than another, 'Ginger is dead.'

'Good God,' said Henry, who had envisaged some cosmic nuclear disturbance especially aimed at him. 'Good God!' he repeated, with intense relief. And then he remembered Ginger last night, sitting on the hearth-rug and purring loudly whenever Henry vouchsafed a look at him. 'Poor Ginger!' he said.

'Yes, sir, and I feel very sorry about him too. Ginger was a good old cat. Would you like to see him, Mr Kitson?'

'What, now?'

'Now, or any time. He's there, he isn't far away.'

Henry got out of bed. He put on his dressing-gown and followed Bill downstairs.

'The usual place,' said Bill.

It was dark down there, so they turned on the light. Ginger was lying in his sawdust box, looking quite comfortable and life-like, except that his head seemed to be twisted over.

Henry stooped down and stroked his cold fur and half listened for the purr that didn't come; then he led the way upstairs.

'He seemed so well last night,' he said to Bill.

'Oh yes, sir, but animals are like that, just like human beings, if you know what I mean. Here today and gone tomorrow.'

Henry felt the bitter sensation of loss that we are all bound to feel at one time or another.

'But he seemed so well last night,' he repeated.

'Yes,' replied Bill, 'but he was very old. We all have to go sometime.'

An unworthy suspicion stirred in Henry's mind, but he stifled it.

'And now I've got to lose you, too, Bill,' he said.

'Oh no, sir,' said Bill, promptly, 'I've thought it over, and I don't want to go, that is, unless you want me to.'

A wave of relief – there was no other word for it – swept over Henry.

'Please stay,' he said, 'please stay, Bill.'

'Yes, I will, Mr Kitson,' Bill answered and there was a surge and an uplift in his voice. 'We've got cutlets for lunch – will that be all right?'

His pronunciation was rather odd, and he made it sound like 'catlets'.

*

'Would you like a drink now, Bill?' Henry asked. 'Or is it too early?'

'I won't say no,' said Bill, and the light began to glow behind his coal-black eyes.

THE CAT THAT WALKED BY HIMSELF

Rudyard Kipling

Hear and attend and listen; for this befell and behappened and became and was, O my Best Beloved, when the Tame animals were wild. The Dog was wild, and the Horse was wild, and the Cow was wild, and the Sheep was wild, and the Pig was wild – as wild as wild could be – and they walked in the Wet Wild Woods by their wild lones. But the wildest of all the wild animals was the Cat. He walked by himself, and all places were alike to him.

Of course the Man was wild too. He was dreadfully wild. He didn't even begin to be tame till he met the Woman, and she told him that she did not like living in his wild ways. She picked out a nice dry Cave, instead of a heap of wet leaves, to lie down in; and she strewed clean sand on the floor; and she lit a nice fire of wood at the back of the Cave; and she hung a dried wild-horse skin, tail-down, across the opening of the Cave; and she said, 'Wipe your feet, dear, when you come in, and now we'll keep house.'

That night, Best Beloved, they ate wild sheep roasted on the hot stones, and flavoured with wild garlic and wild pepper; and wild duck stuffed with wild rice and wild fenugreek and wild coriander and marrow-bones of wild oxen; and wild cherries, and wild grenadillas. Then the Man went to sleep in front of the fire ever so happy; but the Woman sat up, combing her hair. She took the bone of the shoulder of mutton – the big flat blade-bone – and she looked at the wonderful marks on it, and she threw more wood on the fire, and she made a Magic. She made the First Singing Magic in the world.

Out in the Wet Wild Woods all the wild animals gathered together where they could see the light of the fire a long way off, and they wondered what it meant.

Then Wild Horse stamped with his wild foot and said, 'O my Friends and O my Enemies, why have the Man and the Woman made that great light in that great Cave, and what harm will it do us?'

Wild Dog lifted up his wild nose and smelled the smell of the roast mutton, and said, 'I will go up and see and look, and say; for I think it is good. Cat, come with me.'

'Nenni!' said the Cat. 'I am the Cat who walks by himself, and all places are alike to me. I will not come.'

'Then we can never be friends again,' said Wild Dog, and he trotted off to the Cave. But when he had gone a little way the Cat said to himself, 'All places are alike to me. Why should I not go too and see and look and come away at my own liking?' So he slipped after Wild Dog softly, very softly, and hid himself where he could hear everything.

When Wild Dog reached the mouth of the Cave he lifted up the dried horse-skin with his nose and sniffed the beautiful smell of the roast mutton, and the Woman, looking at the blade-bone, heard him, and laughed, and said, 'Here comes the first. Wild Thing out of the Wild Woods, what do you want?'

Wild Dog said, 'O my Enemy and Wife of my Enemy, what is this that smells so good in the Wild Woods?'

Then the Woman picked up a roasted mutton-bone and threw it to Wild Dog, and said, 'Wild Thing out of the Wild Woods, taste and try.' Wild Dog gnawed the bone, and it was more delicious than anything he had ever tasted, and he said, 'O my Enemy and Wife of my Enemy, give me another.'

The Woman said, 'Wild Thing out of the Wild Woods, help my Man to hunt through the day and guard this Cave at night, and I will give you as many roast bones as you need.'

'Ah!' said the Cat, listening. 'This is a very wise Woman, but she is not so wise as I am.'

Wild Dog crawled into the Cave and laid his head on the Woman's lap, and said, 'O my Friend and Wife of my Friend, I will

The Cat that Walked by Himself

help your Man to hunt through the day, and at night I will guard your Cave.'

'Ah!' said the Cat, listening. 'That is a very foolish Dog.' And he went back through the Wet Wild Woods waving his wild tail, and walking by his wild lone. But he never told anybody.

When the Man waked up he said, 'What is Wild Dog doing here?' And the Woman said, 'His name is not Wild Dog any more, but the First Friend, because he will be our friend for always and always and always. Take him with you when you go hunting.'

Next night the Woman cut great green armfuls of fresh grass from the water-meadows, and dried it before the fire, so that it smelt like new-mown hay, and she sat at the mouth of the Cave and plaited a halter out of horse-hide, and she looked at the shoulder-of-mutton bone – at the big broad blade-bone – and she made a Magic. She made the Second Singing Magic in the world.

Out in the Wild Woods all the wild animals wondered what had happened to Wild Dog, and at last Wild Horse stamped with his foot and said, 'I will go and see and say why Wild Dog has not returned. Cat, come with me.'

'Nenni!' said the Cat. 'I am the Cat who walks by himself, and all places are alike to me. I will not come.' But all the same he followed Wild Horse softly, very softly, and hid himself where he could hear everything.

When the Woman heard Wild Horse tripping and stumbling on his long mane, she laughed and said, 'Here comes the second. Wild Thing out of the Wild Woods, what do you want?'

Wild Horse said, 'O my Enemy and Wife of my Enemy, where is Wild Dog?'

The Woman laughed, and picked up the blade-bone and looked at it, and said, 'Wild Thing out of the Wild Woods, you did not come here for Wild Dog, but for the sake of this good grass.'

And Wild Horse, tripping and stumbling on his long mane, said, 'That is true; give it me to eat.'

The Woman said, 'Wild Thing out of the Wild Woods, bend your wild head and wear what I give you, and you shall eat the wonderful grass three times a day.'

'Ah!' said the Cat, listening. 'This is a clever Woman, but she is not so clever as I am.'

Wild Horse bent his wild head, and the Woman slipped the plaited-hide halter over it, and Wild Horse breathed on the Woman's feet and said, 'O my Mistress, and Wife of my Master, I will be your servant for the sake of the wonderful grass.'

'Ah!' said the Cat, listening. 'That is a very foolish Horse.' And he went back through the Wet Wild Woods, waving his wild tail and walking by his wild lone. But he never told anybody.

When the Man and the Dog came back from hunting, the Man said, 'What is Wild Horse doing here?' And the Woman said, 'His name is not Wild Horse any more, but the First Servant, because he will carry us from place to place for always and always and always. Ride on his back when you go hunting.'

Next day, holding her wild head high that her wild horns should not catch in the wild trees, Wild Cow came up to the Cave, and the Cat followed, and hid himself just the same as before; and everything happened just the same as before; and the Cat said the same things as before; and when Wild Cow had promised to give her milk to the Woman every day in exchange for the wonderful grass, the Cat went back through the Wet Wild Woods waving his wild tail and walking by his wild lone, just the same as before. But he never told anybody. And when the Man and the Horse and the Dog came home from hunting and asked the same questions the same as before, the Woman said, 'Her name is not Wild Cow any more, but the Giver of Good Food. She will give us the warm white milk for always and always and always, and I will take care of her while you and the First Friend and the First Servant go hunting.'

Next day the Cat waited to see if any other Wild Thing would go up to the Cave, but no one moved in the Wet Wild Woods, so the Cat walked there by himself; and he saw the Woman milking the Cow, and he saw the light of the fire in the Cave, and he smelt the smell of the warm white milk.

Cat said, 'O my Enemy and Wife of my Enemy, where did Wild Cow go?'

The Woman laughed and said, 'Wild Thing out of the Wild Woods, go back to the Woods again, for I have braided up my hair, and I have put away the magic blade-bone, and we have no more need of either friends or servants in our Cave.'

The Cat that Walked by Himself

Cat said, 'I am not a friend, and I am not a servant. I am the Cat who walks by himself, and I wish to come into your Cave.'

Woman said, 'Then why did you not come with First Friend on the first night?'

Cat grew very angry and said, 'Has Wild Dog told tales of me?'

Then the Woman laughed and said, 'You are the Cat who walks by himself, and all places are alike to you. You are neither a friend nor a servant. You have said it yourself. Go away and walk by yourself in all places alike.'

Then Cat pretended to be sorry and said, 'Must I never come into the Cave? Must I never sit by the warm fire? Must I never drink the warm white milk? You are very wise and very beautiful. You should not be cruel even to a Cat.'

Woman said, 'I knew I was wise, but I did not know I was beautiful. So I will make a bargain with you. If ever I say one word in your praise, you may come into the Cave.'

'And if you say two words in my praise?' said the Cat.

'I never shall,' said the Woman, 'but if I say two words in your praise, you may sit by the fire in the Cave.'

'And if you say three words?' said the Cat.

'I never shall,' said the Woman, 'but if I say three words in your praise, you may drink the warm white milk three times a day for always and always and always.'

Then the Cat arched his back and said, 'Now let the Curtain at the mouth of the Cave, and the Fire at the back of the Cave, and the Milk-pots that stand beside the Fire, remember what my Enemy and the Wife of my Enemy has said.' And he went away through the Wet Wild Woods waving his wild tail and walking by his wild lone.

That night when the Man and the Horse and the Dog came home from hunting, the Woman did not tell them of the bargain that she had made with the Cat, because she was afraid that they might not like it.

Cat went far and far away and hid himself in the Wet Wild Woods by his wild lone for a long time till the Woman forgot all about him. Only the Bat – the little upside-down Bat – that hung inside the Cave knew where Cat hid; and every evening Bat would fly to Cat with news of what was happening.

One evening Bat said, 'There is a Baby in the Cave. He is new and pink and fat and small, and the Woman is very fond of him.'

'Ah,' said the Cat, listening. 'But what is the Baby fond of?'

'He is fond of things that are soft and tickle,' said the Bat. 'He is fond of warm things to hold in his arms when he goes to sleep. He is fond of being played with. He is fond of all those things.'

'Ah,' said the Cat, listening. 'Then my time has come.'

Next night Cat walked through the Wet Wild Woods and hid very near the Cave till morning-time, and Man and Dog and Horse went hunting. The Woman was busy cooking that morning, and the Baby cried and interrupted. So she carried him outside the Cave and gave him a handful of pebbles to play with. But still the Baby cried.

Then the Cat put out his paddy paw and patted the Baby on the cheek, and it cooed; and the Cat rubbed against its fat knees and tickled it under its fat chin with his tail. And the Baby laughed; and the Woman heard him and smiled.

Then the Bat – the little upside-down Bat – that hung in the mouth of the Cave said, 'O my Hostess and Wife of my Host and Mother of my Host's Son, a Wild Thing from the Wild Woods is most beautifully playing with your Baby.'

'A blessing on that Wild Thing whoever he may be,' said the Woman, straightening her back, 'for I was a busy woman this morning and he has done me a service.'

That very minute and second, Best Beloved, the dried horse-skin Curtain that was stretched tail-down at the mouth of the Cave fell down – *whoosh!* – because it remembered the bargain she had made with the Cat; and when the Woman went to pick it up – lo and behold! – the Cat was sitting quite comfy inside the Cave.

'O my Enemy and Wife of my Enemy and Mother of my Enemy,' said the Cat, 'it is I: for you have spoken a word in my praise, and now I can sit within the Cave for always and always and always. But still I am the Cat who walks by himself, and all places are alike to me.'

The Woman was very angry, and shut her lips tight and took up her spinning-wheel and began to spin.

But the Baby cried because the Cat had gone away, and the Woman could not hush it, for it struggled and kicked and grew black in the face.

The Cat that Walked by Himself

'O my Enemy and Wife of my Enemy and Mother of my Enemy,' said the Cat, 'take a strand of the thread that you are spinning and tie it to your spindle-whorl and drag it along the floor, and I will show you a Magic that shall make your Baby laugh as loudly as he is now crying.'

'I will do so,' said the Woman, 'because I am at my wits' end; but I will not thank you for it.'

She tied the thread to the little clay spindle-whorl and drew it across the floor, and the Cat ran after it and patted it with his paws and rolled head over heels, and tossed it backward over his shoulder and chased it between his hind legs and pretended to lose it, and pounced down upon it again, till the Baby laughed as loudly as it had been crying, and scrambled after the Cat and frolicked all over the Cave till it grew tired and settled down to sleep with the Cat in its arms.

'Now,' said Cat, 'I will sing the Baby a song that shall keep him asleep for an hour.' And he began to purr, loud and low, low and loud, till the Baby fell fast asleep. The Woman smiled as she looked down upon the two of them, and said, 'That was wonderfully done. No question but you are very clever, O Cat.'

That very minute and second, Best Beloved, the smoke of the Fire at the back of the Cave came down in clouds from the roof – *puff!* – because it remembered the bargain she had made with the Cat; and when it had cleared away – lo and behold! – the Cat was sitting quite comfy close to the Fire.

'O my Enemy and Wife of my Enemy and Mother of my Enemy,' said the Cat, 'it is I: for you have spoken a second word in my praise, and now I can sit by the warm Fire at the back of the Cave for always and always and always. But still I am the Cat who walks by himself, and all places are alike to me.'

Then the Woman was very very angry, and let down her hair and put more wood on the Fire and brought out the broad blade-bone of the shoulder of mutton and began to make a Magic that should prevent her from saying a third word in praise of the Cat. It was not a Singing Magic, Best Beloved, it was a Still Magic; and by and by the Cave grew so still that a little wee-wee mouse crept out of a corner and ran across the floor.

'O my Enemy and Wife of my Enemy and Mother of my Enemy,'

said the Cat, 'is that little mouse part of your Magic?'

'Ouh! Chee! No indeed!' said the Woman, and she dropped the blade-bone and jumped upon the footstool in front of the fire and braided up her hair very quick for fear that the mouse should run up it.

'Ah,' said the Cat, watching. 'Then the mouse will do me no harm if I eat it?'

'No,' said the Woman, braiding up her hair, 'eat it quickly and I will ever be grateful to you.'

Cat made one jump and caught the little mouse, and the Woman said, 'A hundred thanks. Even the First Friend is not quick enough to catch little mice as you have done. You must be very wise.'

That very minute and second, O Best Beloved, the Milk-pot that stood by the fire cracked in two pieces – *ffft!* – because it remembered the bargain she had made with the Cat; and when the Woman jumped down from the footstool – lo and behold! – the Cat was lapping up the warm white milk that lay in one of the broken pieces.

'O my Enemy and Wife of my Enemy and Mother of my Enemy,' said the Cat, 'it is I: for you have spoken three words in my praise, and now I can drink the warm white milk three times a day for always and always and always. But *still* I am the Cat who walks by himself, and all places are alike to me.'

Then the Woman laughed and set the Cat a bowl of the warm white milk and said, 'O Cat, you are as clever as a man, but remember that your bargain was not made with the Man or the Dog, and I do not know what they will do when they come home.'

'What is that to me?' said the Cat. 'If I have my place in the Cave by the Fire and my warm white milk three times a day I do not care what the Man or the Dog can do.'

That evening when the Man and the Dog came into the Cave, the Woman told them all the story of the bargain, while the Cat sat by the Fire and smiled. Then the Man said, 'Yes, but he has not made a bargain with me or with all proper Men after me.' Then he took off his two leather boots and he took up his little stone axe (that makes three) and he fetched a piece of wood and a hatchet (that is five altogether), and he set them out in a row and he said, 'Now we will

The Cat that Walked by Himself

make *our* bargain. If you do not catch mice when you are in the Cave for always and always and always, I will throw these five things at you whenever I see you, and so shall all proper Men do after me.'

'Ah!' said the Woman, listening. 'This is a very clever Cat, but he is not so clever as my Man.'

The Cat counted the five things (and they looked very knobby) and he said, 'I will catch mice when I am in the Cave for always and always and always; but *still* I am the Cat who walks by himself, and all places are alike to me.'

'Not when I am near,' said the Man. 'If you had not said that last I would have put all these things away for always and always and always; but now I am going to throw my two boots and my little stone axe (that makes three) at you whenever I meet you. And so shall all proper Men do after me!'

Then the Dog said, 'Wait a minute. He has not made a bargain with *me* or with all proper Dogs after me.' And he showed his teeth and said, 'If you are not kind to the Baby while I am in the Cave for always and always and always, I will hunt you till I catch you, and when I catch you I will bite you. And so shall all proper Dogs do after me.'

'Ah!' said the Woman, listening. 'This is a very clever Cat, but he is not so clever as the Dog.'

Cat counted the Dog's teeth (and they looked very pointed), and he said, 'I will be kind to the Baby while I am in the Cave, as long as he does not pull my tail too hard, for always and always and always. But *still* I am the Cat who walks by himself, and all places are alike to me.'

'Not when I am near,' said the Dog. 'If you had not said that last I would have shut my mouth for always and always and always; but *now* I am going to hunt you up a tree whenever I meet you. And so shall all proper Dogs do after me.'

Then the Man threw his two boots and his little stone axe (that makes three) at the Cat, and the Cat ran out of the Cave and the Dog chased him up a tree; and from that day to this, Best Beloved, three proper Men out of five will always throw things at a Cat whenever they meet him, and all proper Dogs will chase him up a tree. But the Cat keeps his side of the bargain too. He will kill mice, and he will be kind to Babies when he is in the house, just as long as they do not pull his tail too hard. But when he has done that, and between times, and when the moon gets up and night comes, he is the Cat that walks by himself, and all places are alike to him. Then he goes out to the Wet Wild Woods or up the Wet Wild Trees or on the Wet Wild Roofs, waving his wild tail and walking by his wild lone.

ABNER OF THE PORCH
Geoffrey Household

When my voice broke, even Abner and MacGillivray understood my grief. I did not expect sympathy from MacGillivray, for he had no reason to like me. But he knew what it was to be excluded from cathedral ceremonies. He was the bishop's dog.

Abner was masterless. I would not claim that he appreciated the alto's solo in the 'Magnificat' when the organ was hushed and there was no other sound in the million and a half cubic feet of the cathedral but the slender purity of a boy's voice; yet he would patronize me after such occasions with the air of the master alto which he might have been. Though not a full Tom, he knew the ancestral songs which resemble our own. To our ears the scale of cats is distasteful, but one cannot deny them sustained notes of singular loveliness and clarity.

Abner's career had followed a common human pattern. My father was the gardener, responsible for the shaven lawns and discreet flowerbeds of the cathedral close. Some three years earlier he had suffered from an invasion of moles – creatures of ecclesiastical subtlety who avoided all the crude traps set for them by a mere layman. The cat, appearing from nowhere, took an interest. After a week he had caught the lot, laying out his game-bag each morning upon the tarpaulin which covered the mower.

Fed and praised by my father, he began to pay some attention to public relations and attracted the attention of visitors. Officially recognized as an ornament of the cathedral when his photograph appeared in the local paper, he ventured to advance from the lawns and tombstones to the porch. There he captivated the dean, always politely rising from the stone bench and thrusting his noble flanks against the gaitered leg. He was most gracious to the bishop and the higher clergy, but he would only stroke the dean. He knew very well from bearing and tone of voice, gentle though they were, that the cathedral belonged to him. It was the dean who christened him Abner.

To such a personage the dog of our new bishop was a disaster. MacGillivray was of respectable middle age, and had on occasion a sense of dignity; but when dignity was not called for he behaved like any other Aberdeen terrier and would race joyously round the cathedral or across the close, defying whatever human being was in charge of him to catch the lead which bounced and flew behind.

His first meeting with his rival set the future tone of their relations. He ventured with appalling temerity to make sport of the cathedral cat. Abner stretched himself, yawned, allowed MacGillivray's charge to approach within a yard, leaped to the narrow and rounded top of a tombstone and, draping himself over it, went ostentatiously to sleep. MacGillivray jumped and yapped at the tail tip which graciously waved for him, and then realized that he was being treated as a puppy. After that, the two passed each other politely but without remark. In our closed world of the cathedral such coolness between servants of dean and servants of bishop was familiar.

MacGillivray considered that he should be on permanent duty with his master. Since he was black, small and ingenious, it was difficult to prevent him. So devoted a friend could not be cruelly chained – and in summer the french windows of the Bishop's Palace were always open. He first endeared himself to choir and clergy at the ceremony of the bishop's installation. Magnificent in mitre and full robes, the bishop at the head of his procession knocked with his crozier upon the cathedral door to demand admission. MacGillivray, observing that his master was shut out and in need of help, hurtled across the close, bounced at the door and added his excited barks to the formal solemnity of the bishop's order.

Led away in disapproving silence, he took the enormity of his crime more seriously than we did. On his next appearance he behaved with decent humility, following the unconscious bishop down the chancel and into the pulpit with bowed head and tail well below horizontal.

Such anxious piety was even more embarrassing than bounce. It became my duty, laid upon me by the bishop in person, to ensure on all formal occasions that MacGillivray had not evaded the butler and was safely confined. I was even empowered to tie him up to the railings on the north side of the close in cases of emergency.

I do not think the bishop ever realized what was troubling his friend and erring brother, MacGillivray – normally a dog of sense who could mind his own business however great his affection for his master. When he accompanied the bishop around the diocese he never committed the solecism of entering a parish church and never used the vicar's cat as an objective for assault practice.

His indiscipline at home was, we were all sure, due to jealousy of Abner. He resented with Scottish obstinacy the fact that he was ejected in disgrace from the cathedral whereas Abner was not. He could not be expected to understand that Abner's discreet movements were beyond human control.

The dean could and did quite honestly declare that he had never seen that cat in the cathedral. Younger eyes, however, which knew where to look, had often distinguished Abner curled up on the ornate stone canopy over the tomb of a seventeenth-century admiral. In winter, he would sometimes sleep upon the left arm of a stone crusader in the cavity between shield and mailed shirt – a dank spot, I thought, until I discovered that it captured a current of warm air from the grating beside the effigy. In both his resting-places he was, if he chose to be, invisible. He was half Persian, tiger-striped with brownish grey on lighter grey, and he matched the stone of the cathedral.

As the summer went by, the feud between Abner and MacGillivray became more subtle. Both scored points. MacGillivray, if he woke up feeling youthful, used to chase the tame pigeons in the close. One morning, to the surprise of both dog and bird, a pigeon failed to get out of the way in time and broke a wing. MacGillivray was embarrassed. He sniffed the pigeon, wagged his tail to show that there was no ill-feeling and sat down to think.

Abner strolled from the porch and held down the pigeon with a firm, gentle paw. He picked it up in his mouth and presented it with liquid and appealing eyes to an elegant American tourist who was musing sentimentally in the close. She swore that the cat had asked her to heal the bird – which, by remaining a whole week in our town in and out of the vet's consulting room, she did. Personally, I think that Abner was attracted by the feline grace of her walk and was suggesting that, as the pigeon could be of no more use to the cathedral, she might as well eat it. But whatever his motives, he had again made MacGillivray look a clumsy and impulsive fool.

MacGillivray's revenge was a little primitive. He deposited bones and offal in dark corners of the porch and pretended that Abner had put them there. That was the second worst crime he knew – to leave on a human floor the inedible portion of his meals.

The verger was deceived and submitted a grave complaint in writing to the dean. The dean, however, knew very well that Abner had no interest in mutton bones, old or new. He was familiar with the cat's tastes. Indeed, it was rumoured from the deanery that he secreted a little box in his pocket at meals, into which he would drop such delicacies as the head of a small trout or the liver of a roast duck.

I cannot remember all the incidents of the cold war. And, anyway, I could not swear to their truth. My father and the dean read into the animals' behaviour motives which were highly unlikely and then shamelessly embroidered them, creating a whole miscellany of private legend for the canons and the choir. So I will only repeat the triumph of MacGillivray and its sequel, both of which I saw myself.

That fulfilment of every dog's dream appeared at first final and overwhelming victory. It was 1 September, the feast of St Giles, our patron saint. Evensong was a full choral and instrumental service, traditional, exquisite, and attracting a congregation whose interest was in music rather than religion. The bishop was to preach. Perhaps the effort of composition, of appealing to well-read intellectuals without offending the simpler clergy, had created an atmosphere of hard work and anxiety in the bishop's study. At any rate, MacGillivray was nervous and mischievous.

While I was ensuring his comfort before shutting him up, he twitched the lead out of my hand and was off on his quarter-mile course round the cathedral looking for a private entrance. When at last I caught him, the changes of the bells had stopped. I had only five minutes before the processional entry of the choir. There wasn't even time to race across the close and tie him up to the railings.

I rushed into the north transept with MacGillivray under my arm, pushed him down the stairs into the crypt and shut the door behind him. I knew that he could not get out. Our Norman crypt was closed to visitors during the service, and no one on a summer evening would have reason to go down to the masons' and carpenters' stores, the strong-room or the boilers. All I feared was that MacGillivray's yaps might be heard through the gratings in the cathedral floor.

I dived into my ruffled surplice and took my place in the procession, earning the blackest possible looks from the choir-master. I just had time to explain to him that it was the fault of MacGillivray. I was not forgiven, but the grin exchanged between choir-master and precentor suggested that I probably would be – if I wasn't still panting by the time that the alto had to praise all famous men and our fathers that begat us.

St Giles, if he still had any taste for earthly music, must have approved his servants that evening. The bishop, always an effective preacher, surpassed himself. His sinewy arguments were of course beyond me, but I had my eye – vain little beast that I was – on the music critics from the London papers, and I could see that several of them were so interested that they were bursting to take over the pulpit and reply.

Only once did he falter, when the barking of MacGillivray, hardly perceptible to anyone but his master and me, caught the episcopal ear. Even then his momentary hesitation was put down to a search for the right word.

I felt that my desperate disposal of MacGillivray might not be appreciated. He must have been audible to any of the congregation sitting near the gratings of the northern aisle. So I shot down to release him immediately after the recessional. The noise was startling as soon as I opened the door. MacGillivray was holding the stairs against a stranger in the crypt.

The man was good-dogging him and trying to make him shut up. He had a small suitcase by his side. When two sturdy vergers, attracted by the noise, appeared hot on my heels, the intruder tried to bolt – dragging behind him MacGillivray with teeth closed on the turn-ups of his trousers. We detained him and opened the suitcase. It contained twenty pounds' weight of the cathedral silver. During the long service our massive but primitive strong-room door had been expertly opened.

The congregation was dispersing, but bishop, dean, archdeacon and innumerable canons were still in the cathedral. They attended the excitement just as any other crowd. Under the circumstances, MacGillivray was the centre of the most complimentary fuss. The canons would have genially petted any dog. But this was the bishop's dog. The wings of gowns and surplices flowed over him like those of exclamatory seagulls descending upon a stranded fish.

Dignity was represented only by our local superintendent of police and the terrier himself. When the thief had been led away, MacGillivray reverently followed his master out of the cathedral; his whole attitude reproached us for ever dreaming that he might take advantage of his popularity.

At the porch, however, he turned round and loosed one short, triumphant bark into the empty nave. The bishop's chaplain unctuously suggested that it was a little voice of thanksgiving. So it was – but far from pious. I noticed where MacGillivray's muzzle was pointing. That bark was for a softness of outline, a shadow, a striping of small stone pinnacles upon the canopy of the Admiral's Tomb.

For several days – all of ten I should say – Abner deserted both the cathedral and its porch. He then returned to his first friend, helping my father to make the last autumn cut of the grass and offering his catch of small game for approval. The dean suggested that he was in need of sunshine. My father shook his head and said nothing. It was obvious to both of us that for Abner the cathedral had been momentarily defiled. He reminded me of an old verger who gave in his resignation – it was long overdue anyway – after discovering a family party eating lunch from paper bags in the Lady Chapel.

He went back to the porch a little before the harvest festival, for he always enjoyed that. During a whole week while the decorations were in place he could find a number of discreet lairs where it was impossible to detect his presence. There may also have been a little hunting in the night. We did not attempt to fill the vastness of the cathedral with all the garden produce dear to a parish church, but the dean was fond of fat sheaves of wheat, oats and barley, bound round the middle like sheaves on a heraldic shield.

It was his own festival in his own cathedral, so that he, not the bishop, conducted it. He had made the ritual as enjoyable as that of Christmas, reviving ancient customs for which he was always ready to quote authority. I suspect that medieval deans would have denied his interpretation of their scanty records, but they would have recognized a master of stage management.

His most effective revival was a procession of cathedral tenants and benefactors, each bearing some offering in kind which the dean received on the altar steps. Fruit, honey and cakes were common, always with some touch of magnificence in the quality, quantity or container. On one occasion, the landlord of the Pilgrim's Inn presented a roasted peacock set in jelly with tail feathers erect. There was some argument about this on the grounds that it ran close to advertisement. But the dean would not be dissuaded. He insisted that any craftsman had the right to present a unique specimen of his skill.

That year the gifts were more humble. My father, as always, led the procession with a basket tray upon which was a two-foot bunch of black grapes from the vinery in the canons' garden. A most original participant was a dear old nursery gardener who presented a plant of his new dwarf camellia which had been the botanical sensation of the year and could not yet be bought for money. There was also a noble milk-pan of Alpine strawberries and cream – which, we hoped, the cathedral school would share next day with the alms houses.

While the file of some twenty persons advanced into the chancel, the choir full-bloodedly sang the 65th Psalm to the joyous score of our own organist. The dean's sense of theatre was as faultless as ever. Lavish in ritual and his own vestments, he then played his part with the utmost simplicity. He thanked and blessed each giver almost conversationally.

Last in the procession were four boys of the cathedral school bearing a great silver bowl of nuts gathered in the hedgerows. The gift and their movements were traditional. As they separated, two to the right and two to the left, leaving the dean alone upon the altar steps, a shadow appeared at his feet and vanished so swiftly that by the time our eyes had registered its true, soft shape it was no longer there.

The dean bent down and picked up a dead field-mouse. He was not put out of countenance for a moment. He laid it reverently with the other gifts. No one was present to be thanked; but when the dean left the cathedral after service and stopped in the porch to talk to Abner he was – to the surprise of the general public – still wearing his full vestments, stiff, gorgeous and suggesting the power of the Church to protect and armour with its blessing the most humble of its servants.

MING'S BIGGEST PREY
Patricia Highsmith

Ming was resting comfortably on the foot of his mistress's bunk, when the man picked him up by the back of the neck, stuck him out on the deck and closed the cabin door. Ming's blue eyes widened in shock and brief anger, then nearly closed again because of the brilliant sunlight. It was not the first time Ming had been thrust out of the cabin rudely, and Ming realized that the man did it when his mistress, Elaine, was not looking.

The sailboat now offered no shelter from the sun, but Ming was not yet too warm. He leapt easily to the cabin roof and stepped on to the coil of rope just behind the mast. Ming liked the rope coil as a couch, because he could see everything from the height, the cup shape of the rope protected him from strong breezes, and also minimized the swaying and sudden changes of angle of the *White Lark*, since it was more or less the centre point. But just now the sail had been taken down, because Elaine and the man had eaten lunch, and often they had a siesta afterwards during which time, Ming knew, that man didn't like him in the cabin. Lunchtime was all right. In fact, Ming had just lunched on delicious grilled fish and a bit of lobster. Now, lying in a relaxed curve on the coil of rope, Ming opened his mouth in a great yawn, then with his slant eyes almost closed against the strong sunlight, gazed at the beige hills and the white and pink houses and hotels that circled the bay of Acapulco. Between the *White Lark* and the shore where people splashed inaudibly, the sun twinkled on the water's surface like thousands of tiny electric lights going on and off. A water-skier went by, skimming up minute spray behind him. Such activity! Ming half dozed, feeling the heat of the sun sink into his fur. Ming was from

New York, and he considered Acapulco a great improvement over his environment in the first weeks of his life. He remembered a sunless box with straw on the bottom, three or four other kittens in with him, and a window behind which giant forms paused for a few moments, tried to catch his attention by tapping, then passed on. He did not remember his mother at all. One day a young woman who smelled of something pleasant came into the place and took him away – away from the ugly, frightening smell of dogs, of medicine and parrot dung. Then they went on what Ming now knew was an aeroplane. He was quite used to aeroplanes now and rather liked them. On aeroplanes he sat on Elaine's lap, or slept on her lap, and there were always titbits to eat if he was hungry.

Elaine spent much of the day in a shop in Acapulco, where dresses and slacks and bathing suits hung on all the walls. This place smelled clean and fresh, there were flowers in pots and in boxes out front, and the floor was of cool blue and white tile. Ming had perfect freedom to wander out into the patio behind the shop, or to sleep in his basket in a corner. There was more sunlight in front of the shop, but mischievous boys often tried to grab him if he sat in front, and Ming could never relax there.

Ming liked best lying in the sun with his mistress on one of the long canvas chairs on their terrace at home. What Ming did not like were the people she sometimes invited to their house, people who spent the night, people by the score who stayed up very late eating and drinking, playing the gramophone or the piano – people who separated him from Elaine. People who stepped on his toes, people who sometimes picked him up from behind before he could do anything about it, so that he had to squirm and fight to get free, people who stroked him roughly, people who closed a door somewhere, locking him in. *People!* Ming detested people. In all the world, he liked only Elaine. Elaine loved him and understood him.

Especially this man called Teddie Ming detested now. Teddie was around all the time lately. Ming did not like the way Teddie looked at him, when Elaine was not watching. And sometimes Teddie, when Elaine was not near, muttered something which Ming knew was a threat. Or a command to leave the room. Ming took it calmly.

Dignity was to be preserved. Besides, wasn't his mistress on his side? The man was the intruder. When Elaine was watching, the man sometimes pretended a fondness for him, but Ming always moved gracefully but unmistakably in another direction.

Ming's nap was interrupted by the sound of the cabin door opening. He heard Elaine and the man laughing and talking. The big red-orange sun was near the horizon.

'Ming!' Elaine came over to him. 'Aren't you getting *cooked*, darling? I thought you were *in*!'

'So did I!' said Teddie.

Ming purred as he always did when he awakened. She picked him up gently, cradled him in her arms, and took him below into the suddenly cool shade of the cabin. She was talking to the man, and not in a gentle tone. She set Ming down in front of his dish of water, and though he was not thirsty, he drank a little to please her. Ming did feel addled by the heat, and he staggered a little.

Elaine took a wet towel and wiped Ming's face, his ears and his four paws. Then she laid him gently on the bunk that smelled of Elaine's perfume but also of the man whom Ming detested.

Now his mistress and the man were quarrelling, Ming could tell from the tone. Elaine was staying with Ming, sitting on the edge of the bunk. Ming at last heard the splash that meant Teddie had dived into the water. Ming hoped he stayed there, hoped he drowned, hoped he never came back. Elaine wet a bathtowel in the aluminium sink, wrung it out, spread it on the bunk, and lifted Ming on to it. She brought water, and now Ming was thirsty, and drank. She left him to sleep again while she washed and put away the dishes. These were comfortable sounds that Ming liked to hear.

But soon there was another *splash* and *plop*, Teddie's wet feet on the deck, and Ming was awake again.

The tone of quarrelling recommenced. Elaine went up the few steps on to the deck. Ming, tense but with his chin still resting on the moist bathtowel, kept his eyes on the cabin door. It was Teddie's feet that he heard descending. Ming lifted his head slightly, aware that there was no exit behind him, that he was trapped in the cabin. The man paused with a towel in his hands, staring at Ming.

Ming relaxed completely, as he might do preparatory to a yawn, and this caused his eyes to cross. Ming then let his tongue slide a little way out of his mouth. The man started to say something, looked as if he wanted to hurl the wadded towel at Ming, but he wavered, whatever he had been going to say never got out of his mouth, and he threw the towel in the sink, then bent to wash his face. It was not the first time Ming had let his tongue slide out at Teddie. Lots of people laughed when Ming did this, if they were people at a party, for instance, and Ming rather enjoyed that. But Ming sensed that Teddie took it as a hostile gesture of some kind, which was why Ming did it deliberately to Teddie, whereas among other people, it was often an accident when Ming's tongue slid out.

The quarrelling continued. Elaine made coffee. Ming began to feel better, and went on deck again, because the sun had now set. Elaine had started the motor, and they were gliding slowly towards the shore. Ming caught the song of birds, the odd screams, like shrill phrases, of certain birds that cried only at sunset. Ming looked forward to the adobe house on the cliff that was his and his mistress's home. He knew that the reason she did not leave him at home (where he would have been more comfortable) when she went on the boat, was because she was afraid that people might trap him, even kill him. Ming understood. People had tried to grab him from almost under Elaine's eyes. Once he had been suddenly hauled away in a cloth bag, and though fighting as hard as he could, he was not sure he would have been able to get out, if Elaine had not hit the boy herself and grabbed the bag from him.

Ming had intended to jump up on the cabin roof again, but after glancing at it, he decided to save his strength, so he crouched on the warm, gently sloping deck with his feet tucked in, and gazed at the approaching shore. Now he could hear guitar music from the beach. The voices of his mistress and the man had come to a halt. For a few moments, the loudest sound was the *chug-chug-chug* of the boat's motor. Then Ming heard the man's bare feet climbing the cabin steps. Ming did not turn his head to look at him, but his ears twitched back a little, involuntarily. Ming looked at the water just the distance of a short leap in front of him and below him. Strangely, there was no sound from the man behind him. The hair on Ming's neck prickled, and Ming glanced over his right shoulder.

At that instant, the man bent forward and rushed at Ming with his arms outspread.

Ming was on his feet at once, darting straight towards the man, which was the only direction of safety on the railless deck, and the man swung his left arm and cuffed Ming in the chest. Ming went flying backwards, claws scraping the deck, but his hind legs went over the edge. Ming clung with his front feet to the sleek wood which gave him little hold, while his hind legs worked to heave him up, worked at the side of the boat which sloped to Ming's disadvantage.

The man advanced to shove a foot against Ming's paws, but Elaine came up the cabin steps just then.

'What's happening? *Ming!*'

Ming's strong hind legs were getting him on to the deck little by little. The man had knelt as if to lend a hand. Elaine had fallen on to her knees also, and had Ming by the back of the neck now.

Ming relaxed, hunched on the deck. His tail was wet.

'He fell overboard!' Teddie said. 'It's true, he's groggy. Just lurched over and fell when the boat gave a dip.'

'It's the sun. Poor *Ming*!' Elaine held the cat against her breast, and carried him into the cabin. 'Teddie – could you steer?'

The man came down into the cabin. Elaine had Ming on the bunk and was talking softly to him. Ming's heart was still beating fast. He was alert against the man at the wheel, even though Elaine was with him. Ming was aware that they had entered the little cove where they always went before getting off the boat.

Here were the friends and allies of Teddie, whom Ming detested by association, although these were merely Mexican boys. Two or three boys in shorts called 'Señor Teddie!' and offered a hand to Elaine to climb on to the dock, took the rope attached to the front of the boat, offered to carry '*Ming! – Ming!*' Ming leapt on to the dock himself and crouched, waiting for Elaine, ready to dart away from any other hand that might reach for him. And there were several brown hands making a rush for him, so that Ming had to keep jumping aside. There were laughs, yelps, stomps of bare feet on wooden boards. But there was also the reassuring voice of Elaine warning them off. Ming knew she was busy carrying off the plastic satchels, locking the cabin door. Teddie with the aid of one of the Mexican boys was stretching the canvas over the cabin now. And Elaine's sandalled feet were beside Ming. Ming followed her as she walked away. A boy took the things Elaine was carrying, then she picked Ming up.

They got into the big car without a roof that belonged to Teddie, and drove up the winding road towards Elaine's and Ming's house. One of the boys was driving. Now the tone in which Elaine and Teddie were speaking was calmer, softer. The man laughed. Ming sat tensely on his mistress's lap. He could feel her concern for him in the way she stroked him and touched the back of his neck. The man reached out to put his fingers on Ming's back, and Ming gave a low growl that rose and fell and rumbled deep in his throat.

'Well, well,' said the man, pretending to be amused, and took his hand away.

Elaine's voice had stopped in the middle of something she was saying. Ming was tired, and wanted nothing more than to take a nap on the big bed at home. The bed was covered with a red-and-white striped blanket of thin wool.

Hardly had Ming thought of this, when he found himself in the cool, fragrant atmosphere of his own home, being lowered gently on to the bed with the soft woollen cover. His mistress kissed his cheek, and said something with the word 'hungry' in it. Ming understood, at any rate. He was to tell her when he was hungry.

Ming dozed, and awakened at the sound of voices on the terrace a couple of yards away, past the open glass doors. Now it was dark. Ming could see one end of the table, and could tell from the quality of the light that there were candles on the table. Concha, the servant who slept in the house, was clearing the table. Ming heard her voice, then the voices of Elaine and the man. Ming smelled cigar smoke. Ming jumped to the floor and sat for a moment looking out of the door towards the terrace. He yawned, then arched his back and stretched, and limbered up his muscles by digging his claws into the thick straw carpet. Then he slipped out to the right on the terrace and glided silently down the long stairway of broad stones to the garden below. The garden was like a jungle or a forest. Avocado trees and mango trees grew as high as the terrace itself, there were bougainvillaea against the wall, orchids in the trees, and magnolias and several camellias which Elaine had planted. Ming could hear birds twittering and stirring in their nests. Sometimes he climbed trees to get at their nests, but tonight he was not in the mood, though he was no longer tired. The voices of his mistress and the man disturbed him. His mistress was not a friend of the man's tonight, that was plain.

Concha was probably still in the kitchen, and Ming decided to go in and ask her for something to eat. Concha liked him. One maid who had not liked him had been dismissed by Elaine. Ming thought he fancied barbecued pork. That was what his mistress and the man had eaten tonight. The breeze blew fresh from the ocean, ruffling Ming's fur slightly. Ming felt completely recovered from the awful experience of nearly falling into the sea.

Now the terrace was empty of people. Ming went left, back into the bedroom, and was at once aware of the man's presence, though there was no light on and Ming could not see him. The man was standing by the dressing-table, opening a box. Again involuntarily Ming gave a low growl which rose and fell, and Ming remained frozen in the position he had been in when he first became aware of the man, his right front paw extended for the next step. Now his ears were back, he was prepared to spring in any direction, although the man had not seen him.

'*Ssss-st!* Damn you!' the man said in a whisper. He stamped his foot, not very hard, to make the cat go away.

Ming did not move at all. Ming heard the soft rattle of the white necklace which belonged to his mistress. The man put it into his pocket, then moved to Ming's right, out of the door that went into the big living-room. Ming now heard the clink of a bottle against glass, heard liquid being poured. Ming went through the same door and turned left towards the kitchen.

Here he miaowed, and was greeted by Elaine and Concha. Concha had her radio turned on to music.

'Fish? – Pork. He likes pork,' Elaine said, speaking the odd form of words which she used with Concha.

Ming, without much difficulty, conveyed his preference for pork, and got it. He fell to with a good appetite. Concha was exclaiming 'Ah-eee-ee!' as his mistress spoke with her, spoke at length. Then Concha bent to stroke him, and Ming put up with it, still looking down at his plate, until she left off and he could finish his meal. Then Elaine left the kitchen. Concha gave him some of the tinned milk, which he loved, in his now empty saucer, and Ming lapped this up.

Then he rubbed himself against her bare leg by way of thanks, and went out of the kitchen, made his way cautiously into the living-room en route to the bedroom. But now Elaine and the man were out on the terrace. Ming had just entered the bedroom, when he heard Elaine call:

'Ming? Where are you?'

Ming went to the terrace door and stopped, and sat on the threshold.

Elaine was sitting sideways at the end of the table, and the candlelight was bright on her long fair hair, on the white of her trousers. She slapped her thigh, and Ming jumped on to her lap.

The man said something in a low tone, something not nice.

Elaine replied something in the same tone. But she laughed a little.

Then the telephone rang. Elaine put Ming down, and went into the living-room towards the telephone.

The man finished what was in his glass, muttered something at Ming, then set the glass on the table. He got up and tried to circle Ming, or to get him towards the edge of the terrace, Ming realized, and Ming also realized that the man was drunk – therefore moving slowly and a little clumsily. The terrace had a parapet about as high as the man's hips, but it was broken by grilles in three places, grilles with bars wide enough for Ming to pass through, though Ming never did, merely looked through the grilles sometimes. It was plain to Ming that the man wanted to drive him through one of the grilles, or grab him and toss him over the terrace parapet. There was nothing easier for Ming than to elude him. Then the man picked up a chair and swung it suddenly, catching Ming on the hip. That had been quick, and it hurt. Ming took the nearest exit which was down the outside steps that led to the garden

The man started down the steps after him. Without reflecting, Ming dashed back up the few steps he had come, keeping close to the wall which was in shadow. The man hadn't seen him, Ming knew. Ming leapt to the terrace parapet, sat down and licked a paw once to recover and collect himself. His heart beat fast as if he were in the middle of a fight. And hatred ran in his veins. Hatred burned his eyes as he crouched and listened to the man uncertainly climbing the steps below him. The man came into view.

Ming tensed himself for a jump, then jumped as hard as he could, landing with all four feet on the man's right arm near the shoulder. Ming clung to the cloth of the man's white jacket, but they were both falling. The man groaned. Ming hung on. Branches crackled. Ming could not tell up from down. Ming jumped off the man, became aware of direction and of the earth too late, and landed on his side. Almost at the same time, he heard the thud of the man hitting the ground, then of his body rolling a little way; then there was silence. Ming had to breathe fast with his mouth open until his chest stopped hurting. From the direction of the man, he could smell drink, cigar, and the sharp odour that meant fear. But the man was not moving.

Ming could now see quite well. There was even a bit of moonlight. Ming headed for the steps again, had to go a long way through the bush, over stones and sand, to where the steps began. Then he glided up and arrived once more upon the terrace.

Elaine was just coming on to the terrace.

'Teddie?' she called. Then she went back into the bedroom where she turned on a lamp. She went into the kitchen. Ming followed her. Concha had left the light on, but Concha was now in her own room, where the radio played.

Elaine opened the front door.

The man's car was still in the driveway, Ming saw. Now Ming's hip had begun to hurt, or now he had begun to notice it. It caused him to limp a little. Elaine noticed this, touched his back, and asked him what was the matter. Ming only purred.

'Teddie? – Where are you?' Elaine called.

She took a torch and shone it down into the garden, down among the great trunks of the avocado trees, among the orchids and the lavender and pink blossoms of the bougainvillaeas. Ming, safe beside her on the terrace parapet, followed the beam of the torch with his eyes and purred with content. The man was not below here, but below and to the right. Elaine went to the terrace steps and carefully, because there was no rail here, only broad steps, pointed the beam of the light downward. Ming did not bother looking. He sat on the terrace where the steps began.

'Teddie!' she said. '*Teddie!*' Then she ran down the steps.

Ming still did not follow her. He heard her draw in her breath. Then she cried:

'*Concha!*'

Elaine ran back up the steps.

Concha had come out of her room. Elaine spoke to Concha. Then Concha became excited. Elaine went to the telephone, and spoke for a short while, then she and Concha went down the steps together. Ming settled himself with his paws tucked under him on the terrace, which was still faintly warm from the day's sun. A car arrived. Elaine came up the steps, and went and opened the front door. Ming kept out of the way on the terrace, in a shadowy corner, as three or four strange men came out on the terrace and tramped down the steps. There was a great deal of talk below, noises of feet, breaking of bushes, and then the smell of all of them mounted the steps, the smell of tobacco, sweat, and the familiar smell of blood. The man's blood. Ming was pleased, as he was pleased when he killed a bird and created this smell of blood under his own teeth. This was big prey. Ming, unnoticed by any of the others, stood up to his full height as the group passed with the corpse, and inhaled the aroma of his victory with a lifted nose.

Then suddenly the house was empty. Everyone had gone, even Concha. Ming drank a little water from his bowl in the kitchen, then went to his mistress's bed, curled against the slope of the pillows, and fell fast asleep. He was awakened by the *rr-rr-rr* of an unfamiliar car. Then the front door opened, and he recognized the step of Elaine and then Concha. Ming stayed where he was. Elaine and Concha talked softly for a few minutes. Then Elaine came into the bedroom. The lamp was still on. Ming watched her slowly open the box on her dressing-table, and into it she let fall the white necklace that made a little clatter. Then she closed the box. She began to unbutton her shirt, but before she had finished, she flung herself on the bed and stroked Ming's head, lifted his left paw and pressed it gently so that the claws came forth.

'Oh, Ming – Ming,' she said.

Ming recognized the tones of love.

THE WHITE CAT
Countess D'Aulnoy

Once upon a time there was a king who had three brave and handsome sons. He feared they might be seized with the desire of reigning before his death. Certain rumours were abroad that they were trying to gain adherents to assist them in depriving him of his kingdom. The king was old, but as vigorous in mind as ever, and had no desire to yield them a position he filled so worthily. He thought, therefore, the best way of living in peace was to divert them by promises he could always escape fulfilling.

He summoned them to his closet, and after speaking kindly, added: 'You will agree with me, my dear children, that my advanced age does not permit me to attend to state affairs so closely as formerly; I fear my subjects may suffer, and wish therefore to give one of you my crown, but it is only fair that in return for such a gift you should seek ways of making my intention of retiring into the country pleasing to me. It seems to me that a clever, pretty, and faithful little dog would be a pleasant companion for me; so without choosing my eldest son rather than my youngest, I declare that whichever of the three brings me the most beautiful dog shall be my heir.' The princes were surprised at their father's desire for a little dog, but the two youngest thought they could turn it to their advantage, and gladly accepted the commission; the eldest was too timid and too respectful to press his rights. They took leave of the king; he gave them money and jewels, adding that in a year, without fail, they must return, and on the same day, and at the same hour bring him their little dogs.

Before their departure they repaired to a castle about a league from the town; there they brought their most intimate friends, and gave a great feast, at which the three brothers swore eternal friendship, that they would conduct the matter in hand without jealousy and annoyance, and that the successful one should share his fortune with the others. At length they set out, deciding that on their return they would meet at the same castle, and go together to the king; they would take no attendants with them, and changed their names in order not to be recognized.

Each took a different route. The two eldest had many adventures, but I shall only relate those of the youngest. He was handsome, and of a gay and merry disposition; he had a well-shaped head, great stature, regular features, beautiful teeth and was very skilful in all exercises befitting a prince. He sang pleasantly, and played charmingly on the lute and theorbo. He could also paint; in short, he was extremely accomplished, and his valour reached almost to rashness.

A day scarcely passed that he did not buy dogs – big, little, greyhounds, bull-dogs, boar-hounds, harriers, spaniels, poodles, lap-dogs; as soon as he had a very fine one, he found one still finer, and therefore let the first go and kept the other: for it would have been impossible to take about with him, quite alone, thirty or forty thousand dogs, and he did not wish to have gentlemen-in-waiting, valets or pages in his suite. He was walking on without knowing where he was going, when night, accompanied by thunder and rain, overtook him in a forest where he could no longer see the paths.

He took the first road that offered, and after he had walked for a long time, saw a light, and felt sure there was a house near in which he could take shelter till the next day. Guided by the light, he came to the gates of a castle, the most magnificent imaginable. The gate was of gold covered with carbuncles, whose bright and pure brilliancy lighted up all the surroundings. That was the light the prince had seen from afar; the walls were of transparent porcelain painted in many colours, illustrating the history of the fairies from the creation of the world: the famous adventures of Peau d'Ane, of Finette, of Orange Tree, of Gracieuse, of the Sleeping Beauty in the Wood, of Green Serpent, and a hundred others were not omitted. He was delighted to recognize Prince Lutin, who was a sort of Scotch uncle. The rain and the bad weather prevented him remaining longer in a place where he was getting wet through, and besides, in those places where the light of the carbuncles did not reach, he could not see at all.

He returned to the gold door; he saw a stag's foot fastened to a diamond chain: he admired its magnificence, and the security in which the inhabitants of the castle must live; for he said: 'What is there to keep thieves from cutting the chain and tearing out the carbuncles? they would be rich for ever.'

He pulled the stag's foot and heard a bell ring, and from its sound judged it to be of gold or silver: in an instant the door was opened, he saw a dozen hands in the air, each holding a torch. He was so astonished that he hesitated to enter, when he felt other hands pushing him from behind somewhat violently. He walked on very uneasily and at great risk; he put his hand on his sword hilt. On entering a vestibule encrusted with porphyry and lapis lazuli, he heard two enchanting voices singing these words:

> Within the bounds of this bright place
> Is nought to fear and nought to flee,
> Save the enchantment of a face,
> If you would live still fancy-free.

He could not imagine that if harm was intended to him later, so kind an invitation should be given now, and feeling himself pushed towards a big coral door that opened as soon as he approached it, he entered a saloon of mother-of-pearl, and then several rooms variously decorated, but so rich in paintings and precious stones that he was as if enchanted. Thousands and thousands of lights, hanging from the roof of the room, lighted some of the other apartments, which contained just the same lustres, girandoles and shelves full of wax candles; indeed, such was the magnificence that it is difficult to believe it possible.

After passing through sixty rooms, the hands that were guiding him stopped; he saw a big and commodious armchair approach the fireplace quite alone. At the same moment the fire was lighted, and the hands, which seemed to him very beautiful, white, small, plump and well-proportioned, undressed him, for, as I already said, he was wet, and they feared he might take cold. He was presented, without seeing anyone, with a shirt beautiful enough for a wedding-day, with a dressing-gown of some material frosted with gold, embroidered with small emeralds to form monograms. The bodiless hands pushed him to a table where everything necessary for the toilet was set out. Nothing could be more magnificent. They combed his hair with a lightness and skill that were delightful. Then they dressed him, but not in his own clothes; they brought him others much richer. He silently wondered at all that was taking place, and sometimes could not quite control a certain impulse of fear.

When he was powdered, curled, perfumed, adorned and made more beautiful than Adonis, the hands led him into a hall resplendent with gildings and furniture. Looking round you saw the histories of the most famous cats: Rodillardus hung up by the feet at the Council of Rats, Puss in Boots, Marquis of Carabas, the cat who wrote, the cat who became a woman, the sorcerers who became cats, their nocturnal revels and all their ceremonies; nothing could be more curious than these pictures.

The table was laid for two, with gold knife, fork and spoon for each; the sideboard was magnificent with a number of rock-crystal vases and a thousand precious stones. The prince did not know for whom the two covers were intended; he perceived cats taking their places in a little orchestra built on purpose; one held a book in which was written the most extraordinary music imaginable, another a roll of paper with which he beat time, and the rest had small guitars. Suddenly each began to mew in a different key, and to strike the strings of their guitars with their sharp claws; it was the strangest music ever heard. The prince would have thought himself in hell, if the palace had not been too wonderful to give probability to such a thought, but he stuffed up his ears and laughed heartily at the different postures and grimaces of the novel musicians.

He was thinking over his various adventures since his entrance into the castle, when he saw a little figure no bigger than your arm enter the hall. The little creature was shrouded in a long, black crêpe veil. Two cats conducted her; they were in mourning, with cloaks and swords at their sides; a numerous procession of cats followed; some carried rat-traps full of rats and others mice in cages.

The prince was more astonished than ever; he did not know what

The White Cat

to think. The little black figure approached him, and raising her veil, he saw the most beautiful white cat that ever was or ever will be. She looked very young and sad; she began to mew so softly and prettily that it went straight to the heart. She said to the prince: 'King's son, you are welcome; my cat-like majesty is glad to see you.' 'Madam Cat,' said the prince, 'it is very kind of you to receive me so cordially, but you do not appear an ordinary animal; your gift of speech and your magnificent castle are strong proofs to the contrary.' 'King's son,' replied White Cat, 'I beg you to leave off making me compliments; I am very simple in speech and manner, but I have a kind heart. Come,' she continued, 'let supper be served and the musicians cease, because the prince does not understand what they say.' 'Are they singing anything, madam?' he replied. 'Certainly,' she went on, 'we have excellent poets here, and if you stay with us a little while you will be convinced of it.' 'It is only necessary to hear you to believe it,' said the prince, politely; 'you seem to be a most rare cat.'

Supper was brought, the bodiless hands waited at table. First two dishes were put on the tables, one of young pigeons and the other of fat mice. The sight of the one prevented the prince from eating the other, imagining that the same cook had prepared them both. But the little cat, guessing by his expression what was passing in his mind, assured him that his kitchen was separate, and that he might eat what was given him without fear of its being rats or mice.

There was no need to repeat it; the prince felt quite sure the beautiful little cat would not deceive him. He was surprised to see that on her paw she wore a miniature. He asked her to show it him, thinking it would be Master Minagrobis. He was astonished to see a young man so handsome that it was scarcely creditable nature could have formed one like him and who resembled him so closely that it would not have been possible to paint his portrait better. She sighed, and becoming more melancholy, remained perfectly silent. The prince saw there was something extraordinary beneath; however, fearing to displease or annoy the cat, he dared not ask. He told her all the news he could think of, and found her well informed about the various interests of princes, and other things that happened in the world.

After supper White Cat invited her guest to enter a hall

containing a stage on which twelve cats and twelve monkeys danced a ballet. The former were dressed as Moors and the latter as Chinese. Their leaps and capers may easily be imagined, and now and again they exchanged blows with their paws. Thus the evening ended. White Cat bade her guest good-night; the hands which had been his guides all along took charge of him again, and led him to an apartment just opposite the one he had seen. It was less magnificent than elegant. It was carpeted with butterflies' wings, whose varied colours formed a thousand different flowers. There were also very rare birds' feathers, never seen perhaps except in this place. The beds were of gauze, fastened by a thousand knots of ribbons. There were large mirrors reaching from the ceiling to the floor, and the chased gold frames represented a thousand little Cupids.

The prince went to bed in silence, for he could not carry on a conversation with the hands; he did not sleep well and was awakened by a confused noise. The hands took him out of bed, and dressed him in hunting costume. He looked out into the courtyard, and saw more than five hundred cats, some of whom led hounds in the leash, others sounded the horn; it was a great fête. White Cat was going hunting and wished the prince to join her. The helpful hands gave him a wooden horse, which galloped at full speed, and stepped grandly. He made some difficulty about mounting, saying that he was far from being a knight-errant like Don Quixote; but his resistance was of no avail, and he was put on the wooden horse. It had housings and saddle of gold and diamond embroidery. White Cat was mounted on the handsomest and finest monkey ever seen. She did not wear her long veil, but a dragoon hat, which lent her such a determined expression that all the mice of the neighbourhood were in terror. Never was there a pleasanter hunt; the cats ran quicker than the rabbits and the hares, so that when they caught them White Cat had the quarry made in front of her, and a thousand skilful and delightful tricks were done. The birds, too, were scarcely safe, for the cats climbed the trees, and the wonderful monkey carried White Cat even into the eagles' nests, so that she might dispose of the eaglets according to her pleasure.

The hunt ended, she blew a horn about a finger's length, but with so loud and clear a sound that it could easily be heard ten leagues off. When she had blown it two or three times, she was surrounded

The White Cat

by all the cats of the country: some were in the air driving chariots, others in boats came by water; never had so many been seen before. They were all dressed differently. White Cat returned to the castle with the pompous procession, and begged the prince to come too. He was most willing, although it seemed to him that so many cats savoured somewhat of uproar and sorcery, and the cat who could speak astonished him more than all the rest.

As soon as she reached home she put on her long black veil; she supped with the prince. He was hungry and ate with a good appetite; liqueurs were served him which he drank with great pleasure, and immediately forgot the little dog he was to take the king. He only thought of mewing with the White Cat, that is, to keep her pleasant and faithful company; the days passed in pleasant fêtes, fishing, hunting, ballets, feasts, and many other ways in which he amused himself capitally; sometimes the White Cat composed verses and songs of so passionate a character that it seemed she must have a tender heart, and that she could not speak as she did without loving; but her secretary, an elderly cat, wrote so badly that although her works have been preserved, it is impossible to read them.

The prince had forgotten even his country. The hands of which I spoke continued to serve him. He sometimes regretted he was not a cat, in order that he might spend his life in that pleasant company. 'Alas!' he said to White Cat, 'how grieved I shall be to leave you, I love you so dearly! Either become a woman or make me a cat.' She was much amused at his wish, and made mysterious answers of which he understood nothing.

A year passes so quickly when you have neither cares nor troubles, and are in good health. White Cat knew when he ought to return, and as he had quite forgotten it, she reminded him. 'Do you know,' she said, 'that you have only three days in which to find the little dog your father wants, and your brothers have found beauties?' The prince then remembered, and astonished at his carelessness, exclaimed: 'By what secret charm have I forgotten the thing more important to me than anything in the world? Unless I procure a dog wonderful enough to win me a kingdom, and a horse speedy enough to travel so long a distance in time, it is all up with my fame and fortune.' He began to feel very anxious and distressed.

White Cat to comfort him said: 'King's son, do not vex yourself, I am your friend. You can stay here another day, and although it is five hundred leagues from here to your country, the wooden horse will take you there in less than twelve hours.' 'I thank you, beautiful cat,' said the prince; 'but it is not enough to return to my father: I must take him a little dog.' 'Stay,' said White Cat, 'here is an acorn which contains one more beautiful than the dog-star.' 'Oh!' said the prince, 'Madam Cat, you are laughing at me.' 'Put the acorn to your ear,' she continued, 'you will hear it bark.' He obeyed, and heard the little dog say bow-wow; the prince was overjoyed, because a dog that could get into an acorn must be very tiny. He was so anxious to see it that he wanted to open it, but White Cat told him it might be cold on the journey, and it would therefore be better to wait till he was with his father. He thanked her a thousand times, and bade her a tender farewell. 'I assure you,' he added, 'time has passed so quickly with you that I somewhat regret leaving you, and although you are queen here, and the cats who form your court are more intelligent and more gallant than ours, I cannot help inviting you to come with me.' The cat's only reply to this was a deep sigh.

They parted; the prince was the first to arrive at the castle where the meeting with his brothers had been arranged to take place. They joined him very soon, and were surprised to see a wooden horse in the courtyard that leaped better than all those in the riding schools.

The prince came to meet them. They embraced each other affectionately, and related their adventures; but our prince did not tell his brothers his real adventures, and showed them a wretched dog which served as turnspit, saying he considered it so pretty that it was the one he destined for the king. No matter how they loved one another, the two eldest were secretly glad of the youngest's foolish choice; being at dinner, one trod on the other's foot as if to say there was nothing to fear on that score.

The next day they went on together in the same coach. The king's two eldest sons brought little dogs in baskets, so beautiful and delicate that one scarcely dared to touch them; the youngest brought the miserable turnspit, which was so dirty that no one could bear it. When they reached the palace, they were greeted and welcomed by all; they entered the king's rooms. He did not know in whose favour to decide, for the dogs brought by his two eldest sons were almost equally beautiful, and they were already disputing the succession, when the youngest brought them into harmony by drawing out of his pocket the acorn White Cat had given him. He quickly opened it, and they saw a little dog lying on cotton wool. He passed through a ring without touching it. The prince put him on the ground, and he began to dance with castanets as lightly as the most famous Spanish girl. He was of a thousand different colours, his silky hair and ears dragged on the ground. The king was greatly puzzled, for it was impossible to find anything to say against the beauty of the little dog.

But he had not the least desire to give away his crown. The tiniest gem of it was dearer to him than all the dogs in the world. He told his children he was pleased with their labours, and they had succeeded so well in the first thing he had asked of them that he wished to prove their skill further before fulfilling his promise; so that he gave them a year to look by sea and land for a piece of linen so fine that it would pass through the eye of a needle used for making Venice point-lace. They were all vastly distressed to be obliged to go on a new quest. The two princes, whose dogs were not so beautiful as that of the youngest, agreed. Each departed his own way without so much affection as the former time, because the turnspit had greatly cooled their love.

Our prince mounted his wooden horse again, and without caring to find other help than that he might hope from White Cat's friendliness, he speedily departed, and returned to the castle where he had been so kindly entertained. He found all the doors open, the windows, roofs, towers and walls were lighted by a hundred thousand lamps that produced a marvellous effect. The hands that had waited on him so well came to meet him, took the bridle of the wooden horse and led it to the stable, while the prince entered White Cat's room. She was lying in a little basket on a very nice white satin mattress. Her toilette was neglected and she looked out of spirits; but when she saw the prince, she leaped and jumped to show him her joy. 'Whatever reason I had,' she said, 'to hope that you would return, king's son, I dared not expect too much, and I am usually so unfortunate in the things I wish that this event surprises me.' The grateful prince caressed her; he related the success of his journey, which she knew probably better than he, and that the king wanted a piece of linen fine enough to go through a needle's eye;

that in truth he thought the thing impossible, but he intended to rely on her friendship and help. White Cat, looking serious, said she would think over the matter; fortunately, there were cats in the castle who spun excellently; she would see that what he wanted was prepared, thus he would have no need to go further afield in search of what he could more easily procure in her palace than in any other place in the world.

The hands appeared, carrying torches, and the prince and White Cat following them, entered a magnificent gallery that extended along the bank of a river, where a splendid display of fireworks took place. Four cats, who had been duly tried with all the usual formalities, were to be burned. They were accused of eating the roast meat provided for White Cat's supper, her cheese, her milk, and of having plotted against her person with Martafax and L'Hermite, famous rats of the country, and held as such by La Fontaine, a truthful writer; but all the same it was known that there was a good deal of treachery in the matter, and that most of the witnesses were bribed. However it might have been, the prince obtained their pardon. The fireworks did no one any harm, and there never were more beautiful rockets.

A very excellent supper was afterwards served, which pleased the prince more than the fireworks, for he was very hungry, and his wooden horse travelled at the greatest speed possible. The days that followed were spent in the same way as those that preceded, with a thousand different fêtes devised by White Cat's ingenuity to amuse the prince. He is perhaps the first man who entertained himself so well in the company of cats.

It is true that White Cat had a charming, flexible and versatile mind. She was more learned than cats usually are. The prince was sometimes astonished. 'No,' he said, 'what I see so surprising in you is not a natural thing; if you love me, charming puss, tell me by what miracle you think and speak so correctly that you would be received into the most famous academies of learned men?' 'Cease to ask questions, king's son,' she said, 'I am not allowed to reply: you can carry your conjectures as far as you please, I shall not oppose them: be contented that I never show my claws to you, and take a tender interest in all that concerns you.'

The second year passed as quickly as the first; everything the prince wished for was immediately brought him by the hands; whether it was books, jewels, pictures, antique medals, he had only to say I want such and such a jewel that is in the cabinet of the Mogul or of the King of Persia, such a statue from Corinth or Greece, and he immediately saw before him what he desired, without knowing who brought it or whence it came. That was not without its charms, and it is sometimes a pleasant diversion to become possessed of the most beautiful treasures of the earth.

White Cat, who never ceased to watch over the prince's interests, warned him that the time of his departure was drawing near, that he need not be anxious about the linen he wanted, since she had had made for him a most wonderful piece; she added that she wished this time to give him an equipage worthy of his rank, and without awaiting his reply, she made him look out into the courtyard. He saw an open barouche enamelled with flame-coloured gold, with a thousand elegant devices that pleased the intelligence as well as the eye. Twelve snow-white horses yoked together in fours drew it, harnessed in flame-coloured velvet embroidered with diamonds, and decorated with gold plates. The inside of the barouche was equally magnificent, and a hundred coaches, with eight horses, filled with nobles of fine appearance, superbly dressed, accompanied the barouche. It was also attended by a thousand bodyguards, whose coats were so thickly embroidered that you could not see the material; and what was strangest, White Cat's portrait appeared everywhere: in the decoration of the barouche, on the coats of the guards, or fastened with a ribbon, like an order, round the necks of those who formed the procession.

'Go,' she said to the prince, 'appear at your father's court in so sumptuous a manner that your magnificence may impress him with awe, so that he will not refuse you the crown you deserve. Here is a walnut; do not crack it until you are before him; it contains the piece of linen you asked of me.'

'Good White Cat,' he said, 'I confess I am so deeply sensible of your kindness that if you would consent, I would rather spend my life with you than amid all the glory I have reason to expect elsewhere.' 'King's son,' she replied, 'I am convinced of your good heart, a very rare commodity among princes: they want to be loved by all without loving anything or anyone themselves, but you are the exception that proves the rule. I shall not forget the affection you show for a little white cat, who is good for nothing but to catch mice.' The prince kissed her paw and departed.

It would be difficult to understand the speed at which he travelled, if we did not know already that the wooden horse had taken less than two days to do the five hundred leagues to the castle, so that the same power that animated that horse worked in the others, and they were only twenty-four hours on the road. They halted nowhere until they reached the king's palace, where the two eldest brothers had already repaired, so that not seeing the youngest they applauded his forgetfulness and whispered: 'This is very fortunate; he is either dead or sick, he will not be our rival in this important business.' They exhibited their pieces of linen, which were indeed so fine that they went through the eye of a big needle, but could not get through that of a small one, and the king, glad of the pretext, showed them the particular needle he meant, and which the magistrates by his orders brought from the treasury of the town, where it had been carefully preserved.

There was much grumbling over this. The princes' friends, and particularly those of the oldest – for his piece of linen was the best – said that it was open chicanery, in which there was great cunning and evasion. The king's supporters upheld that he was not compelled to keep to the proposed conditions. At length, to make them all agree, a delightful sound of trumpets, drums, and hautboys was heard; it was the arrival of the prince and his fine equipage. The king and his two sons were all vastly astonished at its magnificence.

After greeting his father very respectfully and embracing his brothers, he took the walnut out of a box ornamented with rubies, and cracked it, thinking to find in it the famous piece of linen, but instead there was a hazel nut; he cracked that, and was surprised to see a cherry stone. They looked at each other; the king smiled and laughed at his son for being credulous enough to believe a walnut could contain a piece of linen; but why should he not have believed it, since he had already found a little dog contained in an acorn? He cracked the cherry stone, which contained its kernel; then a loud murmur arose in the room, and nothing could be heard but that the youngest prince had been duped. He made no reply to the courtiers' jests; he opened the kernel and found a grain of wheat, and in the grain of wheat a millet seed. In truth, he began to get distrustful, and murmured between his teeth: 'Why, cat, White Cat, you have made game of me.' He felt at that moment a cat's claw on his hand, which scratched him so severely that he bled. He did not know if this was to encourage him or to make him lose heart. However, he opened the millet seed, and the people were no little astonished when he drew from it a piece of linen four hundred ells long, so wonderful that all the birds, beasts, and fishes were painted on it, with trees, fruits, and plants of the earth, the rocks, the curiosities and shells of the sea, the sun, moon, stars and planets of the heavens; further, there were the portraits of the kings and other sovereigns that had reigned in the world, those of their wives, mistresses, children and subjects, not omitting the least important of them. Each in his condition assumed the character that suited him best, and wore the costume of his country. When the king saw the piece of linen, he became as pale as the prince was red from his prolonged efforts to find it. The needle was brought, the piece of linen passed backwards and forwards through the eye six times. The king and the two eldest princes preserved a dismal silence, although the beauty and rarity of the linen compelled them to say that nothing in the world could be compared to it.

The king uttered a deep sigh, and turning to his children, said: 'Nothing consoles me more in my old age than your deference to my wishes. I therefore desire to put you to a further proof. Go and travel for a year, and at the end of that time he who brings back the most beautiful girl shall marry her and be crowned king on his wedding-day. It is absolutely necessary that my successor should marry. I swear, I promise that I will not again put off the reward.'

Our prince strongly felt the injustice. The little dog and the piece of linen deserved ten kingdoms rather than one, but he was too well-bred to oppose his father's will, and without delay got into the barouche again. The whole procession accompanied him, and he returned to his beloved White Cat. She knew the day and hour of his arrival. The road was strewed with flowers, a thousand perfume burners smoked on all sides, and especially in the castle. She was seated on a Persian carpet, under a canopy of cloth of gold, in a gallery whence she could see him coming. He was received by the hands that had always waited on him. All the cats climbed up to the gutters in order to welcome him with a terrible mewing.

'Well, king's son,' she said, 'you have again returned without a crown?' 'Madam,' he replied, 'your kindness has certainly given me the best chance of gaining it, but I am convinced that the king would have more trouble in giving it away than I should have pleasure in possessing it.' 'No matter,' she said, 'you must neglect nothing that can make you deserve it. I will help you this time, and since you must take a beautiful girl to your father's court, I will find you one who will cause you to win the prize. Now let us amuse ourselves; I have ordered a naval combat between my cats and the terrible rats of the country. My cats will doubtless be uncomfortable, for they fear the water, but otherwise they would have had too great an advantage, and things ought before all to be fair.' The prince admired Madam Puss's prudence; he praised her highly, and accompanied her to a terrace that looked on the sea.

The cats' ships consisted of big pieces of cork, on which they floated comfortably enough. The rats had joined together several egg-shells to form their vessels. The combat was obstinately kept up; the rats threw themselves into the water, and swam far better than the cats; so that twenty times they were conquerors and conquered, but Minagrobis, admiral of the cats' fleet, reduced the rats to the extremity of despair. He greedily ate up the leader of their fleet, an old experienced rat, who had been thrice round the world in good vessels, where he was neither captain nor sailor, but only a parasite.

White Cat did not wish those poor wretches to be entirely destroyed. She knew how to rule her people, and thought that if there should be no more rats or mice in the land, her subjects would live in an idleness very harmful to them. The prince spent that year like the others in hunting, fishing and games, for White Cat played chess extremely well. Now and again he could not help asking her fresh questions as to the miracle by which she was able to speak. He asked her if she was a fairy, or if she had become a cat by some change of shape. But she always said only what she wanted to say, and replied only what she wished; and she did this by so many phrases that meant nothing at all, that he clearly saw she did not wish to share her secret with him.

The White Cat

Nothing passes more swiftly than days spent without trouble or care, and if the cat had not been wise enough to remember the time for returning to the court, it is certain that the prince would have entirely forgotten it. She told him the evening before that it only rested with him to take to his father one of the most beautiful princesses the world had ever seen; that the time for destroying the fatal work of the fairies had at length arrived, and to do that it was necessary for him to cut off her head and tail, and throw them at once into the fire. 'I,' he exclaimed, 'White Cat, my love, am I to be cruel enough to kill you? Ah, you doubtless want to prove my heart, but be sure it will never be wanting in the affection and gratitude it owes you.' 'No, king's son,' she continued, 'I do not suspect you of ingratitude, I know your merit; it is neither you nor I who rule our fate in this matter. Do what I wish; we shall both begin to be happy, and you will know on the faith of a rich and honourable cat that I am indeed your friend.'

The tears came into the prince's eyes at the mere thought of cutting off his cat's pretty little head. He said everything loving and tender he could think of to dissuade her, but she obstinately replied that she wished to die by his hand, and that it was the only way of preventing his brothers from obtaining the crown; in fact, she urged him so ardently that trembling he drew his sword, and with a shaking hand cut off the head and tail of his good friend, the cat. Immediately the most charming change imaginable took place. White Cat's body grew tall, and suddenly turned into a girl, whose beauty cannot be described; never was there any so perfect. Her eyes enchanted all hearts, and her sweetness captivated them. Her stature was majestic, and her bearing noble and modest; her mind was versatile, her manners attractive; indeed, she was superior to everything that was most amiable.

The prince was so agreeably surprised at the sight, that he thought he must be enchanted. He could not speak, he could only look at her, and his tongue was so tied that he could not express his astonishment; but it was a very different thing when he saw an extraordinary number of lords and ladies enter the room, who, with their cats' skins thrown over their shoulders, bowed low to their queen, and testified their joy at seeing her again in her natural state.

She received them with marks of kindness that were enough

to prove the character of her disposition. And after holding her court for a few moments, she gave orders that she should be left alone with the prince, and spoke to him thus:

'Do not imagine, sir, that I have always been a cat. My father ruled over six kingdoms. He loved my mother dearly, and allowed her to do exactly as she liked. Her ruling passion was travel, so that shortly before I was born she set out to visit a certain mountain, of which she had heard the most wonderful accounts. On the way she was told that near the place where she then was, was an ancient fairy castle of very great beauty, so at least report said, for, as no one had ever entered it, it could not be proved a fact; but it was well known that the fairies' garden contained the best and most delicately flavoured fruits ever eaten.

'The queen was seized with a violent desire to taste them, and turned her steps in the direction of the castle. She reached the gate of the magnificent building that shone with gold and azure on all sides. But she knocked in vain; no one appeared, it seemed that everybody was dead. The difficulties only served to increase her desire, and she sent for ladders so that they might get over the garden wall. They would have succeeded if the walls had not visibly increased in height although no one worked at them; they tied the ladders together, but they gave way under the weight of the climbers, who were either crippled for life or killed outright.

'The queen was in despair. She saw big trees loaded with fruits that seemed delicious; she felt she must taste them or die; she ordered sumptuous tents to be pitched before the castle, and she and all her court remained there six weeks. She neither ate nor slept; she did nothing but sigh and talk of the fruit in the inaccessible garden. At length she fell dangerously ill, and no one could cure her, for the inexorable fairies had not as much as appeared since she had established herself near the castle. All her officers were greatly distressed. Only weeping and sighs were heard while the dying queen asked her attendants for fruits, but would only have what was denied her.

'One night, when she was somewhat drowsy, she saw when she woke a little ugly decrepit old woman seated in an armchair by her bedside. She was surprised her attendants should have allowed

The White Cat

anyone she did not know to come so near her. The old dame said: "We consider your majesty very importunate in wishing so obstinately to eat of our fruits, but since your life is in danger my sisters and I have agreed to give you as many as you can carry away, and as many as you like while you remain here, provided you make us a present." "Ah! my dear mother," exclaimed the queen, "speak; I will give you my realms, my heart, my soul, provided I may have the fruit; no price is too great for it!" "We desire your majesty," she said, "to give us the daughter shortly to be born to you; at her birth we shall come and fetch her away and bring her up among us. We shall endow her with all the virtues, with beauty and knowledge; in short, she will be our child; we shall make her happy, but remember you will see her no more until she is married. If you like the proposal I will cure you at once and take you to our orchards; although it is night, you will be able to see clearly enough to choose what you please. If you do not like what I have said – well, good-evening, madam, I shall go home to bed." "Although the conditions you impose on me are very hard, I accept them rather than die, for it is certain I have not a day to live. Cure me, wise fairy," she continued, "and do not let me be a moment longer without enjoying the privilege you have just granted me."

'The fairy touched her with a small gold wand, saying: "May your majesty be freed from the sufferings that keep you in this bed!" It seemed to her immediately as though she had put off a very heavy and uncomfortable gown, which had oppressed her. In some places, seemingly where her malady had been most acute, the burden still weighed upon her. She called her ladies-in-waiting, and told them with cheerful looks that she felt extremely well, was going to get up, and that the gates of the fairy palace, so fast bolted and barricaded, would be open for her to eat and carry away as much of the fruit as she pleased.

'The ladies thought the queen was delirious, and dreaming of the fruits she longed for; instead therefore of answering her, they began to cry and awoke the physicians to come and see in what a condition she was. The delay exasperated the queen: she asked for her clothes and was refused; she got angry and became very flushed. They thought it was the effect of the fever. However, the physicians felt her pulse, went through the usual formalities and could not deny that she was in perfect health. Her ladies, seeing the fault their zeal had made them commit, tried to mend it by dressing her quickly. They asked her pardon and were forgiven: she hastened to follow the old fairy, who had been waiting for her all the time.

'She entered the palace, where nothing was wanting to make it the most beautiful place in the world. This you will easily believe, sir,' said Queen White Cat, 'when I tell you it is the very castle in which we are; two other fairies, a little younger than my mother's guide, received them at the door and welcomed them kindly. She begged them to take her at once into the garden, and show her the trees on which she would find the best fruit. "They are all equally good," they told her, "and if you were not so anxious to pluck them yourself, we have merely to bid them come!" "I entreat you, ladies," said the queen, "give me the pleasure of seeing so extraordinary a thing." The oldest put her fingers to her mouth, and whistled three times; then she shouted: "Apricots peaches, nectarines, cherries, plums, pears, white-heart cherries, melons, grapes, apples, oranges, lemons, currants, strawberries, raspberries, come at my bidding!" "But," said the queen, "those you summon, ripen at different seasons." "It is not so in our orchard," they said. "We have all the fruits the earth produces always ripe, always good; they never go bad!"

'Directly they all came, rolling, creeping along, pell-mell, without getting bruised or harmed; so that the queen, eager to satisfy her longing, took the first that offered, and rather devoured than ate them.

'When she was somewhat satisfied, she asked the fairies to let her go to the trees that she might have the pleasure of choosing the fruit with her eye, before plucking it. "We willingly consent," said the three fairies, "but remember your promise. You can no longer go back from it." "I am sure," she replied, "it is very pleasant here, and if I did not love my husband so dearly, I should ask you to let me live here too; so that you need have no fear I shall retract." The fairies, extremely pleased, opened all their gardens and enclosures; the queen stayed with them three days and three nights without wishing to go, so delicious was the fruit. She gathered some to take with her, and as it never spoiled she loaded four thousand mules with it. The fairies added to the fruit gold baskets of exquisite workmanship to put it in, and several curiosities of great value. They promised to give me the education of a princess, to make me perfect, choose a husband for me, and to inform my mother of the day of the wedding, to which they hoped she would come.

'The king was delighted at the queen's return; the whole court rejoiced with him. There were balls, masquerades, running at the ring, and banquets, where the queen's fruits were served as a delicious feast. The king ate them in preference to everything else that was offered him. He did not know the treaty she had made with the fairies, and he often asked her the name of the land from which she had brought such good things. She told him they were to be found on an almost inaccessible mountain; at another time, that they came from the valleys, then from a garden, or a big forest. So many contradictions surprised the king. He questioned those who had accompanied her, but as she had forbidden them to tell the adventure to anyone, they dared not speak of it. As the time of my birth drew nearer, the queen, anxious about her promise to the fairies, fell into a terrible melancholy; she sighed every moment and changed colour rapidly. The king grew very uneasy, and urged the queen to tell him what distressed her. With great difficulty she told him what had passed between her and the fairies, and how she had promised her daughter to them. "What!" exclaimed the king, "we are to have no children; you know how I long for them, and for the sake of eating two or three apples you were capable of promising your daughter. You cannot have any affection for me." He overwhelmed her with a thousand reproaches, which nearly caused my mother to die of grief; but he was not content with that: he shut her up in a tower and surrounded it with guards to prevent her having communication with anybody but the servants who waited on her, and changed those who had been with her at the fairy castle.

'The bad feeling between the king and queen threw the court into great consternation. Everybody put off his rich clothes in order to don those suitable to the general grief. The king, on his part, seemed inexorable; he never saw his wife, and directly I was born, had me brought to his palace to be fed and cared for, while the queen remained a most unhappy prisoner. The fairies knew everything that was going on; they became angry, they wanted to gain possession of me: they looked upon me as their property, and that it was a theft from them to keep me. Before seeking a revenge in proportion to their anger, they sent an embassy to the king, asking him to set the queen at liberty, and take her into favour again, and to give me to their ambassadors in order to be brought up by them. The ambassadors were so small, and so deformed – they were ugly dwarfs – that they had not the gift of persuading the king to do what they wished. He refused roughly, and if they had not speedily departed worse might have befallen them.

'When the fairies learned my father's course of action, they became very indignant; and after inflicting the most desolating evils on his six kingdoms, they let loose a terrible dragon which poisoned all the places he passed through, devoured men and children, and killed the trees and plants by breathing on them.

'The king was in the depths of despair; he consulted all the wise men in the kingdom about what he ought to do to secure his subjects from these overwhelming misfortunes. They advised him to seek through all the world for the cleverest physicians, and the most excellent remedies, and to promise life to all the condemned criminals who would fight the dragon. The king, pleased with the counsel, followed it, but without result, for the mortality continued, and everyone who went against the dragon was devoured; then he had recourse to a fairy who had protected him from his earliest youth. She was very old, and scarcely ever left her bed; he went to her and reproached her for permitting fate to persecute him thus, and for not coming to his assistance. "What do you want me to do?" she said; "you have annoyed my sisters; they are as powerful as I am, and we seldom act against each other. Appease them by giving them your daughter; the little princess belongs to them. You have closely imprisoned the queen: what has she done that you should treat so amiable a woman so badly? Fulfil the promise she gave, and I undertake that good shall come of it."

'My father loved me dearly, but seeing no other way of saving his kingdoms, and delivering himself from the fatal dragon, he told his friend that he would trust her, and give me to the fairies since she declared I should be cherished, and treated as became a princess of my rank; that he would set the queen free, and that she had only to tell him who was to carry me to the fairy castle. "You must carry her in her cradle," said his fairy friend, "to the mountain of flowers; you can even remain near and see what will happen." The king told her that in a week he would go with the queen; meanwhile she might inform her sisters of his decision, that they might make what preparations they thought proper.

'When he returned to the palace, he released the queen with as much affection and ceremony as he had made her prisoner in anger and rage. She was so dejected and changed that he would hardly have recognized her if his heart had not assured him that it was the same woman he had so deeply loved. He entreated her with tears in his eyes to forget the troubles he had caused her, assuring her that they would be the last she would experience from him. She replied that she had brought them on herself by her imprudence in promising her daughter to the fairies, and if anything could excuse her, it was her present condition. The king then told her he intended to deliver me to their keeping. It was now the queen who objected; it seemed to be fated that I was always to be a subject for discord between my father and mother. She wept and groaned without obtaining her desire, for the king was too well aware of the fatal consequences, and our subjects continued to die as if they had been guilty of the faults of our family. At length she consented, and everything was prepared for the ceremony.

'I was put into a mother-of-pearl cradle ornamented with everything pretty that art could imagine. It was hung with wreaths and festoons of flowers made of precious stones, and the different colours catching the sun's rays became so dazzling that you could not look at them. The magnificence of my clothing surpassed that of the cradle. All the fastenings of my robes were composed of big pearls, and twenty-four princesses of the blood carried me on a sort of light litter; their ornaments were not ordinary, and they were only allowed to wear white, as befitted my innocence. The whole court accompanied me, each in his rank.

'While they were ascending the mountain, the sound of a melodious symphony was heard coming nearer, and at length the fairies, thirty in number, appeared. They had asked their good friend the King's fairy to accompany them; each was seated in a pearly shell bigger than that in which Venus rose from the sea; and the shells were drawn by walruses that moved uneasily on dry land. The fairies were more magnificently escorted than great queens, but they were exceedingly old and ugly. They carried an olive branch to signify to the king that his submission found favour with them, and they covered me with such extraordinary caresses that it seemed they intended to live only to make me happy.

'The dragon who had avenged them on my father followed them fastened in diamond chains. They took me in their arms, kissed me, endowed me with many precious qualities, and then began the fairy dance. It was very merry, and it is incredible how those old ladies leaped and sprang; and the dragon, who had eaten so many people, approached crawling. The three fairies, to whom my mother had promised me, seated themselves on him and placed my cradle in their midst, and striking the dragon with a wand, he unfolded his big, scaly wings, finer than crêpe, and of a thousand different colours; thus they repaired to the castle. My mother, seeing me in the air at the mercy of the furious dragon, could not help uttering loud cries. The king consoled her with the assurance given him by his good friend that no harm should come to me, and that I should be as well taken care of as if I had remained in the palace. She became calmer, although it was very sad to lose me for so long, and to be herself the cause of such a misfortune, for if she had not desired to eat the fruit in the garden, I should have remained in my father's kingdoms and should not have suffered all the misfortunes I have still to relate to you.

'Learn then, king's son, that my guardians had purposely built a tower in which were a thousand beautiful apartments for all the seasons of the year, magnificent furniture, interesting books, but no door, and you had to get in by the windows, which were extremely high up. On the tower was a beautiful garden adorned with flowers, fountains and arbours which procured shade even in the hottest season. Here the fairies brought me up with a care that surpassed everything they had promised the queen. My clothes were always in the fashion, and so splendid that if anyone had seen me they would have thought it was my wedding-day. They taught me everything that belonged to my age and rank. I did not give them much trouble, for there was scarcely anything I did not understand with the greatest ease; they liked my gentleness, and as I had never seen anyone except them I might have lived contented with them for the rest of my life.

The White Cat

'They always visited me, mounted on the furious dragon I have already mentioned; they never spoke of the king or queen; they called me their daughter, and I thought I was. No one lived with me in the tower except a parrot and a little dog they had given me for my amusement, for the animals were endowed with reason, and spoke perfectly.

'One of the sides of the castle was built on a deep road, so full of ruts and trees that it was almost impassable, so that since I had lived in the tower I had never seen anyone there. But one day when I was at the window chatting with the parrot and dog I heard a noise. I looked all round and saw a young knight who had stopped to listen to our conversation; I had never seen anyone like him, except in pictures. I was not sorry that an unexpected meeting should afford me such an opportunity, and having no idea of the danger that is attached to the satisfaction of contemplating a pleasant thing, I came forward to look at him, and the longer I looked, the more pleasure I felt. He made me a low bow, and fixed his eyes on me, and seemed greatly troubled to know how he might speak to me; for my window was very high, and he feared to be overheard, well knowing that I was in the fairy castle.

'Night suddenly came on, or to speak more correctly, it came without our perceiving it. He sounded his horn two or three times very prettily and then departed: it was so dark that I could not see which way he went. I was in a dream and no longer took the same pleasure as before in chatting with my parrot and dog. They told me the prettiest things imaginable, for fairy animals are intelligent, but I was preoccupied and knew not how to dissemble. Parrot noticed it; he was cunning and did not betray what was passing in his mind.

'I did not fail to rise with the dawn. I ran to my window and was agreeably surprised to see the young knight at the foot of the tower. He was magnificently dressed. I flattered myself that it was somewhat on my account, and I was not mistaken. He talked to me through a kind of speaking trumpet, and by its aid told me that, having been hitherto insensible to all the beauties he had seen, he was suddenly so impressed with me, that unless he saw me every day of his life he should die. I was charmed with the compliment, and much distressed at not daring to reply to it, for it would have been necessary to shout with all my might, and so risk being better heard by the fairies than by him. I threw him some flowers I had in my hands: he received them as a marked favour, kissed them several times and thanked me. He then asked me if I should like him to come every day at the same time to my windows, and, if so, I was to throw him something. I took a turquoise ring from my finger and hastily threw it him, signing him to go away quickly because I heard the Fairy Violent mounting her dragon to bring me my breakfast.

'The first words she said on entering the room were: "I smell the voice of a man here; search for him, dragon." Imagine my feelings. I was paralysed with fear lest he should go out by the other window and follow the knight in whom I was already greatly interested. "My dear mamma" (for it was thus the old fairy liked me to call her), "you are joking when you say you smell a man's voice; has a voice any smell? and even if it has, who is the mortal daring enough to ascend this tower?" "What you say is true, my daughter," she replied; "I am delighted you argue so nicely, and I suppose it must be the hatred I have for men which sometimes makes me think they are not far from me." She gave me my breakfast and my distaff. "When you have finished eating, spin," she said, "for you are very idle and my sisters will be angry." I had been so taken up with my unknown knight that I had found it impossible to spin.

'As soon as she was gone, I saucily threw the distaff on the ground, and ascended the terrace to see farther over the country. I had an excellent spyglass; nothing impeded my view; I looked on all sides, and discovered my knight on the top of a mountain. He was resting under a rich pavilion of some gold material, and was surrounded by a large court. I supposed he must be the son of some king who was a neighbour of the fairies' palace. As I feared if he returned to the tower he would be discovered by the terrible dragon, I told my parrot to fly to the mountain, seek out the man who had spoken to me, and beg him on my part not to return, because I dreaded my guardians' vigilance, and that they might do him some mischief.

'Parrot acquitted himself of the mission like a parrot of intelligence. It surprised everybody to see him come swiftly and perch on the prince's shoulder and whisper in his ear. The prince felt both pleasure and pain at the message; my anxiety for his welfare flattered him, but the difficulty of seeing and speaking to me overwhelmed him, without, however, turning him from his purpose of pleasing me. He asked Parrot a hundred questions, and Parrot in his turn asked him a hundred, for he was curious by nature. The king entrusted him with a ring for me instead of my turquoise; it was formed of the same stones, but was much more beautiful than mine; it was cut in the shape of a heart, and ornamented with diamonds. "It is only right," he added, "that I should treat you as an ambassador; here is my portrait, only show it to your charming mistress." He fastened the portrait under his wing and brought the ring in his beak.

'I awaited my little messenger's return with an impatience I had never before felt. He told me my knight was a great king; that he had received him most kindly, and that I might rest assured he only wished to live for me; that in spite of the danger he ran in coming to my tower, he was determined to risk everything rather than give up the pleasure of seeing me. That news worried me greatly, and I began to weep. Parrot and Bow-wow consoled me as well as they could, for they loved me dearly; then Parrot gave me the prince's ring and showed me the portrait. I confess I was extremely glad to be able to examine closely the man I had only seen in the distance. He seemed even more charming than I had imagined; a thousand thoughts, some pleasant, others sad, came into my mind, and gave me an extraordinary look of anxiety. The fairies perceived it, and said to each other that doubtless I was feeling bored, and they must, therefore, think about finding me a husband of fairy race. They spoke of several, and fixed on the little King Migonnet, whose kingdom was five hundred thousand leagues from their palace, but that was of no consequence. Parrot overheard this fine advice, and told me of it. "Ah!" he said, "I pity you, my dear mistress, if you become Migonnet's queen; his appearance is enough to frighten anyone. I regret to say it, but truly the king who loves you would not have him for a footman." "Have you seen him, Parrot?" I asked. "I should think so," continued he; "I have been on a branch with him." "What! on a branch?" I replied. "Yes," he said; "he has the claws of an eagle."

'Such a tale distressed me strangely. I looked at the charming portrait of the king: I thought he could only have given it to Parrot so that I might have an opportunity of seeing him, and when I compared him with Migonnet I could hope for nothing more in life, and determined to die rather than marry him.

'I did not sleep the whole night through. Parrot and Bow-wow talked to me. I slept a little towards morning; and as my dog had a keen scent he smelt that the king was at the bottom of the tower. He woke Parrot. "I bet," he said, "the king is down below." Parrot replied: "Be quiet, chatterbox; because your eyes are always open and your ear on the alert, you object to others resting." "But let us bet," said Bow-wow again; "I know he is there." Parrot replied: "And I know very well he is not; did I not carry a message from my mistress forbidding him to come?" "Truly, you're imposing nicely on me with your prohibitions," exclaimed the dog. "A passionate man only consults his heart"; and thereupon he began to pull his wings about so roughly that Parrot grew angry. Their cries awoke me; they told me the cause of the dispute: I ran, or rather flew, to the window. I saw the king, who stretched out his arms, and told me, by means of his trumpet, that he could not live without me, and implored me to find means to get out of the tower, or for him to enter it: he called all the gods and the elements to witness that he would marry me and make me one of the greatest queens in the world.

'I told Parrot to go and tell him that what he hoped seemed to me almost impossible; but that relying on the promise he had made me and on his oaths, I would attempt to do what he wished. But I implored him not to come every day, because he might be seen, and the fairies would give no quarter.

'He went away greatly rejoiced at the hope I held out; but when I thought over what I had just promised, I was in the greatest possible embarrassment. How to get out of a tower that had no doors, the only assistance being Parrot and Bow-wow! to be so young, inexperienced, and timid! I therefore determined not to attempt a thing in which I could never succeed, and sent Parrot to tell the king so. He almost killed himself then and there; but at length he ordered him to persuade me either to come and see him die, or to console him. "Sire," exclaimed the feathered ambassador, "my mistress has the will but lacks the power."

'When he related to me all that had taken place I was more distressed than ever. Fairy Violent came and found my eyes red and swollen; she declared I had been crying, and that if I did not tell her the reason she would burn me, for her threats were always terrible. I replied, trembling, that I was tired of spinning, and that I wanted some small nets to catch the little birds that pecked the fruit in my garden. "What you desire," she said, "need cost you no more tears. I will bring you as much twine as you like"; and in fact I had it the same evening; but she advised me to think less of working than of making myself beautiful, because King Migonnet was expected shortly. I shuddered at the terrible news and said nothing.

'When she was gone, I began to make two or three pieces of netting; but what I really worked at was a rope ladder, and, although I had never seen one, it was very well made. The fairy did not provide me with as much twine as I wanted, and continually said: "But, my daughter, your work is like Penelope's, it never advances, and you are never tired of asking me for more material." "Oh! my dear mamma," I said, "it is all very well to talk, but don't you see that I am not very skilful, and burn it all? Are you afraid I shall ruin you in twine?" My look of simplicity rejoiced her, although she was of a very disagreeable and cruel disposition.

'I sent Parrot to tell the king to come one evening, under the windows of the tower, that he would find a ladder there, and would know the rest when he arrived. I made it fast; determined to fly with him; but when he saw it he did not wait for me to come down but eagerly ascended it, and rushed into my room just as I was preparing for my flight.

'I was so delighted to see him that I forgot the danger we were in. He repeated his oaths, and implored me not to delay making him my husband. Parrot and Bow-wow were witnesses of our marriage; never was a wedding between people of such high rank concluded with less splendour and fuss, and never was any couple happier than we were.

'Day had scarcely dawned when the king left me: I told him the fairies' terrible plan of marrying me to the little Migonnet; I described his appearance, and he was as horrified as I was. After his departure the hours seemed to me as long as years. I ran to the window, I followed him with my eyes in spite of the darkness, but what was my astonishment to see in the air a fiery chariot drawn by winged salamanders who travelled at such speed that the eye could scarcely follow them. The chariot was accompanied by several guards mounted on ostriches. I had not leisure enough to examine the creature which thus traversed the air; but I imagined it must be a fairy or a sorcerer.

'Soon after Fairy Violent entered my room. "I bring you good news," she said: "your lover has been here for some hours; prepare to receive him; here are clothes and jewels." "Who told you," I exclaimed, "that I wanted to be married? it is not at all my desire; send King Migonnet away. I shall not put on a pin more, whether he thinks me beautiful or ugly; I am not for him." "Oh! indeed," said the fairy, what a little rebel! what a little idiot! I do not permit such conduct, and I will make you..." "What will you do to me?" I asked, quite red with the names she had called me. "Could anyone be worse treated than I was, in a tower with a parrot and a dog, seeing every day the hideous and terrible dragon?" "Oh! you ungrateful little thing," said the fairy, "did you deserve so much care and trouble? I have often told my sisters we should have a poor reward." She sought them and told them our dispute; they were all greatly surprised.

'Parrot and Bow-wow remonstrated with me, and said if I persisted in rebelling, they foresaw that bitter misfortunes would happen to me. I was so proud of possessing the heart of a great king that I despised the fairies, and the advice of my poor little companions. I did not dress myself, and did my hair all crooked so that Migonnet might find me unpleasing. Our interview took place on the terrace. He came there in his fiery chariot. Never since there were dwarfs had one so small been seen. He walked on his eagle's feet and on his knees all at the same time, because he had no bones in his legs, and he supported himself on diamond crutches. His royal cloak was only half-an-ell long, and a third of it dragged along the ground. His head was as big as a bushel measure, and his nose so big that he carried a dozen birds on it, in whose chirping he delighted. His beard was so tremendous that canaries made their nests in it, and his ear projected an arm's length beyond his head, but it was scarcely noticed because of a high, pointed crown he wore to make himself appear taller. The flame of his chariot roasted the fruits, and dried up the flowers and fountains of my garden. He came to me, arms open to embrace me; I held myself so upright that his chief squire had to lift him up, but directly he was near me I fled into my room, shut the door and windows, so that Migonnet went back to the fairies very angry with me.

'They asked him to forgive my rudeness, and to appease him – for he was to be feared – they determined to bring him into my room at night while I was asleep, to tie my hands and feet, and put me with him into his burning chariot, so that he might take me away with him. The matter once decided, they scarcely scolded me for my rudeness; they only said I must think how to make up for it. Parrot and Bow-wow were surprised at this gentleness. "Do you know, my mistress," said the dog, "I do not augur well from it; the fairies are strange creatures, and very violent." I laughed at these fears, and awaited my beloved husband most impatiently; he was too anxious to see me to be late. I let down the rope ladder, fully resolved to return with him; he ascended with light step, and spoke to me so tenderly that I dare not recall to memory what he said.

'While we were talking with as much security as if we had been in his palace, suddenly the windows of the room were darkened. The fairies entered on their horrible dragon, Migonnet followed in his fiery chariot, with all his guards and their ostriches. The king, without fear, laid hold of his sword, and only thought of protecting me from the most horrible calamity, for, shall I tell you, sir? the savage creatures set their dragon on him, and it devoured him before my very eyes.

'In despair at his misfortune and mine, I threw myself into the horrid monster's mouth, wishing him to swallow me as he had just swallowed all I loved best in the world. He was very willing, but not so the fairies, who were more cruel than he was. "We must reserve her," they said, "for longer torment; a speedy death is too good for that unworthy girl." They touched me and I at once became a white cat. They brought me to this magnificent palace, which belonged to my father. They changed all the lords and ladies into cats; of some they allowed only the hands to be seen, and reduced me to the deplorable condition in which you found me, informing me of my rank, of the death of my father and mother, and that I could only be delivered from my cat-form by a prince who should exactly resemble the husband they had torn from me. You, sir, possess that likeness,' she continued, 'the same features, same expression, the same tone of voice. I was struck by it directly I saw you. I was informed of all that had happened and will happen; my troubles are at an end.' 'And mine, beautiful queen,' said the prince, throwing himself at her feet, 'will they be of long duration?' 'I already love you more than my life, sir,' said the queen. 'We must go to your father and see what he thinks of me, and if he will consent to what you desire.'

She went out, the prince took her hand, and she stepped into a chariot more magnificent than those he had hitherto seen. The rest of the equipage equalled it in such a degree that all the horses' shoes were of emerald with diamond nails. Probably that is the only time such a thing was seen. I do not relate the pleasant conversation of the queen and the prince; it was unique in its charm and intelligence, and the young prince was as perfect as she was: so that their thoughts were most beautiful.

When they were near the castle where the prince was to meet his two eldest brothers, the queen went inside a little crystal rock whose points were all adorned with rubies and gold. It had curtains all round, so that you could not see it, and it was carried by handsome young men magnificently attired. The prince remained in the chariot, and perceived his brothers walking with very beautiful princesses. When they recognized him they drew near to receive him, and asked him if he had brought a mistress with him. He said he had been unfortunate enough during all his travels only to meet ugly women, and the most beautiful thing he had brought was a little white cat. They began to laugh at his simplicity. 'A cat!' they said, 'are you afraid that our palace will be eaten up by mice.' The prince replied that he was certainly not wise to make his father such a present, and each then took his way to town.

The elder princes and their princesses got into barouches of gold and azure, the horses wore feathers and aigrettes on their heads, and nothing could have been more brilliant than the cavalcade. Our young prince followed, and then the crystal rock that everybody looked at with admiration.

The courtiers hastened to tell the king that the three princes had arrived. 'Do they bring beautiful women with them?' asked the king. 'It is impossible that they should be surpassed,' was their reply. He seemed vexed at the answer. The two princes eagerly entered with their wonderful princesses. The king welcomed them kindly, and did not know to which to award the prize. He looked at the youngest, and said: 'This time you come alone?' 'Your majesty will see in that rock a little white cat,' replied the prince, 'which mews so prettily and is so gentle that she will charm you.' The king smiled, and himself opened the rock, but, as he approached it, the queen by a spring shattered it to pieces, and appeared like the sun which has been for some time hidden by a cloud; her fair hair was flowing over her shoulders, and fell in long curls to her feet; her head was encircled with flowers; her gown was of a light white gauze, lined with pink silk; she rose and made the king a low curtsey, who, in the excess of his admiration could not help exclaiming: 'This is the matchless woman who deserves my crown.'

'Sire,' she said, 'I am not come to take from you a throne you fill so worthily. I possess, by inheritance, six kingdoms: allow me to offer you one, and give the same to each of your sons. As a reward, I only ask for your affection, and this young prince for my husband. We shall have quite enough with three kingdoms.' The king and the court uttered cries of joy and astonishment. The marriage was celebrated at once, and also the marriage of the two princes, so that the court spent many months in amusements and delights. Then each went to rule his own kingdom. The beautiful White Cat was immortalized as much by her goodness and generosity as by her rare merit and beauty.

THE CYPRIAN CAT
Dorothy L. Sayers

It's extraordinarily decent of you to come along and see me like this, Harringay. Believe me, I do appreciate it. It isn't every busy KC who'd do as much for such a hopeless sort of client. I only wish I could spin you a more workable kind of story, but honestly, I can only tell you exactly what I told Peabody. Of course, I can see he doesn't believe a word of it, and I don't blame him. He thinks I ought to be able to make up a more plausible tale than that – and I suppose I could, but where's the use? One's almost bound to fall down somewhere if one tries to swear to a lie. What I'm going to tell you is the absolute truth. I fired one shot and one shot only, and that was at the cat. It's funny that one should be hanged for shooting at a cat.

Merridew and I were always the best of friends; school and college and all that sort of thing. We didn't see very much of each other after the war, because we were living at opposite ends of the country; but we met in Town from time to time and wrote occasionally and each of us knew that the other was there in the background, so to speak. Two years ago, he wrote and told me he was getting married. He was just turned forty and the girl was fifteen years younger, and he was tremendously in love. It gave me a bit of a jolt – you know how it is when your friends marry. You feel they will never be quite the same again; and I'd got used to the idea that Merridew and I were cut out to be old bachelors. But of course I congratulated him and sent him a wedding present, and I did sincerely hope he'd be happy. He was obviously over head and ears; almost dangerously so, I thought, considering all things. Though except for the difference of age it seemed suitable enough. He told me he had met her at – of all places – a rectory garden-party down in Norfolk, and that she had actually never been out of her native village. I mean, literally – not so much as a trip to the nearest town. I'm not trying to convey that she wasn't pukka, or anything like that. Her father was some queer sort of recluse – a medievalist, or something – desperately poor. He died shortly after their marriage.

I didn't see anything of them for the first year or so. Merridew is a civil engineer, you know, and he took his wife away after the honeymoon to Liverpool, where he was doing something in connection with the harbour. It must have been a big change for her from the wilds of Norfolk. I was in Birmingham, with my nose kept pretty close to the grindstone, so we only exchanged occasional letters. His were what I can only call deliriously happy, especially at first. Later on, he seemed a little worried about his wife's health. She was restless; town life didn't suit her; he'd be glad when he could finish up his Liverpool job and get her away into the country. There wasn't any doubt about their happiness, you understand – she'd got him body and soul as they say, and as far as I could make out it was mutual. I want to make that perfectly clear.

Well, to cut a long story short, Merridew wrote to me at the beginning of last month and said he was just off to a new job – a waterworks extension scheme down in Somerset; and he asked if I could possibly cut loose and join them there for a few weeks. He wanted to have a yarn with me, and Felice was longing to make my acquaintance. They had got rooms at the village inn. It was rather a remote spot, but there was fishing and scenery and so forth, and I should be able to keep Felice company while he was working up at the dam. I was about fed up with Birmingham, what with the heat and one thing and another, and it looked pretty good to me, and I was due for a holiday anyhow, so I fixed up to go. I had a bit of business to do in Town, which I calculated would take me about a week, so I said I'd go down to Little Hexham on June 20th.

As it happened, my business in London finished itself off unexpectedly soon, and on the sixteenth I found myself absolutely free and stuck in an hotel with road-drills working just under the windows and a tar-spraying machine to make things livelier. You remember what a hot month it was – flaming June and no mistake about it. I didn't see any point in waiting, so I sent off a wire to

Merridew, packed my bag and took the train for Somerset the same evening. I couldn't get a compartment to myself, but I found a first-class smoker with only three seats occupied, and stowed myself thankfully into the fourth corner. There was a military-looking old boy, an elderly female with a lot of bags and baskets, and a girl. I thought I should have a nice, peaceful journey.

So I should have, if it hadn't been for the unfortunate way I'm built. It was quite all right at first – as a matter of fact, I think I was half asleep, and I only woke up properly at seven o'clock, when the waiter came to say that dinner was on. The other people weren't taking it, and when I came back from the restaurant car I found that the old boy had gone, and there were only the two women left. I settled down in my corner again, and gradually, as we went along, I found a horrible feeling creeping over me that there was a cat in the compartment somewhere. I'm one of those wretched people who can't stand cats. I don't mean just that I prefer dogs – I mean that the presence of a cat in the same room with me makes me feel like nothing on earth. I can't describe it, but I believe quite a lot of people are affected that way. Something to do with electricity, or so they tell me. I've read that very often the dislike is mutual, but it isn't so with me. The brutes seem to find me abominably fascinating – make a bee-line for my legs every time. It's a funny sort of complaint, and it doesn't make me at all popular with dear old ladies.

Anyway, I began to feel more and more awful and I realized that the old girl at the other end of the seat must have a cat in one of her innumerable baskets. I thought of asking her to put it out in the corridor, or calling the guard and having it removed, but I knew how silly it would sound and made up my mind to try and stick it. I couldn't say the animal was misbehaving itself or anything, and she looked a pleasant old lady; it wasn't her fault that I was a freak. I tried to distract my mind by looking at the girl.

She was worth looking at, too – very slim, and dark with one of those dead-white skins that make you think of magnolia blossom. She had the most astonishing eyes, too – I've never seen eyes quite like them; a very pale brown, almost amber, set wide apart and a little slanting, and they seemed to have a kind of luminosity of their own, if you get what I mean. I don't know if this sounds – I don't want you to think I was bowled over, or anything. As a matter of fact she held no sort of attraction for me, though I could imagine a different type of man going potty about her. She was just unusual, that was all. But however much I tried to think of other things I couldn't get rid of the uncomfortable feeling, and eventually I gave it up and went out into the corridor. I just mention this because it will help you to understand the rest of the story. If you can only realize how perfectly awful I feel when there's a cat about – even when it's shut up in a basket – you'll understand better how I came to buy the revolver.

Well, we got to Hexham Junction, which was the nearest station to Little Hexham, and there was old Merridew waiting on the platform. The girl was getting out too – but not the old lady with the cat, thank goodness – and I was just handing her traps out after her when he came galloping up and hailed us.

'Hullo!' he said, 'why that's splendid! Have you introduced yourselves?' So I tumbled to it then that the girl was Mrs Merridew, who'd been up to Town on a shopping expedition, and I explained to her about my change of plans and she said how jolly it was that I could come – the usual things. I noticed what an attractive low voice she had and how graceful her movements were, and I understood – though, mind you, I didn't share – Merridew's infatuation.

We got into his car – Mrs Merridew sat in the back and I got up beside Merridew, and was very glad to feel the air and to get rid of the oppressive electric feeling I'd had in the train. He told me the place suited them wonderfully, and had given Felice an absolutely new lease of life, so to speak. He said he was very fit, too, but I thought myself that he looked rather fagged and nervy.

You'd have liked that inn, Harringay. The real, old-fashioned stuff, as quaint as you make 'em, and everything genuine – none of your Tottenham Court Road antiques. We'd all had our grub, and Mrs Merridew said she was tired; so she went up to bed early and Merridew and I had a drink and went for a stroll round the village. It's a tiny hamlet quite at the other end of nowhere; lights out at ten, little thatched houses with pinched-up attic windows like furry ears – the place purred in its sleep. Merridew's working gang didn't sleep there, of course – they'd run up huts for them at the dams, a mile beyond the village.

The Cyprian Cat

The landlord was just locking up the bar when we came in – a block of a man with an absolutely expressionless face. His wife was a thin, sandy-haired woman who looked as though she was too downtrodden to open her mouth. But I found out afterwards that was a mistake, for one evening when he'd taken one or two over the eight and showed signs of wanting to make a night of it, his wife sent him off upstairs with a gesture and a look that took the heart out of him. That first night she was sitting in the porch, and hardly glanced at us as we passed her. I always thought her an uncomfortable kind of woman, but she certainly kept her house most exquisitely neat and clean.

They'd given me a noble bedroom, close under the eaves with a long, low casement window overlooking the garden. The sheets smelt of lavender, and I was between them and asleep almost before you could count ten. I was tired, you see. But later in the night I woke up. I was too hot, so took off some of the blankets and then strolled across to the window to get a breath of air. The garden was bathed in moonshine and on the lawn I could see something twisting and turning oddly. I stared a bit before I made it out to be two cats. They didn't worry me at that distance, and I watched them for a bit before I turned in again. They were rolling over one another and jumping away again and chasing their own shadows on the grass, intent on their own mysterious business – taking themselves seriously, the way cats always do. It looked like a kind of ritual dance. Then something seemed to startle them, and they scampered away.

I went back to bed, but I couldn't get to sleep again. My nerves seemed to be all on edge. I lay watching the window and listening to a kind of soft rustling noise that seemed to be going on in the big wisteria that ran along my side of the house. And then something landed with a soft thud on the sill – a great Cyprian cat.

What did you say? Well, one of those striped grey-and-black cats. Tabby, that's right. In my part of the country they call them Cyprus cats, or Cyprian cats. I'd never seen such a monster. It stood with its head cocked sideways, staring into the room and rubbing its ears very softly against the upright bar of the casement.

Of course, I couldn't do with that. I shooed the brute away, and it made off without a sound. Heat or no heat, I shut and fastened the window. Far out in the shrubbery I thought I heard a faint miauling; then silence. After that, I went straight off to sleep again and lay like a log till the girl came in to call me.

The next day, Merridew ran us up in his car to see the place where they were making the dam, and that was the first time I realized that Felice's nerviness had not been altogether cured. He showed us where they had diverted part of the river into a swift little stream that was to be used for working the dynamo of an electrical plant. There were a couple of planks laid across the stream, and he wanted to take us over to show us the engine. It wasn't extraordinarily wide or dangerous, but Mrs Merridew peremptorily refused to cross it, and got quite hysterical when he tried to insist. Eventually he and I went over and inspected the machinery by ourselves. When we got back she had recovered her temper and apologized for being so silly. Merridew abased himself, of course, and I began to feel a little *de trop*. She told me afterwards that she had once fallen into a river as a child, and been nearly drowned, and it had left her with a what d'ye call it – a complex about running water. And but for this one trifling episode, I never heard a single sharp word pass between them all the time I was there; nor, for a whole week, did I notice anything else to suggest a flaw in Mrs Merridew's radiant health. Indeed, as the days wore on to midsummer and the heat grew more intense, her whole body seemed to glow with vitality. It was as though she was lit up from within.

Merridew was out all day and working very hard. I thought he was overdoing it and asked him if he was sleeping badly. He told me that, on the contrary, he fell asleep every night the moment his head touched the pillow, and – what was most unusual with him – had no dreams of any kind. I myself felt well enough, but the hot weather made me languid and disinclined for exertion. Mrs Merridew took me out for long drives in the car. I would sit for hours, lulled into a half-slumber by the rush of warm air and the purring of the engine, and gazing at my driver, upright at the wheel, her eyes fixed unwaveringly upon the spinning road. We explored the whole of the country to the south and east of Little Hexham, and once or twice went as far north as Bath. Once I suggested that we should turn eastward over the bridge and run down into what looked like rather beautiful wooded country, but Mrs Merridew didn't care for the idea; she said it was a bad road and that the scenery on that side was disappointing.

Altogether, I spent a pleasant week at Little Hexham, and if it had not been for the cats I should have been perfectly comfortable. Every night the garden seemed to be haunted by them – the Cyprian cat that I had seen the first night of my stay, and a little ginger one and a horrible stinking black Tom were especially tiresome, and one night there was a terrified white kitten that mewed for an hour on end under my window. I flung boots and books at my visitors till I was heartily weary, but they seemed determined to make the inn garden their rendezvous. The nuisance grew worse from night to night; on one occasion I counted fifteen of them, sitting on their hinder-ends in a circle, while the Cyprian cat danced her shadow-dance among them, working in and out like a weaver's shuttle. I had to keep my window shut, for the Cyprian cat evidently made a habit of climbing up by the wisteria. The door, too; for once when I had gone down to fetch something from the sitting-room, I found her on my bed, kneading the coverlet with her paws – *pr'rp, pr'rp, pr'rp* – with her eyes closed in a sensuous ecstasy. I beat her off, and she spat at me as she fled into the dark passage.

I asked the landlady about her, but she replied rather curtly that they kept no cat at the inn, and it is true that I never saw any of the beasts in the daytime; but one evening about dusk I caught the landlord in one of the outhouses. He had the ginger cat on his shoulder, and was feeding her with something that looked like strips of liver. I remonstrated with him for encouraging the cats about the place and asked whether I could have a different room, explaining that the nightly caterwauling disturbed me. He half opened his slits of eyes and murmured that he would ask his wife about it; but nothing was done, and in fact I believe there was no other bedroom in the house.

And all this time the weather got hotter and heavier, working up for thunder, with the sky like brass and the earth like iron, and the air quivering over it so that it hurt your eyes to look at it.

All right, Harringay – I am trying to keep to the point. And I'm not concealing anything from you. I say that my relations with Mrs Merridew were perfectly ordinary. Of course I saw a good deal of her because, as I explained, Merridew was out all day. We went up to the dam with him in the morning and brought the car back, and naturally we had to amuse one another as best we could till the evening. She seemed quite pleased to be in my company, and I couldn't dislike her. I can't tell you what we talked about – nothing in particular. She was not a talkative woman. She would sit or lie for hours in the sunshine, hardly speaking – only stretching out her body to the light and heat. Sometimes she would spend a whole afternoon playing with a twig or a pebble, while I sat by and smoked. Restful! No. No – I shouldn't call her a restful personality, exactly. Not to me, at any rate. In the evening she would liven up and talk a little more, but she generally went up to bed early, and left Merridew and me to yarn together in the garden.

Oh! about the revolver. Yes. I bought that in Bath, when I had been at Little Hexham exactly a week. We drove over in the morning, and while Mrs Merridew got some things for her husband I prowled round the second-hand shops. I had intended to get an air-gun or a pea-shooter or something of that kind, when I saw this. You've seen it, of course. It's very tiny – what people in books describe as 'little more than a toy', but quite deadly enough. The old boy who sold it to me didn't seem to know much about firearms. He'd taken it in pawn some time back, he told me, and there were ten rounds of ammunition with it. He made no bones about a licence or anything – glad enough to make a sale, no doubt, without putting difficulties in a customer's way. I told him I knew how to handle it, and mentioned by way of a joke that I meant to take a pot-shot or two at the cats. That seemed to wake him up a bit. He was a dried-up little fellow, with a scrawny grey beard and a stringy neck. He asked me where I was staying. I told him at Little Hexham.

'You better be careful, sir,' he said. 'They think a heap of their cats down there, and it's reckoned unlucky to kill them.' And then he added something I couldn't quite catch, about a silver bullet. He was a doddering old fellow, and he seemed to have some sort of scruple about letting me take the parcel away, but I assured him that I was perfectly capable of looking after it and myself. I left him standing in the door of his shop, pulling at his beard and staring after me.

That night the thunder came. The sky had turned to lead before evening, but the dull heat was more oppressive than the sunshine.

Both the Merridews seemed to be in a state of nerves – he sulky and swearing at the weather and the flies, and she wrought up to a queer kind of vivid excitement. Thunder affects some people that way. I wasn't much better, and to make things worse I got the feeling that the house was full of cats. I couldn't see them but I knew they were there, lurking behind the cupboards and flitting noiselessly about the corridors. I could scarcely sit in the parlour and I was thankful to escape to my room. Cats or no cats I had to open the window, and I sat there with my pyjama jacket unbuttoned, trying to get a breath of air. But the place was like the inside of a copper furnace. And pitch-dark. I could scarcely see from my window where the bushes ended and the lawn began. But I could hear and feel the cats. There were little scrapings in the wisteria and scufflings among the leaves, and about eleven o'clock one of them started the concert with a loud and hideous wail. Then another and another joined in – I'll swear there were fifty of them. And presently I got that foul sensation of nausea, and the flesh crawled on my bones, and I knew that one of them was slinking close to me in the darkness. I looked round quickly, and there she stood, the great Cyprian; right against my shoulder, her eyes glowing like green lamps. I yelled and struck out at her, and she snarled as she leaped out and down. I heard her thump the gravel, and the yowling burst out all over the garden with renewed vehemence. And then all in a moment there was utter silence, and in the far distance there came a flickering blue flash and then another. In the first of them I saw the far garden wall, topped along all its length with cats, like a nursery frieze. When the second flash came the wall was empty.

At two o'clock the rain came. For three hours before that I had sat there, watching the lightning as it spat across the sky and exulting in the crash of the thunder. The storm seemed to carry off all the electrical disturbance in my body; I could have shouted with excitement and relief. Then the first heavy drops fell; then a steady downpour; then a deluge. It struck the iron-baked garden with a noise like steel rods falling. The smell of the ground came up intoxicatingly, and the wind rose and flung the rain in against my face. At the other end of the passage I heard a window thrown to and fastened, but I leaned out into the tumult and let the water drench my head and shoulders. The thunder still rumbled intermittently, but with less noise and farther off, and in an occasional flash I saw the white grille of falling water drawn between me and the garden.

It was after one of these thunder-peals that I became aware of a knocking at my door. I opened it, and there was Merridew. He had a candle in his hand, and his face was terrified.

'Felice!' he said, abruptly. 'She's ill. I can't wake her. For God's sake, come and give me a hand.'

I hurried down the passage after him. There were two beds in his room – a great four-poster, hung with crimson damask, and a small camp bedstead drawn up near to the window. The small bed was empty, the bedclothes tossed aside; evidently he had just risen from it. In the four-poster lay Mrs Merridew, naked, with only a sheet upon her. She was stretched flat upon her back, her long black hair in two plaits over her shoulders. Her face was waxen and shrunk, like the face of a corpse, and her pulse, when I felt it, was so faint that at first I could scarely feel it. Her breathing was very slow and shallow and her flesh cold. I shook her, but there was no response at all. I lifted her eyelids, and noticed how the eyeballs were turned up under the upper lid, so that only the whites were visible. The touch of my finger-tip upon the sensitive ball evoked no reaction. I immediately wondered whether she took drugs.

Merridew seemed to think it necessary to make some explanation. He was babbling about the heat – she couldn't bear so much as a silk nightgown – she had suggested that he should occupy the other bed – he had slept heavily – right through the thunder. The rain blowing in on his face had aroused him. He had got up and shut the window. Then he had called to Felice to know if she was all right – he thought the storm might have frightened her. There was no answer. He had struck a light. Her condition had alarmed him – and so on.

I told him to pull himself together and to try whether, by chafing his wife's hands and feet, we could restore the circulation. I had it firmly in my mind that she was under the influence of some opiate. We set to work, rubbing and pinching and slapping her with wet towels and shouting her name in her ear. It was like handling a dead woman, except for the very slight but perfectly regular rise and fall of her bosom, on which – with a kind of surprise that there should be any flaw on its magnolia whiteness – I noticed a large brown mole, just over the heart. To my perturbed fancy it suggested a wound and a menace. We had been hard at it for some time, with the sweat pouring off us, when we became aware of something going on outside the window – a stealthy bumping and scraping against the panes. I snatched up the candle and looked out.

On the sill, the Cyprian cat sat and clawed at the casement. Her drenched fur clung limply to her body, her eyes glared into mine, her mouth was opened in protest. She scrabbled furiously at the latch, her hind claws slipping and scratching on the woodwork. I hammered on the pane and bawled at her, and she struck back at the glass as though possessed. As I cursed her and turned away she set up a long, despairing wail.

Merridew called to me to bring back the candle and leave the brute alone. I returned to the bed, but the dismal crying went on and on incessantly. I suggested to Merridew that he should wake the landlord and get hot-water bottles and some brandy from the bar and see if a messenger could not be sent for a doctor. He departed on this errand, while I went on with my massage. It seemed to me that the pulse was growing still fainter. Then I suddenly recollected that I had a small brandy-flask in my bag. I ran out to fetch it, and as I did so the cat suddenly stopped its howling.

As I entered my own room the air blowing through the open window struck gratefully upon me. I found my bag in the dark and was rummaging for the flask among my shirts and socks when I heard a loud, triumphant mew, and turned round in time to see the Cyprian cat crouched for a moment on the sill, before it sprang in past me and out at the door. I found the flask and hastened back with it, just as Merridew and the landlord came running up the stairs.

We all went into the room together. As we did so, Mrs Merridew stirred, sat up, and asked us what in the world was the matter.

I have seldom felt quite such a fool.

Next day the weather was cooler; the storm had cleared the air. What Merridew had said to his wife I do not know. None of us made any public allusion to the night's disturbance, and to all appearances Mrs Merridew was in the best of health and spirits. Merridew took a day off from the waterworks, and we all went for a long drive and picnic together. We were on the best of terms with one another. Ask Merridew – he will tell you the same thing. He would not – he could not, surely – say otherwise. I can't believe, Harringay, I simply cannot believe that he could imagine or suspect me – I say, there was nothing to suspect. Nothing.

Yes – this is the important date – the 24th of June. I can't tell you any more details; there is nothing to tell. We came back and had dinner just as usual. All three of us were together all day, till bed-time. On my honour I had no private interview of any kind that day, either with him or with her. I was the first to go to bed, and I heard the others come upstairs about half an hour later. They were talking cheerfully.

It was a moonlight night. For once, no caterwauling came to trouble me. I didn't even bother to shut the window or the door. I put the revolver on the chair beside me before I lay down. Yes, it was loaded. I had no special object in putting it there, except that I meant to have a go at the cats if they started their games again.

I was desperately tired, and thought I should drop off to sleep at once, but I didn't. I must have been overtired, I suppose. I lay and looked at the moonlight. And then, about midnight, I heard what I had been half expecting: a stealthy scrabbling in the wisteria and a faint miauling sound.

I sat up in bed and reached for the revolver. I heard the 'plop' as the big cat sprang up on to the window-ledge; I saw her black and silver flanks, and the outline of her round head, pricked ears and upright tail. I aimed and fired, and the beast let out one frightful cry and sprang down into the room.

I jumped out of bed. The crack of the shot had sounded terrific in the silent house, and somewhere I heard a distant voice call out. I pursued the cat into the passage, revolver in hand – with some idea of finishing it off, I suppose. And then, at the door of the Merridews' room, I saw Mrs Merridew. She stood with one hand on each doorpost, swaying to and fro. Then she fell down at my feet. Her bare breast was all stained with blood. And as I stood staring at her, clutching the revolver, Merridew came out and found us – like that.

Well, Harringay, that's my story, exactly as I told it to Peabody.

The Cyprian Cat

I'm afraid it won't sound very well in Court, but what can I say? The trail of blood led from my room to hers; the cat must have run that way; I *know* it was the cat I shot. I can't offer any explanation. I don't know who shot Mrs Merridew, or why. I can't help it if the people at the inn say they never saw the Cyprian cat; Merridew saw it that other night, and I know he wouldn't lie about it. Search the house, Harringay – that's the only thing to do. Pull the place to pieces, till you find the body of the Cyprian cat. It will have my bullet in it.

THE YELLOW TERROR
W. L. Alden

'Speaking of cats,' said Captain Foster, 'I'm free to say that I don't like 'em. I don't care to be looked down on by any person, whether he be man or cat. I know I ain't the President of the United States, nor yet a millionaire, nor yet the Boss of New York, but all the same I calculate that I'm a man, and entitled to be treated as such. Now, I never knew a cat yet that didn't look down on me, same as cats do on everybody. A cat considers that men are just dirt under his or her paws, as the case may be. I can't see what it is that makes a cat believe that he is so everlastingly superior to all the men that have ever lived, but there's no denying the fact that such is his belief, and he acts accordingly. There was a professor here one day, lecturing on all sorts of animals, and I asked him if he could explain this aggravating conduct of cats. He said that it was because cats used to be gods, thousands of years ago in the land of Egypt; but I didn't believe him. Egypt is a Scripture country, and consequently we ought not to believe anything about it that we don't read in the Bible. Show me anywhere in the Bible that Egyptian cats are mentioned as having practised as gods, and I'll believe it. Till you show it to me, I'll take the liberty of disbelieving any worldly statements that professors or anybody else may make about Egypt.

'The most notorious cat I ever met was old Captain Smedley's Yellow Terror. His real legal name was just plain Tom: but being yellow, and being a holy terror in many respects, it got to be the fashion among his acquaintances to call him "The Yellow Terror". He was a tremendous big cat, and he had been with Captain Smedley for five years before I saw him.

'Smedley was one of the best men I ever knew. I'll admit that he was a middling hard man on his sailors, so that his ship got the reputation of being a slaughter-house, which it didn't really deserve. And there is no denying that he was a very religious man, which was another thing which made him unpopular with the men. I'm a religious man myself, even when I'm at sea, but I never held with serving out religion to a crew, and making them swallow it with belaying pins. That's what old Smedley used to do. He was in command of the barque *Medford*, out of Boston, when I knew him. I mean the city of Boston in Massachusetts, and not the little town that folks over in England call Boston: and I must say that I can't see why they should copy the names of our cities, no matter how celebrated they may be. Well! The *Medford* used to sail from Boston to London with grain, where she discharged her cargo and loaded again for China. On the outward passage we used to stop at Madeira, and the Cape, and generally Bangkok, and so on to Canton, where we filled up with tea, and then sailed for home direct.

'Now thishyer Yellow Terror had been on the ship's books for upwards of five years when I first met him. Smedley had him regularly shipped, and signed his name to the ship articles, and held a pen in his paw while he made a cross. You see, in those days the underwriters wouldn't let a ship go to sea without a cat, so as to keep the rats from getting at the cargo. I don't know what a land cat may do, but there ain't a seafaring cat that would look at a rat. What with the steward, and the cook and the men forrard, being always ready to give the ship's cat a bite, the cat is generally full from kelson to deck, and wouldn't take the trouble to speak to a rat, unless one was to bite her tail. But, then, underwriters never know anything about what goes on at sea, and it's a shame that a sailorman should be compelled to give in to their ideas. The Yellow Terror had the general idea that the *Medford* was his private yacht, and that all hands were there to wait on him. And Smedley sort of confirmed him in that idea, by treating him with more respect than he treated his owners, when he was ashore. I don't blame the cat, and after I got to know what sort of a person the cat really was, I can't say as I blamed Smedley to any great extent.

'Tom, which I think I told you was the cat's real name, was far and away the best fighter of all cats in Europe, Asia, Africa and

The Yellow Terror

America. Whenever we sighted land he would get himself up in his best fur, spending hours brushing and polishing it, and biting his claws so as to make sure that they were as sharp as they could be made. As soon as the ship was made fast to the quay, or anchored in the harbour, the Yellow Terror went ashore to look for trouble. He always got it too, though he had such a reputation as a fighter, that whenever he showed himself, every cat that recognized him broke for cover. Why, the gatekeeper at the London Docks – I mean the one at the Shadwell entrance – told me that he always knew when the *Medford* was warping into dock, by the stream of cats that went out out of the gate, as if a pack of hounds were after them. You see that as soon as the *Medford* was reported, and word passed among the cats belonging to the ships in dock that the Yellow Terror had arrived, they judged that it was time for them to go ashore, and stop till the *Medford* should sail. Whitechapel used to be regularly overflowed with cats, and the newspapers used to have letters from scientific chaps trying to account for what they called the wave of cats that had spread over East London.

'I remember that once we laid alongside of a Russian brig, down in the basin by Old Gravel Lane. There was a tremendous big black cat sitting on the poop, and as soon as he caught sight of our Tom, he sung out to him, remarking that he was able and ready to wipe the deck up with him at any time. We all understood that the Russian was a new arrival who hadn't ever heard of the Yellow Terror, and we knew that he was, as the good book says, rushing on his fate. Tom was sitting on the rail near the mizzen rigging when the Russian made his remarks, and he didn't seem to hear them. But presently we saw him going slowly aloft till he reached our crossjack yard. He laid out on the yard arm till he was near enough to jump on to the mainyard of the Russian, and the first thing that the Russian cat knew Tom landed square on his back. The fight didn't last more than one round, and at the end of that, the remains of the Russian cat sneaked behind a water cask, and the Yellow Terror came back by the way of the crossjack yard and went on fur brushing, as if nothing had happened.

'When Tom went ashore in a foreign port he generally stopped ashore till we sailed. A few hours before we cast off hawsers, Tom would come aboard. He always knew when we were going to sail, and he never once got left. I remember one time when we were just getting up anchor in Cape Town harbour, and we all reckoned that this time we should have to sail without Tom, he having evidently stopped ashore just a little too long. But presently alongside comes a boat, with Tom lying back at full length in the sternsheets, for all the world like a drunken sailor who has been delaying the ship, and is proud of it. The boatman said that Tom had come down to the pier and jumped into his boat, knowing that the man would row him off to the ship, and calculating that Smedley would be glad to pay the damage. It's my belief that if Tom hadn't found a boatman, he would have chartered the government launch. He had the cheek to do that or anything else.

'Fighting was really Tom's only vice; and it could hardly be called a vice, seeing as he always licked the other cat, and hardly ever came out of a fight with a torn ear or a black eye. Smedley always said that Tom was religious. I used to think that was rubbish; but after I had been with Tom for a couple of voyages I began to believe what Smedley said about him. Every Sunday when the weather permitted, Smedley used to hold service on the quarter-deck. He was a Methodist, and when it came to ladling out Scripture, or singing a hymn, he could give odds to almost any preacher. All hands, except the man at the wheel, and the lookout, were required to attend service on Sunday morning, which naturally caused considerable grumbling, as the watch below considered they had a right to sleep in peace, instead of being dragged aft for service. But they had to knock under, and what they considered even worse, they had to sing, for the old man kept a bright lookout while the singing was going on, and if he caught any man malingering and not doing his full part of the singing he would have a few words to say to that man with a belaying pin, or a rope's end, after the service was over.

'Now Tom never failed to attend service, and to do his level best to help. He would sit somewhere near the old man and pay attention to what was going on better than I've seen some folks do in first-class churches ashore. When the men sang, Tom would start in and let out a yell here and there, which showed that he meant well even if he had never been to a singing-school, and didn't exactly understand singing according to Gunter. First along, I thought that it was all an accident that the cat came to service, and I calculated that his yelling during the singing meant that he didn't like it. But after a while I had to admit that Tom enjoyed the Sunday service as much as the captain himself, and I agreed with Smedley that the cat was a thoroughgoing Methodist.

'Now after I'd been with Smedley for about six years, he got married all of a sudden. I didn't blame him, for in the first place it wasn't any of my business; and, in the next place, I hold that a ship's captain ought to have a wife, and the underwriters would be a sight wiser if they insisted that all captains should be married, instead of insisting that all ships should carry cats. You see that if a ship's captain has a wife, he is naturally anxious to get back to her, and have his best clothes mended, and his food cooked to suit him. Consequently he wants to make good passages and he don't want to run the risk of drowning himself, or of getting into trouble with his owners, and losing his berth. You'll find, if you look into it, that married captains live longer, and get on better than unmarried men, as it stands to reason that they ought to do.

'But it happened that the woman Smedley married was an Agonyostic, which is a sort of person that doesn't believe in anything, except the multiplication table, and such-like human vanities. She didn't lose any time in getting Smedley round to her way of thinking, and instead of being the religious man he used to be, he chucked the whole thing, and used to argue with me by the hour at a time, to prove that religion was a waste of time, and that he hadn't any soul, and had never been created, but had just descended from a family of seafaring monkeys. It made me sick to hear a respectable sailorman talking such rubbish, but of course, seeing as he was my commanding officer, I had to be careful about contradicting him. I wouldn't ever yield an inch to his arguments, and I told him as respectfully as I could, that he was making the biggest mistake of his life. "Why, look at the cat," I used to say, "he's got sense enough to be religious, and if you was to tell him that he was descended from a monkey, he'd consider himself insulted." But it wasn't any use. Smedley was full of his new agonyostical theories, and the more I disagreed with him, the more set he was in his way.

'Of course he knocked off holding Sunday-morning services; and the men ought to have been delighted, considering how they used to grumble at having to come aft and sing hymns, when they wanted to be below. But there is no accounting for sailors. They were actually disappointed when Sunday came and there wasn't any service. They said that we should have an unlucky voyage, and that the old man, now that he had got a rich wife, didn't consider sailors good enough to come aft on the quarter-deck, and take a hand in singing. Smedley didn't care for their opinion, but he was some considerable worried about the Yellow Terror. Tom missed the Sunday morning service, and he said so as plain as he could. Every Sunday, for three or four weeks, he came on deck, and took his usual seat near the captain, and waited for the service to begin. When he found out that there was no use in waiting for it, he showed that he disapproved of Smedley's conduct in the strongest way. He gave up being intimate with the old man, and once when Smedley tried to pat him, and be friendly, he swore at him, and bit him on the leg – not in an angry way, you understand, but just to show his disapproval of Smedley's irreligious conduct.

'When we got to London, Tom never once went ashore, and he hadn't a single fight. He seemed to have lost all interest in worldly things. He'd sit on the poop in a melancholy sort of way, never minding how his fur looked, and never so much as answering if a strange cat sang out to him. After we left London he kept below most of the time, and finally, about the time that we were crossing the line, he took to his bed, as you might say, and got to be as thin and weak as if he had been living in the forecastle of a lime-juicer. And he was that melancholy that you couldn't get him to take an interest in anything. Smedley got to be so anxious about him that he read up in his medical book to try and find out what was the matter with him; and finally made up his mind that the cat had a first-class disease with a big name something like spinal menagerie. That was some little satisfaction to Smedley, but it didn't benefit the cat any; for nothing that Smedley could do would induce Tom to take medicine. He wouldn't so much as sniff at salts, and when Smedley tried to poultice his neck, he considered himself insulted, and roused up enough to take a piece out of the old man's ear.

'About that time we touched at Funchal, and Smedley sent ashore to lay in another tom-cat, thinking that perhaps a fight would brace Tom up a little. But when the new cat was put down alongside of Tom, and swore at him in the most impudent sort of way, Tom just turned over on his other side, and pretended to go asleep. After that we all felt that the Yellow Terror was done for. Smedley sent the new cat ashore again, and told me that Tom was booked for the other world, and that there wouldn't be any more luck for us on that voyage.

'I went down to see the cat, and though he was thin and weak, I couldn't see any signs of serious disease about him. So I says to Smedley that I didn't believe the cat was sick at all.

'"Then what's the matter with him?" says the old man. "You saw yourself that he wouldn't fight, and when he's got to that point I consider that he is about done with this world and its joys and sorrows."

'"His nose is all right," said I. "When I felt it just now it was as cool as a teetotaller's."

'"That does look as if he hadn't any fever to speak of," says Smedley, "and the book says that if you've got spinal menagerie you're bound to have a fever."

'"The trouble with Tom," says I, "is mental: that's what it is. He's got something on his mind that is wearing him out."

'"What can he have on his mind?" says the captain. "He's got everything to suit him aboard this ship. If he was a millionaire he couldn't be better fixed. He won all his fights while we were in Boston, and hasn't had a fight since, which shows that he can't be low-spirited on account of a licking. No, sir! You'll find that Tom's mind is all right."

'"Then what gives him such a mournful look out of his eyes?" says I. "When you spoke to him this morning he looked at you as if he was on the point of crying over your misfortunes – that is to say, if you've got any. Come to think of it, Tom begun to go into thishyer decline just after you were married. Perhaps that's what's the matter with him."

'But there was no convincing Smedley that Tom's trouble was mental, and he was so sure that the cat was going to die, that he got to be about as low-spirited as Tom himself. "I begin to wish," says Smedley to me one morning, "that I was a Methodist again, and believed in a hereafter. It does seem kind of hard that a first-class cat-fighter like Tom shouldn't have a chance when he dies. He was a good religious cat if ever there was one, and I'd like to think that he was going to a better world."

'Just then an idea struck me. "Captain Smedley," says I, "you remember how Tom enjoyed the meetings that we used to have aboard here on Sunday mornings!"

'"He did so," said Smedley. "I never saw a person who took more pleasure in his Sunday privileges than Tom did."

'"Captain Smedley," says I, putting my hand on the old man's sleeve. "All that's the matter with Tom is seeing you deserting the religion that you was brought up in, and turning agonyostical, or whatever you call it. I call it turning plain infidel. Tom's mourning about your soul, and he's miserable because you don't have any more Sunday-morning meetings. I told you the trouble was mental, and now you know it is.'

'"Mebbe you're right," says Smedley, taking what I'd said in a peaceable way, instead of flying into a rage, as I expected he would. "To tell you the truth, I ain't so well satisfied in my own mind as I used to be, and I was thinking last night, when I started in to say 'Now I lay me' – just from habit you know – that if I'd stuck to the Methodist persuasion I should be a blamed sight happier than I am now."

'Tomorrow's Sunday," says I, "and if I was you, captain, I should have the bell rung for service, same as you used to do, and bring Tom up on deck, and let him have the comfort of hearing the rippingest hymns you can lay your hand to. It can't hurt you, and it may do him a heap of good. Anyway, it's worth trying, if you really want the Yellow Terror to get well."

'"I don't mind saying," says Smedley, "that I'd do almost anything to save his life. He's been with me now going on for seven years, and we've never had a hard word. If a Sunday morning meeting will be any comfort to him, he shall have it. Mebbe if it doesn't cure him, it may sort of smooth his hatchway to the tomb."

'Now the very next day was Sunday, and at six the captain had the bell rung for service, and the men were told to lay aft. The bell hadn't fairly stopped ringing, when Tom comes up the companion way, one step at a time, looking as if he was on his way to his own funeral. He came up to his usual place alongside of the captain, and lay down on his side at the old man's feet, and sort of looked up at him with what anybody would have said was a grateful look. I could see that Smedley was feeling pretty serious. He understood what the cat wanted to say, and when he started in to give out a hymn, his voice sort of choked. It was a ripping good hymn, with a regular hurricane chorus, and the men sung it for all they were worth, hoping that it would meet Tom's views. He was too weak to join in with any of his old-time yells, but he sort of flopped the deck with his tail, and you could see he was enjoying it down to the ground.

'Well, the service went on just as it used to do in old times, and Smedley sort of warmed up as it went along, and by and by he'd got the regular old Methodist glow on his face. When it was all through, and the men had gone forrard again, Smedley stooped down, and picked up Tom, and kissed him, and the cat nestled up in the old man's neck and licked his chin. Smedley carried Tom down into the saloon, and sung out to the steward to bring some fresh meat. The cat turned to and ate as good a dinner as he'd ever eaten in his best days, and after he was through, he went into Smedley's own cabin, and curled up in the old man's bunk, and went to sleep purring fit to take the deck off. From that day Tom improved steadily, and by the time we got to Cape Town he was well enough to go ashore, though he was still considerable weak. I went ashore at the same time, and kept an eye on Tom, to see what he would do. I saw him pick out a small measly-looking cat, that couldn't have stood up to a full-grown mouse, and lick him in less than a minute. Then I knew that Tom was all right again, and I admired his judgement in picking out a small cat that was suited to his weak condition. By the time that we got to Canton, Tom was as well in body and mind as he had ever been; and when we sailed, he came aboard with two inches of his tail missing, and his starboard ear carried away, but he had the air of having licked all creation, which I don't doubt he had done, that is to say, so far as all creation could be found in Canton.

'I never heard any more of Smedley's agonyostical nonsense. He went back to the Methodists again, and he always said that Tom had been the blessed means of showing him the error of his ways. I heard that when he got back to Boston, he gave Mrs Smedley notice that he expected her to go to the Methodist meeting with him every Sunday, and that if she didn't, he should consider that it was a breach of wedding articles, and equivalent to mutiny. I don't know how she took it, or what the consequences were, for I left the *Medford* just then, and took command of a barque that traded between Boston and the West Indies. And I never heard of the Yellow Terror after that voyage, though I often thought of him, and always held that for a cat he was the ablest cat, afloat or ashore, that any man ever met.'

EDWARD THE CONQUEROR
Roald Dahl

Louisa, holding a dishcloth in her hand, stepped out of the kitchen door at the back of the house into the cool October sunshine.

'Edward!' she called. '*Ed-ward!* Lunch is ready!'

She paused a moment, listening; then she strolled out on to the lawn and continued across it – a little shadow attending her – skirting the rose bed and touching the sundial lightly with one finger as she went by. She moved rather gracefully for a woman who was small and plump, with a lilt in her walk and a gentle swinging of the shoulders and the arms. She passed under the mulberry tree on to the brick path, then went all the way along the path until she came to the place where she could look down into the dip at the end of this large garden.

'*Edward!* Lunch!'

She could see him now, about eighty yards away, down in the dip on the edge of the wood – the tallish narrow figure in khaki slacks and dark-green sweater, working beside a big bonfire with a fork in his hands, pitching brambles on to the top of the fire. It was blazing fiercely, with orange flames and clouds of milky smoke, and the smoke was drifting back over the garden with a wonderful scent of autumn and burning leaves.

Louisa went down the slope towards her husband. Had she wanted, she could easily have called again and made herself heard, but there was something about a first-class bonfire that impelled her towards it, right up close so she could feel the heat and listen to it burn.

'Lunch,' she said, approaching.

'Oh, hello. All right – yes. I'm coming.'

'*What* a good fire.'

'I've decided to clear this place right out,' her husband said. 'I'm sick and tired of all these brambles.' His long face was wet with perspiration. There were small beads of it clinging all over his moustache like dew, and two little rivers were running down his throat on to the turtleneck of the sweater.

'You better be careful you don't overdo it, Edward.'

'Louisa, I do wish you'd stop treating me as though I were eighty. A bit of exercise never did anyone any harm.'

'Yes, dear, I know. Oh, Edward! Look! Look!'

The man turned and looked at Louisa, who was pointing now to the far side of the bonfire.

'Look, Edward! The cat!'

Sitting on the ground, so close to the fire that the flames sometimes seemed actually to be touching it, was a large cat of a most unusual colour. It stayed quite still, with its head on one side and its nose in the air, watching the man and woman with a cool yellow eye.

'It'll get burnt!' Louisa cried, and she dropped the dishcloth and darted swiftly in and grabbed it with both hands, whisking it away and putting it on the grass well clear of the flames.

'You crazy cat,' she said, dusting off her hands. 'What's the matter with you?'

'Cats know what they're doing,' the husband said. 'You'll never find a cat doing something it doesn't want. Not cats.'

'Whose is it? You ever seen it before?'

'No, I never have. Damn peculiar colour.'

The cat had seated itself on the grass and was regarding them with a sidewise look. There was a veiled inward expression about the eyes, something curiously omniscient and pensive, and around the nose a most delicate air of contempt, as though the sight of these two middle-aged persons – the one small, plump, and rosy, the other lean and extremely sweaty – were a matter of some surprise but very little importance. For a cat, it certainly had an unusual colour – a pure silvery grey with no blue in it at all – and the hair was very long and silky.

Louisa bent down and stroked its head. 'You must go home,' she said. 'Be a good cat now and go on home to where you belong.'

Edward the Conqueror

The man and wife started to stroll back up the hill towards the house. The cat got up and followed, at a distance first, but edging closer and closer as they went along. Soon it was alongside them, then it was ahead, leading the way across the lawn to the house, walking as though it owned the whole place, holding its tail straight up in the air, like a mast.

'Go home,' the man said. 'Go on home. We don't want you.'

But when they reached the house, it came in with them, and Louisa gave it some milk in the kitchen. During lunch, it hopped up on to the spare chair between them and sat through the meal with its head just above the level of the table, watching the proceedings with those dark-yellow eyes which kept moving slowly from the woman to the man and back again.

'I don't like this cat,' Edward said.

'Oh, I think it's a beautiful cat. I do hope it stays a little while.'

'Now, listen to me, Louisa. The creature can't possibly stay here. It belongs to someone else. It's lost. And if it's still trying to hang around this afternoon, you'd better take it to the police. They'll see it gets home.'

After lunch, Edward returned to his gardening. Louisa, as usual, went to the piano. She was a competent pianist and a genuine music-lover, and almost every afternoon she spent an hour or so playing for herself. The cat was now lying on the sofa, and she paused to stroke it as she went by. It opened its eyes, looked at her a moment, then closed them again and went back to sleep.

'You're an awfully nice cat,' she said. 'And such a beautiful colour. I wish I could keep you.' Then her fingers, moving over the fur on the cat's head, came into contact with a small lump, a little growth just above the right eye.

'Poor cat,' she said. 'You've got bumps on your beautiful face. You must be getting old.'

She went over and sat down on the long piano stool but she didn't immediately start to play. One of her special little pleasures was to make every day a kind of concert day, with a carefully arranged programme which she worked out in detail before she began. She never liked to break her enjoyment by having to stop while she wondered what to play next. All she wanted was a brief pause after each piece while the audience clapped enthusiastically and called for more. It was so much nicer to imagine an audience, and now and again while she was playing – on the lucky days, that is – the room would begin to swim and fade and darken, and she would see nothing but row upon row of seats and a sea of white faces upturned towards her, listening with a rapt and adoring concentration.

Sometimes she played from memory, sometimes from music. Today she would play from memory; that was the way she felt. And what should the programme be? She sat before the piano with her small hands clasped on her lap, a plump rosy little person with a round and still quite pretty face, her hair done up in a neat bun at the back of her head. By looking slightly to the right, she could see the cat curled up asleep on the sofa, and its silvery-grey coat was beautiful against the purple of the cushion. How about some Bach to begin with? Or, better still, Vivaldi. The Bach adaptation for organ of the D minor Concerto Grosso. Yes – that first. Then perhaps a little Schumann. *Carnaval*? That would be fun. And after that – well, a touch of Liszt for a change. One of the *Petrarch Sonnets*. The second one – that was the loveliest – the E major. Then another Schumann, another of his gay ones, *Kinderscenen*. And lastly, for the encore, a Brahms waltz, or maybe two of them if she felt like it.

Vivaldi, Schumann, Liszt, Schumann, Brahms. A very nice programme, one that she could play easily without the music. She moved herself a little closer to the piano and paused a moment while someone in the audience – already she could feel that this was one of the lucky days – while someone in the audience had his last cough; then, with the slow grace that accompanied nearly all her movements, she lifted her hands to the keyboard and began to play.

She wasn't, at that particular moment, watching the cat at all – as a matter of fact she had forgotten its presence – but as the first deep notes of the Vivaldi sounded softly in the room, she became aware, out of the corner of one eye, of a sudden flurry, a flash of movement on the sofa to her right. She stopped playing at once. 'What is it?' she said, turning to the cat. 'What's the matter?'

The animal, who a few seconds before had been sleeping peacefully, was now sitting bolt upright on the sofa, very tense, the whole body aquiver, ears up and eyes wide open, staring at the piano.

'Did I frighten you?' she asked gently. 'Perhaps you've never heard music before.'

No, she told herself. I don't think that's what it is. On second thoughts, it seemed to her that the cat's attitude was not one of fear. There was no shrinking or backing away. If anything, there was a leaning forward, a kind of eagerness about the creature, and the face – well, there was rather an odd expression on the face, something of a mixture between surprise and shock. Of course, the face of a cat is a small and fairly expressionless thing, but if you watch carefully the eyes and ears working together, and particularly that little area of mobile skin below the ears and slightly to one side, you can occasionally see the reflection of very powerful emotions. Louisa was watching the face closely now, and because she was curious to see what would happen a second time, she reached out her hands to the keyboard and began again to play the Vivaldi.

This time the cat was ready for it, and all that happened to begin with was a small extra tensing of the body. But as the music swelled and quickened into that first exciting rhythm of the introduction to the fugue, a strange look that amounted almost to ecstasy began to settle upon the creature's face. The ears, which up to then had been pricked up straight, were gradually drawn back, the eyelids drooped, the head went over to one side, and at that moment Louisa could have sworn that the animal was actually *appreciating* the work.

What she saw (or thought she saw) was something she had noticed many times on the faces of people listening very closely to a piece of music. When the sound takes complete hold of them and drowns them in itself, a peculiar, intensely ecstatic look comes over them that you can recognize as easily as a smile. So far as Louisa could see, the cat was now wearing almost exactly this kind of look.

Louisa finished the fugue, then played the siciliana, and all the way through she kept watching the cat on the sofa. The final proof for her that the animal was listening came at the end, when the music stopped. It blinked, stirred itself a little, stretched a leg, settled into a more comfortable position, took a quick glance round the room, then looked expectantly in her direction. It was precisely the way a concert-goer reacts when the music momentarily releases him in the pause between two movements of a symphony. The behaviour was so thoroughly human it gave her a queer agitated feeling in the chest.

'You like that?' she asked. 'You like Vivaldi?'

The moment she'd spoken, she felt ridiculous, but not – and this to her was a trifle sinister – not quite so ridiculous as she knew she should have felt.

Well, there was nothing for it now except to go straight ahead with the next number on the programme, which was *Carnaval*. As soon as she began to play, the cat again stiffened and sat up straighter; then, as it became slowly and blissfully saturated with the sound, it relapsed into that queer melting mood of ecstasy that seemed to have something to do with drowning and with dreaming. It was really an extravagant sight – quite a comical one, too – to see this silvery cat sitting on the sofa and being carried away like this. And what made it more screwy than ever, Louisa thought, was the fact that this music, which the animal seemed to be enjoying so much, was manifestly too *difficult*, too *classical*, to be appreciated by the majority of humans in the world.

Maybe, she thought, the creature's not really enjoying it at all. Maybe it's a sort of hypnotic reaction, like with snakes. After all, if you can charm a snake with music, then why not a cat? Except that millions of cats hear the stuff every day of their lives, on radio and gramophone and piano, and, as far as she knew, there'd never yet been a case of one behaving like this. This one was acting as though it were following every single note. It was certainly a fantastic thing.

But was it not also a wonderful thing? Indeed it was. In fact, unless she was much mistaken, it was a kind of miracle, one of those animal miracles that happen about once every hundred years.

'I could see you *loved* that one,' she said when the piece was over. 'Although I'm sorry I didn't play it any too well today. Which did you like best – the Vivaldi or the Schumann?'

The cat made no reply, so Louisa, fearing she might lose the attention of her listener, went straight into the next part of the programme – Liszt's second *Petrarch Sonnet*.

And now an extraordinary thing happened. She hadn't played more than three or four bars when the animal's whiskers began perceptibly to twitch. Slowly it drew itself up to an extra height, laid its head on one side, then on the other, and stared into space with a kind of frowning concentrated look that seemed to say, 'What's this? Don't tell me. I know it so well, but just for the moment I don't seem to be able to place it.' Louisa was fascinated, and with her little mouth half open and half smiling, she continued to play, waiting to see what on earth was going to happen next.

The cat stood up, walked to one end of the sofa, sat down again, listened some more; then all at once it bounded to the floor and leaped up on to the piano stool beside her. There it sat, listening intently to the lovely sonnet, not dreamily this time, but very erect, the large yellow eyes fixed upon Louisa's fingers.

'Well!' she said as she struck the last chord. 'So you came up to sit beside me, did you? You like this better than the sofa? All right, I'll let you stay, but you must keep still and not jump about.' She put out a hand and stroked the cat softly along the back, from head to tail. 'That was Liszt,' she went on. 'Mind you, he can sometimes be quite horribly vulgar, but in things like this he's really charming.'

She was beginning to enjoy this odd animal pantomime, so she went straight on into the next item on the programme, Schumann's *Kinderscenen*.

She hadn't been playing for more than a minute or two when she realized that the cat had again moved, and was now back in its old place on the sofa. She'd been watching her hands at the time, and presumably that was why she hadn't even noticed its going; all the same, it must have been an extremely swift and silent move. The cat was still staring at her, still apparently attending closely to the music, and yet it seemed to Louisa that there was not now the same rapturous enthusiasm there'd been during the previous piece, the Liszt. In addition, the act of leaving the stool and returning to the sofa appeared in itself to be a mild but positive gesture of disappointment.

'What's the matter?' she asked when it was over. 'What's wrong with Schumann? What's so marvellous about Liszt?' The cat looked straight back at her with those yellow eyes that had small jet-black bars lying vertically in their centres.

This, she told herself, is really beginning to get interesting – a trifle spooky, too, when she came to think of it. But one look at the cat sitting there on the sofa so bright and attentive, so obviously waiting for more music, quickly reassured her.

'All right,' she said. 'I'll tell you what I'm going to do. I'm going to alter my programme specially for you. You seem to like Liszt so much, I'll give you another.'

She hesitated, searching her memory for a good Liszt; then softly she began to play one of the twelve little pieces from *Der Weihnachtsbaum*. She was now watching the cat very closely, and the first thing she noticed was that the whiskers again began to twitch. It jumped down to the carpet, stood still a moment, inclining its head, quivering with excitement, and then, with a slow, silky stride, it walked around the piano, hopped up on the stool, and sat down beside her.

They were in the middle of all this when Edward came in from the garden.

'Edward!' Louisa cried, jumping up. 'Oh, Edward, darling! Listen to this! Listen what's happened!'

'What is it now?' he said. 'I'd like some tea.' He had one of those narrow, sharp-nosed, faintly magenta faces, and the sweat was making it shine as though it were a long wet grape.

'It's the cat!' Louisa cried, pointing to it sitting quietly on the piano stool. 'Just *wait* till you hear what's happened!'

'I thought I told you to take it to the police.'

'But, Edward, *listen* to me. This is *terribly* exciting. This is a *musical* cat.'

'Oh, yes?'

'This cat can appreciate music, and it can understand it too.'

'Now stop this nonsense, Louisa, and for God's sake let's have some tea. I'm hot and tired from cutting brambles and building bonfires.' He sat down in an armchair, took a cigarette from a box beside him, and lit it with an immense patent lighter that stood near the box.

'What you don't understand,' Louisa said, 'is that something extremely exciting has been happening here in our own house while you were out, something that may even be ... well ... almost momentous.'

'I'm quite sure of that.'

'Edward, *please*!'

Louisa was standing by the piano, her little pink face pinker than ever, a scarlet rose high up on each cheek. 'If you want to know,' she said, 'I'll tell you what I think.'

'I'm listening, dear.'

'I think it might be possible that we are at this moment sitting in the presence of—' She stopped, as though suddenly sensing the absurdity of the thought.

'Yes?'

'You may think it silly, Edward, but it's honestly what I think.'

'In the presence of whom, for heaven's sake?'

'Of Franz Liszt himself!'

Her husband took a long slow pull at his cigarette and blew the smoke up at the ceiling. He had the tight-skinned, concave cheeks of a man who has worn a full set of dentures for many years, and every time he sucked at a cigarette, the cheeks went in even more, and the bones of his face stood out like a skeleton's. 'I don't get you,' he said.

'Edward, listen to me. From what I've seen this afternoon with my own eyes, it really looks as though this might be some sort of a reincarnation.'

'You mean this lousy cat?'

'Don't talk like that, dear, please.'

'You're not ill, are you, Louisa?'

'I'm perfectly all right, thank you very much. I'm a bit confused – I don't mind admitting it, but who wouldn't be after what's just happened? Edward, I swear to you—'

'What did happen, if I may ask?'

Louisa told him, and all the while she was speaking, her husband lay sprawled in the chair with his legs stretched out in front of him, sucking at his cigarette and blowing the smoke up at the ceiling. There was a thin cynical smile on his mouth.

'I don't see anything very unusual about that,' he said when it was over. 'All it is – it's a trick cat. It's been taught tricks, that's all.'

'Don't be so silly, Edward. Every time I play Liszt, he gets all excited and comes running over to sit on the stool beside me. But only for Liszt, and nobody can teach a cat the difference between Liszt and Schumann. You don't even know it yourself. But this one can do it every single time. Quite obscure Liszt, too.'

'Twice,' the husband said. 'He's only done it twice.'

'Twice is enough.'

'Let's see him do it again. Come on.'

'No,' Louisa said. 'Definitely not. Because if this *is* Liszt, as I believe it is, or anyway the soul of Liszt or whatever it is that comes back, then it's certainly not right or even very kind to put him through a lot of silly undignified tests.'

'My dear woman! This is a *cat* – a rather stupid grey cat that nearly got its coat singed by the bonfire this morning in the garden. And anyway, what do you know about reincarnation?'

'If the soul is there, that's enough for me,' Louisa said firmly. 'That's all that counts.'

'Come on, then. Let's see him perform. Let's see him tell the difference between his own stuff and someone else's.'

'No, Edward. I've told you before, I refuse to put him through any more silly circus tests. He's had quite enough of that for one day. But I'll tell you what I *will* do. I'll play him a little more of his own music.'

'A fat lot that'll prove.'

'You watch. And one thing is certain – as soon as he recognizes it, he'll refuse to budge off that stool where he's sitting now.'

Louisa went to the music shelf, took down a book of Liszt, thumbed through it quickly, and chose another of his finer compositions – the B minor Sonata. She had meant to play only the first part of the work, but once she got started and saw how the cat was sitting there literally quivering with pleasure and watching her hands with that rapturous concentrated look, she didn't have the heart to stop. She played it all the way through. When it was finished, she glanced up at her husband and smiled. 'There you are,' she said. 'You can't tell me he wasn't absolutely loving it.'

'He just likes the noise, that's all.'

'He was *loving* it. Weren't you, darling?' she said, lifting the cat in her arms. 'Oh, my goodness, if only he could talk. Just think of it, dear – he met Beethoven in his youth! He knew Schubert and Mendelssohn and Schumann and Berlioz and Grieg and Delacroix and Ingres and Heine and Balzac. And let me see . . . My heavens, he was Wagner's father-in-law! I'm holding Wagner's father-in-law in my arms!'

'Louisa!' her husband said sharply, sitting up straight. 'Pull yourself together.' There was a new edge to his voice now, and he spoke louder.

Louisa glanced up quickly. 'Edward, I do believe you're jealous!'

'Of a miserable grey cat!'

'Then don't be so grumpy and cynical about it all. If you're going to behave like this, the best thing you can do is to go back to your gardening and leave the two of us together in peace. That will be best for all of us, won't it, darling?' she said, addressing the cat, stroking its head. 'And later on this evening, we shall have some more music together, you and I, some more of your own work. Oh, yes,' she said, kissing the creature several times on the neck, 'and we might have a little Chopin, too. You needn't tell me – I happen to know you adore Chopin. You used to be great friends with him, didn't you, darling? As a matter of fact – if I remember rightly – it was in Chopin's apartment that you met the great love of your life, Madame Something-or-Other. Had three illegitimate children by her, too, didn't you? Yes, you did, you naughty thing, and don't go trying to deny it. So you shall have some Chopin,' she said, kissing the cat again, 'and that'll probably bring back all sorts of lovely memories to you, won't it?'

'Louisa, stop this at once!'

'Oh, don't be so stuffy, Edward.'

'You're behaving like a perfect idiot, woman. And anyway, you forget we're going out this evening, to Bill and Betty's for canasta.'

'Oh, but I couldn't *possibly* go out now. There's no question of that.'

Edward got up slowly from his chair, then bent down and stubbed his cigarette hard into the ash-tray. 'Tell me something,' he said quietly. 'You don't really believe this – this twaddle you're talking, do you?'

'But of *course* I do. I don't think there's any question about it now. And, what's more, I consider that it puts a tremendous responsibility upon us, Edward – upon both of us. You as well.'

'You know what I think,' he said. 'I think you ought to see a doctor. And damn quick, too.'

With that, he turned and stalked out of the room, through the french windows, back into the garden.

Louisa watched him striding across the lawn towards his bonfire and his brambles, and she waited until he was out of sight before she turned and ran to the front door, still carrying the cat.

Soon she was in the car, driving to town.

She parked in front of the library, locked the cat in the car, hurried up the steps into the building, and headed straight for the reference room. There she began searching the cards for books on two subjects – REINCARNATION and LISZT.

Under REINCARNATION she found something called *Recurring Earth-Lives – How and Why*, by a man called F. Milton Willis, published in 1921. Under LISZT she found two biographical volumes. She took out all three books, returned to the car, and drove home.

Back in the house, she placed the cat on the sofa, sat herself down beside it with her three books, and prepared to do some serious reading. She would begin, she decided, with Mr F. Milton Willis's work. The volume was thin and a trifle soiled, but it had a good heavy feel to it, and the author's name had an authoritative ring.

The doctrine of reincarnation, she read, states that spiritual souls pass from higher to higher forms of animals. 'A man can, for instance, no more be reborn as an animal than an adult can re-become a child.'

She read this again. But how did he know? How could he be so sure? He couldn't. No one could possibly be certain about a thing like that. At the same time, the statement took a good deal of the wind out of her sails.

'Around the centre of consciousness of each of us, there are, besides the dense outer body, four other bodies, invisible to the eye of flesh, but perfectly visible to people whose faculties of perception of superphysical things have undergone the requisite development . . .'

She didn't understand that one at all, but she read on, and soon she came to an interesting passage that told how long a soul usually stayed away from the earth before returning in someone else's body. The time varied according to type, and Mr Willis gave the following breakdown:

Edward the Conqueror

Drunkards and the unemployable	40/50	YEARS
Unskilled labourers	60/100	"
Skilled workers	100/200	"
The *bourgeoisie*	200/300	"
The upper-middle classes	500	"
The highest class of gentleman farmers	600/1,000	"
Those in the Path of Initiation	1,500/2,000	"

Quickly she referred to one of the other books, to find out how long Liszt had been dead. It said he died in Bayreuth in 1886. That was sixty-seven years ago. Therefore, according to Mr Willis, he'd have to have been an unskilled labourer to come back so soon. That didn't seem to fit at all. On the other hand, she didn't think much of the author's methods of grading. According to him, 'the highest class of gentleman farmer' was just about the most superior being on the earth. Red jackets and stirrup cups and the bloody, sadistic murder of the fox. No, she thought, that isn't right. It was a pleasure to find herself beginning to doubt Mr Willis.

Later in the book, she came upon a list of some of the more famous reincarnations. Epictetus, she was told, returned to earth as Ralph Waldo Emerson. Cicero came back as Gladstone, Alfred the Great as Queen Victoria, William the Conqueror as Lord Kitchener. Ashoka Vardhana, King of India in 272 B.C., came back as Colonel Henry Steel Olcott, an esteemed American lawyer. Pythagoras returned as Master Koot Hoomi, the gentleman who founded the Theosophical Society with Mme Blavatsky and Colonel H. S. Olcott (the esteemed American lawyer, alias Ashoka Vardhana, King of India). It didn't say who Mme Blavatsky had been. But 'Theodore Roosevelt,' it said, 'has for numbers of incarnations played great parts as a leader of men ... From him descended the royal line of ancient Chaldea, he having been, about 30,000 B.C., appointed Governor of Chaldea by the Ego we know as Caesar who was then ruler of Persia ... Roosevelt and Caesar have been together time after time as military and administrative leaders; at one time, many thousands of years ago, they were husband and wife ...'

That was enough for Louisa. Mr F. Milton Willis was clearly nothing but a guesser. She was not impressed by his dogmatic assertions. The fellow was probably on the right track, but his pronouncements were extravagant, especially the first one of all, about animals. Soon she hoped to be able to confound the whole Theosophical Society with her proof that man could indeed reappear as a lower animal. Also that he did not have to be an unskilled labourer to come back within a hundred years.

She now turned to one of the Liszt biographies, and she was glancing through it casually when her husband came in again from the garden.

'What are you doing now?' he asked.

'Oh – just checking up a little here and there. Listen, my dear, did you know that Theodore Roosevelt once was Caesar's wife?'

'Louisa,' he said, 'look – why don't we stop this nonsense? I don't like to see you making a fool of yourself like this. Just give me that goddamn cat and I'll take it to the police station myself.'

Louisa didn't seem to hear him. She was staring open-mouthed at a picture of Liszt in the book that lay on her lap. 'My God!' she cried. 'Edward, look!'

'What?'

'Look! The warts on his face! I forgot all about them! He had these great warts on his face and it was a famous thing. Even his students used to cultivate little tufts of hair on their own faces in the same spots, just to be like him.'

'What's that got to do with it!'

'Nothing. I mean not the students. But the warts have.'

'Oh, Christ,' the man said. 'Oh, Christ God Almighty.'

'The cat has them too! Look, I'll show you.'

She took the animal on to her lap and began examining its face. 'There! There's one! And there's another! Wait a minute! I do believe they're in the same places! Where's that picture?'

It was a famous portrait of the musician in his old age, showing the fine powerful face framed in a mass of long grey hair that covered his ears and came half-way down his neck. On the face itself, each large wart had been faithfully reproduced, and there were five of them in all.

'Now, in the picture there's *one* above the right eyebrow.' She looked above the right eyebrow of the cat. 'Yes! It's there! In exactly the same place! And another on the left, at the top of the nose. That one's there, too! And one just below it on the cheek.

And two fairly close together under the chin on the right side. Edward! Edward! Come and look! They're exactly the same.'

'It doesn't prove a thing.'

She looked up at her husband who was standing in the centre of the room in his green sweater and khaki slacks, still perspiring freely. 'You're scared, aren't you, Edward? Scared of losing your precious dignity and having people think you might be making a fool of yourself just for once.'

'I refuse to get hysterical about it, that's all.'

Louisa turned back to the book and began reading some more. 'This is interesting,' she said. 'It says here that Liszt loved all of Chopin's work except one – the Scherzo in B flat minor. Apparently he hated that. He called it the "Governess Scherzo", and said that it ought to be reserved solely for people in that profession.'

'So what?'

'Edward, listen. As you insist on being so horrid about all this, I'll tell you what I'm going to do. I'm going to play this scherzo right now and you can stay here and see what happens.'

'And then maybe you will deign to get us some supper.'

Louisa got up and took from the shelf a large green volume containing all of Chopin's works. 'Here it is. Oh yes, I remember it. It *is* rather awful. Now, listen – or, rather, watch. Watch to see what he does.'

She placed the music on the piano and sat down. Her husband remained standing. He had his hands in his pockets and a cigarette in his mouth, and in spite of himself he was watching the cat, which was now dozing on the sofa. When Louisa began to play, the first effect was as dramatic as ever. The animal jumped up as though it had been stung, and it stood motionless for at least a minute, the ears pricked up, the whole body quivering. Then it became restless and began to walk back and forth along the length of the sofa. Finally, it hopped down on to the floor, and with its nose and tail held high in the air, it marched slowly, majestically, from the room.

'There!' Louisa cried, jumping up and running after it. 'That does it! That really proves it!' She came back carrying the cat which she put down again on the sofa. Her whole face was shining with excitement now, her fists were clenched white, and the little bun on top of her head was loosening and going over to one side. 'What about it, Edward? What d'you think?' She was laughing nervously as she spoke.

'I must say it was quite amusing.'

'*Amusing!* My dear Edward, it's the most wonderful thing that's ever happened! Oh, goodness me!' she cried, picking up the cat again and hugging it to her bosom. 'Isn't it marvellous to think we've got Franz Liszt staying in the house?'

'Now, Louisa. Don't let's get hysterical.'

'I can't help it, I simply can't. And to *imagine* that he's actually going to live with us for always!'

'I beg your pardon?'

'Oh, Edward! I can hardly talk from excitement. And d'you know what I'm going to do next? Every musician in the whole world is going to want to meet him, that's a fact, and ask him about the people he knew – about Beethoven and Chopin and Schubert—'

'He can't talk,' her husband said.

'Well – all right. But they're going to want to meet him anyway, just to see him and touch him and to play their own music to him, modern music he's never heard before.'

'He wasn't that great. Now, if it had been Bach or Beethoven...'

'Don't interrupt, Edward, please. So what I'm going to do is to notify all the important living composers everywhere. It's my duty. I'll tell them Liszt is here, and invite them to visit him. And you know what? They'll come flying in from every corner of the earth!'

'To see a grey cat?'

'Darling, it's the same thing. It's *him*. No one cares what he *looks* like. Oh, Edward, it'll be the most exciting thing there ever was!'

'They'll think you're mad.'

'You wait and see.' She was holding the cat in her arms and petting it tenderly but looking across at her husband, who now walked over to the french windows and stood there staring out into the garden. The evening was beginning, and the lawn was turning slowly from green to black, and in the distance he could see the smoke from his bonfire rising up in a white column.

'No,' he said, without turning round, 'I'm not having it. Not in this house. It'll make us both look perfect fools.'

'Edward, what do you mean?'

'Just what I say. I absolutely refuse to have you stirring up a lot of publicity about a foolish thing like this. You happen to have found a trick cat. O.K. – that's fine. Keep it, if it pleases you. I don't mind. But I don't wish you to go any further than that. Do you understand me, Louisa?'

'Further than what?'

'I don't want to hear any more of this crazy talk. You're acting like a lunatic.'

Louisa put the cat slowly down on the sofa. Then slowly she raised herself to her full small height and took one pace forward. '*Damn* you, Edward!' she shouted, stamping her foot. 'For the first time in our lives something really exciting comes along and you're scared to death of having anything to do with it because someone may laugh at you! That's right, isn't it? You can't deny it, can you?'

'Louisa,' her husband said. 'That's quite enough of that. Pull yourself together now and stop this at once.' He walked over and took a cigarette from the box on the table, then lit it with the enormous patent lighter. His wife stood watching him, and now the tears were beginning to trickle out of the inside corners of her eyes, making two little shiny rivers where they ran through the powder on her cheeks.

'We've been having too many of these scenes just lately, Louisa,' he was saying. 'No no, don't interrupt. Listen to me. I make full allowance for the fact that this may be an awkward time of life for you, and that—'

'Oh, my God! You idiot! You pompous idiot! Can't you see that this is different, this is – this is something miraculous? Can't you see that?'

At that point, he came across the room and took her firmly by the shoulders. He had the freshly lit cigarette between his lips, and she could see faint contours on his skin where the heavy perspiration had dried in patches. 'Listen,' he said. 'I'm hungry. I've given up my golf and I've been working all day in the garden, and I'm tired and hungry and I want some supper. So do you. Off you go now to the kitchen and get us both something good to eat.'

Louisa stepped back and put both hands to her mouth. 'My heavens!' she cried. 'I forgot all about it. He must be absolutely famished. Except for some milk, I haven't given him a thing to eat since he arrived.'

'Who?'

'Why, *him*, of course. I must go at once and cook something really special. I wish I knew what his favourite dishes used to be. What do you think he would like best, Edward?'

'*Goddamn* it, Louisa!'

'Now, Edward, please. I'm going to handle this *my* way just for once. You stay here,' she said, bending down and touching the cat gently with her fingers. 'I won't be long.'

Louisa went into the kitchen and stood for moment, wondering what special dish she might prepare. How about a soufflé? A nice cheese soufflé? Yes, that would be rather special. Of course, Edward didn't much care for them, but that couldn't be helped. She was only a fair cook, and she couldn't be sure of always having a soufflé come out well, but she took extra trouble this time and waited a long while to make certain the oven had heated fully to the correct temperature. While the soufflé was baking and she was searching around for something to go with it, it occurred to her that Liszt had probably never in his life tasted either avocado pears or grapefruit, so she decided to give him both of them at once in a salad. It would be fun to watch his reaction. It really would.

When it was all ready, she put it on a tray and carried it into the living-room. At the exact moment she entered, she saw her husband coming in through the french windows from the garden.

'Here's his supper,' she said, putting it on the table and turning towards the sofa. 'Where is he?'

Her husband closed the garden door behind him and walked across the room to get himself a cigarette.

'Edward, where is he?'

'Who?'

'You know who.'

'Ah, yes. Yes, that's right. Well – I'll tell you.' He was bending forward to light the cigarette, and his hands were cupped around the enormous patent lighter. He glanced up and saw Louisa looking at him – at his shoes and the bottoms of his khaki slacks, which were damp from walking in long grass.

'I just went out to see how the bonfire was going,' he said.

Her eyes travelled slowly upward and rested on his hands.

'It's still burning fine,' he went on. 'I think it'll keep going all night.'

But the way she was staring made him uncomfortable.

'What is it?' he said, lowering the lighter. Then he looked down and noticed for the first time the long thin scratch that ran diagonally clear across the back of one hand, from the knuckle to the wrist.

'*Edward!*'

'Yes,' he said, 'I know. Those brambles are terrible. They tear you to pieces. Now, just a minute, Louisa. What's the matter?'

'*Edward!*'

'Oh, for God's sake, woman, sit down and keep calm. There's nothing to get worked up about. Louisa! Louisa, *sit down*!'

THE SQUAW
Bram Stoker

Nurnberg at the time was not so much exploited as it has been since then. Irving had not been playing *Faust*, and the very name of the old town was hardly known to the great bulk of the travelling public. My wife and I being in the second week of our honeymoon, naturally wanted someone else to join our party, so that when the cheery stranger, Elias P. Hutcheson, hailing from Isthmian City, Bleeding Gulch, Maple Tree County, Neb., turned up at the station at Frankfurt, and casually remarked that he was going on to see the most all-fired old Methusaleh of a town in Yurrup, and that he guessed that so much travelling alone was enough to send an intelligent, active citizen into the melancholy ward of a daft house, we took the pretty broad hint and suggested that we should join forces. We found, on comparing notes afterwards, that we had each intended to speak with some diffidence or hesitation so as not to appear too eager, such not being a good compliment to the success of our married life; but the effect was entirely marred by our both beginning to speak at the same instant – stopping simultaneously and then going on together again. Anyhow, no matter how, it was done; and Elias P. Hutcheson became one of our party. Straightway Amelia and I found the pleasant benefit; instead of quarrelling, as we had been doing, we found that the restraining influence of a third party was such that we now took every opportunity of spooning in odd corners. Amelia declares that ever since she has, as the result of that experience, advised all her friends to take a friend on the honeymoon. Well, we 'did' Nurnberg together, and much enjoyed the racy remarks of our Transatlantic friend, who, from his quaint speech and his wonderful stock of adventures, might have stepped out of a novel. We kept for the last object of interest in the city to be visited the Burg, and on the day appointed for the visit strolled round the outer wall of the city by the eastern side.

The Burg is seated on a rock dominating the town, and an immensely deep fosse guards it on the northern side. Nurnberg has been happy in that it was never sacked; had it been it would certainly not be so spick and span perfect as it is at present. The ditch has not been used for centuries, and now its base is spread with tea-gardens and orchards, of which some of the trees are of quite respectable growth. As we wandered round the wall, dawdling in the hot July sunshine, we often paused to admire the views spread before us, and in especial the great plain covered with towns and villages and bounded with a blue line of hills, like a landscape of Claude Lorraine. From this we always turned with new delight to the city itself, with its myriad of quaint old gables and acre-wide red roofs dotted with dormer windows, tier upon tier. A little to our right rose the towers of the Burg, and nearer still, standing grim, the Torture Tower, which was, and is, perhaps, the most interesting place in the city. For centuries the tradition of the Iron Virgin of Nurnberg has been handed down as an instance of the horrors of cruelty of which man is capable; we had long looked forward to seeing it; and here at last was its home.

In one of our pauses we leaned over the wall of the moat and looked down. The garden seemed quite fifty or sixty feet below us, and the sun pouring into it with an intense, moveless heat like that of an oven. Beyond rose the grey, grim wall seemingly of endless height, and losing itself right and left in the angles of bastion and counterscarp. Trees and bushes crowned the wall, and above again towered the lofty houses on whose massive beauty Time has only set the hand of approval. The sun was hot and we were lazy; time was our own, and we lingered, leaning on the wall. Just below us was a pretty sight – a great black cat lying stretched in the sun, whilst round her gambolled prettily a tiny black kitten. The mother would wave her tail for the kitten to play with, or would raise her feet and push away the little one as an encouragement to further play. They were just at the foot of the wall, and Elias P. Hutcheson, in order to help the play, stooped and took from the walk a moderate-sized pebble.

'See!' he said, 'I will drop it near the kitten, and they will both wonder where it came from.'

'Oh, be careful,' said my wife; 'you might hit the dear little thing!'

'Not me, ma'am,' said Elias P. 'Why, I'm as tender as a Maine cherry-tree. Lor, bless ye, I wouldn't hurt the poor pooty little critter more'n I'd scalp a baby. An' you may bet your variegated socks on that! See, I'll drop it fur away on the outside so's not to go near her!' Thus saying, he leaned over and held his arm out at full length and dropped the stone. It may be that there is some attractive force which draws lesser matters to greater; or more probably that the wall was not plumb but sloped to its base – we not noticing the inclination from above; but the stone fell with a sickening thud that came up to us through the hot air, right on the kitten's head, and shattered out its little brains then and there. The black cat cast a swift upward glance, and we saw her eyes like green fire fixed an instant on Elias P. Hutcheson; and then her attention was given to the kitten, which lay still with just a quiver of her tiny limbs, whilst a thin red stream trickled from a gaping wound. With a muffled cry, such as a human being might give, she bent over the kitten, licking its wound and moaning. Suddenly she seemed to realize that it was dead, and again threw her eyes up at us. I shall never forget the sight, for she looked the perfect incarnation of hate. Her green eyes blazed with lurid fire, and the white, sharp teeth seemed to almost shine through the blood which dabbled her mouth and whiskers. She gnashed her teeth, and her claws stood out stark and at full length on every paw. Then she made a wild rush up the wall as if to reach us, but when the momentum ended fell back, and further added to her horrible appearance for she fell on the kitten, and rose with her back fur smeared with its brains and blood. Amelia turned quite faint, and I had to lift her back from the wall. There was a seat close by in shade of a spreading plane-tree, and here I placed her whilst she composed herself. Then I went back to Hutcheson, who stood without moving, looking down on the angry cat below.

As I joined him, he said:

'Wall, I guess that air the savagest beast I ever see – 'cept once when an Apache squaw had an edge on a half-breed what they nicknamed "Splinters" 'cos of the way he fixed up her papoose which he stole on a raid just to show that he appreciated the way they had given his mother the fire torture. She got that kinder look so set on her face that it just seemed to grow there. She followed Splinters more'n three year till at last the braves got him and handed him over to her. They did say that no man, white or Injun, had ever been so long a-dying under the tortures of the Apaches. The only time I ever see her smile was when I wiped her out. I kem on the camp just in time to see Splinters pass in his checks, and he wasn't sorry to go either. He was a hard citizen, and though I never could shake with him after that papoose business – for it was bitter bad, and he should have been a white man, for he looked like one – I see he had got paid out in full. Durn me, but I took a piece of his hide from one of his skinnin posts an' had it made into a pocket-book. It's here now!' and he slapped the breast pocket of his coat.

Whilst he was speaking the cat was continuing her frantic efforts to get up the wall. She would take a run back and then charge up, sometimes reaching an incredible height. She did not seem to mind the heavy fall which she got each time but started with renewed vigour; and at every tumble her appearance became more horrible. Hutcheson was a kind-hearted man – my wife and I had both noticed little acts of kindness to animals as well as to persons – and he seemed concerned at the state of fury to which the cat had wrought herself.

'Wall now!' he said, 'I du declare that that poor critter seems quite desperate. There! there! poor thing, it was all an accident – though that won't bring back your little one to you. Say! I wouldn't have had such a thing happen for a thousand! Just shows what a clumsy fool of a man can do when he tries to play! Seems I'm too darned slipperhanded to even play with a cat. Say Colonel!' – it was a pleasant way he had to bestow titles freely – 'I hope your wife don't hold no grudge against me on account of this unpleasantness? Why, I wouldn't have had it occur on no account.'

He came over to Amelia and apologized profusely, and she with her usual kindness of heart hastened to assure him that she quite understood that it was an accident. Then we all went again to the wall and looked over.

The cat, missing Hutcheson's face, had drawn back across the moat, and was sitting on her haunches as though ready to spring. Indeed, the very instant she saw him she did spring, and with a blind

The Squaw

unreasoning fury, which would have been grotesque, only that it was so frightfully real. She did not try to run up the wall, but simply launched herself at him as though hate and fury could lend her wings to pass straight through the great distance between them. Amelia, womanlike, got quite concerned, and said to Elias P. in a warning voice:

'Oh! you must be very careful. That animal would try to kill you if she were here; her eyes look like positive murder.'

He laughed out jovially. 'Excuse me, ma'am,' he said, 'but I can't help laughin'. Fancy a man that has fought grizzlies an' Injuns bein' careful of bein' murdered by a cat!'

When the cat heard him laugh, her whole demeanour seemed to change. She no longer tried to jump or run up the wall, but went quietly over, and sitting again beside the dead kitten began to lick and fondle it as though it were alive. 'See!' said I, 'the effect of a really strong man. Even that animal in the midst of her fury recognizes the voice of a master, and bows to him!'

'Like a squaw!' was the only comment of Elias P. Hutcheson, as we moved on our way round the city fosse. Every now and then we looked over the wall and each time saw the cat following us. At first she had kept going back to the dead kitten, and then as the distance grew greater took it in her mouth and so followed. After a while, however, she abandoned this, for we saw her following all alone; she had evidently hidden the body somewhere. Amelia's alarm grew at the cat's persistence, and more than once she repeated her warning; but the American always laughed with amusement, till finally, seeing that she was beginning to be worried, he said:

'I say, ma'am, you needn't be skeered over that cat. I go heeled, I du!' Here he slapped his pistol pocket at the back of his lumbar region. 'Why sooner'n have you worried, I'll shoot the critter, right here, an' risk the police interferin' with a citizen of the United States for carryin' arms contrary to reg'lations!' As he spoke he looked over the wall, but the cat, on seeing him, retreated, with a growl, into a bed of tall flowers, and was hidden. He went on: 'Blest if that ar critter ain't got more sense of what's good for her than most Christians. I guess we've seen the last of her! You bet, she'll go back now to that busted kitten and have a private funeral of it, all to herself!'

Amelia did not like to say more, lest he might, in mistaken kindness to her, fulfil his threat of shooting the cat: and so we went on and crossed the little wooden bridge leading to the gateway whence ran the steep paved roadway between the Burg and the pentagonal Torture Tower. As we crossed the bridge we saw the cat again down below us. When she saw us her fury seemed to return, and she made frantic efforts to get up the steep wall. Hutcheson laughed as he looked down at her, and said:

'Good-bye, old girl. Sorry I in-jured your feelin's, but you'll get over it in time! So long!' And then we passed through the long, dim archway and came to the gate of the Burg.

When we came out again after our survey of this most beautiful old place which not even the well-intended efforts of the Gothic restorers of forty years ago have been able to spoil – though their restoration was then glaring white – we seemed to have quite forgotten the unpleasant episode of the morning. The old lime-tree with its great trunk gnarled with the passing of nearly nine centuries, the deep well cut through the heart of the rock by those captives of old, and the lovely view from the city wall whence we heard, spread over almost a full quarter of an hour, the multitudinous chimes of the city, had all helped to wipe out from our minds the incident of the slain kitten.

We were the only visitors who had entered the Torture Tower that morning – so at least said the old custodian – and as we had the place all to ourselves were able to make a minute and more satisfactory survey than would have otherwise been possible. The custodian, looking to us as the sole source of his gains for the day, was willing to meet our wishes in any way. The Torture Tower is truly a grim place, even now when many thousands of visitors have sent a stream of life, and the joy that follows life, into the place; but at the time I mention it wore its grimmest and most gruesome aspect. The dust of ages seemed to have settled on it, and the darkness and the horror of its memories seem to have become sentient in a way that would have satisfied the Pantheistic souls of Philo or Spinoza. The lower chamber where we entered was seemingly, in its normal state, filled with incarnate darkness; even the hot sunlight streaming in through the door seemed to be lost in the vast thickness of the walls, and only showed the masonry rough as when the builder's scaffolding had come down, but coated with dust and marked here and there with patches of dark stain which, if walls could speak, could have given their own dread memories of fear and pain. We were glad to pass up the dusty wooden staircase, the custodian leaving the outer door open to light us somewhat on our way; for to our eyes the one long-wick'd, evil-smelling candle stuck in a sconce on the wall gave an inadequate light. When we came up through the open trap in the corner of the chamber overhead, Amelia held on to me so tightly that I could actually feel her heart beat. I must say for my own part that I was not surprised at her fear, for this room was even more gruesome than that below. Here there was certainly more light, but only just sufficient to realize the horrible surroundings of the place. The builders of the tower had evidently intended that only they who should gain the top should have any of the joys of light and prospect. There, as we had noticed from below, were ranges of windows, albeit of mediæval smallness, but elsewhere in the tower were only a very few narrow slits such as were habitual in places of mediæval defence. A few of these only lit the chamber, and these so high up in the wall that from no part could the sky be seen through the thickness of the walls. In racks, and leaning in disorder against the walls, were a number of headsmen's swords, great double-handed weapons with broad blade and keen edge. Hard by were several blocks whereon the necks of the victims had lain, with here and there deep notches where the steel had bitten through the guard of flesh and shored into the wood. Round the chamber, placed in all sorts of irregular ways, were many implements of torture which made one's heart ache to see – chairs full of spikes which gave instant and excruciating pain; chairs and couches with dull knobs whose torture was seemingly less, but which, though slower, were equally efficacious; racks, belts, boots, gloves, collars, all made for compressing at will; steel baskets in which the head could be slowly crushed into a pulp if necessary; watchmen's hooks with long handle and knife that cut at resistance – this a speciality of the old Nurnberg police system; and many, many other devices for man's injury to man. Amelia grew quite pale with the horror of the things, but fortunately did not faint, for being a little overcome she sat down on a torture chair, but jumped up again with a shriek, all tendency to faint gone. We both pretended that it was the injury done to her dress by the dust of the chair, and the rusty spikes which had upset her, and Mr Hutcheson acquiesced in accepting the explanation with a kind-hearted laugh.

But the central object in the whole of this chamber of horrors was the engine known as the Iron Virgin, which stood near the centre of the room. It was a rudely shaped figure of a woman, something of the bell order, or, to make a closer comparison, of the figure of Mrs Noah in the children's Ark, but without that slimness of waist and perfect *rondeur* of hip which marks the æsthetic type of the Noah family. One would hardly have recognized it as intended for a human figure at all had not the founder shaped on the forehead a rude semblance of a woman's face. This machine was coated with rust without, and covered with dust; a rope was fastened to a ring in the front of the figure, about where the waist should have been, and was drawn through a pulley, fastened on the wooden pillar which sustained the flooring above. The custodian pulling this rope showed that a section of the front was hinged like a door at one side; we then saw that the engine was of considerable thickness, leaving just room enough inside for a man to be placed. The door was of equal thickness and of great weight, for it took the custodian all his strength, aided though he was by the contrivance of the pulley, to open it. This weight was partly due to the fact that the door was of manifest purpose hung so as to throw its weight downwards, so that it might shut of its own accord when the strain was released. The inside was honeycombed with rust – nay more, the rust alone that comes through time would hardly have eaten so deep into the iron walls; the rust of the cruel stains was deep indeed! It was only, however, when we came to look at the inside of the door that the diabolical intention was manifest to the full. Here were several long spikes, square and massive, broad at the base and sharp at the points, placed in such a position that when the door should close the upper ones would pierce the eyes of the victim, and the lower ones his heart and vitals. The sight was too much for poor Amelia and this time she fainted dead off, and I had to carry her down the stairs, and place her on a bench outside till she recovered. That she felt it to the quick was afterwards shown by the fact that my eldest son bears to this day a rude birthmark on his breast, which has, by family consent, been accepted as representing the Nurnberg Virgin.

The Squaw

When we got back to the chamber we found Hutcheson still opposite the Iron Virgin; he had been evidently philosophizing, and now gave us the benefit of his thought in the shape of a sort of exordium.

'Wall, I guess I've been learnin' somethin' here while madam has been gettin' over her faint. 'Pears to me that we're a long way behind the times on our side of the big drink. We uster think out on the plains that the Injun could give us points in tryin' to make man oncomfortable; but I guess your old mediæval law-and-order party could raise him every time. Splinters was pretty good in his bluff on the squaw, but this here young miss held a straight flush all high on him. The points of them spikes air sharp enough still, though even the edges air eaten out by what uster be on them. It'd be a good thing for our Indian section to get some specimens of this here play-toy to send round to the Reservations jest to knock the stuffin' out of the bucks, and the squaws too, by showing them as how old civilization lays over them at their best. Guess but I'll get in that box a minute jest to see how it feels!'

'Oh no! no!' said Amelia. 'It is too terrible!'

'Guess, ma'am, nothin's too terrible to the explorin' mind. I've been in some queer places in my time. Spent a night inside a dead horse while a prairie fire swept over me in Montana Territory – an' another time slept inside a dead buffler when the Comanches was on the war path an' I didn't keer to leave my kyard on them. I've been two days in a caved-in tunnel in the Billy Broncho gold mine in New Mexico, an' was one of the four shut up for three parts of a day in the caisson what slid over on her side when we was settin' the foundations of the Buffalo Bridge. I've not funked an odd experience yet, an' I don't propose to begin now!'

We saw that he was set on the experiment, so I said: 'Well, hurry up, old man, and get through it quick?'

'All right, General,' said he, 'but I calculate we ain't quite ready yet. The gentlemen, my predecessors, what stood in that thar canister, didn't volunteer for the office – not much! And I guess there was some ornamental tyin' up before the big stroke was made. I want to go into this thing fair and square, so I must get fixed up proper first. I dare say this old galoot can rise some string and tie me up accordin' to sample?'

This was said interrogatively to the old custodian, but the latter, who understood the drift of his speech, though perhaps not appreciating to the full the niceties of dialect and imagery, shook his head. His protest was, however, only formal and made to be overcome. The American thrust a gold piece into his hand, saying, 'Take it, pard! it's your pot; and don't be skeer'd. This ain't no necktie party that you're asked to assist in!' He produced some thin frayed rope and proceeded to bind our companion, with sufficient strictness for the purpose. When the upper part of his body was bound, Hutcheson said:

'Hold on a moment, Judge. Guess I'm too heavy for you to tote into the canister. You jest let me walk in, and then you can wash up regardin' my legs!'

Whilst speaking he had backed himself into the opening which was just enough to hold him. It was a close fit and no mistake. Amelia looked on with fear in her eyes, but she evidently did not like to say anything. Then the custodian completed his task by tying the American's feet together so that he was now absolutely helpless and fixed in his voluntary prison. He seemed to really enjoy it, and the incipient smile which was habitual to his face blossomed into actuality as he said:

'Guess this here Eve was made out of the rib of a dwarf! There ain't much room for a full-grown citizen of the United States to hustle. We uster make our coffins more roomier in Idaho territory. Now, Judge, you just begin to let this door down, slow, on to me. I want to feel the same pleasure as the other jays had when those spikes began to move toward their eyes!'

'Oh no! no! no!' broke in Amelia hysterically. 'It is too terrible! I can't bear to see it! – I can't! I can't!'

But the American was obdurate. 'Say, Colonel,' said he, 'Why not take madam for a little promenade? I wouldn't hurt her feelin's for the world; but now that I am here, havin' kem eight thousand miles, wouldn't it be too hard to give up the very experience I've been pinin' an' pantin' fur? A man can't get to feel like canned goods every time! Me and the Judge here'll fix up this thing in no time, an' then you'll come back, an' we'll all laugh together!'

Once more the resolution that is born of curiosity triumphed, and

The Squaw

Amelia stayed holding tight to my arm and shivering whilst the custodian began to slacken slowly inch by inch the rope that held back the iron door. Hutcheson's face was positively radiant as his eyes followed the first movement of the spikes.

'Wall!' he said, 'I guess I've not had enjoyment like this since I left Noo York. Bar a scrap with a French sailor at Wapping – an' that warn't much of a picnic neither – I've not had a show fur real pleasure in this dod-rotted Continent, where there ain't no b'ars nor no Injuns, an' wheer nary man goes heeled. Slow there, Judge! Don't you rush this business! I want a show for my money this game – I du!'

The custodian must have had in him some of the blood of his predecessors in that ghastly tower, for he worked the engine with a deliberate and excruciating slowness which after five minutes, in which the outer edge of the door had not moved half as many inches, began to overcome Amelia. I saw her lips whiten, and felt her hold upon my arm relax. I looked around an instant for a place whereon to lay her, and when I looked at her again found that her eye had become fixed on the side of the Virgin. Following its direction I saw the black cat crouching out of sight. Her green eyes shone like danger lamps in the gloom of the place, and their colour was heightened by the blood which still smeared her coat and reddened her mouth. I cried out:

'The cat! look out for the cat!' for even then she sprang out before the engine. At this moment she looked like a triumphant demon. Her eyes blazed with ferocity, her hair bristled out till she seemed twice her normal size, and her tail lashed about as does a tiger's when the quarry is before it. Elias P. Hutcheson when he saw her was amused, and his eyes positively sparkled with fun as he said:

'Darned if the squaw hain't got on all her war paint! Jest give her a shove off if she comes any of her tricks on me, for I'm so fixed everlastingly by the boss, that durn my skin if I can keep my eyes from her if she wants them! Easy there, Judge! Don't you slack that ar rope or I'm euchered!'

At this moment Amelia completed her faint, and I had to clutch hold of her round the waist or she would have fallen to the floor. Whilst attending to her I saw the black cat crouching for a spring, and jumped up to turn the creature out.

But at that instant, with a sort of hellish scream, she hurled herself, not as we expected at Hutcheson, but straight at the face of the custodian. Her claws seemed to be tearing wildly as one sees in the Chinese drawings of the dragon rampant, and as I looked I saw one of them light on the poor man's eye, and actually tear through it and down his cheek, leaving a wide band of red where the blood seemed to spurt from every vein.

With a yell of sheer terror which came quicker than even his sense of pain, the man leaped back, dropping as he did so the rope which held back the iron door. I jumped for it, but was too late, for the cord ran like lightning through the pulley-block, and the heavy mass fell forward from its own weight.

As the door closed I caught a glimpse of our poor companion's face. He seemed frozen with terror. His eyes stared with a horrible anguish as if dazed, and no sound came from his lips.

And then the spikes did their work. Happily the end was quick, for when I wrenched open the door they had pierced so deep that they had locked in the bones of the skull through which they had crushed, and actually tore him – it – out of his iron prison till, bound as he was, he fell at full length with a sickly thud upon the floor, the face turning upward as he fell.

I rushed to my wife, lifted her up and carried her out, for I feared for her very reason if she should wake from her faint to such a scene. I laid her on the bench outside and ran back. Leaning against the wooden column was the custodian moaning in pain whilst he held his reddening handkerchief to his eyes. And sitting on the head of the poor American was the cat, purring loudly as she licked the blood which trickled through the gashed sockets of his eyes.

I think no one will call me cruel because I seized one of the old executioner's swords and shore her in two as she sat.

THE CAT IN THE LIFEBOAT
James Thurber

A feline named William got a job as copy cat on a daily paper and was surprised to learn that every other cat on the paper was named Tom, Dick or Harry. He soon found out that he was the only cat named William in town. The fact of his singularity went to his head, and he began confusing it with distinction. It got so that whenever he saw or heard the name William, he thought it referred to him. His fantasies grew wilder and wilder, and he came to believe that he was the Will of Last Will and Testament, and the Willy of Willy Nilly, and the cat who put the cat in catnip. He finally became convinced that Cadillacs were Catillacs because of him.

William became so lost in his daydreams that he no longer heard the editor of the paper when he shouted, 'Copy cat!' and he became not only a ne'er-do-well, but a ne'er-do-anything. 'You're fired,' the editor told him one morning when he showed up for dreams.

'God will provide,' said William jauntily.

'God has his eye on the sparrow,' said the editor.

'So've I,' said William smugly.

William went to live with a cat-crazy woman who had nineteen other cats, but they could not stand William's egotism or the tall tales of his mythical exploits, honours, blue ribbons, silver cups, and medals, and so they all left the woman's house and went to live happily in huts and hovels. The cat-crazy woman changed her will and made William her sole heir, which seemed only natural to him, since he believed that all wills were drawn in his favour. 'I am eight feet tall,' William told her one day, and she smiled and said, 'I should say you are, and I am going to take you on a trip around the world and show you off to everybody.'

William and his mistress sailed one bitter March day on the S.S. *Forlorna*, which ran into heavy weather, high seas and hurricane. At midnight the cargo shifted in the towering seas, the ship listed menacingly, SOS calls were frantically sent out, rockets were fired into the sky, and the officers began running up and down companionways and corridors shouting, 'Abandon ship!' And then another shout arose, which seemed only natural to the egotistical cat. It was, his vain ears told him, the loud repetition of 'William and Children first!' Since William figured no lifeboat would be launched until he was safe and sound, he dressed leisurely, putting on white tie and tails, and then sauntered out on deck. He leaped lightly into a lifeboat that was being lowered, and found himself in the company of a little boy named Johnny Green and another little boy named Tommy Trout, and their mothers, and other children and their mothers. 'Toss that cat overboard!' cried the sailor in charge of the lifeboat, and Johnny Green threw him overboard, but Tommy Trout pulled him back in.

'Let *me* have that tomcat,' said the sailor, and he took William in his big right hand and threw him, like a long incompleted forward pass, about forty yards from the tossing lifeboat.

When William came to in the icy water, he had gone down for the twenty-fourth time, and had thus lost eight of his lives, so he only had one left. With his remaining life and strength he swam and swam until at last he reached the sullen shore of a sombre island inhabited by surly tigers, lions and other great cats. As William lay drenched and panting on the shore, a jaguar and a lynx walked up to him and asked him who he was and where he came from. Alas William's dreadful experience in the lifeboat and the sea had produced traumatic amnesia, and he could not remember who he was or where he came from.

'We'll call him Nobody,' said the jaguar.

'Nobody from Nowhere,' said the lynx.

And so William lived among the great cats on the island until he lost his ninth life in a bar-room brawl with a young panther who had asked him what his name was and where he came from and got what he considered an uncivil answer.

The great cats buried William in an unmarked grave because, as the jaguar said, 'What's the good of putting up a stone reading "Here lies Nobody from Nowhere"?'

THE PARADISE OF CATS
Emile Zola

An aunt bequeathed me an Angora cat, which is certainly the most stupid animal I know of. This is what my cat related to me, one winter night, before the warm embers.

I

I was then two years old, and I was certainly the fattest and most simple cat anyone could have seen. Even at that tender age I displayed all the presumption of an animal that scorns the attractions of the fireside. And yet what gratitude I owed to Providence for having placed me with your aunt! The worthy woman idolized me. I had a regular bedroom at the bottom of a cupboard, with a feather pillow and a triple-folded rug. The food was as good as the bed; no bread or soup, nothing but meat, good underdone meat.

Well! amidst all these comforts, I had but one wish, but one dream, to slip out by the half-open window, and run away on to the tiles. Caresses appeared to me insipid, the softness of my bed disgusted me, I was so fat that I felt sick, and from morn till eve I experienced the weariness of being happy.

I must tell you that by straining my neck I had perceived the opposite roof from the window. That day four cats were fighting there. With bristling coats and tails in the air, they were rolling on the blue slates, in the full sun, amidst oaths of joy. I had never witnessed such an extraordinary sight. From that moment my convictions were settled. Real happiness was upon that roof, in front of that window which the people of the house so carefully closed. I found the proof of this in the way in which they shut the doors of the cupboards where the meat was hidden.

I made up my mind to fly. I felt sure there were other things in life than underdone meat. There was the unknown, the ideal. One day they forgot to close the kitchen window. I sprang on to a small roof beneath it.

II

How beautiful the roofs were! They were bordered by broad gutters exhaling delicious odours. I followed those gutters in raptures of delight, my feet sinking into fine mud, which was deliciously warm and soft. I fancied I was walking on velvet. And the generous heat of the sun melted my fat.

I will not conceal from you the fact that I was trembling in every limb. My delight was mingled with terror. I remember, particularly, experiencing a terrible shock that almost made me tumble down into the street. Three cats came rolling over from the top of a house towards me, mewing most frightfully, and as I was on the point of fainting away, they called me a silly thing, and said they were mewing for fun. I began mewing to them. It was charming. The jolly fellows had none of my stupid fat. When I slipped on the sheets of zinc heated by the burning sun, they laughed at me. An old tom, who was one of the band, showed me particular friendship. He offered to teach me a thing or two, and I gratefully accepted. Ah! your aunt's cat's-meat was far from my thoughts! I drank in the gutters, and never had sugared milk seemed so sweet to me. Everything appeared nice and beautiful. A she-cat passed by, a charming she-cat, the sight of her gave me a feeling I had never experienced before. Hitherto, I had only seen these exquisite creatures, with such delightfully supple backbones, in my dreams. I and my three companions rushed forward to meet the newcomer. I was in front of the others, and was about to pay my respects to the bewitching thing, when one of my comrades cruelly bit my neck. I cried out with pain.

'Bah!' said the old tom, leading me away; 'you will meet with stranger adventures than that.'

III

After an hour's walk I felt as hungry as a wolf.

'What do you eat on the roofs?' I enquired of my friend the tom.

'What you can find,' he answered shrewdly.

This reply caused me some embarrassment, for though I carefully searched I found nothing. At last I perceived a young work-girl in a garret preparing her lunch. A beautiful chop of a tasty red colour was lying on a table under the window.

'That's the very thing I want,' I thought, in all simplicity.

And I sprang on to the table and took the chop. But the work-girl, having seen me, struck me a fearful blow with a broom on the spine, and I fled, uttering a dreadful oath.

'You are fresh from your village, then?' said the tom. 'Meat that is on tables is there for the purpose of being longed for at a distance. You must search in the gutters.'

I could never understand that kitchen meat did not belong to cats. My stomach was beginning to get seriously angry. The tom put me completely to despair by telling me it would be necessary to wait until night. Then we would go down into the street and turn over the heaps of muck. Wait until night! He said it quietly, like a hardened philosopher. I felt myself fainting at the mere thought of this prolonged fast.

IV

Night came slowly, a foggy night that chilled me to the bones. It soon began to rain, a fine, penetrating rain, driven by sudden gusts of wind. We went down along the glazed roof of a staircase. How ugly the street appeared to me! It was no longer that nice heat, that beautiful sun, those roofs white with light where one rolled about so deliciously. My paws slipped on the greasy stones. I sorrowfully recalled to memory my triple blanket and feather pillow.

We were hardly in the street when my friend the tom began to tremble. He made himself small, very small, and ran stealthily along beside the houses, telling me to follow as rapidly as possible. He rushed in at the first street door he came to, and purred with satisfaction as he sought refuge there. When I questioned him as to the motive of his flight, he answered:

'Did you see that man with a basket on his back and a stick with an iron hook at the end?'

'Yes.'

'Well! if he had seen us he would have knocked us on the heads and roasted us!'

'Roasted us!' I exclaimed. 'Then the street is not ours? One can't eat, but one's eaten!'

V

However, the boxes of kitchen refuse had been emptied before the street doors. I rummaged in the heaps in despair. I came across two or three bare bones that had been lying among the cinders, and then understood what a succulent dish fresh cat's-meat made. My friend the tom scratched artistically among the muck. He made me run about until morning, inspecting each heap, and without showing the least hurry. I was out in the rain for more than ten hours, shivering in every limb. Cursed street, cursed liberty, and how I regretted my prison!

At dawn the tom, seeing I was staggering, said to me with a strange air:

'Have you had enough of it?'

'Oh yes,' I answered.

'Do you want to go home?'

'I do, indeed; but how shall I find the house?'

'Come along. This morning, when I saw you come out, I understood that a fat cat like you was not made for the lively delights of liberty. I know your place of abode and will take you to the door.'

The worthy tom said this very quietly. When we had arrived, he bid me 'Good-bye', without betraying the least emotion.

'No,' I exclaimed, 'we will not leave each other so. You must accompany me. We will share the same bed and the same food. My mistress is a good woman—'

He would not allow me to finish my sentence.

'Hold your tongue,' he said sharply, 'you are a simpleton. Your effeminate existence would kill me. Your life of plenty is good for bastard cats. Free cats would never purchase your cat's-meat and feather pillow at the price of a prison. Good-bye.'

And he returned up on to the roofs, where I saw his long outline quiver with joy in the rays of the rising sun.

When I got in, your aunt took the whip and gave me a thrashing which I received with profound delight. I tasted in full measure the pleasure of being beaten and being warm. Whilst she was striking me, I thought with rapture of the meat she would give me afterwards.

VI

You see – concluded my cat, stretching itself out in front of the embers – real happiness, paradise, my dear master, consists of being shut up and beaten in a room where there is meat.

I am speaking from the point of view of cats.

PUSS IN BOOTS
Charles Perrault

There was a miller, who had left no more estate to the three sons he had, than his mill, his ass and his cat. The partition was soon made. Neither the scrivener nor attorney were sent for. They would soon have eaten up all the patrimony. The eldest had the mill, the second the ass and the youngest nothing but the cat.

The poor young fellow was quite comfortless at having so poor a lot. 'My brothers [said he] may get their living handsomely enough, by joining their stocks together; but for my part, when I have eaten up my cat, and made me a muff of his skin, I must die with hunger.' The Cat, who heard all this, but made as if he did not, said to him with a grave and serious air, 'Do not thus afflict yourself, my good master; you have nothing else to do, but to give me a bag, and get a pair of boots made for me, that I may scamper through the dirt and brambles, and you shall see that you have not so bad a portion of me as you imagine.'

Though the Cat's master did not build very much upon what he said, he had, however, often seen him play a great many cunning tricks to catch rats and mice; as when he used to hang by the heels, or hide himself in the meal, and make as if he were dead; so that he did not altogether despair of his affording him some help in his miserable condition. When the Cat had what he asked for, he booted himself very gallantly; and putting his bag about his neck, he held the strings of it in his forepaws, and went into a warren where was great abundance of rabbits. He put bran and sow-thistle into his bag, and stretching himself out at length, as if he had been dead, he waited for some young rabbits, not yet acquainted with the deceits of the world, to come and rummage his bag for what he had put into it.

Scarce was he laid down, but he had what he wanted; a rash and foolish young rabbit jumped into his bag, and Monsieur Puss, immediately drawing close the strings, took and killed him without pity. Proud of his prey, he went with it to the palace, and asked to speak with his Majesty. He was shown upstairs into the King's apartments and, making a low reverence, said to him, 'I have brought you, sir, a rabbit of the warren, which my noble Lord, the Marquis of Carabas [for that was the title which Puss was pleased to give his master] has commanded me to present to your Majesty from him.'

'Tell thy master [said the King] that I thank him, and that he does me a great deal of pleasure.'

Another time he went and hid himself among some standing corn, holding still his bag open; and when a brace of partridges ran into it, he drew the strings, and so caught them both. He went and made a present of them to the King, as he had done before of the rabbits which he took in the warren. The King, in like manner, received the partridges with great pleasure, and ordered him some money for drink.

The Cat continued for two or three months thus to carry his Majesty, from time to time, game of his master's taking. One day in particular, when he knew for certain that he was to take the air, along the riverside, with his daughter, the most beautiful princess in the world, he said to his master, 'If you will follow my advice, your fortune is made; you have nothing else to do, but go and wash yourself in the river, in that part I shall show you, and leave the rest to me.' The Marquis of Carabas did what the Cat advised him to, without knowing why or wherefore.

While he was washing, the King passed by, and the Cat began to cry out as loud as he could, 'Help, help, my Lord Marquis of Carabas is going to be drowned.' At this noise the King put his head out of the coach window and, finding it was the Cat who had often brought him such good game, he commanded his guards to run immediately to the assistance of his Lordship the Marquis of Carabas.

While they were drawing the poor Marquis out of the river, the Cat came up to the coach, and told the King that, 'While his master was washing there came by some rogues, who went off with his

Puss in Boots

clothes, though he had cried out, "Thieves! Thieves!" several times, as loud as he could.' This cunning Cat had hidden them under a great stone. The King immediately commanded the officers of his wardrobe to run and fetch one of his best suits for the Lord Marquis of Carabas.

The King caressed him after a very extraordinary manner; and as the fine clothes he had given him extremely set off his good mien (for he was well made and very handsome in his person), the King's daughter took a secret inclination to him, and the Marquis of Carabas had no sooner cast two or three respectful and somewhat tender glances, but she fell in love with him to distraction. The King would needs have him come into the coach, and partake of the airing. The Cat, quite overjoyed to see his project begin to succeed, marched on before and, meeting some countrymen who were mowing a meadow, he said to them, 'Good people, you who are mowing, if you do not tell the King that the meadow you mow belongs to my Lord Marquis of Carabas, you shall be chopped as small as herbs for the pot.'

The King did not fail of asking of the mowers, to whom the meadow they were mowing belonged; 'To my Lord Marquis of Carabas,' answered they all together; for the Cat's threats had made them terribly afraid. 'You see, sir [said the Marquis], this is a meadow which never fails to yield a plentiful harvest every year.' The Master Cat, who went still on before, met with some reapers, and said to them, 'Good people, you who are reaping, if you do not tell the King that all this corn belongs to the Marquis of Carabas, you shall be chopped as small as herbs for the pot.'

The King, who passed by a moment after, would needs know to whom all that corn, which he then saw, did belong; 'To my Lord Marquis of Carabas,' replied the reapers; and the King was very well pleased with it, as well as the Marquis, whom he congratulated thereupon. The Master Cat, who went always before, said the same words to all he met; and the King was astonished at the vast estates of my Lord Marquis of Carabas.

Monsieur Puss came at last to a stately castle, the master of which was an Ogre, the richest that had ever been known; for all the lands which the King had then gone over belonged, with this castle, to him. The Cat, who had taken care to inform himself who this Ogre was, and what he could do, asked to speak to him, saying, 'he could not pass so near the castle without having the honour of paying his respects to him'.

The Ogre received him as civilly as an Ogre could do, and made him sit down. 'I have been assured [said the Cat] that you have the gift of being able to change yourself into all sorts of creatures you have a mind to; you can, for example, transform yourself into a lion, or elephant, and the like.'

'This is true [answered the Ogre very briskly], and to convince you, you shall see me now become a lion.' Puss was so sadly terrified at the sight of a lion so near him, that he immediately got into the gutter, not without abundance of trouble and danger, because of his boots, which were of no use at all to him in walking upon the tiles. A little while after, when Puss saw that the Ogre had resumed his natural form, he came down, and owned he had been very much frightened.

'I have been moreover informed [said the Cat], but I know not how to believe it, that you have also the power to take upon you the shape of the smallest animals; for example, to change yourself into a rat or a mouse; but I must own to you, I take this to be impossible.'

'Impossible! [cried the Ogre]. You shall see that presently,' and at the same time changed himself into a mouse, and began to run about the floor. Puss no sooner perceived this, but he fell upon him and ate him up.

Meanwhile the King, who saw, as he passed, this fine castle of the Ogre, had a mind to go into it. Puss, who heard the noise of his Majesty's coach running over the drawbridge, ran out, and said to the King, 'Your Majesty is welcome to the castle of my Lord Marquis of Carabas.'

'What! my Lord Marquis [cried the King], and does this castle also belong to you? There can be nothing finer than this court, and all the stately buildings which surround it; let us go into it, if you please.' The Marquis gave his hand to the Princess, and followed the King, who went up first. They passed into a spacious hall, where they found a magnificent collation, which the Ogre had prepared for his friends, who were that very day to visit him, but dared not to enter, knowing the King was there.

His Majesty was perfectly charmed with the good qualities of my

Puss in Boots

Lord Marquis of Carabas, as was his daughter, who was fallen violently in love with him; and seeing the vast estate he possessed, said to him, after having drank five or six glasses, 'It will be owing to yourself only, my Lord Marquis, if you are not my Son-in-Law.' The Marquis, making several low bows, accepted the honour which his Majesty conferred upon him, and forthwith, that very same day, married the Princess.

Puss became a great Lord and never ran after mice any more, only for his diversion.

LILLIAN
Damon Runyon

What I always say is that Wilbur Willard is nothing but a very lucky guy, because what is it but luck that has been teetering along Forty-ninth Street one cold snowy morning when Lillian is mer-owing around the sidewalk looking for her mamma?

And what is it but luck that has Wilbur Willard all mulled up to a million, what with him having been sitting out a few seidels of Scotch with a friend by the name of Haggerty in an apartment over in Fifty-ninth Street? Because if Wilbur Willard is not mulled up he will see Lillian as nothing but a little black cat, and give her plenty of room, for everybody knows that black cats are terribly bad luck, even when they are only kittens.

But being mulled up like I tell you, things look very different to Wilbur Willard, and he does not see Lillian as a little black kitten scrabbling around in the snow. He sees a beautiful leopard, because a copper by the name of O'Hara, who is walking past about then, and who knows Wilbur Willard, hears him say:

'Oh, you beautiful leopard!'

The copper takes a quick peek himself, because he does not wish any leopards running around his beat, it being against the law, but all he sees, as he tells me afterwards, is this rumpot ham, Wilbur Willard, picking up a scrawny little black kitten and shoving it in his overcoat pocket, and he also hears Wilbur say:

'Your name is Lillian.'

Then Wilbur teeters on up to his room on the top floor of an old fleabag in Eighth Avenue that is called the Hotel de Brussels, where he lives quite a while, because the management does not mind actors, the management of the Hotel de Brussels being very broad-minded, indeed.

There is some complaint this same morning from one of Wilbur's neighbours, an old burlesque doll by the name of Minnie Madigan, who is not working since Abraham Lincoln is assassinated, because she hears Wilbur going on in his rooms about a beautiful leopard, and calls up the clerk to say that an hotel which allows wild animals is not respectable. But the clerk looks in on Wilbur and finds him playing with nothing but a harmless-looking little black kitten, and nothing comes of the old doll's beef, especially as nobody ever claims the Hotel de Brussels is respectable anyway, or at least not much.

Of course when Wilbur comes out from under the ether next afternoon he can see Lillian is not a leopard, and in fact Wilbur is quite astonished to find himself in bed with a little black kitten, because it seems Lillian is sleeping on Wilbur's chest to keep warm. At first Wilbur does not believe what he sees, and puts it down to Haggerty's Scotch, but finally he is convinced, and so he puts Lillian in his pocket, and takes her over to the Hot Box night club and gives her some milk, of which it seems Lillian is very fond.

Now where Lillian comes from in the first place of course nobody knows. The chances are somebody chucks her out of a window into the snow, because people are always chucking kittens, and one thing and another, out of windows in New York. In fact, if there is one thing this town has plenty of, it is kittens, which finally grow up to be cats, and go snooping around ash cans, and mer-owing on roofs, and keeping people from sleeping good.

Personally, I have no use for cats, including kittens, because I never see one that has any too much sense, although I know a guy by the name of Pussy McGuire who makes a first-rate living doing nothing but stealing cats, and sometimes dogs, and selling them to old dolls who like such things for company. But Pussy only steals Persian and Angora cats, which are very fine cats, and of course Lillian is no such cat as this. Lillian is nothing but a black cat, and nobody will give you a dime a dozen for black cats in this town, as they are generally regarded as very bad jinxes.

Furthermore, it comes out in a few weeks that Wilbur Willard can just as well name her Herman, or Sidney, as not, but Wilbur sticks to Lillian, because this is the name of his partner when he is in vaudeville years ago. He often tells me about Lillian Withington when he is mulled up, which is more often than somewhat, for Wilbur is a great hand for drinking Scotch, or rye, or bourbon, or gin, or whatever else there is around for drinking, except water. In fact, Wilbur Willard is a high-class drinking man, and it does no good to tell him it is against the law to drink in this country, because it only makes him mad, and he says to the dickens with the law, only Wilbur Willard uses a much rougher word than dickens.

'She is like a beautiful leopard,' Wilbur says to me about Lillian Withington. 'Black-haired, and black-eyed, and all ripply, like a leopard I see in an animal act on the same bill at the Palace with us once. We are headliners then,' he says, 'Willard and Withington, the best singing and dancing act in the country.

'I pick her up in San Antonio, which is a spot in Texas,' Wilbur says. 'She is not long out of a convent, and I just lose my old partner, Mary McGee, who ups and dies on me of pneumonia down there. Lillian wishes to go on the stage, and joins out with me. A natural-born actress with a great voice. But like a leopard,' Wilbur says. 'Like a leopard. There is cat in her, no doubt of this, and cats and women are both ungrateful. I love Lillian Withington. I wish to marry her. But she is cold to me. She says she is not going to follow the stage all her life. She says she wishes money, and luxury, and a fine home and of course a guy like me cannot give a doll such things.

'I wait on her hand and foot,' Wilbur says. 'I am her slave. There is nothing I will not do for her. Then one day she walks in on me in Boston very cool and says she is quitting me. She says she is marrying a rich guy there. Well, naturally it busts up the act and I never have the heart to look for another partner, and then I get to belting that old black bottle around, and now what am I but a cabaret performer?'

Then sometimes he will bust out crying, and sometimes I will cry with him, although the way I look at it, Wilbur gets a pretty fair break, at that, in getting rid of a doll who wishes things he cannot give her. Many a guy in this town is tangled up with a doll who wishes things he cannot give her, but who keeps him tangled up just the same and busting himself trying to keep her quiet.

Wilbur makes pretty fair money as an entertainer in the Hot Box, though he spends most of it for Scotch, and he is not a bad entertainer, either. I often go to the Hot Box when I am feeling blue to hear him sing Melancholy Baby, and Moonshine Valley and other sad songs which break my heart. Personally, I do not see why any doll cannot love Wilbur, especially if they listen to him sing such songs as Melancholy Baby when he is mulled up good, because he is a tall, nice-looking guy with long eyelashes, and sleepy brown eyes, and his voice has a low moaning sound that usually goes very big with the dolls. In fact, many a doll does do some pitching to Wilbur when he is singing in the Hot Box, but somehow Wilbur never gives them a tumble, which I suppose is because he is thinking only of Lillian Withington.

Well, after he gets Lillian, the black kitten, Wilbur seems to find a new interest in life, and Lillian turns out to be right cute, and not bad-looking after Wilbur gets her fed up good. She is blacker than a yard up a chimney, with not a white spot on her, and she grows so fast that by and by Wilbur cannot carry her in his pocket any more, so he puts a collar on her and leads her round. So Lillian becomes very well known on Broadway, what with Wilbur taking her many places, and finally she does not even have to be led around by Willard, but follows him like a pooch. And in all the Roaring Forties there is no pooch that cares to have any truck with Lillian, for she will leap aboard them quicker than you can say scat, and scratch and bite them until they are very glad indeed to get away from her.

But of course the pooches in the Forties are mainly nothing but Chows, and Pekes, and Poms, or little woolly white poodles, which are led around by blonde dolls, and are not fit to take their own part against a smart cat. In fact, Wilbur Willard is finally not on speaking terms with any doll that owns a pooch between Times Square and Columbus Circle, and they are all hoping that both Wilbur and Lillian will go lay down and die somewhere. Furthermore, Wilbur has a couple of battles with guys who also belong to the dolls, but Wilbur is no sucker in a battle if he is not mulled up too much and leg-weary.

After he is through entertaining people in the Hot Box, Wilbur generally goes around to any speakeasies which may still be open, and does a little off-hand drinking on top of what he already drinks down in the Hot Box, which is plenty, and although it is considered very risky in this town to mix Hot Box liquor with any other, it never seemed to bother Wilbur. Along towards daylight he takes a couple of bottles of Scotch over to his room in the Hotel de Brussels and uses them for a nightcap, so by the time Wilbur Willard is ready to slide off to sleep he has plenty of liquor of one kind and another inside him, and he sleeps pretty.

Of course nobody on Broadway blames Wilbur so very much for being such a rumpot, because they know about him loving Lillian Withington, and losing her, and it is considered a reasonable excuse in this town for a guy to do some drinking when he loses a doll, which is why there is so much drinking here, but it is a mystery to one and all how Wilbur stands off all this liquor without croaking. The cemeteries are full of guys who do a lot less drinking than Wilbur, but he never even seems to feel extra tough, or if he does he keeps it to himself and does not go around saying it is the kind of liquor you get nowadays.

He costs some of the boys around Mindy's plenty of dough one winter, because he starts in doing most of his drinking after hours in Good Time Charley's speakeasy, and the boys lay a price of four to one against him lasting until spring, never figuring a guy can drink very much of Good Time Charley's liquor and keep on living. But Wilbur Willard does it just the same, so everybody says the guy is naturally superhuman, and lets it go at that.

Sometimes Wilbur drops into Mindy's with Lillian following him on the lookout for pooches, or riding on his shoulder if the weather is bad, and the two of them will sit with us for hours chewing the rag about one thing and another. At such times Wilbur generally has a bottle on his hip and takes a shot now and then, but of course this does not come under the head of serious drinking with him. When Lillian is with Wilbur she always lays as close to him as she can get and anybody can see that she seems to be very fond of Wilbur, and that he is very fond of her, although he sometimes forgets himself and speaks of her as a beautiful leopard. But of course this is only a slip of the tongue, and anyway if Wilbur gets any pleasure out of thinking Lillian is a leopard, it is nobody's business but his own.

'I suppose she will run away from me some day,' Wilbur says, running his hand over Lillian's back until her fur crackles. 'Yet, although I give her plenty of liver and catnip, and one thing and another, and all my affection, she will probably give me the shake. Cats are like women, and women are like cats. They are both very ungrateful.'

'They are both generally bad luck,' Big Nig, the crap shooter, says. 'Especially cats, and most especially black cats.'

Many other guys tell Wilbur about black cats being bad luck, and advise him to slip Lillian into the North River some night with a sinker on her, but Wilbur claims he already has all the bad luck in the world when he loses Lillian Withington, and that Lillian, the cat, cannot make it any worse, so he goes on taking extra good care of her, and Lillian goes on getting bigger and bigger, until I commence thinking maybe there is some St Bernard in her.

Finally I commence to notice something funny about Lillian. Sometimes she will be acting very loving towards Wilbur, and then again she will be very unfriendly to him, and will spit at him, and snatch at him with her claws, very hostile. It seems to me that she is all right when Willard is mulled up, but is as sad and fretful as he is himself when he is only a little bit mulled. And when Lillian is sad and fretful she makes it very tough indeed on the pooches in the neighbourhood of the Brussels.

In fact, Lillian takes to pooch-hunting, sneaking off when Wilbur is getting his rest, and running pooches bow-legged, especially when she finds one that is not on a leash. A loose pooch is just naturally cherry pie for Lillian.

Well, of course, this causes great indignation among the dolls who own the pooches, particularly when Lillian comes home one day carrying a Peke as big as she is herself by the scruff of the neck, and with a very excited blonde doll following her and yelling bloody murder outside Wilbur Willard's door when Lillian pops into Wilbur's room through a hole he cuts in the door for her, still lugging the Peke. But it seems that instead of being mad at Lillian and giving her a pasting for such goings on, Wilbur is somewhat pleased, because he happens to be still in a fog when Lillian arrives with the Peke, and is thinking of Lillian as a beautiful leopard.

'Why,' Wilbur says, 'this is devotion, indeed. My beautiful leopard goes off into the jungle and fetches me an antelope for dinner.'

Now of course there is no sense whatever to this, because a Peke is certainly not anything like an antelope, but the blonde doll outside Wilbur's door hears Wilbur mumble, and gets the idea that he is going to eat her Peke for dinner and the squawk she puts up is very terrible. There is plenty of trouble around the Brussels in chilling the blonde doll's beef over Lillian snagging her Peke, and what is more the blonde doll's ever-loving guy, who turns out to be a tough Ginney bootlegger by the name of Gregorio, shows up at the Hot Box the next night and wishes to put the slug on Wilbur Willard.

But Wilbur rounds him up with a few drinks and by singing Melancholy Baby to him, and before he leaves the Ginney gets very sentimental towards Wilbur, and Lillian, too, and wishes to give Wilbur five bucks to let Lillian grab the Peke again, if Lillian will promise not to bring it back. It seems Gregorio does not really care for the Peke, and is only acting quarrelsome to please the blonde doll and make her think he loves her dearly.

But I can see Lillian is having different moods, and finally I ask Wilbur if he notices it.

'Yes,' he says, very sad, 'I do not seem to be holding her love. She is getting very fickle. A guy moves on to my floor at the Brussels the other day with a little boy and Lillian becomes very fond of this kid at once. In fact they are great friends. Ah, well,' Wilbur says, 'cats are like women. Their affection does not last.'

I happen to go over to the Brussels a few days later to explain to a guy by the name of Crutchy, who lives on the same floor as Wilbur Willard, that some of our citizens do not like his face and that it may be a good idea for him to leave town, especially if he insists on bringing ale into their territory, and I see Lillian out in the hall with a youngster which I judge is the kid Wilbur is talking about. This kid is maybe three years old, and very cute, what with black hair, and black eyes, and he is woolling Lillian around the hall in a way that is most surprising, for Lillian is not such a cat as will stand for much woolling around, not even from Wilbur Willard.

I am wondering how anybody comes to take such a kid to a joint like the Brussels, but I figure it is some actor's kid, and that maybe there is no mamma for it. Later I am talking to Wilbur about this, and he says:

'Well, if the kid's old man is an actor, he is not working at it. He sticks close to his room all the time, and he does not allow the kid to go anywhere but in the hall, and I feel sorry for the little guy, which is why I allow Lillian to play with him.'

Now it comes on a very cold spell, and a bunch of us are sitting in Mindy's along towards five o'clock in the morning when we hear fire engines going past. By and by in comes a guy by the name of Kansas, who is named Kansas because he comes from Kansas, and who is a crap-shooter by trade.

'The old Brussels is on fire,' this guy Kansas says.

'She is always on fire,' Big Nig says, meaning there is always plenty of hot stuff going on around the Brussels.

About this time who walks in but Wilbur Willard, and anybody can see he is just naturally floating. The chances are he comes from Good Time Charley's, and he is certainly carrying plenty of pressure. I never see Wilbur Willard mulled up more. He does not have Lillian with him, but then he never takes Lillian to Good Time Charley's, because Charley hates cats.

'Hey, Wilbur,' Big Nig says, 'your joint, the Brussels, is on fire.'

'Well,' Wilbur says, 'I am a little firefly, and I need a light. Let us go where there is fire.'

The Brussels is only a few blocks from Mindy's, and there is nothing else to do just then, so some of us walk over to Eighth Avenue with Wilbur teetering along ahead of us. The old shack is certainly roaring good when we get in sight of it, and the firemen are tossing water into it, and the coppers have the fire lines out to keep the crowd back, although there is not much of a crowd at such an hour in the morning.

'Is it not beautiful?' Wilbur Willard says, looking up at the flames. 'Is it not like a fairy palace all lighted up this way?'

You see, Wilbur does not realize the joint is on fire, although guys and dolls are running out of it every which way, most of them half dressed, or not dressed at all, and the firemen are getting out the life nets in case anybody wishes to hop out of the windows.

'It is certainly beautiful,' Wilbur says. 'I must get Lillian so she can see this.'

And before anybody has time to think, there is Wilbur Willard walking into the front door of the Brussels as if nothing happens. The firemen and the coppers are so astonished all they can do is holler at Wilbur, but he pays no attention whatever. Well, naturally everybody figures Wilbur is a gone gosling, but in about ten minutes he comes walking out of this same door through the fire and smoke as cool as you please, and he has Lillian in his arms.

'You know,' Wilbur says, coming over to where we are standing with our eyes popping out, 'I have to walk all the way up to my floor because the elevators seem to be out of commission. The service is getting terrible in this hotel. I will certainly make a strong beef to the management about it as soon as I pay something on my account.'

Then what happens but Lillian lets out a big mer-ow, and hops out of Wilbur's arms and skips past the coppers and the firemen with her back all humped up, and the next thing anybody knows she is tearing through the front door of the old hotel and making plenty of speed.

'Well, well,' Wilbur says, looking much surprised, 'there goes Lillian.'

And what does this daffy Wilbur Willard do but turn and go marching back into the Brussels again, and by this time the smoke is pouring out of the front doors so thick he is out of sight in a second. Naturally he takes the coppers and firemen by surprise, because they are not used to guys walking in and out of fires on them.

This time anybody standing around will lay you plenty of odds – two and a half and maybe three to one that Wilbur never shows up again, because the old Brussels is now just popping with fire and smoke from the lower windows, although there does not seem to be quite so much fire in the upper storey. Everybody seems to be out of the joint, and even the firemen are fighting the blaze from the outside because the Brussels is so old and ramshackly there is no sense in them risking the floors.

I mean everybody is out of the joint except Wilbur Willard and Lillian, and we figure they are getting a good frying somewhere inside, although Feet Samuels is around offering to take thirteen to five for a few small bets that Lillian comes out okay, because Feet claims that a cat has nine lives and that is a fair bet at the price.

Well, up comes a swell-looking doll all heated up about something and pushing and clawing her way through the crowd up to the ropes and screaming until you can hardly hear yourself think, and about this same minute everybody hears a voice going *ai-lee-hi-heé-hoo*, like a Swiss yodeller, which comes from the roof of the Brussels, and looking up what do we see but Wilbur Willard standing up there on the edge of the roof, high above the fire and smoke, and yodelling very loud.

Under one arm he has a big bundle of some kind, and under the other he has the little kid I see playing in the hall with Lillian. As he stands up there going *ai-lee-hi-heé-hoo*, the swell-dressed doll near us begins yipping louder than Wilbur is yodelling, and the firemen rush over under him with a life net.

Wilbur lets go another *ai-lee-hi-heé-hoo*, and down he comes all spraddled out, with the bundle and the kid, but he hits the net sitting down and bounces up and back again for a couple of minutes before he finally settles. In fact, Wilbur is enjoying the bouncing, and the chances are he will be bouncing yet if the firemen do not drop their hold on the net and let him fall to the ground.

Then Wilbur steps out of the net, and I can see the bundle is a rolled-up blanket with Lillian's eyes peeking out of one end. He still had the kid under the other arm with his head stuck out in front, and his legs stuck out behind, and it does not seem to me that Wilbur is handling the kid as careful as he is handling Lillian. He stands there looking at the firemen with a very sneering look, and finally he says:

'Do not think you can catch me in your net unless I wish to be caught. I am a butterfly, and very hard to overtake.'

Then all of a sudden the swell-dressed doll who is doing so much hollering, piles on top of Wilbur and grabs the kid from him and begins hugging and kissing it.

'Wilbur,' she says, 'God bless you, Wilbur, for saving my baby! Oh, thank you, Wilbur, thank you! My wretched husband kidnaps and runs away with him, and it is only a few hours ago that my detectives find out where he is.'

Wilbur gives the doll a funny look for about half a minute and starts to walk away, but Lillian comes wiggling out of the blanket, looking and smelling pretty much singed up, and the kid sees Lillian and begins hollering for her, so Wilbur finally hands Lillian over to the kid. And not wishing to leave Lillian, Wilbur stands around somewhat confused, and the doll gets talking to him, and finally they go away together, and as they go Wilbur is carrying the kid, and the kid is carrying Lillian, and Lillian is not feeling so good from her burns.

Furthermore, Wilbur is probably more sober than he ever is before in years at this hour in the morning, but before they go I get a chance to talk some to Wilbur when he is still rambling somewhat, and I make out from what he says that the first time he goes to get Lillian he finds her in his room and does not see hide or hair of the little kid and does not even think of him, because he does not know what room the kid is in, anyway, having never noticed such a thing.

But the second time he goes up, Lillian is sniffing at the crack under the door of a room down the hall from Wilbur's and Wilbur says he seems to remember seeing a trickle of something like water coming out of the crack.

'And,' Wilbur says, 'as I am looking for a blanket for Lillian, and it will be a bother to go back to my room, I figure I will get one out of this room. I try the knob but the door is locked, so I kick it in, and walk in to find the room full of smoke, and fire is shooting through the windows very lovely, and when I grab a blanket off the bed for Lillian, what is under the blanket but the kid?

'Well,' Wilbur says, 'the kid is squawking, and Lillian is merowing, and there is so much confusion generally that it makes me nervous, so I figure we better go up on the roof and let the stink blow off us, and look at the fire from there. It seems there is a guy stretched out on the floor of the room alongside an upset table between the door and the bed. He has a bottle in one hand, and he is dead. Well, naturally there is no percentage in lugging a dead guy along, so I take Lillian and the kid and go up on the roof, and we just naturally fly off like humming birds. Now I must get a drink,' Wilbur says, 'I wonder if anybody has anything on their hip? '

Well, the papers are certainly full of Wilbur and Lillian the next day, especially Lillian, and they are both great heroes.

But Wilbur cannot stand the publicity very long, because he never has any time to himself for his drinking, what with the scribes and the photographers hopping on him every few minutes wishing to hear his story, and to take more pictures of him and Lillian, so one night he disappears, and Lillian disappears with him.

About a year later it comes out that he marries his old doll, Lillian Withington-Harmon, and falls into a lot of dough, and what is more he cuts out the liquor and becomes quite a useful citizen one way and another. So everybody has to admit that black cats are not always bad luck, although I say Wilbur's case is a little exceptional because he does not start out knowing Lillian is a black cat, but thinking she is a leopard.

I happen to run into Wilbur one day all dressed up in good clothes and jewellery and chucking quite a swell.

'Wilbur,' I say to him, 'I often think how remarkable it is the way Lillian suddenly gets such an attachment for the little kid and remembers about him being in the hotel and leads you back there a second time to the right room. If I do not see this come off with my own eyes, I will never believe a cat has brains enough to do such a thing, because I consider cats extra dumb.'

'Brains nothing,' Wilbur says. 'Lillian does not have brains enough to grease a gimlet. And what is more, she has no more attachment for the kid than a jack rabbit. The time has come,' Wilbur says, 'to expose Lillian. She gets a lot of credit which is never coming to her. I will now tell you about Lillian, and nobody knows this but me.

'You see,' Wilbur says, 'when Lillian is a little kitten I always put a little Scotch in her milk, partly to help make her good and strong, and partly because I am never no hand to drink alone, unless there is nobody with me. Well, at first Lillian does not care so much for this Scotch in her milk, but finally she takes a liking to it, and I keep making her toddy stronger until in the end she will lap up a good big snort without any milk for a chaser, and yell for more. In fact, I suddenly realize that Lillian becomes a rumpot, just like I am in those days, and simply must have her grog, and it is when she is good and rummed up that Lillian goes off snatching Pekes, and acting tough generally.

'Now,' Wilbur says, 'the time of the fire is about the time I get home every morning and give Lillian her schnapps. But when I go into the hotel and get her the first time I forget to Scotch her up, and the reason she runs back into the hotel is because she is looking for her shot. And the reason she is sniffing at the kid's door is not because the kid is in there but because the trickle that is coming through the crack under the door is nothing but Scotch that is running out of the bottle in the dead guy's hand. I never mention this before because I figure it may be a knock to a dead guy's memory,' Wilbur says. 'Drinking is certainly a disgusting thing, especially secret drinking.'

'But how is Lillian getting along these days?' I ask Wilbur Willard.

'I am greatly disappointed in Lillian,' he says. 'She refuses to reform when I do, and the last I hear of her she takes up with Gregorio, the Ginney bootlegger, who keeps her well Scotched up all the time so she will lead his blonde doll's Peke a dog's life.'

THE BLACK CAT
Edgar Allan Poe

For the most wild yet most homely narrative which I am about to pen, I neither expect nor solicit belief. Mad indeed would I be to expect it, in a case where my very senses reject their own evidence. Yet, mad I am not – and very surely do I not dream. But tomorrow I die, and today I would unburden my soul. My immediate purpose is to place before the world, plainly, succinctly, and without comment, a series of mere household events. In their consequences, these events have terrified – have tortured – have destroyed me. Yet I will not attempt to expound them. To me, they have presented little but horror – to many they will seem less terrible than *baroques*.

Hereafter, perhaps, some intellect may be found which will reduce my phantasm to the commonplace – some intellect more calm, more logical, and far less excitable than my own, which will perceive, in the circumstances I detail with awe, nothing more than an ordinary succession of very natural causes and effects.

From my infancy I was noted for the docility and humanity of my disposition. My tenderness of heart was even so conspicuous as to make me the jest of my companions. I was especially fond of animals, and was indulged by my parents with a great variety of pets. With these I spent most of my time, and never was so happy as when feeding and caressing them. This peculiarity of character grew with my growth, and, in my manhood, I derived from it one of my principal sources of pleasure. To those who have cherished an affection for a faithful and sagacious dog, I need hardly be at the trouble of explaining the nature or the intensity of the gratification thus derivable. There is something in the unselfish and self-sacrificing love of a brute, which goes directly to the heart of him who has had frequent occasion to test the paltry friendship and gossamer fidelity of mere *Man*.

I married early, and was happy to find in my wife a disposition not uncongenial with my own. Observing my partiality for domestic pets, she lost no opportunity of procuring those of the most agreeable kind. We had birds, goldfish, a fine dog, rabbits, a small monkey, and a *cat*.

This latter was a remarkably large and beautiful animal, entirely black, and sagacious to an astonishing degree. In speaking of his intelligence, my wife, who at heart was not a little tinctured with superstition, made frequent allusion to the ancient popular notion, which regarded all black cats as witches in disguise. Not that she was ever *serious* upon this point – and I mention the matter at all for no better reason than that it happens, just now, to be remembered.

Pluto – this was the cat's name – was my favourite pet and playmate. I alone fed him, and he attended me wherever I went about the house. It was even with difficulty that I could prevent him from following me through the streets.

Our friendship lasted, in this manner, for several years, during which my general temperament and character – through the instrumentality of the Fiend Intemperance – had (I blush to confess it) experienced a radical alteration for the worse. I grew, day by day, more moody, more irritable, more regardless of the feelings of others. I suffered myself to use intemperate language to my wife. At length, I even offered her personal violence. My pets, of course, were made to feel the change in my disposition. I not only neglected, but ill-used them. For Pluto, however, I still retained sufficient regard to restrain me from maltreating him, as I made no scruple of maltreating the rabbits, the monkey, or even the dog, when, by accident, or through affection, they came in my way. But my disease grew upon me – for what disease is like Alcohol! – and at length even Pluto, who was now becoming old, and consequently somewhat peevish – even Pluto began to experience the effects of my ill temper.

One night, returning home, much intoxicated, from one of my haunts about town, I fancied that the cat avoided my presence. I seized him; then, in his fright at my violence, he inflicted a slight wound upon my hand with his teeth. The fury of a demon instantly possessed me. I knew myself no longer. My original soul seemed, at once, to take its flight from my body; and a more than fiendish malevolence, gin-nurtured, thrilled every fibre of my frame. I took from my waistcoat-pocket a penknife, opened it, grasped the poor beast by the throat and deliberately cut one of its eyes from the socket! I blush, I burn, I shudder, while I pen the damnable atrocity.

When reason returned with the morning – when I had slept off the fumes of the night's debauch – I experienced a sentiment half of horror, half of remorse, for the crime of which I had been guilty; but it was, at best, a feeble and equivocal feeling, and the soul remained untouched. I again plunged into excess, and soon drowned in wine all memory of the deed.

In the meantime the cat slowly recovered. The socket of the lost eye presented, it is true, a frightful appearance, but he no longer appeared to suffer any pain. He went about the house as usual, but, as might be expected, fled in extreme terror at my approach. I had so much of my old heart left, as to be at first grieved by this evident dislike on the part of a creature which had once so loved me. But this feeling soon gave place to irritation. And then came, as if to my final and irrevocable overthrow, the spirit of PERVERSENESS. Of this spirit philosophy takes no account. Yet I am not more sure that my soul lives, than I am that perverseness is one of the primitive impulses of the human heart – one of the indivisible primary faculties, or sentiments, which give direction to the character of Man. Who has not, a hundred times, found himself committing a vile or a stupid action, for no other reason than because he knows he should *not*? Have we not a perpetual inclination, in the teeth of our best judgement, to violate that which is *Law*, merely because we understand it to be such? This spirit of perverseness, I say, came to my final overthrow. It was this unfathomable longing of the soul *to vex itself* – to offer violence to its own nature – to do wrong for the wrong's sake only – that urged me to continue and finally to consummate the injury I had inflicted upon the unoffending brute. One morning, in cold blood, I slipped a noose about its neck and hung it to the limb of a tree – hung it with the tears streaming from my eyes, and with the bitterest remorse at my heart; hung it *because* I knew that it had loved me, and *because* I felt it had given me no reason of offence; hung it *because* I knew that in so doing I was committing a sin – a deadly sin that would so jeopardize my immortal soul as to place it – if such a thing were possible – even beyond the reach of the infinite mercy of the Most Merciful and Most Terrible God.

On the night of the day on which this most cruel deed was done, I was aroused from sleep by the cry of 'Fire!' The curtains of my bed were in flames. The whole house was blazing. It was with great difficulty that my wife, a servant, and myself, made our escape from the conflagration. The destruction was complete. My entire worldly wealth was swallowed up, and I resigned myself thenceforward to despair.

I am above the weakness of seeking to establish a sequence of cause and effect, between the disaster and the atrocity. But I am detailing a chain of facts – and wish not to leave even a possible link imperfect. On the day succeeding the fire, I visited the ruins. The walls, with one exception, had fallen in. This exception was found in a compartment wall, not very thick, which stood about the middle of the house, and against which had rested the head of my bed. The plastering had here, in great measure, resisted the action of the fire – a fact which I attributed to its having been recently spread. About this wall a dense crowd were collected, and many persons seemed to be examining a particular portion of it with very minute and eager attention. The words 'strange!' 'singular!' and other similar expressions, excited my curiosity. I approached and saw, as if graven in bas-relief upon the white surface, the figure of a gigantic *cat*. The impression was given with an accuracy truly marvellous. There was a rope about the animal's neck.

When I first beheld this apparition – for I could scarcely regard it as less – my wonder and my terror were extreme. But at length reflection came to my aid. The cat, I remembered, had been hung in a garden adjacent to the house. Upon the alarm of fire, this garden had been immediately filled by the crowd – by some one of whom the animal must have been cut from the tree and thrown, through an open window, into my chamber. This had probably been done with the view of arousing me from sleep. The falling of other walls had compressed the victim of my cruelty into the substance of the freshly spread plaster; the lime of which, with the flames, and the ammonia from the carcass, had then accomplished the portraiture as I saw it.

Although I thus readily accounted to my reason, if not altogether to my conscience, for the startling fact just detailed, it did not the less fail to make a deep impression upon my fancy. For months I could not rid myself of the phantasm of the cat; and, during this period, there came back into my spirit a half-sentiment that seemed, but was not, remorse. I went so far as to regret the loss of the animal, and to look about me, among the vile haunts which I now habitually frequented, for another pet of the same species, and of somewhat similar appearance, with which to supply its place.

One night as I sat, half stupefied, in a den of more than infamy, my attention was suddenly drawn to some black object, reposing upon the head of one of the immense hogsheads of gin, or of rum, which constituted the chief furniture of the apartment. I had been looking steadily at the top of this hogshead for some minutes, and what now caused me surprise was the fact that I had not sooner perceived the object thereupon. I approached it, and touched it with my hand. It was a black cat – a very large one – fully as large as Pluto, and closely resembling him in every respect but one. Pluto had not a white hair upon any portion of his body; but this cat had a large, although indefinite splotch of white, covering nearly the whole region of the breast.

Upon my touching him, he immediately arose, purred loudly, rubbed against my hand, and appeared delighted with my notice. This, then, was the very creature of which I was in search. I at once tried to purchase it of the landlord; but this person made no claim to it – knew nothing of it – had never seen it before.

I continued my caresses, and when I prepared to go home, the animal evinced a disposition to accompany me. I permitted it to do so; occasionally stooping and patting it as I proceeded. When it reached the house it domesticated itself at once, and became immediately a great favourite with my wife.

For my own part, I soon found a dislike to it arising within me. This was just the reverse of what I had anticipated; but – I knew not how or why it was – its evident fondness for myself rather disgusted and annoyed me. By slow degrees these feelings of disgust and annoyance rose into the bitterness of hatred. I avoided the creature; a certain sense of shame, and the remembrance of my former deed of cruelty, preventing me from physically abusing it. I did not, for some weeks, strike, or otherwise violently ill use it; but gradually – very gradually – I came to look upon it with unutterable loathing, and to flee silently from its odious presence, as from the breath of a pestilence.

What added, no doubt, to my hatred of the beast, was the discovery, on the morning after I brought it home, that, like Pluto, it also had been deprived of one of its eyes. This circumstance, however, only endeared it to my wife, who, as I have already said, possessed, in a high degree, that humanity of feeling which had once been my distinguishing trait, and the source of many of my simplest and purest pleasures.

With my aversion to this cat, however, its partiality for myself seemed to increase. It followed my footsteps with a pertinacity which it would be difficult to make the reader comprehend. Whenever I sat, it would crouch beneath my chair, or spring upon my knees, covering me with its loathsome caresses. If I arose to walk it would get between my feet and thus nearly throw me down, or, fastening its long and sharp claws in my dress, clamber, in this manner, to my breast. At such times, although I longed to destroy it with a blow, I was yet withheld from so doing, partly by a memory of my former crime, but chiefly – let me confess it at once – by absolute *dread* of the beast.

This dread was not exactly a dread of physical evil – and yet I should be at a loss how otherwise to define it. I am almost ashamed to own – yes, even in this felon's cell, I am almost ashamed to own – that the terror and horror with which the animal inspired me, had been heightened by one of the merest chimeras it would be possible to conceive. My wife had called my attention, more than once, to the character of the mark of white hair, of which I have spoken, and which constituted the sole visible difference between the strange beast and the one I had destroyed. The reader will remember that this mark, although large, had been originally very indefinite; but, by slow degrees – degrees nearly imperceptible, and which for a long time my reason struggled to reject as fanciful – it had, at length, assumed a rigorous distinctness of outline. It was now the representation of an object that I shudder to name – and for this, above all, I loathed and dreaded, and would have rid myself of the monster *had I dared* – it was now, I say, the image of a hideous – of a ghastly thing – of the GALLOWS! – oh, mournful and terrible engine of Horror and of Crime – of Agony and of Death!

And now was I indeed wretched beyond the wretchedness of mere Humanity. And *a brute beast* – whose fellow I had contemptuously destroyed – *a brute beast* to work out for *me* – for me, a man fashioned in the image of the High God – so much of insufferable woe! Alas! neither by day nor by night knew I the blessing of rest any more! During the former the creature left me no moment alone, and in the latter I started hourly from dreams of unutterable fear to find the hot breath of *the thing* upon my face, and its vast weight – an incarnate nightmare that I had no power to shake off – incumbent eternally upon my *heart*!

Beneath the pressure of torments such as these the feeble remnant of the good within me succumbed. Evil thoughts became my sole intimates – the darkest and most evil of thoughts. The moodiness of my usual temper increased to hatred of all things and of all mankind; while from the sudden, frequent, and ungovernable outbursts of a fury to which I now blindly abandoned myself, my uncomplaining wife, alas, was the most usual and the most patient of sufferers.

One day she accompanied me, upon some household errand, into the cellar of the old building which our poverty compelled us to inhabit. The cat followed me down the steep stairs, and, nearly throwing me headlong, exasperated me to madness. Uplifting an axe, and forgetting in my wrath the childish dread which had hitherto stayed my hand, I aimed a blow at the animal, which, of course, would have proved instantly fatal had it descended as I wished. But this blow was arrested by the hand of my wife. Goaded by the interference into a rage more than demoniacal, I withdrew my arm from her grasp and buried the axe in her brain. She fell dead upon the spot without a groan.

This hideous murder accomplished, I set myself forthwith, and with entire deliberation, to the task of concealing the body. I knew that I could not remove it from the house, either by day or by night, without the risk of being observed by the neighbours. Many projects entered my mind. At one period I thought of cutting the corpse into minute fragments, and destroying them by fire. At another, I resolved to dig a grave for it in the floor of the cellar. Again, I deliberated about casting it in the well in the yard – about packing it in a box, as if merchandise, with the usual arrangements, and so getting a porter to take it from the house. Finally I hit upon what I considered a far better expedient than either of these. I determined to wall it up in the cellar, as the monks of the Middle Ages are recorded to have walled up their victims.

For a purpose such as this the cellar was well adapted. Its walls were loosely constructed, and had lately been plastered throughout with a rough plaster, which the dampness of the atmosphere had prevented from hardening. Moreover, in one of the walls was a projection, caused by a false chimncy, or fireplace, that had been filled up and made to resemble the rest of the cellar. I made no doubt that I could readily displace the bricks at this point, insert the corpse, and wall the whole up as before, so that no eye could detect anything suspicious.

And in this calculation I was not deceived. By means of a crowbar I easily dislodged the bricks, and, having carefully deposited the body against the inner wall, I propped it in that position, while with little trouble I relaid the whole structure as it originally stood. Having procured mortar, sand and hair, with every possible precaution, I prepared a plaster which could not be distinguished from the old, and with this I very carefully went over the new brickwork. When I had finished, I felt satisfied that all was right. The wall did not present the slightest appearance of having been disturbed. The rubbish on the floor was picked up with the minutest care. I looked around triumphantly, and said to myself: 'Here at least, then, my labour has not been in vain.'

My next step was to look for the beast which had been the cause of so much wretchedness; for I had, at length, firmly resolved to put it to death. Had I been able to meet with it at the moment, there could have been no doubt of its fate; but it appeared that the crafty animal had been alarmed at the violence of my previous anger, and forbore to present itself in my present mood. It is impossible to describe or to imagine the deep, the blissful sense of relief which the absence of the detested creature occasioned in my bosom. It did not make its appearance during the night; and thus for one night, at least, since its introduction into the house, I soundly and tranquilly slept; aye, *slept* even with the burden of murder upon my soul.

The second and the third day passed, and still my tormentor came not. Once again 1 breathed as a free man. The monster, in terror, had fled the premises for ever! I should behold it no more! My happiness was supreme! The guilt of my dark deed disturbed me but little. Some few enquiries had been made, but these had been readily answered. Even a search had been instituted – but of course nothing was to be discovered. I looked upon my future felicity as secured.

Upon the fourth day of the assassination, a party of the police came, very unexpectedly, into the house, and proceeded again to make rigorous investigation of the premises. Secure, however, in the inscrutability of my place of concealment, I felt no embarrassment whatever. The officers bade me accompany them in their search. They left no nook or corner unexplored. At length, for the third or fourth time, they descended into the cellar. I quivered not in a muscle. My heart beat calmly as that of one who slumbers in innocence. I walked the cellar from end to end. I folded my arms upon my bosom, and roamed easily to and fro. The police were thoroughly satisfied and prepared to depart. The glee at my heart was too strong to be restrained. I burned to say if but one word, by way of triumph, and to render doubly sure their assurance of my guiltlessness.

'Gentlemen,' I said at last, as the party ascended the stairs, 'I delight to have allayed your suspicions. I wish you all health and a little more courtesy. By the bye, gentlemen, this – this is a very well-constructed house,' (in the rabid desire to say something easily, I scarcely knew what I uttered at all) – 'I may say an excellently well-constructed house. These walls – are you going, gentlemen? – these walls are solidly put together'; and here, through the mere frenzy of bravado, I rapped heavily with a cane which I held in my hand, upon that very portion of the brickwork behind which stood the corpse of the wife of my bosom.

But may God shield and deliver me from the fangs of the Arch-Fiend! No sooner had the reverberation of my blows sunk into silence, than I was answered by a voice from within the tomb! – by a cry, at first muffled and broken, like the sobbing of a child, and then quickly swelling into one long, loud and continuous scream, utterly anomalous and inhuman – a howl – a wailing shriek, half of horror and half of triumph, such as might have arisen only out of hell, conjointly from the throats of the damned in their agony and of the demons that exult in the damnation.

Of my own thoughts it is folly to speak. Swooning, I staggered to the opposite wall. For one instant the party on the stairs remained motionless, through extremity of terror and awe. In the next a dozen stout arms were toiling at the wall. It fell bodily. The corpse, already greatly decayed and clotted with gore, stood erect before the eyes of the spectators. Upon its head with red extended mouth and solitary eye of fire, sat the hideous beast whose craft had seduced me into murder, and whose informing voice had consigned me to the hangman. I had walled the monster up within the tomb.

SPIEGEL THE CAT
Gottfried Keller

When a Seldwyler has made a bad bargain, or been outwitted, the Seldwylers say of him, 'He's bought the fat off the cat.' This saying is certainly to be heard elsewhere, but nowhere as often as here: the reason may be that there exists in the town an old legend on its origin and meaning.

    Some hundreds of years ago, they say, an elderly lady lived alone in Seldwyla with a fine tabby cat, the very picture of sagacity and content, who shared her life and never did any harm to anyone who left him alone. His one passion was hunting, but he indulged it within the bounds of reason and temperance, taking no credit to himself for the fact that his passion also served a useful purpose and pleased his mistress, and never giving way to undue cruelty. He accordingly caught and killed only the most intrusive and shameless mice who were found trespassing on a certain part of the house, but, having decided to kill, he did so with reliable skill. It was but rarely that he pursued some particularly cunning mouse, which had provoked his wrath, beyond this pale. When such a case arose, he most politely asked permission from the neighbours to do a little mousing in their homes, and the permission was willingly given, for he never touched the milkjugs, nor jumped up at the hams which hung on the walls, but went about his business quietly and attentively, and having despatched it, withdrew discreetly with the mouse in his mouth. Nor was the cat shy and cross: he was friendly to everybody, and never ran away from sensible people: on the contrary, he would put up with a joke from them, and even let them pull his ears a bit without scratching. But a certain type of silly folk he could not bear, declaring that their silliness was the sign of a puerile and worthless nature, and he would get out of their way or give them a good scratch on the hand if they molested him with their clumsy pleasantries.

Thus Spiegel[1] – for so the cat was called from his smooth and glossy coat – lived, cheerful, comely and contemplative, in decent ease and without arrogance. He would not sit too often on his kind mistress's shoulder, snatching the bits from her fork, but would wait until she was in the mood for fun, and during the day he seldom lay and slept on his warm cushion behind the stove, but preferred to take his rest on the narrow banisters on the stairs, or in the roof gutter, there to give himself up to meditation and the contemplation of the world. This quiet life, however, was interrupted for a week each spring and autumn, when the violets were blooming or when, in the mild warmth of St Martin's summer, a mimic violet-time returned. Then Spiegel went his own way, roamed in love-born rapture over the most distant roofs, and sang the loveliest songs. In true Don Juan fashion, he carried on the gravest adventures by day and night, and when by chance he showed himself at home, he looked so bold, so jovial, so debauched and so unkempt that his gentle mistress would exclaim almost angrily, 'Spiegel, Spiegel, aren't you ashamed to lead such a life?' But it never occurred to Spiegel to be ashamed. Like the man of principle he was, knowing how far he could go in the way of healthy change, he quite quietly set about restoring the sheen of his coat and the innocent gaiety of his expression, and passed his damp paw over his nose with as little embarrassment as if nothing had happened.

But a sad event suddenly broke the even tenor of his days. Just as Spiegel was in the prime of life, his mistress unexpectedly died of old age, leaving the handsome puss orphaned and alone. It was the first sorrow he had known, and with the piercing wails which anxiously question whether a great grief has a real and just cause, he followed the body to the door, and wandered helplessly in and about the house for the rest of the day. But the natural soundness of his nature, his common sense and philosophic habit made him pull himself together, face the inevitable, and prove his grateful affection to his dead mistress by offering his services to her rejoicing heirs, and he prepared to support them in word and deed, to keep

---

[1] Looking-glass.

the mice down and to give them many a sound piece of advice which the silly people would not have scorned if they had not been silly. But they never gave Spiegel a chance. They threw the slippers and the pretty footstool of the deceased at his head whenever he appeared, quarrelled with each other for a week, began a law-suit and shut up the house until further notice, so that it now stood quite empty.

So there poor Spiegel sat on the doorstep, sad and forlorn, and there was nobody to let him in. At night he certainly crept in by devious ways under the house roof, and at the beginning, he spent the best part of the day there, trying to sleep away his grief. But hunger soon drove him into the light of day and forced him to reappear in the warm sunlight, among the people, to be on the spot and ready if any poor mouthful of food should show itself. The more rarely this happened, the more watchful Spiegel grew, and soon all his moral qualities were so absorbed in this watchfulness that his own mistress would not have known him. He made many a sally from his doorstep, and slunk hastily across the street, only to return, now with some poor unwholesome scraps such as he would never have looked at formerly, now with nothing at all. He grew thinner and more unkempt from day to day, and greedy too, and cringing and cowardly: all his courage, his dainty feline dignity, his good sense and philosophy disappeared. When the boys came home from school, he would creep into a dark corner as soon as he heard them coming, only peeping out to see if one of them might throw away a crust of bread and to note the place where it fell. At the approach of the most miserable cur he would scuttle off, while before, he had looked danger in the face, and often chastised vicious dogs with a firm hand. Yet when some uncouth yokel came along, whom at one time he would have cautiously avoided, he would stay where he was, although, poor cat, he could well size up the wretch with the remainder of his intelligence; necessity forced Spiegel to deceive himself and hope that the man would, as an exception, stroke him kindly and give him something to eat. Even when no such thing happened, and he was only beaten or had his tail pulled, he would not scratch, but would turn aside without a word and look longingly at the hand which had struck him or pulled his tail, and which smelt of sausage or herring.

One day, when the noble and intelligent Spiegel had come so far down in the world, he was sitting, thin and dejected, on his doorstep, blinking at the sun. Then the Town Wizard, Master Pineiss, came along and stopped in front of him. Hoping for something good, although he knew the canny creature well enough, Spiegel sat meekly on his doorstep and waited for what Master Pineiss might say or do. But when he addressed him with the words, 'Well, Cat, shall I buy your fat off you?' Spiegel's heart sank, for he thought the Town Wizard was making fun of his leanness. Still, not wishing to fall out with anybody, he replied with a modest smile, 'You do like your little joke, Master Pineiss!'

'Not at all!' cried Pineiss. 'I really mean it. Above all things I need cat's fat for my sorcery, but it must be voluntarily ceded to me by legal agreement with the gentlemen in question, otherwise it is powerless. I do think that if ever a stout puss was by way of making a good bargain you are the one. Come into my service. I will make you round and fat with sausage and roast quail. On the sunniest heights of the enormously high roof of my house – which, by the way, is the most alluring roof in the world for cats, being full of interesting nooks and crannies – fine grass, emerald green, waves delicately in the breeze, inviting you to nibble off its most tender tips if all my tit-bits should prove too much for your digestion. In this way you will remain in the best of health, and, when the time comes, yield rich and valuable fat.'

Spiegel had long since pricked up his ears and was listening with watering mouth. Yet to his weakened intelligence, the thing was not yet clear, so he replied, 'So far, so good, Master Pineiss. But what I can't make out is this. How can I, since my life goes with my fat, get possession of the price agreed upon, and enjoy it when I am no more?'

'Get your price?' said the wizard in astonishment. 'Why, you will be getting your price all the time in the rich, copious food with which I shall fatten you, of course! Still, I won't force you!' and he began to move off.

But Spiegel said, hastily and anxiously, 'You must at least grant me a moderate respite beyond the period of my greatest fatness and rotundity, so that I shall not suddenly be called upon to lay down my life when that agreeable and alas! so mournful moment has arrived and been recognized.'

'So be it!' said Master Pineiss, with apparent good nature. 'You shall be allowed to enjoy your pleasant condition until the following full moon, but not a day longer, for the matter must not drag on into the waning moon, since that would tend to reduce my legitimate profit.'

The cat hastened to agree, and signed a spare contract which the wizard had on him with the pointed handwriting which was his last possession and sign of better days.

'You can come to dinner, Cat!' said the wizard. 'I dine at twelve sharp.'

'I will make so free, if I may,' said Spiegel, and presented himself punctually at twelve at the wizard's house.

Then there began a few highly agreeable months for the cat, for he had nothing whatever to do save to consume the good things which were set before him, to watch his master making magic whenever he got the chance, and to go walking on the roof. This roof was like an enormous chimney-pot hat, or one of those tricornes which the Swabian peasants wear, and just as such a hat covers a head full of tricks and shifts, so this roof covered a great, gloomy, cornery house full of all manner of hocus-pocus. Master Pineiss was a jack of all trades and did a thousand odd jobs. He cured various ailments, exterminated bugs, pulled out teeth, and lent money on interest: he was the guardian of all widows and children, cut quill pens in his spare time at a penny the dozen, and made fine black ink: he dealt in ginger and pepper, in waggon-grease and rosoli,[1] in little note-books and hobnails: he mended the town clock, and drew up the almanack for the year with the phases of the moon, the laws of husbandry and the bloodletting manikins.[2] He did a thousand perfectly lawful things by day for small pay, and

---

[1] AUTHOR'S NOTE. – Fine Italian liqueur, made of orange-blossoms, now usually called Maraschino.

[2] In the old popular calendars, the days on which bleeding was considered advisable were marked with a particular sign generally a little man. (Tr.)

just a few unlawful ones by night for his personal satisfaction, or clipped on to the lawful ones, before he despatched them, a tiny unlawful tail, as tiny as a young frog's, just out of natural waggishness. Moreover, he made the weather in difficult times, kept a knowing eye on the witches, and when they were ripe, he had them burned. So far as he was concerned, he carried on witchcraft as a scientific experiment and for domestic use: and he privately tested and twisted the town laws, which he drafted and copied out with his own hand, to make sure of their durability. As the Seldwylers always needed someone to do their disagreeable jobs for them, big or little, he had been appointed Town Wizard, and had already filled this office for many years, early and late, with indefatigable devotion and efficiency, so that his house was full, from garret to cellar, with all manner of things, and Spiegel found it most entertaining to examine and sniff at everything. But at first all his attention was concentrated on food. He gobbled up everything which Pineiss set before him, and could scarcely wait from one meal to the next. In this way he overloaded his stomach and was really obliged to go on to the roof to eat some of the fine green grass to cure himself of all manner of sickness.

When the wizard saw this ravening, he was glad, and thought to himself that Spiegel would soon grow fat in this way, and that the more he spent now, the craftier he really was and the more he would save in the long run. So he made quite a little landscape for Spiegel in his room, setting up a forest of miniature pine-trees with diminutive hills of stones and moss and a tiny lake. On the trees he hung roasted larks, chaffinches, tits and sparrows, so that Spiegel always found something there to pull down and pick at. He made artificial mouse-holes in the mountains and in them he hid fine mice, which he carefully fattened on cornflour, then drew, larded with tender strips of bacon, and fried. Spiegel could reach out a few of these with his paws; the others were put further in to increase the fun, but these were tied to a string and Spiegel had to draw them out cautiously when he wished to enjoy the pleasures of a mimic hunt. The basin of the lake, however, Pineiss filled daily with fresh milk so that Spiegel might quench his thirst in the sweet liquid, and sometimes he put fried gudgeon to float in it, for he knew that cats like to fish from time to time. But since Spiegel was leading such a fine life, and could do or leave undone, eat or drink, whatever he liked and when he liked, he visibly flourished as to the outer man, his coat once more became sleek and glossy and his eye bright; at the same time, his mental powers being restored in a like degree, his manners improved, his wild craving subsided, and, as he had a bitter experience behind him, his wits grew keener than ever. He moderated his desires and ate no more than was good for him, while he resumed his habit of sage and profound reflection and began to see things more clearly. Thus one day he took down a pretty little fieldfare from the branches and as he pensively tore it to pieces he found its little stomach quite round and full with fresh, undigested food. Little green herbs, prettily rolled up, seeds, black and white, and a shining red berry were packed in as daintily and as close as if a mother had packed her son's knapsack for a journey. When Spiegel had slowly devoured the bird, he took the pleasantly filled little stomach on his claws and contemplated it philosophically. He was moved by the fate of the poor fieldfare, who, having peacefully done his work, had to quit life so suddenly that he could not even digest the things he had swallowed. 'What did he have of it, poor fellow?' meditated Spiegel, 'feeding so eagerly and so busily that this little paunch looks like a well-spent day? It was that red berry which decoyed him out of the free life of the woods into the snare of the fowler. But he thought, at least, that he was doing well for himself and prolonging his life with such berries, while I, who have just eaten the unhappy bird, have simply eaten myself a step nearer death. Can a man conclude a more miserable and cowardly contract than to save his life for a little while, only to lose it for the price of saving it? Would not a quick and voluntary death have been better for a resolute cat? But my wits were all confused, and now that I can think again, I can see nothing before me but the fate of this wild bird. When I am fat enough, I must go hence, simply because I am fat! Is that a reason for a lusty and nimble-witted he-cat? If only I could get out of the trap!'

He brooded this way and that as to how it could be done, but as the time of danger was not yet at hand, he could not see things clearly enough to find a way out. Like the wise man he was, however, he devoted himself to virtue and self-control, which is always the best way of passing the time while preparing a decision.

He spurned the soft cushion which Pineiss had laid down for him to lie and grow fat on, and again preferred to lie on narrow ledges and high, dangerous places when he wanted to rest. He scorned the roasted birds and larded mice, and, having now a regular hunting ground, he chose rather to exercise his own cunning and agility by catching a simple, living sparrow on the roof, or a nimble mouse in the attics. Such prey tasted far better than the roasted game in Pineiss's artificial preserves, while it did not make him too fat: and the exercise, with his return to virtue and philosophy, prevented him from putting on flesh too rapidly, so that Spiegel looked healthy and sleek, but, to Pineiss's astonishment, remained at a fixed point of embonpoint which was far from that which the wizard proposed to reach with his benevolent fattening, for he had in mind a great obese animal, as round as a ball, which would not move from its cushion and literally consisted of fat. But here his witchcraft had gone wrong, and for all his cunning he did not know that, if you feed an ass, it remains an ass, but if you feed a fox, it will never be anything but a fox, for each animal grows according to its own nature. When it was borne in upon Master Pineiss that Spiegel remained at the same point of well-nourished but lithe and vigorous slimness, he suddenly attacked him one evening and said rudely, 'Well, Spiegel, what about it? Why don't you eat the good food which I cook so well and set down for you? Why don't you catch the roasted birds on the trees? Why don't you hunt the tasty mice in the caves? Why don't you fish in the lake? Why do you rush about the whole time, so that you don't get fat?'

'Why, Master Pineiss, because I feel better so! Shall I not pass the short remainder of my life in the way I like best?'

'What's that?' cried Pineiss. 'You shall live so as to get round and fat and not wear yourself out hunting! But I know what you're after. You think you're going to play your monkey tricks on me, and that I'm going to let you run about for ever in that condition, neither fat nor lean? But you may just make up your mind to it. You shan't get the better of me! It's your duty to eat and drink and look after yourself so as to put on flesh and acquire fat. Have the goodness to give up this deceitful and fraudulent temperance on the spot, or I shall have something to say to you!'

Spiegel interrupted the comfortable purring he had set going to keep himself in hand and said, 'This is the first I have heard of anything in the contract about giving up temperance and a healthy life. If you, Master Pineiss, counted on my being a lazy glutton, that's not my fault. You do a thousand lawful things by day, so add this to them and let us both stick to our rights, for you know that my fat is only of use to you if it has grown legitimately.'

'Chattering beast!' said Pineiss. 'Do you think you can teach me? Let's see how far you've got, you idle devil. Perhaps we could deal with you soon.' He caught hold of the cat by the stomach, but Spiegel, feeling an unpleasant irritation, gave the wizard a good scratch across the hand. Pineiss looked at it reflectively, then said, 'Is that the way of it, you beast? Good! I solemnly declare you, in virtue of the contract, fat enough. I am satisfied with the result and will see that I get it! Full moon is in five days. Till then you can enjoy life, as stipulated in the contract, but not a day longer.' And thereupon he turned his back and left Spiegel to his thoughts.

These were heavy and sombre. The hour was then near when the good Spiegel must lay down his life. With all his wits, was there no way out? Sighing, he climbed on to the high roof, the ridge of which loomed dark in the autumn evening sky. Then the moon rose over the town and cast its beams on the dark mossy tiles of the old roof; a lovely song fell on Spiegel's ears, and a snow-white she-cat passed shining over a neighbouring roof-top. Spiegel at once forgot his approaching death, and raised his noblest caterwaul in answer to the beauty's hymn of praise. He hurled himself towards her, and was straightway engaged in hot combat by three strange tom-cats, whom he put to flight with a wild courage. Then he paid fiery and humble court to the lady, and passed his days and nights by her side without thinking of Pineiss or showing himself at home. He sang like a nightingale through the long moonlight nights, dashed headlong after his lady-love over the roofs and through the gardens, and more than once, in the jousts of love, or in fights with his rivals, he rolled off high roofs and tumbled into the street, but only to pick himself up, shake himself and dash off again in hot pursuit of his love. Hours of turmoil and hours of ease, the sweetness of passion and the heat of battle, graceful conversation and witty discussions, the machinations of love and jealousy, caresses and scuffles, the elation of success and the misery of mischance – all this filled up the love-sick Spiegel's time so completely that, by the time the moon's disc gleamed full, he was so reduced by all these excitements and passions that he looked more miserable, emaciated and unkempt than ever. At that moment Pineiss put his head out of an attic window and called to him, 'Spiegel, Spiegel, where are you? Aren't you coming home for a bit?'

Then Spiegel took his leave of his white mistress, who went her way mewing in cool content, and turned proudly to meet his torturer. The latter went down into the kitchen, rustled the contract, and said, 'Come along, Spiegel, my dear!' and Spiegel followed him, and, thin and dishevelled as he was, stood defiantly before him in the wizard's kitchen. When Pineiss saw how scurvily he had been tricked of his profit, he sprang up like one possessed and yelled savagely, 'What's that? You rascal, you unscrupulous rogue! What have you been at?' Beside himself with rage, he snatched up a broom and made as if to beat Spiegel, but Spiegel arched his black back, ruffled up his fur until the sparks flew, laid his ears back, and hissed and spat at the old man with such rage that he, aghast, leapt back three paces. He began to suspect that he was up against some wizard who was fooling him and was more advanced in the art than himself. Dismayed and subdued, he said, 'Can it be that the honourable Master Spiegel is one of us? Has some learned sorcerer deigned to assume his outward form, seeing that he can command his physique at his pleasure and attain precisely the corpulence he desires, not a shade too much or too little, or even waste away to a skeleton to avoid death?'

Spiegel calmed down and said candidly, 'No, I am no sorcerer. The sweet power of passion alone has reduced me to this state and used your fat for my pleasure; but if you like to begin the whole business again, I will do my share stoutly and feed well. Try me with a fine fat sausage, for I am quite weak with hunger.' Then Pineiss took Spiegel wrathfully by the scruff of the neck, shut him up in the goose-house, which was always empty, and shouted, 'Now see if your sweet power of passion will help you out and if it is more potent than the power of sorcery and my lawful contract.'

Then he fried a long sausage which smelt so good that he could not refrain from nibbling a bit off both ends before he stuck it through the netting. Spiegel ate it up from end to end, and as he comfortably stroked his moustache and licked his coat, he said to himself, 'Upon my word, love is a fine thing. It has got me out of the trap again. Now I will rest a bit and see that I come to reasonable thoughts again by meditation and good food. There is a time for everything – today a little passion, tomorrow a little rest and reflection – each is good in its way. This prison is by no means so bad, and I can surely think out something useful here.' But Pineiss pulled himself together, and daily cooked toothsome tit-bits, so wholesome and so varied, that Spiegel in his cage could not resist them, for the wizard's stock of voluntary and legitimate cat's fat was dwindling from day to day, and without this, the chief matter of his trade, the sorcerer was a beaten man. But the good wizard, in feeding Spiegel's body, fed his mind too, and could by no means get rid of this annoying detail, at which point his witchcraft proved itself defective.

When he judged that Spiegel in his cage was fat enough, he hesitated no longer, but before the eyes of the watching cat, arranged all the dishes and made a bright fire on the hearth to boil out the yield he had so ardently longed for. Then he sharpened a great knife, pulled Spiegel out, after having first carefully closed the kitchen door, and said cheerily, 'Come on, you rascal! We'll cut off your head first, then skin you. That will make a nice warm cap for me. Simpleton that I was not to think of that before. Shall I flay you first, then cut off your head?'

'No, if you would be so good,' said Spiegel humbly. 'Please, the head first!'

'Quite right, poor fellow!' said Pineiss. 'We won't torture you for nothing. Anything that's right!'

'That's well said,' replied Spiegel, with a piteous sigh, bending his head in resignation. 'Oh! if I had always done what's right and not frivolously neglected such an important matter, I could die now with a clearer conscience, for I am glad to die; but an evil deed embitters the death which in all else is so welcome. For what does life offer to me? Nothing but care, fear and poverty, with, for a change, a storm of devastating passion, which is worse than quiet, trembling fear!'

'What evil deed – what important matter?' asked Pineiss inquisitively.

'What's the use of talking now?' sighed Spiegel. 'What has happened has happened, and remorse comes too late!'

'Now you see, you rogue, what a sinner you are,' said Pineiss, 'and how you have deserved your death! But what in the world have you been at? Have you purloined, removed, destroyed, something belonging to me? Have you done me some crying wrong of which I know, fear, suspect nothing, you Satan? A pretty business! I'm glad I've got on the track of it. Out with it on the spot or I shall skin and boil you alive!'

'Ah! no,' said Spiegel. 'I have nothing on my conscience so far as you are concerned. It's about the ten thousand guilders of my late mistress – but talking won't mend matters. Yet when I think the matter over and look at you, there may yet be time. When I look at you, I see that you are still a hale and handsome man in the prime of life. Tell me, Master Pineiss, have you never felt you might like to marry, honourably and well? But there, how I do chatter! How could a wise and ingenious man indulge such idle thoughts? How could an adept so usefully employed fill his head with those silly women? Of course, even the worst of them has something about her which might be useful to a man – that one can't deny. And if she is only half a woman, then a good housewife may even be white of body, careful of mind, obliging of manners, faithful of heart, economical in the house but lavish in the care of her husband, entertaining in word and pleasing in deed, and fond in all her doings. She kisses a man with her mouth and strokes his beard and embraces him with her arms and scratches him gently behind the ears – just as he likes it done – in short, she does a thousand things which are not to be despised. She stays near him or withdraws to a modest distance, just as he feels inclined, and when he goes about his business, she does not disturb him but sings meanwhile his praises at home and abroad, for she won't hear a word against him and extols everything about him. But the sweetest thing about her is the wonderful nature of her delicate bodily being, which, for all the apparent human likeness, has been made so different from ours that it works perpetual prodigies in a happy marriage and, in fact, contains the most subtle magic. Yet listen to me, chattering like a fool on the threshold of death! Forgive me, Master Pineiss, and cut off my head!'

But Pineiss cried hotly, 'Have done, you chatterer! and tell me, where is such a woman, and has she ten thousand guilders?'

'Ten thousand guilders?' asked Spiegel.

'Of course,' cried Pineiss, impatiently, 'didn't you begin with that?'

'No,' replied the other. 'That's another story. They are buried somewhere.'

'What are they doing there? Whose are they?' shouted Pineiss.

'They're nobody's. That's just why I am so conscience-stricken about them, for I ought to have disposed of them somehow. They really belong to the man who marries such a woman as I have described. But who could bring three such things together in this godless town – ten thousand guilders, a clever, comely and virtuous housewife, and a wise and upright man? So my sin is not too great, for the task was too heavy for a poor he-cat.'

'If,' yelled Pineiss, 'you don't stick to your subject and explain the thing clearly and in order, I will cut off your tail and both ears at once. Now begin!'

'Well, since you will have it, I must tell the story,' said Spiegel, coolly sitting down on his hind legs, 'although this delay only increases my sufferings!'

Pineiss stuck his knife into the floor between them and, all agog, sat down on a little cask to listen, while Spiegel continued:

'You must know, Master Pineiss, that that good woman, my late mistress, died an old maid, having quietly done a great deal of good, and never hurt anyone. But things had not always been so still and calm about her, and although she was never an ill-natured person, she had done a good deal of harm in her day, for in her youth she was the loveliest young woman far and near, and every gallant gentleman and bold youth living in the neighbourhood or passing by on his travels fell in love with her and wanted to marry her. Now she really wanted to marry, and take a handsome, honest and clever husband, and she had her choice, for men far and wide fought for her and there were duels to the death for the first chance with her. Suitors, bold and faint-hearted, crafty and sincere, rich and poor, flocked to pay court to her, some with good and honest businesses, some who lived delicately on their means like gentlemen. One had this advantage, another that: one was glib, the next silent, a third merry and kind, while yet another seemed to have more in him although he looked a bit simple. In short, she had as perfect a choice as a marriageable spinster could wish.

'However, she possessed, in addition to her beauty, a handsome fortune of many thousand guilders, and that was the reason why she never got so far as making a choice and settling on a husband, for she was remarkably far-sighted and prudent in the care of her property, and thought very much of it, and as we always judge others from the standpoint of our own inclinations, it came about that, as soon as a decent man came near her and she felt half attracted to him, she at once imagined that he only wanted her fortune. If he were rich, she thought he would not want her if she were not rich too, and as for the poor ones, she took it for granted that they were only after her money, and were thinking what a good thing they would make out of it, and the poor young lady, who herself attached so much importance to worldly goods, was quite incapable of distinguishing the love of money in her suitors from their love for herself, or, if they did care for money, of making allowances for it and forgiving them. More than once she was as good as betrothed and her heart at last began to beat faster, but she would suddenly take it into her head from some word or look that she was betrayed and that her lover was thinking only of her fortune, and she would immediately break off the whole matter and withdraw, sorrowful but resolute. All she liked she tested in a thousand ways, and they had to be very adroit not to fall into the trap, and in the end, nobody could have the least hope of her unless he were a thorough-paced rogue and hypocrite, so, for that reason alone, the choice became really difficult, because in the long run such men create a strangely uneasy atmosphere and awake the most painful anxiety in the heart of a lady, the more insidious and clever they are. Her chief way of putting her admirers to the test was to inveigle them into great expenses, rich gifts and charitable actions. But try as they would, they were never right, for if they were generous and devoted, made her fine presents, gave brilliant parties or confided large sums for the poor to her, she would suddenly say they were throwing a sprat to catch a salmon, as the saying goes. And she gave the money and the presents to convents and fed the poor, but she mercilessly dismissed the discomfited suitors. But if they proved a bit economical, or even a little stingy, they had no chance at all, for she thought that much worse, and declared that they were openly base, callous and selfish. So it came about that she, who sought a pure heart, devoted to herself alone, was in the end surrounded by hypocritical, perfidious and self-seeking men, whom she could never make out and who embittered her life.

'One day she felt herself out of humour and depressed, so she turned the whole lot out of the house, locked it up and set out for Milan, where she had a cousin. As she rode over the Gotthard on an ass, her mood was as gloomy and terrifying as the wild rocks which towered from the abyss, and she felt the strongest temptation to throw herself over the Devil's Bridge into the raging waters of the Reuss. It was only with difficulty that she could be pacified and dissuaded from her dark impulse by the guide and the two maids she had with her, whom I knew, though they are long since dead. And she was pale and low-spirited when she arrived in the lovely land of Italy, and however blue the sky, her gloomy thoughts would not brighten. Yet but few days were to pass before another song was to be heard, and a springtime dawn in her heart of which she had known little till then, and for which she had ceased to hope. For a young compatriot came to her cousin's house to whom she took such a liking at first sight that one may say she fell in love for the first time of her own free will. He was a handsome youth, well-bred and of noble manners, and at the time neither rich nor poor, for all he had was ten thousand guilders which he had inherited from his parents, and with which, having learned the trade, he was to set up a silk business in Milan, for he was enterprising and shrewd, and lucky, as simple-minded and honest people often are, and that the young man was. With all his experience, he looked as frank and innocent as a child. And though he was a merchant, yet of so ingenuous a disposition, a combination in itself delightfully rare, he was firm and knightly in his bearing and wore his sword by his side as boldly as only an experienced soldier can do. All this, with his fresh, handsome face, so won the young lady's heart that she could hardly contain her pleasure, and received him with the utmost graciousness. Her spirits rose, and if from time to time she felt sad, her sadness came only from the alternating hopes and fears of love, and that, after all, is a nobler feeling than all the miserable perplexity she had felt among her suitors. Now only one anxious problem faced her – how to find favour in the sight of the handsome and good young man, and the more beautiful she knew herself to be, the more humble and uncertain she felt now that real love had entered her heart.

'But the young merchant himself had never seen so lovely a woman, or been so warmly received by one. Now she, as I have already said, was not only beautiful, but kind of heart and courteous of manners, so it is not to be wondered at that the young man, whose heart was still free and inexperienced, fell in love with her too, as deeply as he knew how. Still, perhaps nobody would ever have known anything about it if he, in his innocence, had not been encouraged by the lady's complaisance, which, with much secret trembling and hesitation, he dared to take for a return of his affection, for he himself knew no pretence. Yet he contained himself for a few weeks and imagined he was keeping it all very dark, although everybody could see from far off that he was in love, and if he happened to be near the lady, or to hear her name mentioned, it was as clear as day with whom. And indeed, he was not long in love, but began really to love with all the passion of his youth so that the young lady became for him the highest and best in the world, and he set upon her once for all the salvation of his soul and the whole worth of his life. This was very delightful to her, for there was in everything he said and did something different from all she had known hitherto, and it exhilarated her and touched her so deeply that she now fell passionately in love herself and there was no further question of choice for her. Everybody saw the little drama being played out, and it was quite openly spoken of and many a joke was made. The young lady was highly pleased with it all, and though her heart was nearly bursting with timid expectation, she did all she could to complicate and spin out the romance from her side, so as to enjoy it to the full. For in his confusion, the young man did the most charming, childish things, the like of which she had never seen, and they were more flattering and sweet to her than anything else could be. But he, in his candour and frankness, could not bear it long, for everyone hinted and joked, and the whole thing seemed to be turning into a farce, and his beloved was too good and too sacred to him for that; what enchanted her, grieved him, and made him sad, perplexed and embarrassed about her. Moreover, he thought that it was insulting and deceitful towards her to be full of passion for her and constantly thinking of her, while she had not the least suspicion of it, and that it was not at all right and proper and not fair to himself! So, one morning, it was quite clear that he had some project on hand, and he confessed his love to her in a few words, never to repeat them if he should not find favour in her sight. For he could not but think that such a beautiful young lady would say what she meant the first time, and pronounce her irrevocable yes or no. He was as sensitive as he was loving, as pure as he was childlike, and as proud as he was candid, and for him it was a matter of life and death. But the very moment the lady heard the declaration she had so longed for, her old suspicion came over her again, and, to her misfortune, it occurred to her that her lover was a merchant who probably only wanted her money to extend his business. After all, if he were a little in love with her at the same time, that was scarcely to his credit, considering her beauty, and really it was all the more revolting that she should represent nothing but a desirable addition to her own money. So, instead of confessing her love to him and receiving him well, she put on a grave, half-sad expression, and confided to him that she was already betrothed to a young man from her native town whom she most dearly loved. She had often wished to tell him – the merchant – that she was very fond of him as a friend, as he had probably seen from her behaviour, and that she trusted him like a brother. But the silly jokes which had been made in their presence had made a confidential conversation impossible; still, as he himself had taken her by surprise, and opened his good and noble heart to her, she could thank him in no better way than by confiding in him just as frankly. Yes, she went on, she could only belong to the man she had once chosen, and she could never turn her heart to another – that was written in flaming golden letters in her soul, and the dear man himself did not know how dear he was to her, however well he might know her. But a sad misfortune had befallen her. Her betrothed was a merchant, but desperately poor, so they had planned to set up business with the bride's money. A start had been made, and everything was going on well, when, as ill-luck would have it, unexpected claims had been made involving her whole property, and perhaps it would be lost for ever, while the poor man had shortly to make his first payments to merchants from Milan and Venice, on which depended his credit, his prosperity and his honour, not to speak of their reunion and happy marriage. She had in all haste to set out for Milan, where she had wealthy relatives, to find ways and means, but she had come at a bad time, for nothing could be arranged: the fateful day was fast approaching and if she could not help her beloved, she must die of sorrow, for he was the dearest and best man in the world and would become a great merchant if he could be helped, and she could imagine no happiness on earth save that of being his wife. When she had finished her story, the poor handsome youth, who had long since turned pale, was as white as a sheet. Yet he uttered no sound of complaint, and spoke no more of his unhappy love, but merely asked sadly what were the liabilities of the happy unhappy betrothed. 'Ten thousand guilders,' she replied, still more sadly. The sad young merchant rose, bade the lady be of good courage as a way out would surely be found, and went away without daring to look at her, so confused and ashamed he felt at having set his heart upon a lady who loved another so faithfully and so passionately. For he took every word of her story for gospel. Then he went straight to his business friends, and by begging, and by forfeiting a certain sum, got them to cancel the orders and purchases which he himself just then wished to pay for with his ten thousand guilders and on which he was founding his whole career, and before six hours had passed, he reappeared before the lady and begged her for God's sake to accept this help from him. Her eyes sparkled with glad surprise and her heart beat furiously. She asked him where he had raised the capital, and he replied that he had borrowed it on the security of his good name and that he would be able to return it without inconvenience, as his own business was going very well. She saw clearly that he was lying and that he was sacrificing his whole fortune and hopes to her happiness, but she pretended to believe him. She gave way to her glee and cruelly gave him to think that it arose from her joy at being able to help her lover and marry the man of her choice, and she could find no words to express her gratitude. Yet suddenly she bethought herself and declared that she could only accept the generous deed on one condition, and that otherwise, all prayers were in vain.

When asked what this condition was, she demanded a sacred promise that he would come to her on a certain day to be present at her wedding and to become the best friend and patron of her future husband and her own most loyal friend, protector and adviser. Blushing, he begged her to give up the idea, but it was in vain that he put forward all possible reasons for making her give it up; in vain he pointed out to her that his own affairs did not permit him to return to Switzerland, and that his business would suffer considerably from such an absence. She stuck to her demand, and when he refused to give in, she even pushed his gold back to him. In the end, he promised, but he had to give her his hand on it and swear it on his honour and salvation. Only then did she accept his sacrifice and have the treasure carried into her bedroom, where she locked it into her travelling-chest with her own hands and put the key in her bosom. Then she delayed no longer in Milan, but travelled as joyously back over the Gotthard as she had come sadly. On the Devil's Bridge, where she had wanted to throw herself down, she laughed like mad, and raising her pleasing voice in a cry of exultation, she cast into the Reuss a bunch of pomegranate flowers she wore in her bosom. In short, her joy knew no bounds, and it was the happiest journey that had ever been made. But once at home, she opened and aired her house from top to bottom as if she were expecting a prince, and at the head of her bed she laid the sack with the ten thousand guilders, and at night she lay and slept on the hard lump as if it had been the softest down pillow.

'As the day approached, she could hardly contain her impatience, for she knew he would not break the simplest promise, let alone an oath, though it should cost him his life. But the day dawned and the beloved did not come, and many days and weeks passed without any news of him. Then she began to tremble in every limb, and fell a prey to the deepest dread and despondency. She sent letter after letter to Milan, but nobody knew where he was. Finally it came out by chance that the young man had had a suit made of a piece of blood-red damask he had had in the house ever since he set up business, and had already paid for, and had gone with the Swiss mercenaries, who were fighting the Milanese wars in the pay of King Francis. After the battle of Pavia, in which so many Swiss lost their lives, he was found lying on a heap of dead Spaniards, mortally wounded, with his fine red suit slashed and torn from top to bottom. But before he died, he dictated to a Seldwyler, who was lying beside him in less desperate case, the following message, made him learn it by heart and begged him to deliver it if he should escape with his life. "Dearest lady, although I swore by my faith, by my honour and by my salvation to come to your wedding, I could not bring myself to see you again, and to see another possess what is for me the greatest happiness in the world. I first felt this when I had left you, and did not know before what a grievous and mysterious thing is such a love as I bear to you, else I had kept it from my heart. But since it is so, I had rather lose my honour in this world and my salvation in the next, and go to eternal damnation for a broken oath, than appear before you with a fire in my breast which is stronger and more unquenchable than hell fire, which it will scarcely let me feel. Do not pray for me, loveliest of women, for I cannot and never shall be happy without you, here or there, and now farewell and my greeting to you." So in that battle, after which King Francis said, "All is lost save honour", the luckless lover had lost everything, hope, honour, life and eternal salvation, but not the love which consumed him. The Seldwyler escaped, and as soon as he had recovered and was out of danger, he wrote the dead man's words on his tablets so as not to forget them, journeyed home, presented himself before the unhappy lady, and read her the message, as stiff and soldierly as he was wont to be when reading the roll of his regiment, for he was a field lieutenant. But the lady tore her hair and rent her clothes, and began to scream and weep so loud that all the people came running. She dragged out the ten thousand guilders like a madwoman, scattered them on the floor, flung herself at full length upon them, and kissed the glittering gold. Completely beside herself, she tried to collect the rolling coins, and to embrace them as if the lost beloved were bodily in them. She lay day and night on the treasure, refused to eat or drink and continually kissed and caressed the cold metal until once, in the dead of night, she suddenly got up, carried the treasure into the garden and there, with bitter tears, threw it into a deep well and laid a curse upon it, that it should not belong to anyone else.'

When Spiegel had got so far, Pineiss said, 'And is all that money still lying in the well?'

'Where else could it lie?' asked Spiegel, 'for only I can get it out, and so far I have not done so.'

'Oh! yes, quite so!' said Pineiss. 'I quite forgot that in your tale. You can tell a story, you vagabond, and really, I quite begin to hanker after a little woman who would be so taken with me. But she would have to be very beautiful! However, go on and tell me how the whole thing hangs together.'

'Many years passed,' continued Spiegel, 'before the lady recovered sufficiently from her bitter anguish to become the quiet old maid that I knew. I may pride myself on being her one consolation and her most trusted friend in her lonely life until her peaceful end. But when she saw death approach, she recalled once more the distant time of her youth and beauty, and suffered again, with milder and more resigned thoughts, the sweet passion and bitter sorrow of that time, and she wept quietly seven days and nights for the love of the youth she had lost through her own suspicions, so that, just before her death, her poor old eyes were blinded. Then she repented of the curse she had laid upon the treasure, and entrusted its disposal to me in these words: 'I direct otherwise now, dear Spiegel, and give you full power to execute my will. Look about until you find a lovely but poor woman who can find no suitor on account of her poverty. Then if you can find a sensible, honest and handsome man with a good income, who will ask the woman to be his wife in spite of her poverty, and moved only by her beauty, make him swear by the most sacred oaths to be as loyal, self-sacrificing and unchangingly devoted to her as my unhappy lover to me. Then give the girl the ten thousand guilders as a dowry, so that she can surprise her bridegroom with them on her wedding-morning.' Thus spoke the deceased, and as, owing to untoward events, I have neglected to carry out her directions, I must fear that the poor woman cannot rest quiet in her grave, and that would not have very pleasant consequences for me.'

Pineiss eyed Spiegel dubiously and said, 'Could you, my good fellow, show me the way to the treasure and let me see it with my own eyes?'

'At any time,' replied Spiegel. 'But you must know, Master Town Wizard, that you cannot simply fish up the treasure like that. You would certainly have your neck wrung, for there is something weird about that well. I have had certain signs of it which I cannot discuss further for reasons of my own.'

'But who said anything about fishing it up?' said Pineiss, with some apprehension. 'Take me there once and show me the treasure – or rather I will take you there at the end of a nice stout string, so that you don't run away.'

'As you like,' rejoined Spiegel. 'But take another long string and a dark lantern with you which you can let down into the well, for it is very deep and dark.'

Pineiss followed his directions, and led the cheery puss to the dead lady's garden. They climbed the wall together, and Spiegel showed the sorcerer the way to the well, which was hidden under wild-growing bushes. There Pineiss let down his lantern, looking greedily after it and keeping a firm hold on Spiegel. But there it was – in the depths, he saw gold glittering under the green water and cried, 'It's perfectly true – I see it! Spiegel, you really are a fine fellow.' Then he peered eagerly down again and said, 'Are there really ten thousand there?'

'Well, I won't swear,' said Spiegel, 'I never was down there, and I haven't counted. It may be that the lady lost a few pieces on the way, for she was very agitated.'

'A dozen more or less,' said Master Pineiss, 'that doesn't matter.' He sat down on the edge of the well. Spiegel did likewise and licked his paw. 'So there's the treasure,' said Pineiss, scratching himself behind the ear. 'And here's the man. We only need the lovely woman.'

'What?' said Spiegel.

'I only mean that we still need the woman who will get the ten thousand guilders as a dowry, to surprise me with on our wedding morning, and who has all the attractive qualities you spoke of.'

'H'm!' said Spiegel. 'That's not quite the point: to speak candidly, I have already unearthed the lovely woman, but the real hitch is the man who would marry her in these difficult circumstances, for nowadays, beauty must be gilded, like nuts at Christmas, and the emptier men's heads get, the harder they try to fill the void with a bit of dowry, so that they may pass their time more pleasantly. For then, they can strut about inspecting a horse or buying a length of velvet, run all over the town to order a fine cross-bow, and the smith is never out of the house. Then "I must get in wine and clean my casks, have my trees pruned or my house roofed, I must send my wife to a watering-place – she isn't very strong and costs a good deal of money; I must cut my wood and call in outstanding debts; I have bought some greyhounds and given away my watchdog; I have bought a fine oak table and given my great walnut chest in part exchange; I have cut my beans and dismissed my gardener, sold my hay and sown my salad" – it's "mine, mine, mine" from morning till night. There are even men who say – "I have my washing next week; I must get a new maid and see about a butcher, for I shall have to get rid of the old one; I have got hold of a fine wafer-iron and sold my spice-box – it wasn't any good to me anyhow." Now all this is the wife's business, and a fellow of that kind passes his time and steals a day from the Lord counting up all these little matters and never doing a hand's turn. At the very outside, if a fellow like that has to knuckle under a bit, he may go so far as to say – 'our cows and our pigs', but—'

Pineiss pulled Spiegel by the string until he miaowed again and bawled 'Enough, out with it! Where is she?' For the tale of all the splendid doings which a wife's property brings with it had made the withered old wizard's mouth water more than ever.

But Spiegel said in surprise, 'Will you really undertake it, Master Pineiss?'

'Of course I will. Who else? So now, out with it! Where is she?'

'So that you can go and court her?'

'Of course!'

'Well, you must realize that you can only act through me! You will have to talk matters over with me if you want the money and the bride,' said Spiegel coolly and indifferently, assiduously passing each paw over his ears in turn, having carefully damped it first.

Pineiss reflected carefully, groaned slightly and said,

'I can see that you want to suppress our contract and save your skin.'

'Do you think that so unfair and unnatural?'

'You'll cheat me in the end, like the rogue you are!'

'That's possible too!'

'I tell you you shan't cheat me!' cried Pineiss, peremptorily.

'Very good, I shan't cheat you.'

'If you do—'

'Then I do.'

'Don't torture me, Pussy,' said Pineiss, almost in tears; and Spiegel now replied gravely:

'You're a funny man, Master Pineiss. Look – you've got me on the end of a string and you're nearly strangling me with it. You've had the sword of death hanging over me for more than two hours – two hours I say! – for six months, and now you say "Don't torture me, Pussy." Now, to put the matter shortly, I should be glad enough to fulfil my loving duty to the dead by finding a good husband for the lady in question, and you seem to me in every way suitable. It's no laughing matter to get a woman settled these days, whatever it may seem, and I tell you once more, I am glad you are ready to undertake it. But it's no use killing me. Before I say another word or take another step, before I even open my mouth again, I must have my freedom and security for my life. So take off this string and lay the contract down here by the well, or cut off my head – one or the other.'

'But why, you bedlamite, you scatter-pate,' said Pineiss, 'you hot-head, you don't really mean it! Come, we must discuss the thing properly, and in any case draw up a new contract.'

Spiegel answered never a word and sat there motionless one, two, three minutes. Then the wizard began to get frightened: he pulled out his letter-case, clawed out the contract, read it through again, then laid it hesitatingly before Spiegel. Scarcely had it left his hand when Spiegel snapped it up and ate it, and although he had to gulp pretty hard to get it down, it seemed to him the most wholesome meal he had ever enjoyed, and he hoped it would agree with him for a long time to come and make him fat and merry. When he had finished this pleasant repast, he bowed politely to the wizard and said, 'You shall certainly hear from me, Master Pineiss, and wife and money you shall have, but you must prepare to fall in love properly, so that you can swear to and fulfil the condition of unchanging devotion to the wife who is as good as yours. And so, for the present, I thank you kindly for board and service, and take my leave.'

Therewith Spiegel went his way, chuckling inwardly over the stupidity of the wizard, who imagined he could take himself and everybody else in by setting out to marry the hoped-for bride, not from disinterested motives and pure love of her beauty, but in full knowledge of the little detail of the ten thousand guilders. Meanwhile, he had someone in mind whom he hoped to foist off on the foolish wizard in return for his roast birds, mice and sausages.

Opposite to Master Pineiss's house there stood another: the front of it was cleanly whitewashed and its windows always glittered with fresh scouring. The modest window-curtains were always snow-white and newly ironed, and equally white were the dress, cap and neckerchief of an old beguine who lived in the house, while the nun-like wimple which covered her bosom always looked as if folded in white writing-paper, so that you couldn't help wanting to write on it, which would have been perfectly easy as far as the bosom was concerned, for it was as flat and hard as a board. As sharp as the white edges and corners of the beguine's clothes were her nose and chin, her tongue and the evil look in her eye, though she spoke little with her tongue and looked little with her eye, for she hated waste and only spent at the right time and after much consideration. She went to church three times a day, and when she went down the street in her fresh white crackling dress, and with her sharp white nose, the children ran frightened away from her and even grown people slipped behind the door if there were time. But she had a great reputation for piety and was much respected by the clergy, though even the priests preferred to deal with her in writing, and when she went to confession, the parson rushed out of the confessional sweating as if he came out of an oven. Thus the pious beguine, who never understood a joke, lived on in profound peace and remained unwed. She would have nothing to do with other people and let them go their own way, provided they kept out of hers. Her neighbour Pineiss, however, she had singled out for a particular hate, for every time he appeared at his window she gave him an evil look and immediately drew the white curtains, and Pineiss dreaded her like fire, and only dared to crack a joke about her right at the back of the house when everything was locked up. But, white and fresh though the beguine's house looked from the street, from behind it was black and smoky, sinister and strange, for there it could hardly be seen at all save by the cats on the roof and the birds in the sky, because it was built into an angle of high blind walls, where never a human face was to be seen. Under the roof there hung old torn petticoats, baskets and bags of herbs, on it there grew regular little oaks and thornbushes, and a great sooty chimney rose eerily into the air. But from this chimney, a witch often rode out on her broom, young and beautiful and stark naked, as God made women and as the devil likes to see them. When she rode out of the chimney, she sniffed the night air with delicate nostrils and smiling red lips, and rode off by the gleam of her white body, while her long black hair streamed behind her like a dusky flag. In a hole in the chimney there sat an old owl, and the liberated Spiegel now paid her a visit with a fat mouse in his mouth which he had caught on the way.

'Good evening to you, Mistress Owl! On the watch, as usual!' he said; and the owl replied, 'Needs must when the devil drives. Good evening to yourself. I haven't seen you this long while, Master Spiegel.'

'And for a good reason. I'll tell you about it. Here's a mouse for you, just what the season offers, if you care for it. Has the mistress gone out riding?'

'Not yet. She will only ride out for an hour or two towards morning. Many thanks for the fine mouse. Always the gentleman, Master Spiegel! Here is a little sparrow which flew too near me today. May I offer it to you? And what has been happening to you?'

'Strange things,' replied Spiegel. 'They were after my life. I should like to tell you all about it.' While they ate their cosy supper, Spiegel told the attentive owl all that had happened to him, and how he had got out of the clutches of Master Pineiss.

'Well, I congratulate you heartily,' said the owl. 'Now you are a man again and can do what you like, after all your varied experiences.'

'Yes, but that isn't the end of the matter,' said Spiegel. 'The man must have his wife and his money.'

'Are you crazy, wanting to do the wretch a good turn when he wanted to flay you?'

'Well, he could have done it legally, according to the contract, and since I can pay him back in the same coin, why shouldn't I? Who said I wanted to do him a good turn? The story was a pure invention of mine. My late mistress, now with God, was a simple person who had never been in love or had admirers in her life, and the treasure is unlawful property which she inherited and threw into the well so that she should come to no harm by it.'

'H'm! That's another story. But where will you find the woman?'

'Here in this chimney! That's why I came – to talk the matter over with you. Wouldn't you like to be free of the witch? Think how we can catch her and marry her to the old scoundrel.'

'Spiegel, the mere sight of you stimulates me!'

'There, I knew I hadn't come to the wrong place. You just bring some new spice into it, and we can't go wrong.'

'Since everything works together so well, I needn't think long. My plans are already laid.'

'How shall we catch her?'

'With a new woodcock snare made of good strong hemp strands. It must have been twisted by a twenty-year-old hunter who has never looked at a woman, and the night dew must have fallen on it three times without a woodcock having been caught in it. The reason for this, however, must be a threefold good action. Such a net is strong enough to catch the witch.'

'Now I wonder where you will get that,' said Spiegel, 'for I trust you not to talk nonsense.'

'It's found already – the very thing. In a wood not far from here there lives a hunter's son who is twenty years old and has never looked at a woman, for he is blind. Therefore he is no use for anything save to twist cord, and a few days ago he made a new and very fine woodcock springe. But when the old hunter wanted to set it for the first time, a woman came along and tried to tempt him to sin, but she was so ugly that he fled appalled, leaving the net on the ground, so that the dew fell on it without a woodcock having been caught, and the cause of that was a good action. The next day, when he went to set it again, a horseman rode by with a heavy sack of gold behind him, out of which a gold coin fell every now and then. And the hunter again left the net lying and ran after the rider, collecting the coins until the horseman turned round, saw what was going on and turned his lance on him in anger. Then the hunter bowed in terror and said, "Allow me, sir. You have dropped a great deal of money which I have picked up for you." That was another good action, honest finding being one of the most difficult and best; but he was so far from his net that he left it lying and took a short cut home. The third day, however, which was yesterday, as he was on the way, he met a pretty woman who used to cajole the old man a good deal and to whom he had given many a little hare. So then he quite forgot the woodcock and said in the morning, "I have spared their poor little lives. One must be merciful, even to animals." And in view of these good deeds, he came to the conclusion that he was too good for this world and went into a monastery early this morning. So the net is still lying unused in the wood. I have only to fetch it.'

'Fetch it quickly, then,' said Spiegel. 'It's the very thing we need.'

'All right,' said the owl. 'Just keep watch for me in this hole and if the mistress calls up the chimney to ask whether the air is clear, you must answer, imitating my voice, "No; there's no stink yet in the fencing school!"' Spiegel took his place in the chimney and the owl flew quietly away over the town and into the wood. She soon returned with the net and asked, 'Has she called up yet?'

'Not yet,' said Spiegel.

Then they stretched the net over the chimney, and sat down warily beside it: the air was dark and in the light morning breeze a few stars were twinkling. 'You should see,' said the owl, 'how cleverly she can ride up the chimney without making her white shoulders black.' 'I have never seen her so close,' whispered Spiegel. 'If only she doesn't catch us.'

Then the witch called up the chimney from below, 'Is the air clear?' The owl cried, 'Quite clear. There's a fine stink in the fencing school,' and forthwith the witch came riding up the chimney and was caught in the net, which the owl and the cat pulled tight and tied. 'Hold firm,' said Spiegel. 'Bind her fast,' said the owl. The witch struggled and writhed speechless like a fish in a net, but the cord held. Only her broom-handle stuck out through the meshes, and Spiegel tried to draw it out quite gently, but got such a crack on his nose that he nearly fainted and realized that it is unwise to come too near a lioness, even in a net. Finally the witch calmed down and said, 'What do you want, you crazy beasts?'

'You are to release me from your service and give me my freedom,' said the owl. 'A lot of trouble for nothing,' said the witch. 'You are free. Untie this cord.'

'Not so fast,' said Spiegel, who was still rubbing his nose. 'You must promise to marry the Town Wizard, Master Pineiss, your neighbour, exactly in the way we tell you and never to leave him.'

Then the witch began to struggle again and to spit like the devil, and the owl said, 'She won't.' But Spiegel said, 'Unless you are quiet and do just what we want, we shall hang the net with you in it in front of the house on the dragon's head on the eaves, so that tomorrow the people will see you and know who is the witch. Now say – would you rather roast under the supervision of Master Pineiss, or roast him by marrying him?'

Then the witch said with a sigh, 'How did you think of doing it?' and Spiegel expounded the whole matter to her delicately, explaining what was to be done and what her part was. 'Well, we can manage that, if there's no other way out,' she said, and pledged herself with the strongest oaths that can bind a witch. Then the animals undid the net and let her out. She at once mounted her broom, the owl got up behind her and Spiegel at the back, and so they set off for the well, into which she rode to fetch up the treasure.

In the morning, Spiegel presented himself at Pineiss's and announced to him that he could visit the lady and pay his respects to her: she was already so poor that she was completely abandoned and forlorn, and was sitting in front of the town gate under a tree and weeping bitterly. Forthwith, Master Pineiss dressed himself in his shabby old yellow velvet doublet, which he only wore on ceremonial occasions, donned his second-best poodle cap and girt on his dagger; in his hand he bore an old green glove, a little balsam-bottle, which had once had balsam in it and still smelt slightly, and a paper carnation; then he set off for the town gate to court the lady. There he saw a woman sitting, more lovely than any he had ever seen before, but her dress was so poor and torn that, however modestly she might bear herself, her white body gleamed through here and there. Pineiss could hardly begin his courting for delight. Then the beauty dried her tears, gave him her hand, thanked him in a voice like heavenly bells for his generosity and swore to be true to him. But at that very moment he conceived such jealousy, such passionate envy of his wife, that he made up his mind never to let her be seen by mortal eyes. He got an old hermit to marry them and celebrated the marriage feast with her in his house with no other guests than Spiegel and the owl, whom Spiegel had asked permission to bring. The ten thousand guilders stood in a dish on the table, and from time to time Pineiss dipped his hand in them and stirred the gold about; then he looked at the lovely woman sitting there in a sea-blue velvet dress, her hair woven through a gold net and adorned with flowers, and with pearls round her lovely neck. He tried to kiss her the whole time, but she modestly held him off and swore that she would never do so in front of strangers and before the fall of night. This made him all the more love-sick and blissful, and Spiegel spiced the feast with charming speeches, which the lady followed up with such pleasant, witty and flattering remarks that the old wizard did not know where he was for joy.

But when darkness fell, the owl and the cat paid their respects and modestly withdrew. Pineiss accompanied them to the front door and thanked Spiegel again, calling him an excellent, polite fellow, and when he returned to the room, there sat the old beguine, his neighbour, leering at him with her evil eye. Pineiss dropped the light and leaned trembling against the wall. His tongue lolled out and his face was as livid as hers. But she rose, and drove him before her to the nuptial chamber, where she tortured him with tortures more fiendish than ever mortal yet experienced.

So now he was irrevocably married to the old woman, and in the town, when the thing got about, they said, 'Still waters run deep. Who would have thought that the Town Wizard and the old beguine would have made a match of it? Well, they are an honest couple, if not particularly attractive.'

But from that time on, Master Pineiss led a wretched life. His wife had got hold of all his secrets and ruled him with a rod of iron. He never had the slightest rest or freedom and had to make magic from morning till night, and when Spiegel went by and saw him, he would call politely, 'Busy as usual, Master Pineiss!'

So from that time on they have said in Seldwyla, 'He has bought the fat off the cat', especially if anyone has married a shrewish and ugly wife.

THE CAT
Mary E. Wilkins Freeman

The snow was falling, and the Cat's fur was stiffly pointed with it, but he was imperturbable. He sat crouched, ready for the death-spring, as he had sat for hours. It was night – but that made no difference – all times were as one to the Cat when he was in wait for prey. Then, too, he was under no constraint of human will, for he was living alone that winter. Nowhere in the world was any voice calling him; on no hearth was there a waiting dish. He was quite free except for his own desires, which tyrannized over him when unsatisfied as now. The Cat was very hungry – almost famished, in fact. For days the weather had been very bitter, and all the feebler wild things which were his prey by inheritance, the born serfs to his family, had kept, for the most part, in their burrows and nests, and the Cat's long hunt had availed him nothing. But he waited with the inconceivable patience and persistency of his race; besides, he was certain. The Cat was a creature of absolute convictions, and his faith in his deductions never wavered. The rabbit had gone in there between those low-hung pine boughs. Now her little doorway had before it a shaggy curtain of snow, but in there she was. The Cat had seen her enter, so like a swift grey shadow that even his sharp and practised eyes had glanced back for the substance following, and then she was gone.

So he sat down and waited, and he waited still in the white night, listening angrily to the north wind starting in the upper heights of the mountains with distant screams, then swelling into an awful crescendo of rage, and swooping down with furious white wings of snow like a flock of fierce eagles into the valleys and ravines. The Cat was on the side of a mountain, on a wooded terrace. Above him a few feet away towered the rock ascent as steep as the wall of a cathedral. The Cat had never climbed it – trees were the ladders to his heights of life. He had often looked with wonder at the rock, and miauled bitterly and resentfully as man does in the face of a forbidding Providence. At his left was the sheer precipice. Behind him, with a short stretch of woody growth between, was the frozen perpendicular wall of a mountain stream. Before him was the way to his home. When the rabbit came out she was trapped; her little cloven feet could not scale such unbroken steeps. So the Cat waited. The place in which he was looked like a maelstrom of the wood. The tangle of trees and bushes clinging to the mountain-side with a stern clutch of roots, the prostrate trunks and branches, the vines embracing everything with strong knots and coils of growth, had a curious effect, as of things which had whirled for ages in a current of raging water, only it was not water, but wind, which had disposed everything in circling lines of yielding to its fiercest points of onset. And now over all this whirl of wood and rock and dead trunks and branches and vines descended the snow. It blew down like smoke over the rock-crest above; it stood in a gyrating column like some death-wraith of nature, on the level, then it broke over the edge of the precipice, and the Cat cowered before the fierce backward set of it. It was as if ice needles pricked his skin through his beautiful thick fur, but he never faltered and never once cried. He had nothing to gain from crying, and everything to lose; the rabbit would hear him cry and know he was waiting.

It grew darker and darker, with a strange white smother, instead of the natural blackness of night. It was a night of storm and death superadded to the night of nature. The mountains were all hidden, wrapped about, overawed, and tumultuously overborne by it, but in the midst of it waited, quite unconquered, this little unswerving, living patience and power under a little coat of grey fur.

A fiercer blast swept over the rock, spun on one mighty foot of whirlwind athwart the level, then was over the precipice.

Then the Cat saw two eyes luminous with terror, frantic with the impulse of flight, he saw a little, quivering, dilating nose, he saw two pointing ears, and he kept still, with every one of his fine nerves and muscles strained like wires. Then the rabbit was out – there was one long line of incarnate flight and terror – and the Cat had her.

The Cat

Then the Cat went home trailing his prey through the snow.

The Cat lived in the house which his master had built, as rudely as a child's block-house, but stanchly enough. The snow was heavy on the low slant of its roof, but it would not settle under it. The two windows and the door were made fast, but the Cat knew a way in. Up a pine-tree behind the house he scuttled, though it was hard work with his heavy rabbit, and was in his little window under the eaves, then down through the trap to the room below, and on his master's bed with a spring and a great cry of triumph, rabbit and all. But his master was not there; he had been gone since early autumn and it was now February. He would not return until spring, for he was an old man, and the cruel cold of the mountains clutched at his vitals like a panther, and he had gone to the village to winter. The Cat had known for a long time that his master was gone, but his reasoning was always sequential and circuitous; always for him what had been would be, and the more easily for his marvellous waiting powers, so he always came home expecting to find his master.

When he saw that he was still gone, he dragged the rabbit off the rude couch which was the bed to the floor, put one little paw on the carcass to keep it steady, and began gnawing with head to one side to bring his strongest teeth to bear.

It was darker in the house than it had been in the wood, and the cold was as deadly, though not so fierce. If the Cat had not received his fur coat unquestioningly of Providence, he would have been thankful that he had it. It was a mottled grey, white on the face and breast, and thick as fur could grow.

The wind drove the snow on the windows with such force that it rattled like sleet, and the house trembled a little. Then all at once the Cat heard a noise, and stopped gnawing his rabbit and listened, his shining green eyes fixed upon a window. Then he heard a hoarse shout, a halloo of despair and entreaty; but he knew it was not his master come home, and he waited, one paw still on the rabbit. Then the halloo came again, and then the Cat answered. He said all that was essential quite plainly to his own comprehension. There was in his cry of response enquiry, information, warning, terror, and finally, the offer of comradeship; but the man outside did not hear him, because of the howling of the storm.

Then there was a great battering pound at the door, then another, and another. The Cat dragged his rabbit under the bed. The blows came thicker and faster. It was a weak arm which gave them, but it was nerved by desperation. Finally the lock yielded, and the stranger came in. Then the Cat, peering from under the bed, blinked with a sudden light, and his green eyes narrowed. The stranger struck a match and looked about. The Cat saw a face wild and blue with hunger and cold, and a man who looked poorer and older than his poor old master, who was an outcast among men for his poverty and lowly mystery of antecedents; and he heard a muttered, unintelligible voicing of distress from the harsh, piteous mouth. There was in it both profanity and prayer, but the Cat knew nothing of that.

The stranger braced the door which he had forced, got some wood from the stock in the corner, and kindled a fire in the old stove as quickly as his half-frozen hands would allow. He shook so pitiably as he worked that the Cat under the bed felt the tremor of it. Then the man, who was small and feeble and marked with the scars of suffering which he had pulled down upon his own head, sat down in one of the old chairs and crouched over the fire as if it were the one love and desire of his soul, holding out his yellow hands like yellow claws, and he groaned. The Cat came out from under the bed and leaped upon his lap with the rabbit. The man gave a great shout and start of terror, and sprang, and the Cat slid clawing to the floor, and the rabbit fell inertly, and the man leaned, gasping with fright, and ghastly, against the wall. The Cat grabbed the rabbit by the slack of its neck and dragged it to the man's feet. Then he raised his shrill, insistent cry, he arched his back high, his tail was a splendid waving plume. He rubbed against the man's feet, which were bursting out of their torn shoes.

The man pushed the Cat away, gently enough, and began searching about the little cabin. He even climbed painfully the ladder to the loft, lit a match, and peered up in the darkness with straining eyes. He feared lest there might be a man, since there was a cat. His experience with men had not been pleasant, and neither had the experience of men been pleasant with him. He was an old wandering Ishmael among his kind; he had stumbled upon the house of a brother, and the brother was not at home, and he was glad.

He returned to the Cat, and stooped stiffly and stroked his back, which the animal arched like the spring of a bow.

Then he took up the rabbit and looked at it eagerly by the firelight. His jaws worked. He could almost have devoured it raw. He fumbled – the Cat close at his heels – around some rude shelves and a table, and found, with a grunt of self-gratulation, a lamp with oil in it. That he lighted; then he found a frying-pan and a knife, and skinned the rabbit, and prepared it for cooking, the Cat always at his feet.

When the odour of the cooking flesh filled the cabin, both the man and the Cat looked wolfish. The man turned the rabbit with one hand and stooped to pat the Cat with the other. The Cat thought him a fine man. He loved him with all his heart, though he had known him such a short time, and though the man had a face both pitiful and sharply set at variance with the best of things.

It was a face with the grimy grizzle of age upon it, with fever hollows in the cheeks, and the memories of wrong in the dim eyes but the Cat accepted the man unquestioningly and loved him. When the rabbit was half cooked, neither the man nor the Cat could wait any longer. The man took it from the fire, divided it exactly in halves, gave the Cat one, and took the other himself. Then they ate.

Then the man blew out the light, called the Cat to him, got on the bed, drew up the ragged coverings, and fell asleep with the Cat in his bosom.

The man was the Cat's guest all the rest of the winter, and winter is long in the mountains. The rightful owner of the little hut did not return until May. All that time the Cat toiled hard, and he grew rather thin himself, for he shared everything except mice with his guest; and sometimes game was wary, and the fruit of patience of days was very little for two. The man was ill and weak, however, and unable to eat much, which was fortunate, since he could not hunt for himself. All day long he lay on the bed, or else sat crouched over the fire. It was a good thing that firewood was ready at hand for the picking up, not a stone's-throw from the door, for that he had to attend to himself.

The Cat foraged tirelessly. Sometimes he was gone for days together, and at first the man used to be terrified, thinking he would never return; then he would hear the familiar cry at the door, and stumble to his feet and let him in. Then the two would dine together, sharing equally; then the Cat would rest and purr, and finally sleep in the man's arms.

Towards spring the game grew plentiful; more wild little quarry were tempted out of their homes, in search of love as well as food. One day the Cat had luck – a rabbit, a partridge, and a mouse. He could not carry them all at once, but finally he had them together at the house door. Then he cried, but no one answered. All the mountain streams were loosened, and the air was full of the gurgle of many waters, occasionally pierced by a bird-whistle. The trees rustled with a new sound to the spring wind; there was a flush of rose and gold-green on the breasting surface of a distant mountain seen through an opening in the wood. The tips of the bushes were swollen and glistening red, and now and then there was a flower; but the Cat had nothing to do with flowers. He stood beside his booty at the house door, and cried and cried with his insistent triumph and complaint and pleading, but no one came to let him in. Then the Cat left his little treasures at the door, and went around to the back of the house to the pine-tree, and was up the trunk with a wild scramble, and in through his little window, and down through the trap to the room, and the man was gone.

The Cat cried again – that cry of the animal for human companionship which is one of the sad notes of the world; he looked in all the corners; he sprang to the chair at the window and looked out, but no one came. The man was gone, and he never came again.

The Cat ate his mouse out on the turf beside the house; the rabbit and the partridge he carried painfully into the house, but the man did not come to share them. Finally, in the course of a day or two, he ate them up himself; then he slept a long time on the bed, and when he waked the man was not there.

Then the Cat went forth to his hunting-grounds again, and came home at night with a plump bird, reasoning with his tireless persistency in expectancy that the man would be there; and there was a light in the window, and when he cried his old master opened the door and let him in.

His master had strong comradeship with the Cat, but not affection. He never patted him like that gentler outcast, but he had a pride in him and an anxiety for his welfare, though he had left him alone all winter without scruple. He feared lest some misfortune might have come to the Cat, though he was so large of his kind, and a mighty hunter. Therefore, when he saw him at the door in all the glory of his glossy winter coat, his white breast and face shining like snow in the sun, his own face lit up with welcome, and the Cat embraced his feet with his sinuous body vibrant with rejoicing purrs.

The Cat had his bird to himself, for his master had his own supper already cooking on the stove. After supper the Cat's master took his pipe, and sought a small store of tobacco which he had left in his hut over winter. He had thought often of it; that and the Cat seemed something to come home to in the spring. But the tobacco was gone; not a dust left. The man swore a little in a grim monotone, which made the profanity lose its customary effect. He had been, and was, a hard drinker; he had knocked about the world until the marks of its sharp corners were on his very soul, which was thereby calloused, until his very sensibility to loss was dulled. He was a very old man.

He searched for the tobacco with a sort of dull combativeness of persistency; then he stared with stupid wonder around the room. Suddenly many features struck him as being changed. Another stove-lid was broken; an old piece of carpet was tacked up over a window to keep out the cold; his firewood was gone. He looked, and there was no oil left in his can. He looked at the coverings on his bed; he took them up, and again he made that strange remonstrant noise in his throat. Then he looked again for his tobacco.

Finally he gave it up. He sat down beside the fire, for May in the mountains is cold; he held his empty pipe in his mouth, his rough forehead knitted, and he and the Cat looked at each other across that impassable barrier of silence which has been set between man and beast from the creation of the world.

Acknowledgements

Italo Calvino: 'The Garden of Stubborn Cats' from *Marcovaldo*, reprinted by permission of Secker & Warburg Ltd., Aitken & Stone Ltd. and Harcourt Brace Inc.

Colette: 'The Tom-Cat' from *Creatures Great and Small*, reprinted by permission of Secker & Warburg Ltd. and Farrar, Strauss & Giroux Inc.

Roald Dahl: 'Edward the Conqueror' from *Kiss, Kiss*, reprinted by permission of Murray Pollinger Ltd. and Alfred A. Knopf Inc., Michael Joseph Ltd., Penguin Books Ltd. Copyright © 1953 by Roald Dahl. First published in *The New Yorker*.

L. P. Hartley: 'Pains and Pleasures' from *The Complete Short Stories of L. P. Hartley*, reprinted by permission of Hamish Hamilton Ltd.

Patricia Highsmith: 'Ming's Biggest Prey' from *The Animal Lover's Book of Beastly Murder*, reprinted by permission of William Heinemann Ltd. and Warner Books Inc.

Geoffrey Household: 'Abner of the Porch' from *The Europe That Was*, reprinted by permission of A. M. Heath Ltd.

Gottfried Keller: 'Spiegel the Cat' from *The People of Seldwyla* translated by M. D. Hottinger, reprinted by permission of J. M. Dent Ltd.

Ellis Peters: 'The Trinity Cat', reprinted by permission of Deborah

Owen Ltd. Copyright © 1976 by Ellis Peters. First published in *Winter's Crimes 8* (Macmillan, 1976).

Damon Runyon: 'Lillian' from *Runyon on Broadway*, reprinted by permission of Constable Ltd. and the American Play Inc.

Dorothy L. Sayers: 'The Cyprian Cat' from *In the Teeth of the Evidence and Other Stories*, reprinted with permission of David Higham Associates Ltd.

James Thurber: 'The Cat in the Lifeboat' from *Further Fables of Our Time*, reprinted by permission of Hamish Hamilton Ltd. and Simon & Schuster Inc. Copyright © 1956 by James Thurber. Copyright © 1984 by Helen Thurber.

DELETED

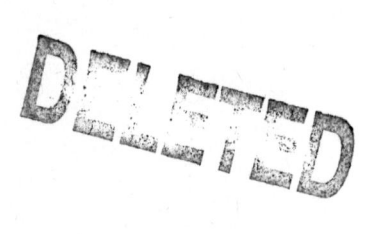